About the Authors

Caroline Anderson's been a nurse, a secretary, a teacher, and has run her own business. Now she's settled on writing. 'I was looking for that elusive something and finally realised it was variety – now I have it in abundance. Every book brings new horizons, new friends, and in between books I juggle! My husband John and I have two beautiful daughters, Sarah and Hannah, umpteen pets, and several acres of Suffolk that nature tries to reclaim every time we turn our backs!'

Deanne Anders was reading romance while her friends were still reading Nancy Drew, and she knew she'd hit the jackpot when she found a shelf of Mills & Boon Modern in her local library. Years later she discovered the fun of writing her own. Deanne lives in Florida, with her husband and their spoiled Pomeranian. During the day she works as a nursing supervisor. With her love of everything medical and romance, writing for Mills & Boon Medical is a dream come true.

Louisa Heaton is a married mother of f_____ _____ding a set of twins) and lives on an isl_____ _____ When not wrangling her child_____ _____mals, she can often _____ the beach mutterin_____ _____ts. In her spare tim_____ _____ally when she ought t_____ _____se!

Midwives' Miracles

Midwives' Miracles: From Midwife to Mum

CAROLINE ANDERSON

DEANNE ANDERS

LOUISA HEATON

MILLS & BOON

First Published in Great Britain 2022
By Mills & Boon, an imprint of HarperCollins*Publishers,* Ltd
1 London Bridge Street, London, SE1 9GF

www.harpercollins.co.uk

HarperCollins*Publishers*
1st Floor, Watermarque Building,
Ringsend Road, Dublin 4, Ireland

MIDWIVES MIRACLES: FROM MIDWIFE TO MUM © 2022 Harlequin Books S.A.

The Midwife's Longed-For Baby © 2017 Caroline Anderson
From Midwife to Mummy © 2019 Denise Chavers
The Baby That Changed Her Life © 2015 Louisa Heaton

ISBN: 978-0-263-30420-6

MIX
Paper from
responsible sources
FSC
www.fsc.org
FSC™ C007454

THE MIDWIFE'S LONGED-FOR BABY

CAROLINE ANDERSON

For all those whose infertility stories have touched my heart, and for the very many more whose stories I have never heard but who are themselves travelling this emotionally challenging road with courage. My heart aches for you.

CHAPTER ONE

'Liv, have you got a minute?'

She hesitated, about to say no, but Ben wasn't one to waste time and if he wanted to talk to her...

'If it really is only that? I need to check on a mum soon.'

'That's fine, it won't take long. I just want to run something by you. Can we go in my office?'

His office?

'Is this about Jen?' she asked as Ben closed the door.

The fleeting smile didn't quite reach his eyes. 'In a way. Did you know she's got cancer?'

'Yes, Simon told me yesterday. I was gutted. She's such a lovely person and it seems so unfair. He said they're moving home so their families can help with the children while she's having treatment. So what is it you want me to do?' she asked, thinking flowers, a gift voucher, something for the kids—

'Nothing, but what I do could affect you, because yesterday was Simon's last day and his compassionate leave's pretty open-ended so we need a locum, and I'd like to talk to Nick about it.'

'Nick?'

Of all the things he'd been going to say, her ex husband's name was so far down the list it wasn't even on it, and just the sound of his name made her heart beat faster. And he wasn't officially ex, because she'd never quite been able to follow through on that—

'Are you still in touch?'

Ben nodded. 'Yes, we're in touch. I speak to him quite often. He always asks about you,' he added gently.

Her heart lurched. 'Does he? How is he?' she asked, trying not to sound too needy and failing hopelessly.

'He's OK. He's well, keeps himself busy.' He frowned, hesitating, then went on, 'I know it's none of my business, Liv, and I'm not asking any questions, but I was really sorry when you two split up.'

She felt her eyes fill and blinked as she looked away. 'Me, too, but it wasn't working.' Any more than this was, this awful aching emptiness where her love for Nick had been...

'I know. I could see there was something wrong, so I wasn't surprised, just saddened for you both. Look, don't worry about it. I'll try and get someone else. I only thought of him because he'd be perfect for the job, but I don't want to make things difficult for you—for either of you, really.'

The shock had worn off now, swamped by a tidal wave of mixed emotions that she couldn't quite work out. Longing? Dread? She didn't have a clue. Both, maybe, but confusion was fighting its way to the top of the pile.

'I don't understand how he could do it anyway. Doesn't he have a job?'

He must have. He was paying the mortgage on their house—

'Not any more, as far as I know. His existing locum post's about to come to an end and I haven't heard that he's got anything else lined up so I wanted to get in soon if we were to stand a chance, but it's probably too late anyway.'

He was *locuming*? He'd been made a consultant at Yoxburgh Park Hospital a few months before they'd split up. How had he ended up working as a locum? Although it was only a year ago since he'd left. Maybe nothing had come up, nothing as good anyway. Nothing that would do him justice...

'Can I think about it? Before you ask him, or get anyone else. It's just—it's the last thing I expected you to say and I can't quite get my head round it.'

'I know, I can see that. And I realise you might need to talk to him first.'

No way. She hadn't spoken to him since that horrible day that she'd regretted ever since, but this wasn't the time or the way to do it. She shook her head. 'No, I don't need to do that. How long can I have?'

Ben shrugged. 'The rest of the morning? I'm sorry, I know it isn't long, but if you think you can deal with it I really don't want to hang about in case we lose him. It's right up his street—mostly obstetrics, but there's some of the fertility clinic work as well, which is why I thought of him.'

That stopped her mind in its tracks, and she felt her jaw drop. She just couldn't picture him in a fertility clinic, of all the ironic places, but of course Simon's job partly involved it.

'I didn't realise he knew anything at all about infertility.'

Apart from their own, but she wasn't saying that to Ben.

'Yes, that's one of the reasons why we want him, because of Simon's role here. Plus he's a damn good obstetrician, of course, but he's a perfect fit. He's been running the fertility clinic in his hospital since last May, and it shuts any day now.'

Her heart was beating so fast she could feel it thudding against her ribs. Of all the things for him to do, running a fertility clinic was so out of left field she'd never have seen it coming. Why would he choose to punish himself in that way? *Unless he'd had no choice.* Had he been driven to it just to earn a living? Her guilt over the mortgage ramped up a notch.

'I had no idea,' she said numbly. She took another moment, letting it all sink in a little, and then took a deep breath and made a decision she just hoped she didn't regret.

'Talk to him, Ben. Ask him if he's interested. If he is—well, I'm sure we can be civilised about it.'

'Are you sure? I realise it's a big decision for you.'

'But it isn't really mine to make. It's yours, and his, and if he's the right man for the job, who am I to stand in the way? And anyway, it's not permanent. Ask him, Ben. Just keep me in the loop, OK? I don't want any surprises.'

'Of course I will.' He opened the door and stared down thoughtfully into her eyes. 'Thank you, Liv. I do appreciate it and I know it can't be easy for you.'

Did he? She wondered how much he knew about their break-up, about the why and the how. Had Nick spoken to him about it? Surely not. If there was one thing her marriage had taught her, it was that Nick didn't talk about his feelings. Not to her, and certainly not to his boss.

She found a smile from somewhere. 'You're welcome. Just let me know his reaction.'

'I will.'

'Nick? It's Ben Walker. Are you OK to talk? I want to ask you something.'

'Yeah, sure. What d'you want to know?' he asked.

'Nothing. I'm headhunting you. I know your clinic's shutting any time now, and we need a full-time locum consultant to cover Obs and Gynae and some of the fertility clinic workload and I thought it sounded right up your street, unless you've got your next job lined up already?'

Ben was asking him to go back? With Liv still there? At least, he assumed she was. He hadn't heard otherwise and Ben would have told him, he was sure. Would he be working with her?

His heart rate rocketed, and he hauled in a deep breath and let it go, consciously engaging his brain instead of his adrenal glands.

'Whose job is it? It sounds like Simon's.'

'It is. His wife's got cancer and he's gone off on compassionate leave with immediate effect. They're moving back to their home town so their parents can help with childcare.'

'Oh, no, that's horrendous. Poor Jen. Poor all of them. And poor you, because it's obviously left you in the lurch, but I'm not sure I'm the man for the job. Does Liv know you're asking me?'

'Yes. I asked her first. She said she thought you could be civilised about it.'

Civilised?

He'd be right under her nose, working with couples to solve the very thing that had left their marriage in tatters. *Civilised* wasn't the word he would have applied to that situation.

A minefield, more likely.

Or an opportunity to build bridges? He knew so much more now than he had then, but the pain was still raw and no amount of knowledge was going to make that go away.

Could he do it? It wasn't as if they'd be working together, and it was only temporary in any case. They could keep out of each other's way if necessary, but it might give them a chance—

'So, are you still free?'

'Yes, technically. I haven't got anything lined up yet, at least, and I'm seeing the last patients today, but I had thought I'd take a break. When would you want me to start?'

Ben made a sound that could have been laughter. 'Tomorrow? And by the way, that was a joke, but—ASAP, really. We can cover it for a few days but after that it'll get really tricky. Every woman in Suffolk seems to be pregnant or trying to be at the moment.'

His chest tightened. Not quite every woman. Not his Liv...

'Why don't you come and talk to me about it?' Ben went on. 'See how you feel?'

He had no idea how he'd feel. Confused? Desperate to see Liv? Afraid to see her, to find that she was happily settled without him when he was still miserable and lonely and struggling to make sense of it all? But maybe she *was* happy, which would mean he'd done the right thing by leaving without a fight. Maybe he needed to know that so he could move on?

There was no real reason why he couldn't go. When the clinic closed its doors at five that evening, he'd be jobless. He'd planned a holiday, something reckless and adrenaline-soaked, but he hadn't booked anything and now Ben was dangling this opportunity to go back to Yoxburgh right in front of his nose.

Yoxburgh, and Liv.

They'd been so happy there at first in the pretty Victorian seaside town, but it had all gone horribly wrong for them and now the only memories he had of it were sad ones. Did he really want to go back?

He'd made changes in his life, tried to get it back on track, but although his diet and lifestyle had undergone a radical overhaul, his heart hadn't moved on. He'd just shut it away, buried it under a massive pile of work and endless runs around an inner-city park, and going back was bound to open a whole new can of worms. Did he really want to do that? The sensible answer was no—or was that just the coward's answer?

And Ben needed him. He had no commitments or ties, no reason why he couldn't go, except that Liv would be there, and maybe that wasn't a good enough reason to stay away.

Even though it was a minefield, even though they hadn't spoken in over a year, even though he knew it was rash and stupid and ill-considered, he realised there was a massive part of him that wanted to see her again.

Needed to see her again.

It was high time they had the conversation he'd been putting off since they'd split up. The conversation he owed her—and the one she owed him, like why after more than a year she still hadn't started divorce proceedings...

'Let's just go for it,' he said, suddenly decisive. 'I can't do tomorrow, but why don't I come up on Friday? That gives me a day to tidy up here and pack, and if I can sort everything out with your HR first thing on Friday morning I can start work right away. My paperwork's all in order, so once HR have seen it I'll be good to go. Then you'll only have to deal with tomorrow, and I can spend the weekend finding somewhere to live.'

'Are you sure?'

'Yes, absolutely,' he said without giving himself time to back out of it. 'Let's do it. I'll drive down early so I'm with you for eight and I can be in HR as soon as they open.'

'Nick, thank you. I can't tell you how grateful I am,' Ben said, and the relief in his voice made Nick realise just how much pressure his old clinical lead was under. 'And don't worry about finding anywhere to live,' Ben added, 'you can stay with us as long as you need to, Daisy'd love to have you. Come here, to the hospital. You know where to find me. They'll page me when you get here.'

'Sure. Thanks. I'll see you then.'

He hung up, slid the phone into his pocket and stared blankly across the room.

He was going back.

He wasn't sure he was ready to see Liv again, because he'd never managed to get any emotional distance and his heart was still as raw as it had been the day she threw him out, so it was going to be tough. Very tough. But maybe he could use the opportunity to find out if she was happy without him, because he sure as hell wasn't happy without her...

There was a knock on the door and a nurse popped her head into the room. 'Mr Jarvis? Mr and Mrs Lyons are waiting to see you.'

He nodded, gave himself a mental shake and got to his feet. 'Show them in, please.'

He was coming back today.

Taking Simon's job, at least in the short term. She still couldn't work out how she felt about that. Confused, more than anything. Confused and nervous and tingling with apprehension. Lots of that.

She found a slot in the staff car park, got out and headed for the maternity unit on autopilot, her mind whirling.

Would she see him today? Did she want to? Did *he* want to see *her*? Their last exchange had hardly been amicable. Well, her side of it anyway. He'd hardly said a word but then he hadn't needed to, the evidence had spoken for itself.

She reached the kerb and glanced up, checking that the road was clear, and saw a car approaching.

Nick's car.

She recognised it instantly, and her heart started to thud as he drew closer, their eyes meeting as he slowed down.

To speak to her?

For a moment she thought he was going to stop, and then he raised his hand in acknowledgement and drove on, and she hauled in a breath and crossed the road on legs like jelly.

Her heart was tumbling in her chest, her lips dry, and she was breathing so fast she could have been running. Ridiculous. He was just a doctor, here to do his job, and she was just a midwife doing hers. The fact that they were still married was neither here nor there. They could do this.

She just had to work out how.

Nick parked the car and sat there for a moment, waiting for his heart to slow down.

He'd known it would be odd to see her again, but he hadn't expected the thunderbolt that had struck him when he'd met her eyes. It was like being punched in the gut, and it had taken his breath away.

Jaws clenched, he took the key out of the ignition, picked up the briefcase containing his stethoscope and the file with all the documentation for HR and got out of the car, following her towards the maternity unit.

Why the hell had he said yes? He could have turned Ben down, walked away, gone and had the holiday he'd been promising himself. Then he wouldn't have been here, he wouldn't have seen her and ripped open the wound left by the abrupt end to their marriage.

Not that it had taken much ripping. It had barely skinned over in the last year and a bit, but he was here now, the damage was done and he might as well just get on with it. And anyway, she needed the truth. They both did, and maybe then they could both move on.

The door slid open and he strode through it, went up to the maternity reception desk and asked them to page Ben.

'Morning, all.'

'Oh, Liv, I'm so glad I've caught you. Can you do us a huge favour? Would you mind covering an antenatal clinic this morning? Jan's called in sick and you're the only person who's not already involved in a delivery.'

She felt a little shaft of relief and smiled at her line manager. 'No, that's fine, I'll head straight down.' And she'd be nicely tucked out of the way so she wouldn't run the risk of bumping into Nick.

Which was stupid, really, because it was going to happen sometime, but she'd had less than forty-eight hours to get used to the idea of him coming back and judging by her reaction to him in the car park, it had been nothing like long enough.

She'd spend the morning giving herself a thorough talking-to, and then by the time he actually started work she'd have herself firmly under control.

Good plan.

Except it wasn't.

The clinic receptionist welcomed her with a smile

of relief and then comprehensively trashed her peace of mind.

'Thank heavens it's you, Liv, we need someone who knows the ropes. There's a bit of a delay because the locum who's covering for Mr Bailey is still in HR, but he'll be down soon, apparently, so if you could make a start that would be amazing.'

Simon's clinic? That meant she'd be working with Nick all morning, before she had a chance to shore up the walls and get all her defences in place. Great. Fabulous.

Her heart had started to pound, and she hauled in a breath, picked up the first set of notes with shaking hands and pasted on a smile.

'No problem. I can do that,' she said, as much to herself as the receptionist. She walked out to the waiting area, glanced at the file and scanned the room.

'Judy Richards?'

'Nick! Welcome back!'

He recognised Jane, the motherly but ruthlessly efficient woman who acted as Ben's secretary as well as Simon's, and greeted her warmly.

'Hello, Jane, it's good to see you again. How are you?'

'I'm fine. I've been expecting you. HR said you'd be up here shortly. They said you were very well organised, ironically.'

He laughed. 'It just so happens I had a file ready with the relevant paperwork in it because I knew I'd need it soon, but don't let that lull you into a false sense of security. I hate admin.'

She smiled knowingly. 'I haven't forgotten that. Don't worry, I'll make sure you do everything you have to do.'

'Can you read my mind?' he asked, and she just laughed.

'If necessary. That's what I'm here for.'

'Good. I don't suppose you've got Simon's schedule handy, have you? I really need to hit the ground running. Ben said something about a clinic and I've got a list this afternoon.'

'Yes, I've printed it all out for you here. First on your list is the antenatal clinic, as you know. It's still in the same place and they're expecting you. And your elective list starts at two, so you should just about have time after the clinic to meet your patients before you start in Theatre. The notes are on the ward.'

'Jane, you're a legend.' He hung his stethoscope round his neck, left his briefcase in her care and went.

At least in the clinic he was less likely to run into Liv, because she'd be safely tucked away on the midwife-led unit. And even though in a way he'd wanted to see her, their brief encounter this morning had shaken him more than he'd expected and he could do without any more surprises.

Yes, a nice, busy clinic was exactly what he needed. Just until he got his head round the idea of working in the same building as her…

'Liv…'

She was standing in the empty corridor with an armful of notes when she heard him say her name, and she turned slowly and met his eyes.

Anguish, love, regret—and then nothing, as he got control of himself again and slammed the shutters down. He'd had plenty of practice at that, he'd got it down to a fine art in the last year of their marriage, but he'd been too slow this time and his reaction exactly mirrored her own.

'Hello, Nick,' she said, her voice sounding scratchy

and unused. The words *how are you* hovered on her tongue, but she couldn't speak because it had glued itself to the roof of her mouth so she just stared at him.

His face was leaner, she realised, the crows' feet more pronounced, the frown lines shallower. Because he was happier? He hadn't looked happy, but he looked more like the old Nick, the man she'd fallen in love with, fit and well and healthy but with a touch of grey at his temples now. Stress, or just age? He was thirty-nine now, nearly forty, and he wore it well apart from that.

Not that the silver threaded through his dark hair did anything to dim his subtle but potent sex appeal—

Her heart was beating so fast it was deafening her, her breath was lodged in her throat, and she had to clamp her lips together to stifle a sudden little sob.

She blinked fiercely and adjusted the folders in her arms before looking back at him, and as she met those beautiful, smoky grey eyes again her heart thudded, but his gaze held her eyes and she was powerless to look away.

'I wasn't expecting to see you down here,' he said after a second of silence that seemed to scream on for eternity, and his gruff voice set her free and she breathed again.

'Ditto, but it's just as well you're here now, we've got a lot of work to do.' She pretended to look at the notes in her arms. Anything to get away from those searching eyes when her own were bound to be too revealing. 'I take it you managed to tick all HR's boxes?'

'Yes. I have a file I keep up to date. It comes in handy when you're a locum.'

That again. *Why hasn't he got a full-time job?*

He hesitated, as if there was something else he wanted to say, but after a moment he looked down at the armful of folders she was holding. 'So, what's that lot?'

'The ladies who've had their BP and fundal height measured and their urine tested, so they're all ready for you.' Her voice was almost normal again, and she nearly laughed. If he had any idea what was going on in her chest—

She led him into the consulting room and handed him the folders, and as he took them his hand brushed lightly against hers and the heat from his skin sent a wave of longing through her. She almost dropped the files but he had them, and he turned swiftly away and dumped them on the desk.

'Anyone I should be particularly aware of?' he asked, his voice a little taut and very businesslike, so she followed his lead. Anything to help get herself back under control before her heart gave out.

'Yes, Judy Richards,' she said briskly. 'She has a history of early miscarriage. This is her fourth pregnancy, she's thirty-two weeks which is the longest she's ever gone, but her fundal height hasn't changed since her last appointment a week ago and that wasn't as much as it should have been, so it might be that the baby's found a new position, or it could be that it's stopped growing for some reason. She's on the top of the pile.'

He frowned thoughtfully, all business now. 'Right. Good. Has she been tested for APS?'

'Yes, after her last miscarriage. The test came back negative.'

'Hmm. OK, well, she'd better have another scan before I see her, if we can do it without worrying her too much.'

'It's done. I knew you'd ask for it so I told her it was because it was a new consultant, and she didn't question it. The results are on here,' she said, handing him the department tablet.

'Great. Thanks.' He scrolled through and studied the results, then handed it back, frowning thoughtfully.

'OK. I think I'm going to admit her. Can you call her in, please, and I'll check her over and break the news?'

'Sure.'

And oddly it was fine, because Judy Richards and her baby needed them, they had a job to do and so they just got on with it, slipping seamlessly back into the familiar routine as if it had been yesterday. Not that she was relaxed in any way, but it was a joy watching him with Judy, and a stark reminder of how good he was at his job.

She'd forgotten how intuitive a doctor he was, and how caring. Kind, gentle, thorough—and from his first greeting onwards, Liv could see Judy had utter faith in him.

'Mrs Richards—I'm Nick Jarvis, I've taken over from Simon Bailey. I've had a look at your notes, and also the scan you had done today. It doesn't really shed any light—which is good news in a way, I suppose, but it still leaves some unanswered questions and I don't like that, so I think I'd like to admit you and do a few more tests, get a closer look at your baby and the placenta and retest you for APS—antiphospholipid syndrome. Has anybody discussed that with you yet?'

'Yes, Mr Bailey did, but he didn't think I'd got it.'

'He may well be right, but I'm erring on the side of caution, so if that's all right with you, I'll ring the ward and make the arrangements for you to be admitted now, and then maybe someone could bring some things in for you later.'

'I can't go home and get them myself?'

'You can, of course, but I'd like to get the tests under way as soon as possible and I'm in Theatre this afternoon, so I'd very much rather you didn't because I'd like to look after you myself rather than hand you over to someone else in my team.'

By the time he'd convinced Judy to come in immediately for closer monitoring, she was still calm and relatively relaxed, which considering her obstetric history was nothing short of a miracle.

If only *they* were as calm and relaxed things would be fine, but they weren't. Liv felt like a cat on hot bricks, and she wasn't sure he was faring any better.

They got through the morning by keeping out of each other's way as much as possible, avoiding eye contact, restricting conversation to a minimum and all work-related, but fun it wasn't and her nerves were in bits, so the second the clinic was finished she made her escape.

He closed the door as Liv went out with the last patient, leant back against the wall and closed his eyes, letting his breath out in a long, slow huff.

Well, they'd survived, if you could call it that.

Not that it had been easy, but they'd got through it by sticking to business and getting on with the job, and they'd done that well, working together as a smooth, well-oiled team just as they had in the old days. Except in the old days they'd enjoyed it, and he was pretty certain neither of them had enjoyed it today, and the tension between them could have been cut with a knife.

It couldn't go on like this, though, and he knew he had to do something to break through the icy politeness and careful distance between them or it wasn't going to work. At all.

He shrugged away from the wall, picked up the last set of notes and left the room, scanning the clinic for Liv, but there was no sign of her.

'Seen Liv?' he asked at Reception as he handed over the file, and was told she'd gone for lunch.

Which meant, unless she'd changed her habits, she'd be in the café that opened onto the park.

Good. He could do with a nice, strong coffee, with caffeine in it for a change. It might help him get through what was sure to be a deeply awkward conversation.

CHAPTER TWO

'MIND IF I join you?'

She might have known he'd find her here. She should have gone to the other café, or the restaurant—or even better, gone off-site.

Too late now. She looked pointedly at the two free tables, then up into those beautiful, unreadable eyes that were studying her knowingly. Too knowingly. She looked away.

'Is this about work?'

'In a way.'

He didn't wait for her to invite him, just put his cup on the table and sat down, his gaze meeting hers again, but this time she didn't look away because his eyes looked guarded and a little wary still, and she realised he was— nervous? No, not nervous, that didn't sound like Nick. Uncomfortable, maybe. That didn't sound like him, either, not the Nick she knew and loved anyway, but maybe he'd changed. Maybe she'd changed him by cutting him so brutally out of her life, but she'd been so hurt...

'Liv, I realise this is awkward, but I do think we need to clear the air if we're going to work together,' he said quietly, 'unless you being in the clinic this morning was just a one-off?'

She shook her head. 'No, it wasn't a one-off, but I

wasn't meant to be doing the clinic today and I didn't realise you'd be starting work so early. I thought it would take longer with HR.'

'Ah, well, that's the file for you,' he said with a slight smile that didn't reach his eyes. 'Answers all the questions in an instant. So, getting back to us, I'd assumed when Ben asked me that you'd still be in the midwife-led unit?'

She shook her head again. 'No, I only moved there while you were working your notice, and after you'd gone there was no point in me staying there, so I switched back to the consultant unit when there was a vacancy. I've been back six months.'

He frowned. 'I didn't know that. I'm sorry, I would have talked to you first if I had. Obviously I knew we'd see each other anyway from time to time, but that's not quite the same as having to work together. Are you going to be OK with that?'

Was she? OK with spending day after day bumping into him, working alongside him on deliveries, their hands, their bodies touching as they brushed against each other in the confines of the delivery room? OK with hearing his voice, catching endless glimpses of him around the maternity unit, hearing him laugh? He had a wonderful laugh, warm and rich and never, never unkind.

Would she really be OK with all of that?

She let out a soft, slightly shaky sigh. 'Nick, it's fine. We managed this morning and as I said to Ben, I'm sure we can be civilised.'

'I'm sure we can, but that still doesn't make it easy.'

The despairing little laugh escaped without her permission. 'What, you thought you could come back into my life after a year and it would be *easy*? Get real, Nick.

We're not married any more, in case you hadn't noticed. Of course it won't be easy.'

He winced slightly—so slightly that anyone who didn't know him as well as she did wouldn't have spotted it, but when he spoke it was without emotion.

'We *are* still married,' he corrected, his voice carefully controlled, 'but I haven't forgotten for a single moment that we're not together. That's not what this is about. But we are going to have to work together, and we never had a problem in the past and I don't want us to have a problem now.'

'Did we have a problem today?'

'With the work? No. With the atmosphere, definitely, and I'm not sure I can do it unless we can find some middle ground. We used to be such a brilliant team, and I want to find a way to get that back.'

'Seriously?' she asked, slightly incredulous, but he nodded.

'Seriously. I realise it's not going to be the same, but it needs to be better than it was this morning, and I just wanted to clear the air, break the ice a bit and get rid of the awkwardness, so that we're more at ease next time.'

In his dreams. There was no way she was going to be at ease with him. She only had to hear his voice or catch a glimpse of him and her heart started racing, but he was here and she was stuck with it, for now at least, and he had a point. They did have to be able to work together, although she still had questions about that, so she went for the first one on the pile.

'How come you were available to locum anyway?' she asked without preamble. 'I'd imagined you tucked up in a nice little consultant's post somewhere picturesque.'

Probably with another woman. She didn't add that, because he was trying to pour oil on troubled waters and it wouldn't help at all if she threw petrol on the fire instead. And besides, it was none of her business any more who he chose to sleep with.

He glanced down, stirring his coffee on autopilot even though she knew it wouldn't have sugar in it.

'I didn't want to tie myself down,' he said, finally putting the spoon back in the saucer and meeting her eyes again. 'After I left here, I just wanted to get away, let the dust settle, work out where I wanted to go. I thought maybe New Zealand, but my parents are still alive and they're getting older, so I took a two-month locum post covering maternity leave fairly close to them while I worked out what I wanted to do, and then when that was coming to an end they asked me to cover the fertility clinic until it shut because the services were being centralised and the consultant had left, so I did. I saw my last patients two days ago, on the day Ben rang, and I had nothing else lined up, so I'm here.'

'Why on earth did you say yes?'

'To Ben? Because I need a job, so I can eat and keep a roof over both our heads.'

She felt another pang of guilt. 'I didn't mean that, Nick, but if the mortgage is an issue—'

'It's not an issue, Liv, it's a fact, and I'm not going to make you homeless under any circumstances so let's just ignore that. So what *did* you mean?'

'I was talking about the fertility clinic job. I couldn't believe it when Ben told me that's what you'd been doing. It seems such an odd choice to make, under the circumstances, and I couldn't understand why on earth you'd do it.'

His eyes flicked away, then back to hers, curiously intent. 'Because I needed a job, as I said, and I was already in the hospital, I'd made a few friends, it meant I wouldn't have to relocate—and maybe, also, because I thought it might help me understand what had happened to us.'

Her heart thumped. 'And did it?'

He smiled sadly. 'Well, let's just say it made it blindingly obvious that we weren't the only couple struggling.'

His expression wasn't guarded now, just full of regret, and she lowered her head, unable to hold those clear grey eyes that seemed to see to the bottom of her insecurities.

'How about you?' he asked softly. 'What have you been up to since I went?'

She picked up her spoon and chased the froth on her cappuccino, stalling just as he had. 'What I'm doing now, pretty much. What did you expect?'

'I didn't. I had no idea what you'd want to do.'

Cry? She'd done so much of that after he'd gone, but she wasn't telling him that, although he could probably work it out. Fix it? Impossible, because the thing that had been wrong was the thing they hadn't been able to fix, so she'd just got on with her life, putting one foot in front of the other, not even trying to make sense of it because there wasn't any sense to be made.

'I didn't want to do anything,' she said sadly, watching the froth slide off the spoon. 'I just wanted peace, that was all. Peace, contentment, and the satisfaction of a job well done instead of the endless spectre of failure—'

'You didn't fail, Liv!'

She dropped the spoon with a clatter. 'Really? So what would you call it? Month after month, all our hopes and dreams flushed away—and then, just to rub my nose in it, you go off and sleep with your ex. That doesn't exactly make it a success in my book—'

She pushed back her chair, grabbed her bag and walked swiftly away from him, out of the café into the park, hauling in the cold air as if she'd just come up from the bottom of the ocean.

Don't cry! Whatever you do, don't cry—

'Liv! Liv, wait!'

She turned and looked up at him, right behind her, his grey eyes troubled, and she had the crazy urge to throw herself into his arms and sob her heart out.

Don't cry!

'Leave it, Nick,' she said, hoping her voice didn't show her desperation. 'Just leave it. I don't mind working with you, I said that to Ben, and I'm sure we can keep it professional, but I don't need any cosy chats or in-depth analysis of where it all went wrong for us. We both know exactly where it all went wrong, and if I'd gone to the conference with you that weekend then you would never have slept with Suzanne—'

'I didn't sleep with her.'

She stared at him, stunned. *'What?'*

'I said, I didn't sleep with her.'

Shock robbed her of breath.

'I don't believe you. You're lying!'

'No, I'm not, Liv. I didn't touch her. Honestly.'

She took a step back, struggling for air, for sense, for understanding, but they all eluded her.

'That's not true. It can't be true. Why would you suddenly come out with this now?'

'Because it *is* true, and I should have told you at the time.'

How did he do that with his eyes? Make them appear utterly unguarded and shining with sincerity?

'But—you admitted it!'

'No. No, I didn't Liv, I just confirmed that she'd spent the night with me in my room,' he told her. 'That was what you asked me, and I said yes because it was the truth. She did spend the night in there with me. You didn't ask why, though, or what for, because by the time I came home you'd spoken to Beth, you'd found the note Suze had left in my luggage and you had me hung, drawn and quartered and hung out to dry before I even stepped over the threshold, so you wouldn't have believed me anyway.

'You just assumed I'd slept with her,' he went on, his voice heavy and tinged with sadness, 'and I let you, because in that split second I felt that you'd thrown me a lifeline, a way out of a marriage that was tearing us both apart, so I just grabbed it and ran. And I'm sorry. I should never have done that to you. I should have told you the truth there and then, and made you listen.'

His words stunned her, the shockwaves rolling through her, bringing a sob to her throat.

'How could you do that?' she asked, her voice a strangled whisper. 'How could you let me believe that for all this time? I've spent a whole, agonising year believing that you slept with her, that I wasn't enough for you, that you didn't truly love me any more—you're right, you should have told me the truth then, Nick, instead of letting me think that you'd spent the night making love to—'

She broke off, unable to say her name. 'You let me end our *marriage*, on the grounds that you'd slept with that *whore*—'

His eyes hardened. 'She's not a whore, she's a friend, a damn good friend, who told me to pull myself together and go home and sort out my marriage.'

A sob rose in her throat, threatening to choke her, but she crushed it down and pulled herself together. 'Well, you did a great job of that—'

Her voice cracked and she pushed past him, shaking his hand off as he tried to stop her. She went back inside, cutting through the café to the main hospital corridor, then out on the other side bordering the car park, deliberately going the wrong way to throw him off the scent and lose him because if she had to spend another moment in his company she was going to cry, and she wasn't prepared to give him the satisfaction.

So she kept on going, and she didn't stop until she was back on the ward.

She'd gone.

The corridor was empty and he stood there, kicking himself for letting the conversation stray into such dangerous territory—especially in a public place and right in the middle of the working day.

Idiot!

He had to talk to her, to explain why he'd let her believe what she had, how he'd felt, why he hadn't stood his ground and told her the truth at the time. The *real* reason.

But not now. This afternoon he had a—mercifully short—elective list, so his first port of call was the wards, to make sure Judy Richards was settled in, and to meet the patients he was going to operate on and read through their notes before he was due in Theatre. And if he was lucky, Liv's shift would be well and truly over by the time he'd finished.

He'd go and see her at home later, to apologise, to explain, to try and help her understand.

If he could get her to listen, and judging by the way she'd just reacted, that was by no means a foregone conclusion.

Liv was tied up in a delivery for the afternoon, the nice straightforward labour of a woman having her sixth baby. She'd haemorrhaged after the last so she'd been admitted directly to the consultant-led unit with this one just in case, but so far everything was going fine.

Just as well, because Liv's concentration was totally shot.

How could he have done that to her? Let her believe he'd betrayed her like that if he hadn't? And why then, when she'd just found out that *yet again* she wasn't pregnant, so she'd been at her most vulnerable? She'd spent over a year living with the bone-deep certainty that he'd been unfaithful to her, and now she didn't know what to believe—

'I need to push.'

'OK, Karen. Nice and steady. That's good.'

But Karen's baby wasn't going for nice and steady, and three minutes later, half an hour before the end of Liv's shift, a lusty, squalling baby was delivered into her father's waiting hands.

'It's a girl,' he said, laughing and crying as he lay their daughter in his wife Karen's outstretched arms. 'Finally, it's a girl!'

Liv's eyes filled, and she had to blink away the tears as she gave Karen the oxytocin injection to help her uterus to contract down.

If this had been them, if she'd been able to give him a child, then maybe that would have been enough to keep him...

Liv checked the baby quickly as she lay in her mother's arms, making sure that all was well, but the baby was lovely and pink, her pulse steady and strong, her skinny little arms and legs moving beautifully. She'd stopped crying now and was staring up at her mother, riveted by the first face she'd ever seen.

It was a beautiful moment, one Liv never tired of seeing, and she watched the two of them staring into each other's eyes and falling in love and felt a familiar lump in her throat.

'Apgar score ten at one minute,' she said, her voice miraculously steady. 'Congratulations. She's lovely.'

She checked her again four minutes later, by which time the cord had stopped pulsating, so Liv clamped and cut it and handed the baby back to her mother.

'I take it this is your first girl?'

Her father's grin was wry. 'Yes, so hopefully we can stop now. Six is getting a little crazy, but we did want a girl so we thought we'd have one last try.'

'We may live to regret it when she hits puberty,' Karen said with a laugh, her hands cradling the naked baby tenderly at her breast.

Liv laid a warm towel back over them both and tucked it round the baby. 'She'll be fine, and she'll have all those big brothers to look after her. She's latched on well,' Liv added, struck yet again by the miracle of birth and the naturalness of this wonderful bond between mother and child. The bond she would never know...

'Yes, and thank goodness I've never had any problems with feeding any of them,' Karen said with a laugh. 'There's way too much to do in our house without sterilising bottles and making up feeds. Ooh, I can feel a contraction.'

'OK, Karen, that's good, you're nearly done. Gentle push for me when you're ready?' she said calmly, but Liv felt her heart rate pick up, because this was the moment, as the placenta separated from the uterine wall, that the haemorrhage would happen, and she really, really didn't feel ready for that.

Didn't feel ready for any more stress today, and the last thing she needed was Nick striding in there to take over like the cavalry after he'd just destabilised her fragile status quo with that bombshell about Suzanne.

Concentrate!

The haemorrhage didn't happen. To everyone's huge relief, the placenta came away cleanly with hardly any blood loss, so after they'd sorted Karen out and Liv was happy that her uterus was contracting down well and that all was as it should be, she left the other midwife to fill out the notes and headed for the changing room, only an hour late.

Tomorrow was Saturday, and with any luck she wouldn't run into Nick again today which meant she was unlikely to see him again until Monday. That would give her two clear days to get her emotions in order.

Except it didn't, because she walked out of the lift at the bottom of the building and ran slap into him.

'Sorry—'

She stepped hastily back, and they stood transfixed in awkward silence as the lift doors hissed shut behind her, cutting off her retreat.

'I gather your delivery was all right?' he asked, breaking the silence. 'I've been on standby in case she haemorrhaged again.'

'Oh—yes, it was fine, thanks. No problems. How's Judy Richards?'

'Settling in. I think I've reassured her.' He paused, his eyes searching hers. 'Look, Liv, are you done for the day?'

'Yes,' she said firmly, holding his eyes with a determined effort and clutching her coat in her arms like a shield. 'And I'm going home.'

'Can we talk?'

Her heart sank. 'Again? Nick, there's nothing you have to say that I need to hear. If there's a shred of truth in what you said, you should have told me then, not saved it for now, and I really don't want to discuss it. For heaven's sake, just leave it. It's not relevant any more anyway.'

She pushed past him and walked out of the door, but of course he couldn't leave it, could he? She could barely hear his footsteps behind her but she knew he was there, his voice calling her name as she made her way across the car park, but it was almost drowned out by the pounding of her heart.

She dodged between the rows of cars, reached the kerb by the access road to the main car park and was about to cross it when she felt his hand on her arm.

'Liv, please, let me talk to you. Give me a chance to explain.'

But she'd had enough to deal with already today, so she turned back to face him and shook her head. 'No. I can't do this now just to ease your guilty conscience, Nick, and I'm not going to. Please, just leave me alone!'

He caught her shoulders and held her. 'Liv, I won't take much of your time, but there's something I need to tell you and you need to hear it—'

'No! No, I don't!'

She tried to spin away from him, but his grip suddenly tightened and he tried to pull her back.

'Liv, no!' he yelled, his voice urgent, but the urgency was lost on her as she wrenched her arm away and stumbled backwards off the kerb out of reach.

She saw the look of horror on his face, heard the blast of a horn, saw the car as it clipped her and sent her spinning, and then her head hit the ground and everything went black...

He watched helplessly as the car struck her, saw her fall, saw her head bouncing off the kerb as she came to rest just inches from the front wheel. The big SUV had ground to a halt and the driver stumbled out, other people ran towards them shouting, but his eyes were only for Liv.

She was lying motionless on the edge of the road like a broken doll, her head level with the front wheel, her feet partly under the car just inches from the rear wheel, and for a terrifying second he thought she was dead.

Her hair had tumbled over her face and he dropped to his knees beside her, sweeping the hair aside to check for a pulse in her neck, but his own heart was beating so hard he could scarcely feel hers and his breath jammed in his throat.

'Liv? Liv, talk to me, for God's sake!'

He found a pulse and dragged in a breath, digging out the doctor instead of the lover, running his hands over her quickly, checking that she was breathing, scanning her for injuries, but her limbs were all straight, her pupils were equal and reactive, her breathing was normal. For now. But she was unconscious, and that could mean anything.

He needed help, and fast. He tugged his phone out of his pocket with shaking fingers and rang the ED direct. 'One of our midwives has been knocked down near the staff car park and she's unconscious. Send a team out here now, please, fast. Tell them they'll need a collar and board and a pelvic band. And hurry.'

She started to stir, and he dropped the phone and reached out, bracketing her head carefully in his hands and holding it steady, feeling the stickiness of blood on his fingers as they burrowed through her hair. No...

'Easy, Liv. Try not to move. I've called for help. Just stay as still as you can.'

'Nick?'

She knew him. Thank God...

'It's OK, Liv, I've got you, my love. I've got you.

They'll be here soon. You'll be OK. Just keep still for me, sweetheart.'

'My head hurts...'

'I know, darling, I know, but they'll be here soon. Just hang on another minute. It won't be long.'

'Over here,' someone yelled, and then the crowd that had gathered around them parted as the trauma team arrived.

He looked up without moving his hands. 'She was KOed briefly, she's got a head wound, and you'll need a collar and a board. GCS three at first, now fourteen. She's concussed, almost certainly whiplashed and she could have pelvic and spinal injuries—and mind her legs. I don't know if they were hit,' he said unsteadily, and then someone took over the control of her head and neck and he found himself gently shifted out of the way. Someone backed the car away very carefully to give them better access, and as soon as her spine was immobilised they moved her onto a stretcher, then up onto the trolley for the short trundle to the ED doors.

He scooped up her bag and coat and went with them, still issuing instructions on autopilot. 'Try and keep it smooth,' he said, putting his free hand on the trolley to steady it. 'She'll need a head and neck CT and a full trauma series—'

'It's OK, you can leave her with us now,' someone said, but he shook his head.

'No way, she's my wife,' he said, for the sake of economy, and he followed them into Resus without waiting to be invited. The team closed around her, nobody he recognised, no one he could connect with, and then a door swished open and someone said, 'OK, what have we got?' and the voice from his youth was so familiar he could have cried with relief.

'Sam,' he said, his voice choked, and Sam stopped in his tracks and did a mild double-take.

'Nick? What are you doing here?'

'My wife was knocked down in the car park, right in front of me. Her name's Olivia—Liv. She's a midwife here.'

'Liv's your wife?' Sam's face creased into a frown and he bent over her so she could see his face without moving. 'Hi, Liv, it's Sam Ryder. Remember me? You delivered our baby last year.'

'Of course I do. How is she?' she mumbled, and Nick let out a sigh of relief because if she remembered that, it was a good sign—wasn't it?

'She's fine. They're both well.' Sam turned to him. 'What can you tell me about the accident? Speed, angle of collision, how far she travelled?'

He made himself focus. 'Um—low speed collision, probably less than ten miles an hour at the most? She stepped out backwards in front of a big SUV. She was hit from her left side and spun as she fell, but not far. Her head hit the kerb pretty hard. There's a cut on the left side just behind the temple. GCS three initially, then fourteen after a brief loss of consciousness—'

'How brief?'

He shrugged. 'I don't know. Not long, but long enough to be significant. A minute, maybe, at the most? I'd done a cursory check and called for help before she stirred.'

'Did her head hit the bonnet before she fell?'

'No. No, it really wasn't that fast and the front wing just clipped her. She just—spun and fell, but really hard so she'll need a CT and her head's bleeding so she could have a fracture there where she hit the kerb, and she might be whiplashed and her spine needs checking thoroughly—'

Sam lifted a hand. 'OK, we're on it. Can you give us her details so we can be getting her notes up? And then maybe you need to go and get a coffee while we check her over.'

'I can't leave her—'

'Yes, you can. Don't worry, we'll keep you updated. Make sure we've got your number.'

Sam turned back to Liv, taking her hand in his, focusing intently on his patient as Nick stood numbly and watched them, hardly daring to breathe.

'OK, Liv, can you tell me where it hurts?' Sam asked softly.

'Everywhere.'

'Well, that's not very useful,' he said with a grin. 'Can you try and be a little more specific?'

'My head?'

'Anywhere else?' He carried on chattily assessing her while Nick watched tensely from the sidelines, then he straightened.

'OK. That's all good. Can we get some IV paracetamol on board, please, and get a full trauma screen to rule out any fractures and then we'll send you down for a head and neck CT, Liv, OK? And can we run a FAST scan, please, while we're waiting?'

Nick felt himself relax a fraction. Despite his light-hearted banter, Sam was looking after her properly, and all the time the nurses had been working, linking her to a monitor, getting IV access ready, cutting her clothes away so Sam could see her injuries.

He could see them, too, and the bruises on her smooth, pale skin made him wince. She could so easily have been killed—

'Mr Jarvis?'

He turned his head, finally becoming aware of the

nurse who'd laid a hand on his arm and was shaking it gently to get his attention.

'If you could give me her details that would be very helpful.'

'Of course. I'm sorry.' He forced himself to focus, rattled off her name, date of birth, address, GP—

'OK, I've got her. You're her next of kin?'

'Yes,' he said firmly, although he didn't know if that was still true, strictly speaking, because the ex-ness made that all a little unclear...

'Same mobile phone number?'

'Yes.'

'Is that her stuff? Would you like me to look after it?'

He looked down and saw the coat and bag, clutched in his hand like a lifeline. He'd forgotten all about them. 'Yeah, thanks.' He handed them over just as the door behind him opened again and swished shut, and he turned his head and met Ben Walker's worried eyes.

'What's going on? I heard Liv had been run over.'

'Not run over,' he said, his voice suddenly hollow. 'She was knocked down. She's got a head injury.'

Ben frowned, crossed over to the bed and exchanged a few words with Sam, then leant over her. 'Hi, Liv. Anything I can do?'

She mumbled something, and Ben nodded and straightened up, squeezing her hand as he left her side.

'Don't worry, I'll look after him.'

He turned to the nurse who was printing up Liv's labels for the notes. 'Page me if you need us,' he said, and hooking his arm around Nick's shoulders, the bluff Yorkshireman gently but firmly led him away.

CHAPTER THREE

BEN STEERED HIM through the department and out of the doors on the park side of the building.

The cold March air hit him, and he hauled in a breath and gagged.

'I feel sick,' he said, and doubled over, retching emptily.

He felt Ben's hand on his back. 'Come on. We'll find a bench where you can sit down and I'll go and get us a drink.'

He nodded and straightened up, following Ben obediently across the grass on legs that weren't quite steady. 'I thought she was dead, Ben. She was about to step out in front of this massive SUV, right in front of my eyes, and I tried to hold her but she pulled away and fell backwards and it smacked into her and then she was lying there, so still, her feet just inches from the wheels—'

'Nick, she's alive and conscious and talking, and Sam will be doing everything he can to make sure she stays that way. Now sit down before you fall down.'

They'd reached a bench, and he didn't need telling twice. He dropped onto it and propped his elbows on his knees, trying to slow his breathing and regain control of his emotions. After a few seconds he straightened up and glanced across at Ben, who was sitting beside him watching him thoughtfully.

'Better?'

He nodded. 'Yeah. Sorry.'

The hand on his shoulder was warm and firm and comforting. 'Don't be. You're in shock, and I'd be just the same if it was Daisy or one of the kids. How do you take your tea?'

'Coffee, for a start, black, no sugar—and if you put a ton of sugar in it, I'll pour it on the grass, so don't even try.'

Ben grunted and got to his feet without bothering to comment. 'Have you eaten today?'

'Not since seven. I didn't manage to get lunch.'

Too busy trashing what was left of his relationship with Liv...

'Right. I'll get you something to eat, as well. Stay here.'

He didn't think he had a choice. He was seriously unsure his legs would hold him if he tried to get up, and he swallowed on another wave of nausea.

Shock, he realised numbly. He was in shock, as Ben had said, but Liv was alive, Sam was looking after her and if he was as good a doctor as he was a sailor, she was in safe hands.

All he could do was wait.

So this is what it's like in a scanner, she thought, but she felt curiously detached, as if it wasn't really happening to her.

It didn't take long, and then she was wheeled back to the ED, lying on her back staring at the ceiling as it whizzed past and feeling disorientated. She knew the route well, but she'd never seen it from this angle. Weird.

They went through several sets of doors, and came to rest at last in Resus. She was glad they'd stopped. Her head was spinning and even the slight jiggle of the trolley along the smooth corridors had made it hurt more.

'OK?' Sam asked, smiling down at her, and she tried to smile back but it felt like a pretty poor effort and she just wanted Nick.

'I think so. My head aches a bit.'

'It will. You've had quite a bump, Liv, but nothing's broken and there's no evidence of a brain injury. You might be pretty sore for a while, though, but your spine's OK and so's your pelvis, so we can get rid of all this stuff and someone'll come and clean you up a bit and then I'll get you moved out of Resus.'

'What happened to my clothes? I don't remember anyone taking them off.'

'We cut them off you,' he said, frowning slightly. 'When you were brought in.'

'Oh.' She thought hard, but came up with nothing. 'I didn't register that. I suppose you had to. Where's Nick?'

'I don't know, but when I find him he's going to ask me questions and I gather from Ben that you're not together any more, so do I have your permission to talk to him about your results, or would you rather I didn't?'

Her results? 'Yes—yes, of course. If you don't tell him he'll only ask me anyway so you might as well.'

Sam chuckled. 'That sounds like him. OK, I'll go and find him while we get you sorted. He won't be far away.'

He was in the relatives' room where Ben had left him when Sam came in. He tried to get up, but Sam put a hand on his shoulder and pushed him gently back down. It wasn't hard. His legs felt like jelly and he thought he was going to be sick again.

He opened his mouth to ask how she was, but he didn't need to, Sam got there before him.

'She's OK, Nick. She's doing all right.'

He let his breath out in a rush and crushed the sudden urge to cry. 'No brain injury?'

Sam sat down beside him and shook his head.

'No. Not as far as we can see but we'll watch that. Her CT was clear, her X-rays didn't reveal any fractures, but she's got a small cut on her scalp which I'm going to glue, and she's going to have some colourful bruises. There's the odd superficial graze from contact with the ground, of course, and she's going to be sore, but all in all she's got away with it pretty lightly. Assuming there's no silent head injury waiting to show itself, she should be fine in a day or so but she might be a bit concussed. She's got a headache, so I want to keep an eye on that, but it's probably a bit of whiplash.'

He nodded, swallowing. 'Can I see her now?'

'In a minute. I'll get someone to take you to her as soon as she's ready. I'm going to keep her on fifteen-minute obs for a while, and I'm probably going to admit her overnight, just in case. She didn't seem to remember we'd cut her clothes off, but that might just be shock. She was still in the neck brace so she might not even have realised what we were doing, but I don't want to make assumptions and miss anything.'

Nick tried to smile. 'Don't worry, I won't let you. I'll be right there by her side and I'll be watching her like a hawk.'

'Good. I'll let you know when she's ready. Oh, and the police want to talk to you about the accident. I'll get them to come and see you now. Don't move.'

It seemed to take an age before the police were finished with him, but finally he was able to go and see Liv. She was in a bed in the small observation ward, her lashes dark against her pale cheeks, and she looked so frail and vulnerable that his heart wrenched. It could so easily have been so much worse. It might yet be...

The chair creaked as he sat down, and her lids fluttered open and her head turned towards him.

'Nick?'

He stood up and moved to her side, gripping the cot sides on the edge of the bed as he stared down at her ashen face. A bruise was coming out on her cheekbone, blue against the pale skin, and he swallowed hard. 'Yes, it's me, Liv. Is that OK, or do you want me to leave?'

'No, stay with me, please?' Her hand fluttered, and he reached down and slipped his fingers through hers and they curled around his and clung.

'How are you feeling?' he asked, aware of how gruff his voice sounded but unable to do anything about it.

She shrugged slightly, and winced. 'Sore?' she said, sounding weak and tired and nothing like his Liv. 'I've got a banging headache and everything's feeling a bit tender. Sam said I was lucky not to break anything, but it doesn't feel lucky from where I'm lying.'

'It's lucky,' he said fervently. 'Trust me, it's lucky. I watched that car hit you, and for a minute there—well, whatever. If I hadn't followed you—'

'Nick, it wasn't your fault I stepped out in front of it.'

'Don't, Liv. I don't want to think about it. It's all I can see as it is, and it *was* my fault, I should have listened to you and let you go.' He lifted her hand to his mouth and pressed a long, lingering kiss to the back of her fingers. 'Is there anything I can do for you, anything I can get you?'

'A taxi?' she joked weakly. 'Not that I can go anywhere. They cut my clothes off.'

He frowned. 'They had to, Liv. They had no idea what

injuries you had, and anyway, hitting the tarmac won't have done them any good. And as for the taxi, you're going nowhere,' he said firmly. 'Sam's talking about admitting you overnight for observation and I think it's a good idea.'

'No-o. I don't want to stay in,' she moaned softly. 'It's so noisy here. I just want my own bed.'

'OK. Maybe later. I'll talk to Sam,' he murmured to stall her, although he knew darned well what Sam would say, and so, apparently, did she.

'My parents used to do that,' she said, her voice tailing off. 'I'll ask your father. I'll see what your mother says. All stalling tactics. The answer never did change...'

Her lids drifted down, her lashes coming to rest against her bleached skin, and as her hand relaxed he laid it down gently, let his breath out on a slow, silent huff and lowered himself onto the chair again, never taking his eyes off her.

She'd get better a lot quicker, Liv thought, if they'd only leave her alone to sleep, but she knew why they were doing it, and it was reassuring in a mildly irritating way.

The nurses came intermittently to do her obs, and after a while Nick told them not to bother, he'd do them. It meant he had to touch her, to feel the pulse beating in her wrist, to check her pupils with a pen light, and although he was doing exactly what the nurses had, somehow his touch was different.

Not quite so clinical as theirs, lingering a little longer than was strictly necessary, and his voice was quiet and soothing but also filled with an emotion that he either didn't or couldn't disguise. And when she had to stare into his eyes so he could test her pupil reflexes, there was a tenderness there that made her want to cry.

A nurse brought him a cup of tea at one point, and a couple of times Sam popped his head round the curtain, glanced at her chart and exchanged a few words with them, asked her questions, made her squeeze his hands, push against him, wiggle her toes, shone a light in her eyes to check her pupil reflexes and accommodation, but all of it with an appropriate clinical detachment which just made Nick's touch all the more obviously different.

It was weird having him there with her. He was so gentle, so quiet and unobtrusive, and yet even when he was sitting silently beside her, she was aware of him with every battered cell in her body. She'd been so desperate to get away from him that she'd nearly died, and now that seemed ridiculous because she actually wanted him there, crazy though it was.

Because she still loved him, despite the lie? Maybe even *because* of it—because of the fact that he hadn't, after all, slept with Suzanne.

Why not? She wouldn't have blamed him—or Suze, come to that. She was a beautiful woman, and he was a beautiful man. Why wouldn't they want each other? It wasn't as if it would have been the first time—and it wasn't as if things had been exactly peachy in the months leading up to it, and that was her own fault as much as his.

She'd spent the last year blaming herself for shutting him out and driving him to it, but he'd shut her out, too, and their relationship had been crumbling for months before it had reached crisis point.

He was right, they did need to talk, but not now, and not here, in probably the busiest department of the hospital. Now, with her head hurting and every part of her starting to ache, all she wanted was to go home.

Sam, though, had other ideas. Before he'd discuss it

he wanted a urine sample to check for blood, presumably to see if she'd sustained kidney damage.

'I'll get a bedpan,' Nick said, but she was ready for that and dismissed it instantly.

'No way. Or a commode. The loo—as in proper plumbing, running water, and a door that shuts.'

'I don't think—'

'Good. Don't bother,' she said, trying to sound firm and failing miserably. 'Seriously, Nick, if you won't let me walk, then get me a wheelchair, and if you won't do that then I'll crawl on my hands and knees. Please don't make me, because I will do it.' Her voice cracked, and she bit her lips and waited.

She watched his internal battle, and then to her relief he sighed quietly and got to his feet. 'Still as stubborn as ever, then,' he said mildly, and went, presumably to find a wheelchair.

'Going somewhere?' Sam asked as Nick wheeled it in.

'Yeah. It has to be the loo, apparently.'

'Well, stay with her.'

'I will.'

'Over my dead body,' she said, and Sam just laughed, but Nick frowned, his face a mask.

'Can we not talk about your dead body, please?' he said tightly, and she felt a chill run over her. If that car had been going a little quicker, she might not be here now. There'd been a fraction of a second when everything had gone into slow motion, and she'd been sure she was going to die. What must it have been like for him to watch it all happen and be unable to prevent it? To feel that he'd caused it, even?

Horrendous, and it was only by the grace of God that she wasn't dead or far more critically injured. No wonder he was fussing over her. After all, he'd loved her once, and maybe, in a way, still did. And despite their problems, he was a good man. Way too good to have deserved the way she'd treated him.

'Sorry,' she said soberly, cutting him some slack. 'If you could just wheel me there, please, I can do the rest.'

He had an opinion, of course, but in the end she won and he hovered outside the door until she'd finished and then took the urine sample off her and wheeled her back to bed.

'OK?' he asked as she sank back against the pillows with relief.

'Mmm. Thanks. Could you give that to Sam and ask him when I can go home?'

'You can ask me yourself,' Sam said, appearing at the foot of the bed and giving her a wry smile. 'You won't like the answer.'

'Oh, no, Sam, really? I'm fine—'

'No, you're not, Liv,' Sam told her gently. 'You're doing OK, but you're not fine, and if you've got a silent head injury—'

'Then I'll call someone.'

'Not if you can't,' Nick growled from beside her. 'You need monitoring all night.'

'No, I don't! I'm fine, Nick, and if you won't discharge me, Sam, I'm going to discharge myself.'

'Liv, I really—'

'No, Nick! This is none of your business. I appreciate your concern, both of you, but I don't want to stay in. I've got a few bruises—'

'You were out cold!'

'For seconds—'

'It still counts, Liv,' Sam interjected, but she just glared at him.

'I. Want. To. Go. Home,' she said, stressing every word

as if she was talking to a pair of idiots, which frankly she felt she was. Her head was killing her, everything hurt and she just wanted out. Now. Before she broke down and let out all the emotions that were building inside her.

Sam looked at her, looked at Nick and looked back at her again—and gave in.

'OK,' he said, to her astonishment. 'On one condition.'

'Anything,' she said rashly.

'Nick stays with you.'

'No!'

They spoke together, but Sam just arched a brow and shrugged. 'Your choice. It's that or nothing.'

'I'll discharge myself.'

Nick felt sick again. She would, he knew that. The woman was stubborn enough for anything, even if it worked against her. He'd learned that years ago, and he'd given up fighting it.

But this was different. This was her life they were talking about, and her safety was more important to him than anything else and he'd done enough to compromise it today already.

'I'll do it,' he said. 'If you insist on going home, I'll do it.'

'No. It's not necessary.'

'Take it or leave it, Liv,' he said flatly. 'Either I'm there with you, or you're here, which is definitely my preferred option.'

'It's not your option to have, and you can't make me—'

'Watch me. I've already seen you nearly get killed once today because of me. I won't stand back and watch you have another go. As I said, take it or leave it, but that's the way it is.'

She frowned, lifting her hand to her head and pressing

it against her forehead as if she was trying to push away the pain. Finally her arm dropped in a gesture of defeat.

'OK. You win. Come home with me if you think you have to, but it's totally unnecessary and I'm not happy about it.'

'Tough. At least I'll be able to live with myself,' he told her.

Sam rolled his eyes and grinned. 'Right. Now that's sorted, I'll go check this urine for blood, and if it's OK I'll authorise your discharge so that we can all go home tonight,' he said, and Nick watched her close her eyes with a sigh.

'I'm still not happy,' she grumbled, but he wasn't going to argue. He'd won this round. For now, that was enough.

It was almost ten that night before he pulled up on the drive of the home they'd shared for three years.

When they'd bought it just over four years ago, a bright future lay ahead of them. Little had they known how it was all going to pan out, but those happy days—and nights—now seemed a lifetime ago and he'd almost forgotten what home meant.

'Keys?' he said to her, and she rummaged in her bag and held them out to him.

'The burglar alarm's set. My code's 0901—and there's a mortice lock on the door now, too.'

The security lights triggered as he got out of the car, which was just as well, as he had to find the new keyhole.

Why the new lock? To stop him getting back in? And changing the code? She hadn't needed to do that. She should have known he wouldn't have invaded her privacy. Maybe he should have done, should have stuck it out and had the rest of the conversation she'd cut off at the ankles when she'd thrown him out, and maybe then he'd still have been with her, instead of drifting around in limbo and living alone in a box no bigger than their double garage.

He let out a tired sigh and swung the door open, stepping into the hall with a curious sense of déjà vu. He didn't know what he'd expected—that she would have changed the decor, or moved the furniture—anything, really, apart from nothing, which was what confronted him.

The same colour walls—not quite white, a soft touch of earthy grey taking the edge off it—the same striped stair carpet in muted greys and neutrals, the chair that sat randomly in the corner for no apparent reason—even the basket of carefully pressed and folded washing on the third step waiting for her to make a journey upstairs and take it with her.

It could have sat there untouched since the day she'd thrown him out—on the ninth of January. Hence the code for the burglar alarm, he realised belatedly.

Swallowing the lump in his throat, he turned it off ran upstairs with the washing basket and put it on the floor in their—correction, *her*—bedroom, and ran back down to help her out of the car.

Too slow.

'Liv, what are you doing?'

She lifted her head and frowned at him. 'What do you think I'm doing?' she asked, levering herself to her feet. 'It's obvious.'

Stubborn woman. 'Here, let me help you—'

Her level stare stopped him in his tracks, her pride obviously overriding common sense. 'Nick, relax, I can manage. You're only here because Sam insisted. I don't *need* you to help me.'

Which would have been fine, had she not then swayed against the car and let out a stifled groan.

He didn't wait to be asked. She'd be on the floor before she admitted she needed him for anything at all, so he just stepped in, laid her right arm carefully over his shoulders and put his other arm around her waist to steady her.

'Headrush?' he asked quietly, and she nodded.

'Mmm. It's OK now.' But she didn't try and shake him off, which she would have done if she'd truly been OK, so he walked her carefully to the front door, helped her over the doorstep, and then lowered her gently to the chair. He'd never seen the point of it until now, he thought wryly, watching as she sat silently on it with her eyes shut and a tiny frown creasing her brow.

The bruise on her cheekbone was spreading, coming out nicely in a black and blue stain that extended up into her hair and round the edge of her eye, steadily creeping across her eyebrow and down onto the lid. The only reason her face wasn't scraped was that her thick, dark hair had tumbled across her cheek and protected it as she'd hit the tarmac, and it had been further back on the side of her head that she'd taken the brunt of the fall. Hence the dried blood matted in her hair—

Her eyes opened again and she lifted her head and looked at him, the frown deepening. 'What?'

'What do you mean, what?'

'You were looking at me funny. You still are.'

He clenched his teeth, swallowing the horror he'd been reliving, the sight of her crashing to the ground, the way her head had bounced off the kerb—

'You're imagining it,' he said dismissively. 'Where to? Up or down?'

She looked at the stairs, her eyes running up the flight as if to assess the enormity of the task, then back to him as the fight went out of her. 'It all looks like too much effort but I suppose I really ought to go to bed before I can't get there.'

'Is there anything I can do to help you?'

She shook her head. 'No. I'll manage, Nick.'

She shrugged off her coat, took a deep breath and tackled the stairs. They seemed endless but she made it, only because she didn't really have a choice if she was going to be comfortable, but her head was pounding and she felt dizzy halfway up and had to lean on him.

'Just a few more steps to go,' Nick murmured, his warm, solid body reassuringly close behind her, and she gritted her teeth and made it up the last ones, pausing to lean on him for another moment before tackling the short distance across the landing to the bed.

He flicked back the covers, and she sat down gingerly on the edge with a sigh of relief, cold sweat beading on her forehead.

'OK?'

'Yes, I'm OK. I'm up here anyway. Maybe I should have some painkillers. My head's banging like a drum now.'

'Maybe you should. Let's get you comfy and I'll sort you out a drink to take them with.'

He shifted the pillows, stacking them up so she could lean back on them while she kicked off her shoes and then swung her legs up.

'Oh, that's better.' She sighed, settling against the pillows. 'I just feel a bit battered all over, and my head aches. I keep telling it I feel better, but it hasn't got the memo yet.'

He gave a wry huff of laughter, and he ran downstairs and brought her back a glass of water to take the paracetamol.

'Have you had any other drugs today? Any other pain relief?'

'No, I haven't. You know I don't take drugs. Only the IV paracetamol they gave me this afternoon, and that was hours ago. Just give it to me, for heaven's sake, and don't fuss.'

'I wouldn't dream of it,' he said drily, handing her the water and holding out his hand with the pills in.

She took them, washed them down with water and handed the glass back with an apologetic sigh. 'Thank you. I'm sorry I've been so bitchy. I just...'

'Forget it,' he said softly. 'Tea? Coffee? Something to eat?'

'Tea would be lovely. And some toast, maybe? I'm starving. I don't know what happened to lunch.'

He did. He'd messed it up, like he'd messed so many things up. He put the glass on the bedside table and went back down to the kitchen. It hadn't changed any more than the rest, and he glanced across to the family room, his eyes settling on the sofa where it had all unravelled.

It could have been yesterday, he thought, if it wasn't for the wrenching heartache that had filled every day since she'd told him she wanted a divorce—a divorce that had never happened, for some reason.

He rested his hands on the edge of the worktop, hung his head and let out a shaky sigh. He so hadn't wanted to do this, to be here with her in this way, forced together by circumstances and Sam's well-meant interference, but he was the best candidate for the job.

He knew every inch of the house, could find his way round the kitchen in the dark, and, more importantly, knew Liv well enough to override her when necessary. That didn't mean he was going to enjoy it, and he knew it wouldn't be easy, not if she had anything to say about it—and he was sure she would, in spades.

Oh, well. One thing at a time.

He straightened up, hauled in a bracing lungful of air and put the kettle on.

CHAPTER FOUR

'DOES BEN KNOW you're not staying there tonight?'

He glanced up at her, taking his eyes off the midwifery journal he'd been pretending to read. As if she hadn't realised that. He hadn't turned a page in the last few minutes and his face had been like a frozen mask.

'Yes. I rang him just before we left the hospital. He's been fretting about you. He took me for coffee and force-fed me a disgustingly sweet chocolate muffin when Sam kicked me out of Resus, but then he had to go back to work. He's been bombarding me with texts ever since, asking how you are.'

She laughed softly and then winced, and he frowned.

'You OK?'

She nodded. 'My stomach muscles hurt a bit. I guess being flung around like that'd cause all sorts of odd aches and pains.'

He frowned again at that, no doubt reliving the accident, and she regretted mentioning it.

'You probably tensed up to protect yourself. Are the painkillers working yet?'

She would have laughed under normal circumstances, but she'd tried that once. 'Not so you'd notice,' she told him. 'I need to get out of this lot,' she said, plucking at the horrible hospital gown and the borrowed scrub bottoms they'd lent her in the ED.

'Really? I thought it was rather fetching. The little NHS logo all over the gown goes really well with your eyes, but it's your choice.'

'Good of you to remember that,' she said drily. 'There's a long pink T-shirt with short sleeves in the second drawer, on the left.'

'Do you really need it?'

He sounded puzzled, and she forced herself to look up and meet his eyes. 'Yes, I do, because you're going to be here and we're not together any more,' she told him bluntly.

He rolled his eyes. 'Jeez, Liv, give me credit. I just thought you'll be more comfortable with nothing on. I'm hardly going to take advantage of it.'

'It's nothing to do with that,' she said, remembering when he'd taken every opportunity to do exactly that, but that was a long time ago, well before she'd thrown him out. Their problems had started long before then. She sighed. So much water under so many bridges…

'Nick, I can't be bothered to argue,' she told him. 'Just find it, please, could you, and then leave me alone? The bathroom's just here, not ten feet from the bed. I'll be fine.'

That sounded churlish, and she didn't mean it to. She let out a shaky sigh and shook her head. 'Sorry. That came out all wrong but I'm too tired to play games and I just want to go to sleep.'

She looked up at him, and saw sorrow etched on his face.

'It's OK, Liv. I understand,' he said softly. 'I know you don't want me here, but it's not for long. You'll be fine in a day or two.'

He was wrong. She did want him there, but not like this. Not shackled by duty and guilt, but there because he loved her.

He found the T-shirt, put it on the bed beside her and went out of the room. Not far, she knew that from the creaks on the landing, but far enough. He was probably sitting on the top step. She swung her legs over the side of the bed as she sat up, then unfastened the hideous hospital gown and tried to peel it off her shoulders, but they protested and she stifled a whimper.

Come on, girl, toughen up.

She got there in the end and pulled the long top on, then stood up, but as she bent over to push the trousers down she felt her head start to swim again.

She let out a little wail of frustration as she sagged back onto the bed, and the door swung open and Nick walked in.

'Feel free to knock,' she grumbled, but he ignored it and crouched down in front of her, his hands resting lightly on her knees as he looked up at her.

'What happened?' he asked gently. 'Another head-rush?'

'Mmm. My head started swimming again when I bent over to take the scrubs off.'

'I'm not surprised, you've got concussion,' he said, easing them off over her feet as his eyes scanned the bruises that were coming out on her legs. His voice was calm, but she was sure he didn't feel calm. She could see the pulse beating in his throat as he looked at the bruises, and she knew he was holding his feelings in. Maybe it was just as well. She was on the brink of losing it as it was, and if he'd been nice to her, shown the slightest sign of caring, she would have crumpled like a wet tissue. Might anyway...

He stood up. 'Let me check your obs again,' he said, all business now suddenly, as if that was the easiest way to cope. He probably wasn't wrong.

He took the pen light he'd raided off Sam out of his pocket and turned it on, crouching down in front of her again. 'OK, look at me,' he said, and flashed it in her eyes in turn while she stared straight back into his. He had such beautiful eyes, and there'd been a time not so very long ago when they'd looked at her lovingly. Now, it was all business.

'OK, follow the pen.'

She followed it dutifully, overwhelmingly conscious of his left hand on the edge of the bed close to her right hip, steadying himself as he balanced on the balls of his feet. He was so close to her that she could feel the warmth coming off his body, smell the faint and yet unmistakable scent that was uniquely him.

She'd missed that, missed snuggling up to him, missed his arms around her, his heart beating under her ear—

'OK, your eyes are fine. Squeeze my hands?'

His grip was sure but gentle, and after she'd squeezed and relaxed he let her fingers lie in his. Only for a moment, but longer than was strictly necessary, then he let them go and stood up briskly, and she felt cool air sweep in where his warmth had been.

'You'll do,' he said, his voice suddenly gruff.

'I could have told you that. I need the loo now.'

'Can you manage on your own or do you need my help?'

'No, I can manage,' she said, mustering her feeble reserves. *Gosh, she was so tired.* She stood up, tugging the long tee down, and headed through the door, closing it behind her and waiting for his voice.

'Don't lock it.'

Right on cue. 'I won't,' she promised wearily. Not so long ago they'd never bothered to shut the bathroom door, but those days were long gone, and for what? Just a lonely, aching wilderness of wasted emotion.

Her eyes prickled and she screwed her eyes up and swallowed hard. She was *not* going to cry. Not, not, not.

And then her head swam again, and the sob she'd tried to suppress wasn't having any of it, and it broke free in an anguished wail.

He opened the door and found her still sitting there, her hand clamped over her mouth. Holding down the sobs? Pointless, because they were escaping anyway and tearing him apart.

The darkening blue tinge of her bruises was starting to show more clearly against the pale skin of her leg. When they really came out it would be black from top to bottom. He dragged his eyes away and swallowed hard. How she hadn't broken anything...

'What's up, sweetheart?' he asked gently, the endearment slipping out past his guard as he went over to her.

'I feel dizzy and I daren't get up and I feel so stupid—'

Her voice cracked, and his hands cradled her head tenderly against him while he told her she wasn't stupid, just hurt, letting her lean on him in a rare moment of weakness while he struggled to keep his own emotions in check. She didn't give him long, though. A few precious seconds at most, and then she pulled herself together, straightening up and using his hands to lever herself to her feet, her independence fighting fit again.

'Thank you,' she said, aiming for the basin, but he headed her off.

'No. Bed,' he told her firmly, wheeling her out of the room towards it. Independence be damned. 'I'll wash your hands, and then I'm going to find us something proper to eat because I think you're probably feeling lightheaded because of low blood sugar as much as anything else. What do you fancy?'

She sat down on the bed and shrugged. 'I don't think there is much. I'd be fine with more toast.'

'That isn't enough, not for either of us, and I haven't eaten all day apart from that muffin which really doesn't count. Don't worry, I'll find something in the freezer. You just settle back and get comfortable and leave it all to me.'

He went back into the bathroom and noticed a tiny crumpled heap of something on the floor beside the pan. The hideous disposable paper pants the hospital had given her, he realised, and stooped slowly and picked them up. She used to wear gorgeous undies—delicate lace that offered tantalising glimpses of her body.

He dropped them in the bin, turned on the tap, ran it until the water was hot and squeezed out her facecloth in the water, adding a touch of soap.

'Here,' he said, picking up her hands one at a time and washing them meticulously. The right one was fine, the left a little grazed and bruised on the outside edge where she must have landed on it, and he worked carefully round the sore place, then rinsed the cloth and wiped them again before patting them dry. Such a simple thing to do, and yet strangely symbolic. If only he could wash away their sadness and make them whole again...

'Thank you,' she whispered, and he looked up and saw the sparkle of tears in her eyes and felt his own fill. 'Thank you for looking after me. I know I've been horribly ungracious, but I really couldn't have managed without you, and I'm sorry.'

'Oh, Liv—' His voice cracked, and he squeezed her

hands in his. 'You don't have to apologise to me for anything.'

'Yes, I do, for so many things—'

'No. Not now. Now, you need to rest, and you need some food, and then you need to sleep,' he said gently, his voice sounding like sandpaper.

He took the towel back into the bathroom and caught sight of his face in the mirror. He looked haggard, his eyes a little wild, his mouth a grim line. No wonder. She could have died under those wheels, so easily. Another foot—

He hung up the towel, rinsed the facecloth and wrung it out so hard he nearly tore it in two.

Nick went downstairs to make some food, and she rested her head back and closed her eyes. She was exhausted, but even on the normally very comfortable bed she couldn't get truly comfortable. She must have dozed off, though, because she woke with a little groan to find he was there again, straddling the small bedroom chair he'd turned around, arms folded across the back, watching her with those intent, searching eyes.

'Hi,' he said, his voice sounding a little rough and unused for some reason.

'Hi. I didn't hear you come back up. Have I been asleep for long?'

'Ten minutes, perhaps?'

'Oh. Right. Not long, then. Did you find any food?'

His mouth kicked up in a wry smile and he shook his head. 'Not really. I had a look in the freezer, but it's not exactly over-stocked. How about a takeaway?'

Her stomach rumbled, and she realised she was ravenous. No wonder she was dizzy. 'That would be lovely.'

'Is the Chinese restaurant on the front still open?'

'Yes. And they deliver free.'

'Special chow mein?' he asked.

Gosh. Had she really been so predictable? It felt odd, especially considering she hadn't had one for at least a year, or maybe two. Not since long before he'd left. She dredged up a smile. 'Please.'

'Banana fritters?'

'That's disgusting,' she said, trying not to be tempted.

'But you love them.'

'Loved,' she corrected. 'I'm eating much more healthily now.'

'Still having chow mein.'

'Says the man whose entire diet today has been a slice of toast, a chocolate muffin and black coffee—and this whole takeaway thing was your idea, remember, not mine.'

His mouth twitched, but he let it go and pulled out his phone, looking for the number.

'Seven six four, three two nine,' she said, and he laughed as he keyed it in, the sound wrapping round her and cloaking her in grief for all they'd lost.

'You always did have the memory of an elephant for irrelevant detail,' he teased, and she felt her smile falter.

'It's not just the irrelevant things I can remember,' she told him sadly, and he swallowed hard and looked away.

'Frankly, today, I'm happy that you can remember anything—yeah, hi, can I order a special chow mein and chicken chop suey with boiled rice, please?'

That made her blink. Normally he'd have had king prawn balls in batter with special fried rice, and drenched the lot in lurid orange sweet and sour sauce, but maybe she wasn't the only one to address her diet. She ran her eyes over him, reassessing the changes she'd noticed earlier. He'd lost a little weight, but it was more than that—

the difference between healthy and letting yourself go. He looked fit and toned again, as if he'd taken up running or rejoined a gym. Gone was the man she'd been married to when it had all fallen apart.

Taking care of himself at last? He must be, and about time. He hung up and turned back to her.

'It'll be here in ten minutes.'

'Great. Thanks. Can you help me sort out the pillows? I can't sit up straight enough to eat and my neck's just not comfortable like this.'

'Sure.'

He sat her up, rearranged the pillows and settled her back against them as if she was made of fragile china.

'Better?' he asked, and she nodded.

'Yes, much. Thank you.' She rested her head back and frowned. 'I feel so guilty. Ben and Daisy were expecting you and she will have cooked, you know what she's like.'

'I know, but it can't be helped and Ben knows I'm staying here and why, and it's just until you're all right.'

'I am all right, Nick. I'm fine—'

His quiet snort of disbelief cut her off. 'Really? So fine you can't get off the loo without help? So fine you can't even move in your sleep without waking up because of the pain?'

He came over to her, perched carefully on the edge of the bed and wrapped her hand in both of his, a frown furrowing his brow.

'Liv, look at yourself,' he said softly, his voice oddly raw. 'You're going to be black and blue, your head's banging like a drum—how bad do you have to be before you'll let go of this ridiculous pretence that you're fine and just accept my help? For God's sake, you could have died—'

His voice cracked, his fingers tightening on hers, and in the moments before he looked away, she saw the fear that he must have felt for her, the guilt that because he'd followed her when she was trying to get away, she'd stepped out in front of the car. And he'd only wanted to talk to her. How much would it have hurt her to stop and listen, give him a chance? Not this much.

'Nick, I didn't look where I was going. It's my fault, not yours.'

He let go of her hand and stood up, pacing to the window.

'Of course it's my fault. It's all my fault. It's my fault our marriage went wrong, it's my fault you threw me out, my fault you got hit—'

'That's rubbish. And it's not your fault our marriage went wrong; I shut you out, I wouldn't let you help me, and if I'd gone to the conference with you instead of sending you on your own, none of this would have happened and I wouldn't have kicked you out. You can't take the blame for everything, Nick. I was horrible to you.'

He sat back down on the bed, taking her hand again, his warmth curiously comforting.

'No, you weren't. You were just unhappy, and so was I, and we took it out on each other instead of getting help, and it just got into a downward spiral and I don't think we knew how to stop it. And it happens so often with couples who have difficulty conceiving, but one thing my job's taught me is that struggling on alone isn't the answer and we were barely even communicating by the end. We got so lost that we couldn't find a way out and we just stopped talking to each other.'

'Why us?' she asked forlornly, but he just shrugged.

'Why anyone? It's the luck of the draw, Liv, and we got unlucky, but it was our own fault we let it destroy us and we both should have known better and tried harder instead of building walls around ourselves.'

The doorbell rang, and he let go of her hand and went downstairs, and she dropped her head back against the pillows.

Was that what they'd done? Built walls? Probably. They'd had an amazing marriage, filled with love and laughter and tenderness, and then bit by bit it had all slowly disappeared, eaten away by the bitter disappointment of their repeated failure to make a baby. And with every bit that went, they'd added another brick to their walls.

Nick was right. It was nobody's fault, and they'd been helpless to help themselves, and by the end they weren't even trying to, they'd just let it all wither away to dust.

A tear trickled out of the corner of her eye, and she swiped it hastily away as he came back into the room with two bowls and a couple of forks.

He plonked himself down on the bed next to her, propped himself up against the headboard and handed her the chow mein. 'There you go, wrap yourself around that.'

It smelt amazing, and there'd be plenty of time to talk later. 'Gosh, I'm ready for this,' she said, finding a smile from somewhere, and dug her fork in.

'Where are you going to sleep?'

He glanced at her, looked around the room and shrugged. 'On the floor, I guess.'

'Nick, there are two other bedrooms—'

'Three.'

She looked away. 'Two. I turned the little room into a study.'

The room that had been destined to be a nursery. The room that had haunted her until she'd had the guts to address it and claim it as her own, instead of waiting for something that would never happen.

He frowned slightly. 'There's a study downstairs.'

'But that's yours,' she said simply, 'and I wanted my own space.' One where she wasn't constantly bombarded by reminders of him. 'I'm doing a course on natural childbirth and pain relief in labour. I'm studying hypnosis at the moment. And it wasn't as if it was needed for anything else.'

He closed his eyes briefly, and when he opened them she could see the anguish in them.

'I'm sorry, Liv,' he said heavily. 'I'm so sorry it didn't work for us, that we never needed that room. I'm sorry I couldn't give you a baby. And I'm so sorry I wasn't there for you, sorry I shut you out, sorry I let you shut me out. It wasn't meant to be like that. Not at all. It was all going to be perfect—'

'Oh, Nick, don't—' She felt her eyes fill and looked away, blinking hard. They'd been so happy, had so many hopes and dreams, and it had all come to nothing and in such a horrible way.

'So anyway,' she went on, putting that firmly out of her mind, 'you have two other rooms to choose from tonight, both of them better than sleeping on the floor.'

'Not for keeping an eye on you, which is after all why I'm here.'

'It's not as if you'll be far away, and anyway, I'm—'

'If you tell me once more that you're fine, I might just strangle you. And I'm not leaving you alone, Liv. Not for anything. I told Sam I'd look after you because otherwise he wouldn't have let you come home, so humour me, for God's sake.'

She gave a choked little laugh. Anyone less physically violent than Nick she'd never met, and he was obviously worried sick about her and she knew he'd only lie awake all night.

'Oh, for goodness' sake, if you're going to insist on

being in here, why don't you just sleep in the bed?' she
said softly.

After a pause so long she thought he hadn't heard, he
turned his head and met her eyes.

'You'd let me do that?'

She frowned. 'Why not? It's not like I can't trust you.
You wouldn't be here if I didn't trust you. I would have
stayed in hospital.'

'That's not what I meant. I just thought you wouldn't
want me that close. It's not much more than an hour since
you insisted you needed nightclothes on, and that's when
you thought I'd be in another room.'

'That's nothing to do with this.'

'Isn't it?'

'No. It's because I didn't want to—' She didn't know
how to describe it. Flaunt herself? In front of Nick? Ridiculous. He knew every inch of her. Expose herself to
humiliation, then, perhaps, because he'd certainly lost
interest in her body by the end...

He let out a weary sigh. 'Liv, it's OK. I'm sorry, I don't
want to argue. Of course you want to wear a nightdress,
you're entitled to your privacy. And it doesn't matter
where I sleep. I'll sleep anywhere.'

'So sleep here,' she said, patting the mattress beside
her. 'Near to me. Just in case—you know...'

He frowned. 'Is your headache worse?'

She tried to shake it, and thought better of it. 'No. No
more than it was, and maybe less, but I know you'll be
getting up and down all night because you'll be worried
about me. If you're here you can just prod me and ask if
I'm all right and go straight back to sleep.'

Fat chance.

He hovered over her while she washed, then did a
quick neuro check before he settled her in bed and lay

down beside her, but he was reluctant to move in case he hurt her or disturbed her, and his head was too full of the endless re-run of the accident to let him sleep.

Beside him Liv was restless and he wasn't sure she was asleep, either, despite the fact that she must be exhausted. Too sore? Or too cold?

The heating must have gone off and the room was growing steadily colder. It hadn't been over-warm in the first place—to save money? He propped himself up on one elbow and peered at her in the dim light spilling in from the landing, and realised she'd kicked the covers off, and she was going to be stiff and sore enough when she woke in the morning.

He checked his phone for the time. Nearly one o'clock. Time for another check. He turned towards her, pulling the covers back over her as he woke her.

'Liv?'

'Mmm?'

'Talk to me, sweetheart. It's time for another check. Are you OK?'

'I'm fine,' she said. She sounded tired rather than sleepy, and he wondered if she'd been awake, too.

'Do you hurt?'

'No, not so much now. I'm a bit cold.'

'You'd kicked the covers off, but I've put them back now, you'll soon warm up.'

He'd propped himself up on one elbow to flash the pen light in her eyes, and it gave him a chance to study her face. The bruise around her eye had invaded the lower lid now, and he could see further bruising along her cheekbone.

Without thinking, he leant over and touched his lips lightly to the bruise. 'You've got a real shiner now,' he said softly. 'The neighbours are going to think I've come back for revenge and beaten you up.'

'You'd never hurt me,' she said quietly. 'Not physically, at least.'

No. She was right, he wouldn't. Couldn't. But it hadn't stopped him walking out on their broken marriage and he knew how badly that had hurt her. Hurt both of them. He sighed softly, lifting his hand and trailing it lightly over her cheekbone and down her jaw. 'Do you need painkillers again?'

'No, not really.' She hesitated, her gaze holding his, then said quietly, as if she was afraid of his reaction, 'Do you know what I really want more than anything? A hug. I've really missed your hugs.'

A tear slid out of the corner of her eye and ran down into her hair, and his eyes blurred.

'Oh, Liv—'

His voice hitched, and he put the pen light back and lay down, reaching out his arms and folding them gently round her, and as she wriggled closer he pressed his lips to her forehead and squeezed his eyes tight shut to try and hold back the tears.

She wasn't the only one who'd missed this, and the feel of her body against his made something deep within him, something that had been out of kilter for one or maybe even two years, fall back into place.

He felt her hand slide up his chest and settle against his jaw, her fingertips resting against his neck, right over the pulse.

'What happened to us, Nick?' she asked sadly, her fingertips stroking soothingly over the beating artery. 'How did we end up in this mess?'

He swallowed hard. 'I have no idea. I just know I miss you every single day.'

'I miss you, too. You were my best friend.'

'Don't—'

His arms tightened round her, cradling her against his heart, and he blinked away the stinging tears and pressed another kiss to her hair.

It was stiff and smelt of blood and antiseptic, and he thought of how close she'd come to death, lying there almost under the wheels of that big, heavy car, and the tears squeezed past his lids and trickled across his temple and onto the pillow by her head.

'I nearly lost you today, Liv,' he whispered into the darkness. 'That car was so close—'

Her arms tightened round him, her lips finding his cheek and feathering soft kisses over the damp skin. 'Oh, Nick. I'm sorry I scared you. I was scared, too. I thought I was going to die—'

Her voice cracked, and he cradled her head tenderly against his shoulder. 'Don't be scared any more. You're not going to die, sweetheart, you're going to be fine,' he murmured gently, 'but you need to rest, my love. Just go to sleep. You're safe now. I've got you.'

She made a sleepy, contented noise and settled against him, and he felt the tension going out of her limbs, her breathing growing slow and deep and regular as she drifted off to sleep, but he didn't sleep for a long, long time.

He just held her, feeling the slow rise and fall of her chest with every breath, the warmth of her body against his, and wondered where on earth they went from here.

CHAPTER FIVE

HE WOKE TO the soft, yielding warmth of Liv's body draped over his.

He'd checked her a couple more times in the night and the last time she'd rolled away, but at some point she must have rolled back. He hadn't woken, but his arm was round her and her head was on his shoulder and it felt so familiar, so *right*...

Her arm lay loosely over his chest, her knee wedged down between his thighs, and her body was so close to his he could feel her heart beat.

Which would have been fine, except his body was apparently very happy to have her pressed up tight against it and he wasn't sure they were quite ready for that yet. At least he'd kept his underwear on. It gave him a little privacy, but not nearly enough, and it wasn't going to get any better unless he could somehow ease his leg out from under hers and move away.

He could always wait, he thought. She'd wake up at some point and then he could get his arm out from under her head and unravel the potentially embarrassing tangle of limbs.

But she didn't wake, and she was overdue for another check. He touched her cheek.

'Liv, wake up.'

She made a funny little noise and snuggled closer, her right arm curving down over his ribs, her fingers tucking under his side.

He closed his eyes, swore softly and took her wrist in his hand and eased it back again. 'Liv! Liv, wake up. I have to check you again.'

But she didn't move, just moaned slightly, and his heart went into overdrive. Why couldn't he wake her? Did she have a brain injury after all, and he'd slept through it and missed the signs?

'Liv! Come on. Wake up. Now!'

He shook her arm roughly and her eyes flickered open, blinking in the daylight that seeped in around the curtained windows. She made a soft noise and shifted her head back so she could get him into focus. 'Don't shout at me. What's the matter?'

Relief flooded him and he closed his eyes and sucked in a breath. 'Sorry. I'm sorry. I couldn't wake you, and I thought...' He couldn't say it, couldn't voice his fears out loud, but he didn't need to.

She blinked again, as if she'd just worked out where she was and what had happened, and she let out her breath on a little sigh and settled back against him. 'Oh, Nick, I'm fine,' she said softly, her hand coming to rest over his heart. 'A bit sore, but my head's much better now. I was just really heavily asleep.'

He felt himself relax, but not much, because their legs were still wrapped together and he really, really needed to get away before she realised quite how much his body was lapping it up.

'Good. I'm glad you're feeling better, but I need to get up. My arm's gone dead and I need to phone the hospital about Judy Richards.'

'Oh. Sorry, you should have said.'

He gave a soft, frustrated laugh. 'I just did. That's why I was trying to wake you.'

'Oh. Right. OK.'

She put her hand on his chest and shifted her leg, and as she moved it she brushed against him and her eyes widened and she froze.

'Nick?' His name was a soft out-breath, teasing against his skin, and her hand curved against his cheek, the delicate touch unbearably erotic.

Damn. He closed his eyes. 'Sorry. Ignore it, it's just a normal, physiological response,' he muttered, his voice gruff. 'It doesn't mean anything—'

Her lips brushed his. 'Oh. And there I thought you were pleased to see me,' she murmured, a hint of mischief in her voice, but it was a touch husky and he knew if he didn't get out of there soon he was going to lose the plot.

'Very funny,' he said, but she just laughed softly and curled her hand around the back of his head, easing him closer. Her lips met his again, the touch so sweet, so familiar, so agonisingly dear that he let out a soft groan and kissed her back.

Not for long. Just long enough that he knew if he didn't get out of there fast this was going to get well out of control and it was every kind of a bad idea.

He dragged his mouth away from temptation. 'Liv, no,' he said, his voice as firm as he could make it. 'I have to get up.'

'I thought you were,' she said mischievously, but before he could react she laughed again and rolled away.

'Better?'

'Yes, thank you.'

Liar. It was much worse, because he wanted her right back where she'd been, and it wasn't going to happen. He retrieved his arm and groaned.

'What?'

'Just my arm dropping off.'

'So long as that's all…'

He gave a despairing chuckle, swung his legs over the side of the bed and stood up with his back firmly towards her. He hadn't seen Liv in this teasing, mischievous mood for years, and the urge to get back into bed and haul her into his arms was killing him.

'I'll go and phone the hospital and I'll get you some tea while I'm at it.' He grabbed his shirt and headed for the door, shaking his right arm to get the circulation going. 'Ah, dammit,' he muttered again as the blood started to flow back into it.

'Wimp,' she called after him, and he paused on the top step, shoving his arms into the shirt.

'Me, a wimp? You should listen to yourself. The fuss you've been making, anybody would think you'd been hit by a car.'

The sound of her laughter followed him down the stairs to the kitchen, and he couldn't help but smile. She sounded so much better and the relief he felt was profound. For a moment there, when he hadn't been able to wake her—

He cut that thought off before it dragged him back in, phoned the hospital about Judy while the kettle boiled and took her tea up to her, his body now back under control.

She was in the bathroom when he got there and he put the mug down on the bedside table as she opened the door and came out.

'Are you OK?'

'I'm fine, considering I was *hit by a car*. Much less sore than I deserve to be,' she said with a wry grin.

'Good. And you don't deser—'

She reached out and pressed a finger to his lips, stopping the words. The grin softened to a smile, and he felt his heart thud against his ribs as she dropped her arm and took another step towards him. She was close enough now that he could smell the toothpaste on her breath and feel the warmth radiating off her skin, and she put her arms around him and rested her head on his chest and hugged him.

'Thank you for looking after me last night,' she murmured, and he wrapped his arms around her and dropped a gentle kiss on her matted, bloodstained hair, every cell in his body aware of the soft press of her breasts against his chest, the warmth of her body luring him, reeling him in. Such a bad idea, but his body thought it was great. He dropped his arms.

'You're welcome,' he said gruffly. 'I've put the tea on your bedside table. I'm going to get my stuff out of the car. I could do with a shower and shave.'

She lifted her hand and rubbed the palm over his jaw against the lie of the hair; he heard the stubble rasp against her skin, saw her pupils darken, felt his body react. 'Shame. I rather like you with the morning-after look,' she said with that slightly wicked smile he'd missed so much for so long now.

Her hand was just there, her thumb against his lips. He could turn his head and press his lips to her palm, ease her back into his arms—or he could just step back out of reach and keep what was left of his sanity.

'Liv, don't do this, please. It's hard enough as it is.'

'Mmm. I noticed.'

He groaned and took a step back out of reach, his control at breaking point. 'It's not funny, Liv,' he said gruffly. 'It's so not a good idea. You're hurt, and it's not what I'm here for.'

Her eyes widened and she blinked, her hand falling slowly to her side.

'No. No, I'm sorry. I wasn't—I didn't mean—'

She couldn't finish the sentence, maybe because like him she didn't know quite what to say, what the protocol was in this really rather awkward situation.

'It's OK. It's just—I don't really think...'

Now it was him who couldn't finish, so he gave up on the conversation, pulled on his trousers, ran downstairs and let himself out of the front door, kicking himself every step of the way.

She watched him go, beating what could only be called a hasty retreat, and bit her lip.

He'd seemed so uncomfortable with her touch, as if she'd crossed an invisible line that had somehow appeared between them since they'd got out of bed. Or maybe it had been there all night, and she'd crossed it then too without realising.

She'd certainly been close enough to him when he'd woken her, close enough to feel his reaction. It wasn't unusual, just a spontaneous physiological response, as he'd said, and in the good old days, before the bad ones, they would have taken advantage of it. But today he couldn't get away fast enough, and he'd seemed embarrassed.

And all she'd done was tease him, when actually she'd wanted him to wrap her in his arms again and make love to her like he used to.

She hadn't even thought about it when she'd suggested he share the bed, and although he'd protested, he hadn't refused, and he'd willingly held her most of the night. He'd obviously only done it out of concern because of her head injury, though, and then she'd gone and wrapped herself all round him, and then hugged him and touched him in a way she no longer had any right to touch him.

And maybe he'd moved on. Maybe there was another woman in his life now, a woman who had those rights?

She felt a wave of humiliation, then a hollow ache inside, and without permission her eyes filled with tears. She hadn't even thought about it, but maybe he'd found someone to love, someone who could give him babies, or just someone to have fun with, as they'd had fun in the early days, before it all became about ovulation tests and body temperature fluctuation and counting days on the calendar?

Not that it was any of her business now, since she'd kicked him out without giving him a second chance.

'Oh, Nick…'

She shifted the pillows into a pile and crawled back onto the bed, leaning back against the pillows and kicking herself for reading too much into his kindness last night. Because that was all it had been, of course. Just kindness.

But he said he'd missed her every single day. Was that kindness talking? It hadn't felt like it, and she was sure there had been tears on his cheeks at one point. That didn't seem like simple kindness, and the way he'd held her, as if she was the most precious thing in the world…

She could hear his voice outside through the bathroom window, and wondered who he was talking to at this time of the morning. Bert, probably. Oh, lord. That would open a whole new can of worms.

It was her own fault. She should have stayed in hospital like Sam had wanted her to instead of making such a fuss—or better still, asked Ben not to contact Nick, and then none of this would have happened.

But then she wouldn't have seen him again, and somehow that felt immeasurably worse…

* * *

'Morning, Nick.'

Damn. He looked up and saw their old neighbour clipping their rose hedge. Liv's rose hedge, he corrected himself. He supposed he should be grateful Bert was looking after her, but instead he felt resentful and distinctly underdressed.

'Morning,' he grunted, unlocking the car and opening the door, wincing as he stepped back onto a sharp stone in his bare feet.

Bert's voice followed his head into the car. 'I see you're back, then. Hope you don't mind, I'm just tidying up a few bits and pieces I missed. First clip of the season, so she gets the best flowers.'

He ducked his head back out as Bert took a step towards him, shears in hand. 'Back for good, are you?'

He gave a mental sigh and put the old man straight.

'No. Liv had an accident yesterday. I'm just looking after her for a day or two.'

Bert lowered the shears, settling in no doubt for a nice long chat and a few juicy details. 'Oh, I'm sorry to hear that. I hope she'll be all right. Car, was it?'

'No.' Well, it wasn't. Not hers. 'She fell,' he said, which was being massively frugal with the truth, but it was none of Bert's business. 'She's just got a few bruises and scrapes.'

'Oh, dear. Poor Liv. I'll tell Gwen, she'll pop round—'

'No, Bert, really, it's fine. She just needs to rest.'

'Oh, well. Give her our best, then. And you'd better get back inside before you catch your death with those bare feet.'

'Yes, indeed.'

He lifted his overnight bag out of the car, locked it and headed back inside, hearing the irritating click-click-click of the shears as Bert went back to work on the immaculate hedge. He ran upstairs, pausing at the bedroom door.

'I'm going to have a shower, if that's OK?'

'Of course. Was that Bert?'

'Yes. He'd obviously spotted the car and he wanted to know if I was back. I told him you'd fallen and got a few bruises. He was threatening to send Gwen round, probably to interrogate you. God knows what she'd make of your black eye, but I'm sure I'd be implicated. I told him you needed to rest.'

Liv rolled her eyes. 'Good. Thank you. They mean well, but—Gwen kept asking questions when you went, saying things like, "It's such a shame he's gone, we were so looking forward to the patter of tiny feet," and I just didn't know what to say to her.'

'Tell her to mind her own business,' he said roughly, the mention of those elusive babies catching him on the raw. 'He's cutting the hedge again, by the way, though why he needs to do it before eight o'clock on a Saturday morning defeats me. It doesn't look as if it needs it anyway.'

'It doesn't. He only did it last week but he was saying he'd missed a bit. I couldn't see it. I've told him not to bother, I can do it myself and anyway, I quite like it when it gets a bit wild, but he insists I won't get the best flowers unless it's done early, and I just can't be that churlish.'

Nick snorted, hefting the bag in his hand. 'I'm damn sure I could. I'm going to shower and get dressed, and then I'd better give Sam an update and phone Ben.'

He scooped up his shoes and socks and took everything to the other bathroom, grabbing a towel on the way and locking the door firmly behind him. Not that she was likely to follow him in, but he just needed some guaranteed privacy while he got his thoughts into order because frankly, between watching her almost get killed and then having her plastered over him all night, his head was a mess and his body wasn't much better.

And her touching him like that, hugging him, kissing him, running her hand over his stubble and looking at him with those melting eyes that threatened to lure him in again—

He stared at the shower controls, contemplated cold and decided against it. He'd never been a masochist, and the last twenty-four hours had been tough enough. He turned on the hot, tested the temperature and stepped into the cubicle under the wall of steaming water.

It pounded down on him, and he dropped his head forwards and felt the tension drain away, but it was replaced by relief that she was still alive, and anguish that she'd been hurt at all, by the deep sorrow left in the wake of their break-up and the grief he still felt that he'd never been able to give her the child she so desperately wanted. Might never be able to.

She'd asked what had happened to them, and the answer was nothing. No pregnancy, no baby, no family.

That, rather than Suzanne, was why their marriage had fallen apart. The business with Suze had just been the trigger, the last straw, and if he was honest, he hadn't cared at that point, because he'd been at the end of his tether with their broken relationship.

By asking for a divorce she'd handed him a perfect way out, or so he'd thought, but then she'd never done it, never started divorce proceedings, just left him in limbo waiting for the other shoe to drop. He'd thought she'd be better off without him, but he hadn't been better off without her, and walking out of her life had left a wound that time didn't seem about to heal.

And getting too close to her again too soon could be

a disaster, so no more snuggling up in the night, no more hugs, no more tender touches breaking through his defences and laying him wide open to hurt again.

And what about the job? How were they going to cope with working together every day when they were obviously still so attracted to each other? Could he manage to keep his distance?

Did he really want to? Or was he just being a coward, afraid to try again? Frankly, he had no idea.

He reached for the soap, scrubbed away the memory of her body against his, towelled himself roughly dry—and discovered he'd forgotten to pack his razor.

Damn.

He ran his hand over his beard, hearing the rasp of it against his skin, feeling the touch of her hand against it earlier, and swore softly and comprehensively at himself.

He could always borrow hers, he supposed, but she'd be unlikely to have a new one and the one in the shower would be worse than useless, he knew that of old. And the intimacy of it...

He'd go and buy some later. Just so she didn't get any more ideas about his morning-after look.

He dressed quickly, packed up his things and took his bag down to the hall. There wasn't really any need to stay here again tonight, he could quite easily go to Ben and Daisy's as planned. Much safer.

He ran back up and stuck his head round the bedroom door. 'OK?'

'Yes, except I'd love more tea. Oh, and Sam rang, by the way. He's on his way over to check up on me. Says he doesn't trust you.'

'Damn cheek. Do you have any decent coffee?'

'I think so, in the freezer. If not there's an unopened packet of ground coffee in the larder cupboard. I might not have a lot of milk. I was going shopping on the way home.'

'I'll check. What do you want for breakfast?'

She shrugged. 'Anything. Toast is easy. And marmalade. It's in the fridge door. And forget the tea, I'll have coffee if you're making it for Sam.'

'OK.'

He ran downstairs and put the kettle on just as the doorbell rang, and he opened the door to his old friend.

'Sam—come in. Thank you so much for yesterday.'

'You're welcome,' Sam said, stepping into the hall and wrapping Nick in a fierce and affectionate hug. Yesterday he'd been a professional but today he was a concerned friend, and he dropped his arms and stepped back with a wry smile, studying his face.

'It's really good to see you again. I'm just sorry it was under those circumstances. How is she? And come to that, how are you? It must have been pretty tough to witness it.'

He shrugged and closed the front door. 'I'm fine. She's a bit sore, but her head seems OK and that was the real worry. I've just put the kettle on. Can I get you anything?'

'Coffee would be good. I've been up since before six with Isadora.'

'Your baby?'

'Yes. She was born last October.' Sam smiled ruefully. 'She's gorgeous, but she's an early riser, and Kate's not a morning person.'

'Are you?'

Sam laughed. 'After years in the army, believe me, getting up for a smiley baby is a walk in the park.'

Nick gave a dutiful laugh, then turned away. 'Yes, I can imagine,' he said. 'Why don't you go on up and see

Liv? She's on the right at the top of the stairs. I'm just getting her breakfast and I'll bring our coffee up.'

He headed back to the kitchen, trying hard not to think of the joy of being woken by a baby with a beaming smile at any time of the day or night.

Liv hadn't wanted to go to the conference because everyone would be talking about their children, and she'd been right. They were at the age where their friends nearly all had families, and the fact that they'd kept their problems a secret just meant there'd been nobody to share it with, no one to offload on when it all became too much.

Except Suze, and look where that had got him.

He put bread in the toaster, checked the milk situation and found the new packet of coffee and the cafetière.

Core business, he told himself. *Stick to what you're here for, and forget the rest.*

'Well, good morning. How's the patient?'

'Much better but cross with myself, thank you,' she told him, and then asked the question that had been niggling at her since yesterday. 'How come you know Nick?'

'We grew up together. He was my best friend, but we drifted apart once life got in the way.'

'Ah. You're that Sam—the one who taught him to sail,' she said, all the little pieces falling neatly into place.

'That's me. Can we talk about you, now?' he said, smiling a little wryly. 'That's a cracking black eye you've got there.'

'Isn't it just? At least it's only the colour. I can still open my eye more or less fully, and I feel fine now.'

'Really? The eye doesn't say so, and I'm pretty sure your body's at least as colourful.'

'I'm fine, Sam. Really. Yes, I hurt a bit here and there, but I'm alive, no fractures, I haven't got a serious head injury—what more could I ask for? Apart from the common sense not to have stepped backwards off the pavement. That would have helped.'

Sam chuckled, then his smile faded as he studied her. 'How is Nick? I haven't seen him for years. The last I knew he was working in Surrey.'

'He was, but that's six or seven years ago. It's where we met.' She swallowed and looked away. 'And I don't really know how he is. I haven't seen him since last March, and I hadn't spoken to him then since we split up in the middle of January because we weren't working together and we were avoiding each other. He came back yesterday because he's going to locum for a bit, but that was the first time we'd spoken, so yesterday was a bit of a trial, one way or another.'

Sam looked shocked. 'Gosh, Liv, I'm sorry. If I'd realised that, I wouldn't have suggested he stayed here with you, but you seemed to want him around and he certainly wasn't going anywhere, but no wonder you both objected. Ben mentioned that you weren't together now, but I just assumed you had a working relationship—kids, probably, and shared custody, not total radio silence.'

She tried to smile, but it was probably a sad little event and she gave up. 'No kids,' she said, trying to keep the wobble out of her voice. 'We just—it wasn't working, so we split up.'

She didn't elaborate, just left him to conclude whatever he liked from that, because by the end nothing had been working for them, not the relentless striving for a child, or their crumbling relationship.

'I'm sorry,' Sam said again. 'I shouldn't have interfered without knowing more about your situation.'

'Sam, it's fine,' she said, swiftly changing the subject to one she was more comfortable with than the slow and painful disintegration of her marriage. 'Tell me about your baby.'

'Isadora?'

'Is that what you called her? What a lovely name. Have you got any photos?'

Of course he did, and he pulled out his phone and scrolled around for a moment and then handed it to her. 'Swipe from right to left. That's her yesterday morning, helping me eat my breakfast. She kept stealing the spoon, so I think we're going to have to start weaning her soon.'

'She's just like you.'

'I generally have better table manners.'

Liv felt a lump in her throat, and with a choked little laugh she scrolled through the photos, only handing the phone back when Nick came in with a tray laden with toast and coffee.

'Room service,' he said lightly, putting the tray down on the top of her chest of drawers and turning to Sam. 'Black, white, sugar?'

But her head was aching, and she knew the men would have lots to talk about, so she caught Nick's eye. 'Actually, I could do with a nap. If you could leave me some toast and coffee, maybe you two would like to catch up downstairs for a while?'

Sam stayed for an hour, telling him about the baby, his wife, their house, the fact that he'd just bought, done up and sold a wooden ketch and was now looking for a much more sensibly sized sailing dinghy.

'I thought I might get a Laser or a Firefly. You'll have to come out with me when I get it. I'd trust you not to tip us both over the side,' he said with a wry grin, and Nick laughed, remembering the time Sam had taken a girl out sailing and she'd done exactly that.

'I can still hear that girl scream as she hit the water,' he said with a chuckle, and Sam grinned.

'Lizzie. Yeah. She never really forgave me for that.'

His smile died, and he searched Nick's face with eyes that knew him far too well.

'I'm sorry about you and Liv. She's a lovely woman.'

'She is,' he said, that lump back in his throat, 'but it just wasn't working any more.'

'Yes, she said. Shame.'

'It is, but it's over, we've moved on, and—well, that's it, really,' he lied, glossing over a whole world of messy emotions.

'So I gather you're going to be locuming here for a bit.'

'Yes.' He looked away, pretending to study his hands. 'I don't know how I feel about it. Coming back here, I mean.'

'How does Liv feel?'

'I don't know. I tried to talk to her about it yesterday but it didn't go well. I didn't realise we'd be working together, I thought she'd be in the midwife-led unit still, so yesterday was a bit fraught, and since I almost killed her by letting her fall under a car, we've had other things to think about.'

Sam put his cup down and got to his feet.

'I'll leave you in peace. It'll be good to have you near for a while, though, and let's not lose touch this time. It's been way, way too long and I didn't realise how much I'd missed you.'

He hugged Nick again, the gesture saying more than words ever could, and Nick waved him off and closed the door. The lump in his throat was so big now he could hardly swallow. What on earth was wrong with him today? He was an emotional wreck—

'Has Sam gone?'

He turned slowly and looked up the stairs at Liv. She must have showered, because her hair was wet and she was wearing a loose, comfortable dress that fell to her ankles. He was glad about that. It covered her bruises, which meant he wouldn't be constantly reminded of them. If he didn't look at her face...

'Yeah, he's gone. I thought you were napping? Did he say it was OK to wash your hair?'

She nodded. 'He said it would be fine so long as I didn't soak in the bath, so I just showered to get the blood off, really. I feel much better now. Much less sore and a lot less grubby.'

'Good. Will you be OK if I go out? I need to see Judy Richards, and Ben wants to talk to me about the job and what it entails which he was going to do yesterday evening, so I thought I'd walk to the hospital, then I can pick up your car after I'm done.'

'Good thinking. I'll get a parking fine if I don't move it but I'm not sure I should drive yet. You know what insurance companies are like,' she said, making her way carefully down the stairs. 'And you also need to apologise to Ben for me for messing up your weekend—and don't tell me again it was your fault.'

He ignored that. 'I'll pick up some more milk while I'm out. Is there anything else you want?'

She nodded. 'Maybe some salad for lunch and something to have with it? Oh, and probably bread. I don't have any decent bread.'

'OK. Text me a shopping list—and I need the car key.'

'I'll just give you my set. There's a house key on there as well, so you'll be able to let yourself back in, just in case I have a nap on the sofa.'

She found them in her bag and then hesitated before

she dropped them into his outstretched hand, as though she was afraid to touch him. Very wise. He closed his fist around them, nodded, and let himself out.

CHAPTER SIX

SHE SPENT THE morning dozing on the sofa in the sitting room.

It was the sofa she'd always thought of as his, the only one she used now. It had the best view of the garden, if you didn't count the one from what they'd optimistically described as the family room, and she hadn't been able to bring herself to sit in there since their final showdown.

Too many painful memories.

But it had been glorious in the sitting room today, the sun streaming in and bringing the promise of spring with it, and between that and her sleepless night she'd struggled to stay awake, but lying awkwardly hadn't done her neck any good so she'd retreated back to the bedroom for a nap.

She was contemplating getting up and taking a walk around the garden when she heard the scrape of the key in the lock and his soft, 'Hello? I'm back,' as he closed the door.

'I'm up here,' she called, and she heard him run lightly up the stairs, tapping on the door as he walked in.

The Nick she'd fallen in love with wouldn't have knocked, and he would have bent down and kissed her, but this Nick didn't, and it was shocking how much she'd missed that. How much she'd missed him.

'I'm sorry I've been so long. Have you been OK?'

'I've been fine. Sleeping, mostly. How's Judy?'

'Good. Everything's stable, the baby's got a lovely strong heartbeat, her blood pressure's fine and the placenta scan was OK. It's just watch and wait until the blood test results come back. I got milk. Do you want a coffee?'

'That would be great. Thanks.'

He disappeared for a little while, and she could hear the kettle boiling and the sound of the fridge door being opened and shut as he put the shopping away, then after a moment he came back up the stairs with the coffee and a packet of almond thins.

'My favourite biscuits!'

He opened the packet and handed them to her, his smile a little crooked. 'We aim to please.'

'How did you get on with Ben?'

'All right,' he said thoughtfully. He put the biscuits down on the bed and propped himself up against the headboard beside her, his face troubled. 'There's a possibility Simon won't come back.'

'I did wonder. Was Ben trying to talk you into staying?'

He chuckled quietly. 'How did you guess? I said I'd do the locum partly to help Ben out of a bind and partly because I knew I needed to see you again, but we haven't exactly got off to a flying start and I wouldn't contemplate coming back permanently if you didn't want me to, Liv. That wouldn't be fair on either of us.'

'No. No, it wouldn't.' She bit her lip, wondering what it would be like if he came back, and she realised she was hoping—desperately hoping—that it would happen. But only if he came back to her as well, and there was a question that was burning a hole in her, even though she wasn't sure she'd want the answer despite agonising over it the whole time he'd been out—well, when she hadn't been asleep, at least—but it was sort of relevant so she said it anyway.

'That would depend on if there's anybody else in your life now, because that would change things a lot. You know—someone you're seeing? Suzanne, perhaps, or someone new?'

His laugh sounded like disbelief, and he shook his head firmly. 'No, Liv. Absolutely not, and certainly not Suze. I haven't even seen her since the conference. I've been working in a different field so our paths don't cross any more, and even if they did, our relationship was over seven years ago. Why would I want to go back to it? And, no, there isn't anyone else, either. There hasn't been anyone else. I'm not interested.'

She stared at him, shocked by that admission. Her relationship with Nick was—or had been—physical. Very physical. Until it all went so horribly wrong.

'No one at all?' she asked incredulously. 'Not even a minor fling, in more than a year?'

He shook his head. 'No. Why would I?'

'For sex?' she offered, stating the obvious, and got the same sad, slightly disbelieving laugh.

'With someone I don't really want? No. Sex is just an itch, Liv. I can scratch it myself, and the only woman I really want threw me out, so that's not a goer.'

He held her eyes with his, the sincerity in them so believable she couldn't doubt it, and after an age she sucked in a breath and looked away, letting it all sink in, but still it didn't quite stack up, because always in the background was this thing with Suzanne that she couldn't quite believe.

'If that's really true, can we scroll back to the conference, because it doesn't seem plausible that you'd be in your room with Suze and not sleep with her, and I'm obviously not the only person who thought that. I knew something had been going on because Beth rang me on Sunday morning and asked if everything was all right, and there was just something in her voice that told me it wasn't, and when she said Suzanne was there and she'd seen you together at breakfast, it all sort of fell into place. But breakfast alone wouldn't make her think that, surely, so she must have seen you going into your room together, and I'm really struggling with that because I know you, Nick, and I know sex is a hugely significant thing in your life, so if it wasn't to sleep with Suze, then what the hell *was* it for?'

He was staring down at his coffee, his face a mask, shutting her out again.

'I just needed to talk to her,' he said eventually.

'So why couldn't you do that downstairs in the bar or something? Why your room? And what on earth were you doing that made Beth suspicious enough to ring me?'

He let out a weary sigh and scrubbed his hand through his hair, then he lifted his head and met her eyes, and his were raw with pain and grief.

'She saw us waiting for the lift. I was in the bar on my own wallowing in self-pity, and Suze came over and asked me if I was all right, and I got so choked I couldn't answer her, so she suggested we took it upstairs. She grabbed the bottle of wine off the table and hauled me out of the bar, and I didn't stop to analyse what anyone might think of it. I just wanted to leave before I made a total idiot of myself, and then we ran into Beth by the lift—me, Suze and the bottle. God knows what she thought we were up to but it must have looked pretty incriminating. Anyway, she asked how we were and I mumbled something and then the lift came and we got in it. Then the following morning she came into the restaurant after we'd already met up there, saw us having breakfast together and I guess put two and two together and came up with five.'

'Well, of course she would—who wouldn't?'

'Exactly. And under any normal circumstances and with anybody else, she would have been right, but it wasn't normal, I wasn't normal, and Suze realised that. That's why she got me out of there, and I can promise you sex was absolutely the last thing on my mind at the time.'

'So why didn't you just tell me that?'

'Because you wouldn't have believed me, and because for that fleeting moment it seemed like an escape route and I was desperate for one. It was a split-second decision, Liv, and I've regretted it ever since, and I know it's too late now to undo all the hurt, but I really need you to believe that nothing happened between me and Suze.'

'So—what did you do? You just drank the bottle of wine and talked? And if so, how did she come to write you that note? "Always here if you need me"? I don't buy it. That's a lover's note, Nick.'

'Or a friend's. If she hadn't been there that night I don't know what would have happened to me, because I was on the brink of a total meltdown and if it hadn't been for her I don't know what I would have done. And I know she's not a saint, but she's not a whore, and that was a cheap shot yesterday, Liv.'

She felt a wash of shame. 'I know. I'm sorry, I should never have said that but I'd spent a year hating her—'

'No. You've spent seven years hating her, being jealous of her, and I've never understood it.'

'What? She's gorgeous, Nick. She's got that amazing lush figure and come-to-bed eyes and you were together for years. And I know she's still in your phone contacts, and she sends you a Christmas card every year—it really wasn't such a stretch to think you would have slept with her again. A lot of people wouldn't even count it, sleeping with an ex.'

'But I would. Which is why I couldn't have done it, because she's a *friend* now—and anyway, what makes you think she's any more desirable than you are?' he asked, shifting so that he was facing her.

'Because I'm not blind?'

He laughed softly and shook his head. 'Liv—seriously, you have nothing to worry about in that department. Yes, we were lovers, of course we were, but she didn't want what I wanted, she didn't see life and family and the future in the same way as me, but you did, and right from the beginning I knew I needed to be with you. You're the one I married, you're the only woman I'll ever want.'

'But you didn't want me then! We hardly ever made love any more, only when the time was right, and it wasn't as if you hadn't slept with her before, so why not?'

'I've just told you that—and I did still want you. I just couldn't touch you without breaking down, and I was trying to be strong for you but I just couldn't do it any longer. I was breaking my heart over us, Liv, and Suze realised it, and the moment the door was shut and she said, "What's wrong?", I fell apart. She sat me on the bed and held me, and I unravelled all over her.

'When I finally ground to a halt she made us coffee and let me talk. Which I did, for hours. I lay on the bed next to her and poured my heart out, told her everything, and then I fell asleep and when I woke up, she was gone. She must have written the note and put it in my bag before she left, but I didn't see it until you showed it to me.

'She told me over breakfast to come home to you and

sort things out, to do what I could to mend our marriage, but I'd hardly got through the door before I had to go into the hospital to deliver Amy Zacharelli's baby, and by the time I got back you'd already spoken to Beth, you'd found the note, and you'd made up your mind. From that point on, I didn't stand a chance.'

Tears welled in her eyes, and she looked down at her hands, the fingers clenched together, trying not to cry for everything they'd lost. Or thrown away.

'I'm so sorry. Sorry I've been mean about her...sorry I didn't trust you. I should have trusted you, but the evidence was so clear, Nick, and I felt like such an idiot. That was why I was so shocked about Suzanne, so angry, because even though I was jealous of her I thought I knew you wouldn't do something like that, not once we were married, and then suddenly it looked as if you'd just run back into her open arms and I wondered if I really knew you at all.'

His hand reached out and cradled her cheek gently. 'Of course you know me. There's not much to know. I'm pretty straightforward. You should have trusted your judgement—and I should have told you the truth there and then.'

'But I didn't make it easy for you, did I? As you said, I'd made up my mind, and I'm so sorry, because it's all my own stupid fault. I should have come with you. It should have been me you broke down with, me you poured your heart out to. If I'd only come with you, maybe you would have done that and then all this business with Suze would never have happened,' she whispered, her voice cracking, but he shifted closer, disentangling her knotted fingers and wrapping them in his warm, strong hands.

'No,' he said gruffly. 'It's not your fault, it's mine. I can't let you take the blame for that. I shouldn't have gone, but I was just at the end of my tether with it all and I couldn't cope with it any more. I'd had the day from hell, and then I came home and found you distraught because you weren't pregnant again and I couldn't take it any more, couldn't bear your pain any more. It was the last straw.

'I never should have left you alone like that. I should have stayed with you, talked about it properly, faced the truth instead of just running away to the conference because it was the easiest thing to do—'

'What could you have done? We'd talked about it endlessly. Every month, for nearly two years. What more was there to say? We'd said it all.'

'No, we hadn't. We'd said the same things over and over. It'll be all right. It'll happen soon, we just need to give it time. We're still young. There's no hurry. Lots of people have this trouble. We've been too busy. We missed the date—every month, the same excuses, the same justification for our failure to conceive, but we never once admitted that we might have a problem, that we needed help, that it wasn't working and wasn't going to work, because we didn't want to admit it. It was as if saying it out loud would make it real, and we couldn't bear to do that.'

She didn't answer, because she didn't need to. He was right, all their talking had got them nowhere because neither of them would admit that they needed help, and maybe there would have been a simple answer if they'd only ever asked the right question.

She'd started running for an hour every day to escape from the truth, from the mess her marriage was in, from the endless recurring sorrow of her infertility, and yet the running itself might have made the situation worse. Why hadn't she realised that? She'd got so thin, scrawny almost. That wasn't healthy, but it hadn't stopped her, and there had been the odd month when the ovulation test hadn't reacted positively. Was that why?

His thumb traced idly over the back of her hand, sweeping backwards and forwards, over and over as the silence hung in the air between them until finally he broke it with a shuddering sigh.

'I wish I'd felt able to talk to you, Liv. I never really told you how I felt, did I? Not really. Not honestly. I never told you how I grieved for us every time we failed, how I ached for you, how I blamed myself for not being able to help you when I was working in the same field. Why couldn't I? I'm a doctor, an obstetrician. My job is babies, and yet I couldn't even give you a baby.'

'You weren't alone, Nick. My job's babies, too, and I couldn't give you one, either. And I couldn't talk about it—not to you, not to anyone. I don't think that helped us.'

'No, I don't think it did. I meant to, when I got back from the conference, but then the whole thing just escalated and overwhelmed me, and I wasn't thinking clearly anyway. I'd had virtually no sleep, I knew I had a mountain to climb to get our marriage back on track, and then you told me to go and I realised there wasn't any point in talking about it, because you'd made up your mind, so I did the easy thing. Again. It was about the only thing I was any good at.'

'So why not talk to me after that?' she asked. 'You were still here for nearly three months, working your notice. You could have given me time to cool off, and then told me the truth. I waited and waited, and you never said a word in your own defence. It felt like you'd slunk away with your tail between your legs, and it just made you look even guiltier, if that was possible.'

'I know, and it was deliberate, even though it was killing me. I thought it would be easier that way, easier for both of us—give us a fresh start. I thought we might be able to move on, but I haven't. I haven't moved on at all. Have you?' he asked, his voice low, the question hardly voiced as if he wasn't sure he wanted the answer. 'Have you met anyone?'

She shook her head. 'No. No, of course not.'

'There's no "of course" about it. You're a beautiful woman, Liv. Why not?'

Because no one else was Nick. She'd had other relationships before she'd met him, but once he'd come into her life she'd realised he was the only man she'd ever really loved, the only man she'd ever really wanted. Nothing would change that.

She shook her head. 'I'm not interested. I've never been one for casual sex, and even if I'd met someone I really liked, I wouldn't have done anything about it, because the last thing I needed was another relationship. I just can't see it happening.'

'Because I hurt you so badly,' he said heavily.

'No, not you. Our marriage. The way it slowly crumbled away beneath us. That was so hard to take, and it wasn't even as if we'd fallen out of love. We'd just stopped communicating.'

'We had, you're right. And we shouldn't have done, but I was afraid if I was honest and told you how desperate I was, you'd just feel even guiltier, and I knew how that felt.'

She looked up at him, searching his eyes while she asked another question, one which had been plaguing her since Ben had told her what he'd been doing.

'I know I've already asked you this, but why *are* you working in infertility? I would have thought you'd run screaming from it, taken any other job in the world, almost, to avoid it.'

He shrugged and shifted on the bed, and she wriggled closer and rested her head on his shoulder.

'I don't know, to be honest,' he murmured. 'It was partly by accident, really. As soon as he knew it was destined for closure the consultant left to set up his own private clinic, and they were left in the lurch without a proper job to offer, so recruiting someone permanent wasn't possible, and I'd just come to the end of one job, it was in the same department, I knew some of the people—I suppose I felt I owed them, in a way, and they talked me into it. I didn't really want to do it, but it wasn't long term, there was a definite end-date, and I thought it would give me time to look for something I really wanted. And it meant I wouldn't have to move again for a while. So I said yes, and then after a bit I realised I'm actually ideally placed to do it.

'I know what it's like, I know what they go through, how hard it can be to cope with the endless see-saw of emotions, the hope, the fear, the despair, and in a way it helped me to understand what had happened to us. As I told you yesterday, I realised we're definitely not alone. There are marriages and relationships falling apart all the time because of the pressure couples put on themselves, and for the ones who stick together, if I can help them get pregnant, then maybe I can save them going through what we did, and if I can't, I can empathise. I can give them advice, point them in the direction of support groups, talking therapies, relationship advice—'

'We never had any of that,' she pointed out sadly.

'No. No, we didn't. Nor did we go through the endless investigations, or try any one of the many options which might have helped us in one way or another, and I'm still not really sure why, because it was getting blindingly obvious that we needed help. Maybe it was because we felt there wasn't enough there to start with, that our marriage just wasn't strong enough to survive what might lie ahead.'

She sucked her breath in, shocked by that. 'Nick, we had a good marriage,' she said, her voice little more than a whisper. 'You know we did.'

'I thought so. I'd always thought so, so why couldn't I support you when you needed me?' he asked despairingly. 'Why wasn't I there for you every time it didn't happen? Why did I go to the conference without you that weekend—and why did you believe the worst of me and not even question me about Suze?'

'I did!'

'No. You asked me if she was in my room. You never asked me why, or what we did. You just assumed I'd slept with her, and yes, I could have explained, but it was as if you'd already made up your mind, and in the next breath you told me you wanted a divorce as if you'd been waiting for a reason to get rid of me. Why would you do that if our marriage was so good?'

'Because it wasn't by then,' she admitted, her eyes filling. 'It was awful. You know what it was like. We hardly spoke to each other, we never hugged or kissed or laughed together. We just had sex at the right time— never at the wrong time, never just because we wanted to. I can't remember when we last made love, but I can remember just about every time we had sex to make a baby that never happened.'

He was silent for an age, and then he drew in a ragged breath and rested his head against hers.

'I'm sorry. I never meant it to be like that, but this room became such an emotional minefield that I almost dreaded going into it. I felt as if that was all you wanted from me, that I was just a sperm donor, that my only reason for being there was to get you pregnant, and I couldn't do that, and when you said you wanted a divorce, it gave me a way out of a situation that was tearing me apart.'

'Which was why you didn't tell me the truth about that night, because you wanted out.'

'Partly. I knew I still loved you, and I was coming home to try and make it work, but in my heart of hearts I knew I couldn't live with you any more, not the way it was. And I don't want to go there again, Liv, I really don't. I won't get back on that merry-go-round of hope and despair until I'm sure we're strong enough to take the next step. It's too destructive, and I can't do it. It just hurts too damn much.'

'Have I asked you to?'

He shook his head. 'No. No, you haven't, but I didn't want you building any dreams of that happening on the vague possibility of me coming back here to work permanently. That's not what I'm here for, and I don't know if we could ever be strong enough to try again for a baby.'

Her heart jolted, a shock of disappointment coursing through her, and she realised she'd foolishly allowed herself to hope…

'So why did you say yes to Ben? Why did you come back?'

'Because I have to earn a living?'

She waited, but he said nothing more for a long time, then eventually he shrugged his shoulders as if he was asking himself the same question.

'I don't know,' he said at last. 'Yes, I needed to work, but I could have taken any one of a number of locum jobs. I wasn't even going to start looking until I'd had a holiday, but then Ben rang, and—I don't know why I'm here really, Liv. I just know I'm not happy, that my life outside work doesn't really exist, that I'm lonely and I miss our old friends.'

He turned towards her, and she shifted her head so she could look into those sad, stormy eyes.

'And I miss you,' he went on softly. 'All the time. I know I hurt you, and I know you hurt me, but I still miss you, and I never stopped loving you, which doesn't mean I see us getting back together, but maybe we can find something else, forge a friendship—I don't know. I don't have the answers, Liv, I wish I did. I just know that what I have now isn't working for me, either in terms of job satisfaction or personally, and I want more. I want something better. And one way or another, I want you in my life.'

She held his eyes, her own filling. 'I want you, too. I've missed you every single day. And even though it was horrible by the end, I still loved you. I'll always love you. And I want something better, too, because there has to be something better than this.'

He gave a quiet, heartfelt sigh. 'That's why I came back, but just because we love each other doesn't mean it works, Liv, and we've hurt each other enough already. The last thing I want is to make it any worse.'

She gave a soft huff of empty laughter. 'I don't think that's possible,' she said honestly, and he sucked in a breath, his fingers tightening on hers.

'Don't say that. I didn't want to hurt you. I never wanted to hurt you.'

Their eyes were locked, his sorrow and regret plain to see until in the end he sucked in a shuddering breath and looked away.

'Oh, Nick. Come here,' she said softly, and he shifted, putting his arms around her with such fierce tenderness it made her want to cry. She turned her face into his chest, breathing in the scent that was so unmistakably Nick, holding him close.

'I miss you so much,' she admitted. 'My life's so empty without you. All I have is my work, and I love it, but I'm still empty because you aren't here.'

His arms tightened a fraction, his chest shifting as he sucked in a deep breath, then let it out on a ragged sigh. 'I'm empty, too, but I don't want to go back to what we had.'

'Then let's not. Maybe we should try again, Nick. Not for a baby, but for us, to see if we can make each other happy like we used to. Because we did. We were very happy, once. Maybe we could be happy again, if we wanted it enough. Maybe we just didn't try hard enough at *that*.'

He lifted his head and searched her eyes, then his closed and he swallowed hard.

'I don't know. I don't know if we can even remember *how* to be happy any more.'

'But we should try. We owe ourselves that much.'

She drew his head down, touching her lips to his, and with a quiet sigh he kissed her back, a gentle, lingering kiss, not platonic but not passionate, either.

An apology, from both of them, for all that had gone before?

Then he pulled back a little, staring down into her eyes. 'I'm sorry I blew it,' he said quietly. 'I honestly never meant to hurt you. I thought leaving would make it easier for you, but it didn't, did it? And I don't want to risk hurting you again.'

She sighed quietly, wishing she could see an easy way forward, dreading how she would feel if they couldn't. 'Life hurt us both, Nick, but only because we let it. We're older now, wiser. Why don't we just see where this takes us? You're here for a while now. Maybe we just need to turn back the clock far enough, rediscover what it was about each other that we fell in love with. Maybe that's all we've ever needed. And if we can't have children, we have our jobs and they're filled with babies, all the babies we could ever want. Maybe that should be enough for us. We need to find what it was we had, and then perhaps we'll be able to make sense of it all.'

'Maybe. But I'm not making any promises. Not yet. And I don't want to rush into anything, either. As you said, I'm here for a while. Let's just take our time.'

He dropped another kiss on her lips before rolling away from her and standing up—to distance himself from a conversation that was becoming uncomfortably deep? Probably, because he changed the subject then, his voice firmer, deceptively casual.

'By the way, did you know Daisy's pregnant again?'

'Yes. I'm really pleased for her. She had a miscarriage a few months back, and they were gutted. It's really good news.'

'Ben didn't tell me that,' he said quietly, his attempt at casual banished in an instant. 'That's really sad. Miscarriage is horrible.'

'It's obstetrics, Nick. It happens. Pregnancy is never a certainty until you've got a healthy baby in your arms, and that's just the start of all the trouble. They have to grow up safely, and that can be a challenge. Their little boy Thomas fell out of a tree last year and broke his arm.'

'I didn't know that, either. I can't believe he's old enough to climb trees.'

'No. You disappeared off the radar, Nick, not just for me but for everybody. It would be so good to have you back, even if it was just as a friend. I've really missed your friendship.'

She reached out a hand and he took it, folding it in both of his, bowing his head to press a firm, lingering kiss on her knuckles.

'Let me think about it, Liv. Don't let's rush this. The last thing I want to do is make any more mistakes.'

She nodded, not wanting to give him time but knowing she had no choice if she was going to stand a chance to win him back. And she really, really wanted him back. She knew that now, with bone-deep certainty.

But first, it was time for a change of scenery, a breath of air, a bit of emotional space for both of them.

'I need to walk around for a bit or I'll just seize up. And I'm starving. How about some lunch?'

CHAPTER SEVEN

SHE WANTED HIM BACK—and he wanted her. That had never changed.

But to try again? He wasn't sure if what he felt was trepidation or anticipation.

Or both. But there were still things she didn't know, things he wasn't sure he wanted to tell her until he knew it was relevant, and the knowledge was eating a hole in him.

He made them lunch, just a simple salad with the things he'd picked up in the local shops on the way back, while she sat in the garden munching almond thins and drinking her tepid coffee on the swing seat under the tree where they'd often sat together in the good old days.

Not so much in the bad old days. She'd tended to retreat to it then, and he'd let her.

A mistake? Probably, but he'd been struggling to stay afloat himself then, and it had all been about self-preservation. He picked up the plates and went out to her.

'Can you manage this on your lap? It's pretty much fork food.'

'That's fine—it looks lovely. Thank you.'

'You're welcome. How are you feeling now?'

'OK. I feel a bit woozy if I bend over, but not bad. I can move around which has to be a good thing. I might go for a stroll later. I don't want to seize up.'

'Don't overdo it.'

She rolled her eyes and went back to her salad, and when she'd finished eating she went into the sitting room to watch the television while he cleared up the kitchen and dealt with his emails.

Mostly spam and trivia, but there was one from Ben with the detailed job description attached, dangling the carrot under his nose again. He read it through carefully, more and more sure that he wanted it if Simon didn't come back—so long as this thing with Liv didn't blow up in both their faces.

He'd do his best to avoid it, but his track record wasn't great. Could they pull it off? He really, really wasn't sure, but the best way to make it work was to take it slowly and give themselves time to adjust, to get used to each other again rather than jumping in the deep end. That way at least they could still be friends, and anything more would just be a bonus.

He stayed there that night, justifying it to himself on the grounds of her head injury—which, considering how well she looked, could have seemed a bogus excuse, but he wasn't prepared to risk it. At the very least she had concussion, and it wasn't too late for a slow, encapsulated bleed to flare into a full-blown crisis, so he talked himself into it and slept in the spare room with the door ajar—just in case.

He woke in the night and went to check on her, and found her fast asleep with her arms wrapped round a pillow.

Better that than him, he thought morosely. A lot, lot safer. Safer still if he found himself a flat. He'd check on-line tomorrow, see what there was. He went back to bed, ridiculously jealous of the pillow, and finally fell asleep again, to be woken by the brush of her hair over his face and the touch of her lips on his cheek.

'Rise and shine, sleepy-head. I've brought you a cup of tea. I thought you might want it before you go back to the hospital to see Judy Richards again.'

Judy! He struggled up out of the bedclothes, stifling a yawn and the urge to pull her down into the bed with him and take advantage of his early-morning erection. 'What's the time?'

'Eight thirty.'

'Damn. No time for tea. Shoo.' He grabbed the bed-clothes, gave her a pointed look and waited until she was out of the room before throwing them off and getting out of bed.

He definitely needed a place of his own.

He showered in record time, went to the hospital and satisfied himself that Judy was all right and her baby was stable, then on the way out his phone rang.

'Nick? It's Sam. What are you up to?'

'I've just seen a patient and I'm leaving the hospital now—why?'

'Because I've been thinking, Ben said you were supposed to be staying with them until you could find a flat, but you didn't sound overjoyed, and after talking to you and Liv yesterday it's pretty obvious you feel awkward staying with her, so why don't you come and live here while you do your locum? We've got a cabin in the garden that's doing nothing and you'll love it—it's right by the sea wall. You probably know it, it used to be James and Connie's house and I lived in the cabin when I first came up here, before I bought the house off them. It's got everything you'd need—a shower room and a small kitchen, a decent bed, free wi-fi, and it would be great for you.'

A place of his own? He felt a wash of relief, but held it

down. For now. 'I didn't know you'd bought it—but then I don't know anything about your life now, so that's hardly a surprise, is it? And hadn't you better ask Kate before you start offering me the cabin? She might hate me.'

'Nah, of course she won't. She's itching to meet you, and anyway, it was her idea. Why don't you come down now? I'll make you a fancy coffee and Kate'll feed you cake while I talk you into it. Five minutes?'

'Sam, I haven't even had breakfast yet!'

'Perfect. Nor have I. You can have a bacon roll *and* cake.'

He laughed and gave in, trying not to let himself get too excited by the idea of a place of his own. 'OK, but I need to tell Liv I'm not going back yet. I'll see you shortly.'

Sam was right.

The cabin was exactly what he needed, bigger than the studio flat he'd lived in for the past two years and right by the sea, as he'd been told. It didn't overlook the water, set down as it was behind the sea wall, but with the windows open he could hear it, and it was instantly soothing.

After he'd been introduced to Kate and the delightfully smiley Isadora, they'd settled down in their big sitting room with the sea stretched out in front of them as far as the eye could see, and eaten fat, juicy bacon rolls followed by cake washed down with copious coffee, and then Sam took him up onto the sea wall.

They strolled along to some railings and leant on them, listening to the soft suck of the sea on the shingle and watching the gulls wheeling over the water. 'Look at that—how can you resist it?' Sam asked with a grin, and Nick laughed.

'I don't even want to try. What sort of rent are we talking about?' he asked, and Sam looked incredulous.

'What? You're the best friend I've ever had. Why the hell would I charge you money to stay here?'

'Because I'll be using electricity for heating and hot water, I'm invading your privacy—it's not fair.'

'It is fair. You can come sailing with me when I find a boat. Then I won't have Kate on my case about going out alone.'

He laughed and gave in. 'Well—if you're sure, and if Kate doesn't mind—'

'She doesn't. She really likes you. She says it'll be fun.'

He smiled at Sam. 'I really like her, too. You're well suited. How long have you known her?'

'Oh, not long. We met last January, but I didn't see her again until I started work here in April. Liv said you left in March, so I must have just missed you.'

'Yes, you must. So how does the maths work?' he asked, his mind ticking. 'Because Isadora's—what, five months old?'

Sam grinned. 'Yeah. Well, let's just say it was love at first sight and leave it at that. Whatever, we couldn't be happier. So, when are you going to move in?' he asked, changing the subject, and Nick shrugged.

'I don't know, but to be honest I need to get out of there, for all sorts of reasons and the sooner the better. I'm working all week and I'm probably on call next weekend, but I'm not doing anything today, and Liv seems fine now. I could go and empty my flat and come straight back here tonight. Is that OK, or is it too soon?'

'No. Whenever. Makes no difference and if Liv's worried she can always call me. I'll give it a clean this morning, and you can have it as soon as you like. Do you need a hand with moving your stuff?'

'No, I'll be fine. I don't have a lot, it'll easily go in the car. And don't worry about sheets and towels, I've got all that.'

'Great. I'll give you the key now and then it's all yours.'

'How did you get on with Sam?'

He smiled fleetingly. 'Good. It was a bit weird going down to the harbour. I didn't realise how much I'd missed the sound of the sea—it sort of felt like I'd come home.'

There was something sad about the way he'd said that which tugged at her heartstrings. 'It could be home again,' she said, a little tentatively because she didn't want to push it, but he just nodded.

'Maybe. I hope so. The cabin's lovely, by the way, and Sam said I can have it as soon as I like, so I thought I'd go and empty my flat and move in there today, if you're feeling OK?'

He was moving out today? She'd thought—or maybe not thought, just hoped—that he'd stay a little longer.

'Yes—yes, of course, if it's what you want, but is there really that much of a rush?' she asked, curiously reluctant to let him go so soon. Or maybe at all? 'Why not leave it till next weekend? And what about Judy Richards?'

He was silent for a moment, then his eyes met hers fleetingly and flicked away again. 'Ben's going to keep an eye on her—he's on call this weekend anyway, and Sam says you can call him if you're worried or need anything. I'm working all week and I might be on call next weekend but I've got the opportunity today and I don't know when I'll get another one. And there's no rush, but now you're feeling better it might be wise for us not to be spending too much time alone together.'

'Wise?' Why *wise*?

'Yes. *Wise*.'

His eyes met hers again, and this time she saw the slow burn deep in the back of them, and heat flooded her body. She looked away hastily.

'I want you, Liv,' he said softly, 'but we're not ready for that yet. We need to take our time, be sure before we commit. And it's not as if we don't know how good it used to be.'

He was right, of course, but she felt a stupid surge of disappointment. 'So how about lunch, then, before you go?'

'Actually, I might just go now,' he said. 'We had bacon rolls and then Kate fed me a ton of cake so I really don't need to eat. Which reminds me, will you have enough food or do you want me to shop for you before I go?'

'No, it's fine, there's still some food in the fridge and I suspect the second your car's off the drive Gwen'll be round with a casserole or an apple pie to get the low-down anyway.'

He gave a wry chuckle. 'I don't know how you tolerate it.'

'Oh, they mean well, and I know it seems nosey but it's quite harmless. They're sweet, really, and they've been very kind to me.'

'Which is more than can be said for the hedge. He's tortured it into submission.'

She laughed, and once again his eyes caught hers and she saw the heat flaring in them. This time it was him who looked away.

'Are you sure you'll be all right if I go?'

'Nick, I'm fine. I'm better. I'm going back to work tomorrow.'

He frowned. 'Really? So soon? Are you sure?'

'Yes, I'm sure. I haven't even got a headache today. And I'll be fine. Go, get your stuff, get settled in. It's a good idea.'

He held her eyes for a second, then nodded. 'OK. Right, I'll get my bag,' he said. He ran upstairs, and she heard the slight creak of the boards as he went into the spare bedroom overhead, then moments later the stairs again as he came back down.

'That was quick.'

'I travel light. Don't get up. I'll let myself out.'

'No. I want to give you a set of keys before you go.'

She found them in the study—his study, in the top drawer of his desk—and handed them to him. It felt weirdly symbolic.

'So you can come and go whenever you want,' she said. 'No strings.'

He hefted them in his hand, met her eyes, his own unreadable again, and slipped them into his pocket.

'Thank you.'

'Don't thank me,' she said, shaking her head. 'I should be thanking you for looking after me—'

'It was my f—'

She cut him off, her fingers pressed over his lips. 'No. No more blame,' she said softly, and then she curved her hand around the back of his neck, drew his head down and kissed him.

For a second he froze, then his mouth softened, coaxing, tempting her until her lips parted to welcome him, his hand cradling her cheek as he deepened the kiss, tasting, searching, his tongue duelling with hers in a gentle, sensuous dance filled with promise.

Then he eased away, long before she was ready to let him go, opened the front door and turned on the step. 'Don't do anything rash, Liv,' he said gruffly. 'Don't forget you've got concussion. The signals in the brain can be disrupted for a month.'

'Nick, I'll be fine. Go. And ring me when you get back.'

He opened his mouth as if he was going to argue, then gave a rueful smile and nodded. 'Will do. Take care.'

And with a fleeting smile, he got into his car, fired up the engine and drove away.

She was on tenterhooks for the next twelve hours. Ridiculous, considering the number of times he must have been on the road in the last two years and she'd never given it a second thought.

It was different now. Now, she was letting herself care about him again, starting to forgive him—not for being unfaithful, because she'd done that long ago when she'd realised that she'd shut him out, but for letting her believe it all this time.

And she had to forgive herself, too—for making their lives a misery, for shutting him out, for putting him in a position where he'd been happy for her to think that he'd betrayed her trust because it gave him a way out of a situation that had become intolerable.

Why hadn't they talked? Because they were talking now. They'd done little else in the past forty-eight hours, and already the wounds hurt a little less.

Like the physical ones, from Friday. Every hour saw another patch of skin go black as the bruising came out, but it looked much worse than it felt and it really didn't hurt any more and nor did her head.

She pottered in the garden, tried a little weeding and

gave up because bending over induced a headache and she didn't want to push it, even though her concussion had only been mild. Maybe Nick was right and she should take it easy.

Her phone pinged at midnight, with a text to say he was back at Sam's and see her tomorrow, and for the first time in hours she let herself relax.

Then on Monday morning just before eight, he rang her.

'Are you really coming in to work?'

'Yes, I am, but only light duties from nine to three. Are you still fretting about me?' she asked mildly.

'No, not at all, but I've put Judy on steroids. I've got a funny feeling about her—until we get the antiphospholipid result we won't know why she's had problems, but at least if the steroids have matured the baby's lungs it'll have more chance if we do need to deliver her in a hurry. I just thought you'd like to know.'

'Mmm. Thanks. Poor Judy. How is she?'

'Scared? She might appreciate a visit, if you've got a minute.'

She smiled. 'I'll drop in on her. And before you ask, no, I'm not driving, I'm going to walk in.'

'Good,' he said, sounding relieved. 'I'll see you later. Text me when you get here.'

So much for keeping their distance, she thought with a smile, but at least if they were at work there'd be no cosy moments to derail them.

To his surprise she walked onto the antenatal ward half an hour later, just as he went to check on Judy again.

'Gosh, two of you! It's like buses.'

'Mine's only a social call, Judy,' Liv said, turning towards her. 'I just popped up to say hi.'

'Oh! Your eye! What have you done?'

'Ah, yes. Minor accident on Friday.'

Nick snorted softly, and Judy glanced from him to Liv and back again, studying their nametags. 'You're both Jarvis,' she said slowly. 'Are you married, or is that just coincidence?'

He opened his mouth, looked at Liv and left it up to her.

'We were married—and no, he didn't hit me, it genuinely was an accident,' she said, and gave Judy a twisted little smile.

'Oh, gosh. Why did you let him go?'

Nick snorted again and picked up the board at the end of the bed, scanning her charts with half an eye while he waited for Liv to reply to that one.

'Yes. Bit silly, wasn't it?' she said eventually, and the silence grew a little awkward.

'Right, now we've established that I'm not a wife-beater, can we get back to business, please? Judy, how are you feeling?'

All trace of humour vanished from her face. 'Worried, if I'm honest, because there's something I didn't tell you that maybe I should have. I've been taking aspirin since just before I got pregnant.'

'Aspirin?' he asked, frowning, and glanced at Liv, who just shrugged and looked as stunned as he felt.

'Yes. I've been really worried about this APS thing but the test I had after my last miscarriage was negative so I thought I'd be all right, but then I read up about OAPS and it just seemed to fit, you know, and it said take aspirin, so I started taking it after my last period, and I don't know if it's coincidence but everything seemed to be going fine until I stopped—'

'You stopped? When?'

She nodded. 'About three weeks ago, because I was bruising so easily and I thought I might be doing more harm than good and I was a bit worried about having a haemorrhage, and it's all gone wrong since then.'

She pressed a hand over her mouth. 'It's my fault, isn't it? I shouldn't have stopped. I should have said something.'

'Yes, you should, because stopping it could certainly explain the baby's slow growth in the last few weeks,' he told her thoughtfully, 'but taking it could also have stopped you miscarrying in the first place, so, no, I don't think it was the wrong thing to do, but yes, you probably should have told us because had we known I would have put you back on aspirin on Friday as a precaution.'

'I'm so sorry—'

'No, don't apologise, Judy, it's OK, because I think it's just made everything a lot clearer, so here's what we'll do. I'm going to chase those results, because it's quite possible you *have* got obstetric antiphospholipid syndrome, which unlike normal APS only affects you when you're pregnant, hence the negative result before. Basically what happens is the blood clots in the capillaries in the uterine wall and can prevent implantation of an embryo, prevent the placenta developing, or cause it to fail later on, which may be what's happening with your baby now, but if that's what it is, it's utterly treatable and we can stop it in its tracks, so I'm going to put you back on aspirin just to be on the safe side, and we'll see what the results come up with and go from there. OK?'

She nodded, looking on the verge of tears. 'I'm sorry. I should have told you I'd been taking it, but I didn't want to look hysterical. I know doctors frown on people self-medicating.'

'There's nothing hysterical about it, Judy, and you

may have done exactly the right thing. You've lost three babies already, but this one's still alive, and I'm going to make very, very sure that we do everything we can to keep it safe. OK?'

Her eyes filled, and she nodded. 'OK. Thank you.'

'My pleasure. Let's just hope we get some answers soon.'

Liv got to her feet. 'I'll leave you to it. I think there's a stack of filing with my name on it. I'll pop back and see you later if I get a minute, Judy.'

'That would be lovely.' Judy watched her walk away, then said, 'You ought to take care of her, she shouldn't be here, not with that eye,' and he met her reproachful eyes over the top of the charts and felt a twinge of guilt mixed with frustration.

'Tell me about it.' He sighed, and hung the charts back on the end of the bed. 'OK. I'll chase up the results, get you some aspirin and I'll be back later. Yell if you feel any different. They'll page me. And don't worry about Liv, I'm keeping an eye on her.'

'You do that. She's a lovely woman.'

As if he hadn't noticed.

He appeared in the ward office some time after she started sifting through the clearly non-essential paperwork, most of which needed shredding, from what she could see.

'Sorted Judy?' she asked, and he nodded.

'I wish she'd told us about the aspirin, I would have put her back on it prophylactically on Friday, but she's on it now and hopefully it won't be too late. Got time for coffee? I haven't had breakfast yet and I've been here since seven.'

'Yes, I've got tons of time,' she said with a wry smile,

getting to her feet. 'Nobody will give me anything to do. I think they're all terrified by the black eye, so it's a good job they can't see my leg.'

'Probably, it was bad enough on Saturday and it can only be worse by now. Judy told me to take care of you, by the way, and said you shouldn't be here with that eye. I agreed with her.'

'Is that why nobody'll give me anything to do except filing, because you've been sticking your oar in?'

'I hardly needed to do that. One look at you is enough.'

She made a disgusted sound. 'Whatever, I'd like to kill whoever invented filing. I'm beginning to think it's possible to die of boredom and I've only been doing it for half an hour.'

He chuckled. 'I think you're trying to get out of a dull job.'

'Rumbled,' she said with a laugh, and they walked down to the café in a companionable silence.

He ordered their coffees and picked up a cereal bar and a banana. 'Want one?' he asked, waggling the banana at her, and she nodded.

'Yes, please. There wasn't much left in the house so I only had toast for breakfast. Gwen didn't rock up with a casserole, by the way, but I did see her through the window and waved. I think the black eye might have scared her off.'

He winced. 'Perhaps you'd better explain about the accident before Bert comes looking for me with his garden shears.'

They found a table by the window, and he sat down and stretched his legs out. 'Before I forget, I put a food order in this morning so you'll have something for breakfast tomorrow. It should arrive at yours this evening between six and seven. I take it you'll be there?'

'You ordered food for me?' she said, puzzled.

'Yes. Well, some staples for you to save you having to shop, but I got some stuff for us to share, as well. I thought, if we're going to take this seriously and try and get to know each other again, maybe we should spend the evenings together when we can, and the kitchen in the cabin's a bit basic so I thought maybe we could do it at the house? I'll do all the cooking, so it should be easier for you, too. Unless you have any objections?'

'No, that sounds great. Why would I object to being waited on? Did you order wine, by the way? I'm sorry I didn't have any over the weekend.'

'I don't drink any more,' he said. 'I still have the odd glass if I'm with friends, but I never buy alcohol routinely, and I absolutely never drink on my own. And I go to the gym, and I'm running again, and I've cleaned up my diet—too little, too late, but...'

He tailed off, leaving her to absorb all that for a second, and she shook her head.

'I thought you looked better,' she said quietly. 'Fitter. Healthier. More like the man I married—except you don't look like the man I married, because the man I married was happy, and you're not happy any more and that's my fault.'

'Liv, it's not your fault.'

'Yes, it is. I've destroyed your life, messed up your career, trashed everything, and I'm so sorry. I shouldn't have believed that you'd been unfaithful to me, because it was so unlike you, but when I thought about it, it didn't seem such a stretch to imagine that you'd turn to someone else, because you weren't showing any interest in me by then and I couldn't see what I had to offer you any longer. It was all so horrible—'

He gave a soft sigh, his voice quiet, his smile gentle,

but he looked troubled, as if there was something he wanted to say. He didn't, though, just took her hand and squeezed it. 'Hey, no more, come on. This isn't the time or the place. Let's concentrate on the here and now—and right now, I'm operating in an hour and I haven't gone through the notes properly yet, so I'll take my coffee and go. You take it easy, I'll catch you later.'

She watched him go and sat there a moment longer, soaking up the sun, but then her phone rang, making her jump. It was Sam, checking up on her and asking if she felt she needed physio.

'No, Sam, I'm fine, but thank you. I'm back at work already.'

'Seriously? You've got concussion, not to mention the bruises.'

'Sam, I'm fine, really. And thank you for putting Nick up. It's very kind of you. He seems really happy with the cabin.'

'Good. You're welcome. Sorry, I've got to go, I'm needed in Resus but you know where I am. Shout if you need anything and don't overdo it.'

The phone went dead, and she slipped it into her pocket, finished her coffee and went back to the tedious filing.

Overdo it? Chance would be a fine thing.

CHAPTER EIGHT

SHE WAS SENT down to cover for Jan again in the antenatal clinic after lunch, and Nick took one look at her and told her to go home. 'You're white as a sheet and you look shattered. Go on, out of here.'

'I'm fine. I'm only working till three. Don't fuss. How's Judy?'

'OK, but she has got antiphospholipid antibodies.'

'So she's definitely got OAPS?'

He gave a frustrated sigh. 'It looks like it, and I'm kicking myself for not putting her on aspirin on Friday when I admitted her. The more I think about it, the crosser I get.'

'Why? She'd already had a test that was negative, and Simon hadn't picked it up.'

'No, but his wife had just been diagnosed with cancer, so I doubt his mind was in the right place, and I wasn't firing on all cylinders either after finding we were working together, but two wrongs don't make a right.'

'No, they don't, but she'd withheld vital information, and anyway, it was a judgement call, Nick.'

'And I made the wrong judgement. Hence the expression "human error", but it's unforgivable when a baby's life's at stake. Still, I'd admitted her and she'd been monitored so we know nothing happened over the weekend. I suppose that's something to be thankful for. Right, Amy Zacharelli.'

She felt her eyes widen. It was Amy's baby he'd gone to deliver by emergency C-section on the day she'd thrown him out. Of all the coincidences...

'Amy's pregnant again already?'

'So it would seem.'

'Is she going for another section?'

'I don't know. I'm going to talk to her now I've seen her latest scan images. I'm hoping not. Simon's written "Query VBAC" in her notes, so it's obviously been discussed. Would you like to call her in?'

'Sure.'

She went out to the waiting room and called Amy, and a good-looking couple got to their feet. She'd never seen Amy, but she would have recognised Leo blindfolded. He was a celebrity chef, and she was a massive fan of his cookery show.

'May I come, too?' he asked with a coaxing smile, and she smiled back and hoped she didn't look too fan-girly.

'Of course, if Amy's happy. Mr Jarvis won't mind,' she said as she ushered them into the consulting room.

'Mr Jarvis?' Amy said, and her face lit up as she saw him in there. 'I thought you'd gone for ever.'

'So did I.' He got to his feet and smiled, shaking their hands. 'It's good to see you again, and not before time. I owe you both a massive apology. I promised to come back and make sure you were OK when I delivered your last baby, but I got caught up in something and then I was off on leave and I didn't even get a message to you. I'm really sorry.'

Caught up in something? On leave? One way of putting it when your wife calls time on your marriage, Liv thought, and wondered if she was the only person who could see what was going on under the surface of his calm, professional demeanour. She hoped so, for his sake, but both she and Nick were well aware that she'd found Suze's note while he'd been delivering Amy's baby.

'There's no need to apologise,' Leo was saying. 'I'm just sorry that we never had a chance to thank you, but I've never forgotten how kind you were to Amy, and how much we owe you.'

'You don't owe me anything,' Nick said, brushing it aside. 'It was a pleasure. So, how is your little girl? Is she doing well?'

'She's wonderful. Naughty, but wonderful,' Amy said with a laugh, 'and she's been fine, thanks to you and Mr Walker.'

'Do you know what this one is?'

'A boy,' Leo told him, his smile saying it all, and Liv felt the familiar shaft of pain like an old friend, but Nick's smile was convincing. If you didn't know better...

'Perfect,' he said. 'So, what are your birth plans? I see from your notes there's a suggestion you want to try for a normal vaginal delivery.'

'I want to, if I can. Mr Bailey said he was prepared to let me try, but he's apparently gone off on indefinite leave so I'm in the lurch again. I seem to have that effect on people.'

His smile was a little strained. 'I'm sure you can't take the blame for either of us abandoning you, but you're not in the lurch, unless I don't count? I'm replacing him for now, so I'll be looking after you for the rest of this pregnancy and I'm happy to let you try if everything looks OK.'

'You are?' Her face lit up, and she pressed her hands to her mouth. 'Oh, that's amazing! I was so worried, I thought his replacement might say no.'

'No. They're going to be close together, of course, only about fifteen months apart, but it's over a year so technically speaking that's not a problem. Why don't you hop up on the couch and let's have a look at your scar?'

All was well, he was relieved to see. The scar was a fine, tidy line, her uterus under the skin felt smooth, with only the slightest hint of a ridge over the incision site, and he could feel nothing to worry him.

'OK, Amy, I'm all done.' He snapped off his gloves and propped himself up on his desk. 'It's looking good,' he said. 'The head's engaged, everything looks fine, and I think I'll be quite happy to let you try. I'll make sure I'm here when you're admitted, but I don't see any reason why you shouldn't succeed. Liv?'

'No, I'd be happy to deliver you, Amy. I might be a bit less happy if it was a home birth, but provided you're here and we're keeping a close eye on things, I don't see a problem at all.'

'Oh, that's brilliant,' Amy said, tugging her clothes straight and picking up her bag. 'I feel so much happier now.'

He grinned at her enthusiasm. 'Good. I like my mums to be happy. I'll definitely make sure I'm around when you go into labour, and I'll do my best to give you the delivery you want, but the safety net is there. We'll make sure of that.'

'Thank you,' she said fervently, and then to his astonishment she went up on tiptoe and kissed his cheek. 'Thank you so much.'

'My pleasure. I'll see you in two weeks, if not before. I wouldn't want you to go over, but we'll see how it's going, and you might need a membrane sweep to chivvy things along, but so far, so good. You take care. It's good to see you both again.'

'You, too,' Leo said. 'Welcome back to Yoxburgh.'

Nick smiled and watched them go, wondering again what it would be like to come back here permanently, to see his patients extending their families, getting to know them over the years.

Maybe he'd get to find out?

He turned to Liv. 'Right, you, time to go home. I can manage the rest. They'll find me a nurse. Shoo. Go.'

She went, much more tired than she'd expected, and the short walk took her twice as long as usual. She let herself in and curled up on the sofa, her body tired and achy, her legs like lead. She'd just got settled when the doorbell rang, and she dragged herself off the sofa and opened the door.

Flowers.

Beautiful flowers, hand-tied and in a lovely vase, so she didn't even have to arrange them. There was a card, and she pulled it out of the envelope.

N xxx

Nothing more, but he didn't need to say more. His phone went straight to voicemail, so she left him a message thanking him, and spent the rest of the afternoon either dozing or staring at them with a silly smile on her face.

He cared. Still, after everything that had happened, he cared. And tonight couldn't come soon enough...

He looked tired but happier when he turned up, and although he'd shaved this morning she could see the dark shadow of stubble on his jaw again, and it sent a shiver through her.

He hugged her briefly, kissed her cheek and let her go, shoving his hands in his back pockets. To keep them out of trouble? Probably wise, she thought regretfully.

'So, did the shopping come?' he asked.

'Yes. And the flowers. They're beautiful. Thank you.'

'You're welcome. How are you?'

'Tired,' she admitted. 'I wasn't expecting to feel like this. It's not even as if my head aches.'

'Concussion's a weird thing. You need to take it easy. What about the rest of you?'

'All right. My bruises hurt if I touch them, but otherwise I'm fine.'

'Well, there's an easy answer to that,' he said with a grin.

He wandered through to the kitchen and started poking about in the fridge.

'So, what did you do this morning while I was filing?' she asked, following him.

'Oh, gynae surgery. All the usual stuff. Pretty dull. I like the babies.'

She laughed sadly. 'Me, too. We really chose the right careers, didn't we? So what do you reckon Amy Zacharelli's chances of delivering successfully are?'

'I don't know. She's due in sixteen days, but I don't want her to go over, really. It would be lovely if she went into labour spontaneously so we don't have to induce her but that could complicate things so I'm not holding my breath.' He pulled his head out of the fridge. 'How do you fancy a Thai chicken curry with cauliflower rice?'

She felt her eyes widen. 'That's a bit healthy. And I noticed everything's organic.'

'I told you I'd turned my life around. Too healthy?'

'No—no, it sounds great. Go for it. Can I do anything?'

'Yes. Sit down on the sofa there and talk to me while I cook.'

She turned her head and looked at it, squatting there in the 'family room' like a malevolent toad, taunting her with horrible memories.

'Do I have to?'

He looked up and met her eyes, and frowned. 'Hey, what's up?' he asked softly, abandoning the food and cradling her cheek in his hand. It was chilly from the fridge, and it sent a shiver down her spine.

'I don't like that sofa. Not since…'

'Oh, Liv.' Her name was a sigh on his lips, and he drew her gently into his arms and hugged her. 'Come on. We'll sit on it together and chase out the demons.'

And he took her hand and led her over to the sofa and sat her down next to him. 'There. See? It's just a sofa.'

She looked at the coffee table, and he followed her eyes and frowned. 'What's that mark?' he asked, leaning forwards and scratching at a dull, pale patch with his nail.

'You slopped your coffee when you stood up when I told you to go, and I put the paper under it to mop it up, and it stuck.'

He turned his head, his eyes shocked as they met hers.

'It's been there all this time?'

She shrugged. 'It didn't matter. I don't use it.'

He got up, found a sponge in the sink and came back, scrubbing at the stuck bits of paper until they dissolved and slid away. He gave the table one last swipe and straightened up to look at it.

'There, that's better,' he said, and bent and caught her chin in his fingers. 'Much better,' he added softly, and lowered his head the last few inches and kissed her.

'Now stay there, and I'll make you supper and you can talk to me.'

She looked at the mark, now nothing more than a slowly drying damp patch, and realised he was right. It was much better, in every way. Amazing what you could wipe away with a damp sponge...

She settled back into the corner, tucked a cushion behind her head and watched him cook while her lips tingled gently from his kiss.

'Thank you. That was amazing. I loved the cauliflower rice.'

They were back on the sofa, the one where her life had fallen apart last January, and he propped his feet up on the coffee table and rolled his head towards her.

'Don't get too addicted to it. I don't want you getting skinny again. You were way too thin, with all that running.'

'I know.' She looked away for a moment, and he caught her chin and gently turned her face towards him, his eyes searching.

'What?'

She shrugged, forcing herself to hold his steady gaze. 'I've wondered—you know, if that was why I never conceived?'

He dropped his hand and this time it was him who looked away. 'Not necessarily.'

She frowned. There was something he wasn't telling her, and she had a sinking feeling in her gut. 'Nick?'

He swallowed, sucked in a breath and let it go again slowly.

'I had semen analysis,' he said eventually, his voice heavy. 'Three years ago, after the second month you weren't pregnant.'

'And?' she prompted, her heart pounding. If they'd been trying for two years, and all that time he'd known—

'Well, I wasn't exactly firing blanks, but my sperm count was down on the optimum, and the quality wasn't stunning. It wasn't that bad, but it wasn't great, either.'

'So you cleaned up your act,' she said slowly, remembering how he'd suddenly stopped drinking wine and eating rubbish, rejoined the hospital gym, started running—but it hadn't lasted.

'Yes. And you still didn't get pregnant, and it was getting tougher and tougher, so I just let it all slide again. And then just before you found out you weren't pregnant, I had another test.'

Her heart thumped. 'And?'

'It was worse. Not catastrophic, but bad enough that it could definitely be an issue by then. I'd already decided that if you weren't pregnant I was going to talk to you, tell you the truth, but then when I got the result I was just numb, so I went to the conference, trying to work up the courage to tell you it was probably all my fault, and then Suze asked me what was wrong and I just lost it. And then when you thought I'd slept with her and kicked me out it seemed like the best idea because I thought if you hated me you'd find it easier to move on, but you haven't, and neither have I. But that's really why I didn't tell you the truth about Suze, because I didn't want you taking me back out of pity and going through endless cycles of IVF when you didn't really love me any more anyway.'

She slid her hand into his, threading their fingers together and holding on. 'I never stopped loving you, Nick.'

His fingers tightened. 'It felt like it, when you said you wanted a divorce. It felt as if you hated me, and I could see why, because I hated myself then and I thought if I got out of your life you'd find someone else and have babies the easy way, because IVF's tough, Liv. It can be really tough, I didn't know how tough until I saw others going through it, and you're younger than me, you've got years to find another man who can give you babies—'

'But I don't want another man, Nick, and I don't want anyone else's babies! I want you, and if it was right for us, down the line, I'd want *your* babies, via IVF or whatever other route we had to take so I could give them to you.'

She lifted her other hand and curled it round his jaw, turning his face back to her. 'That's why I never divorced you, because I love you,' she said softly. 'I'll always love you, and I couldn't bring myself to let you go.'

'Oh, Liv...'

He closed the gap between them, his mouth finding hers, sipping, searching, coaxing. She tipped back her head and his lips trailed down over her jaw, down her throat, over her collarbone until they met the soft, clinging fabric of her top.

And then he stopped, motionless for a moment before he lifted his head and dropped the lightest, sweetest kiss on her lips and moved away.

'Don't stop.'

'I have to. We can't do this now, Liv. Not yet. Apart from anything else you're exhausted, you've had a long day and you need to go to bed.'

'So take me to bed.'

He gave a despairing little laugh and kissed her again. 'Nice try, but I need to go,' he whispered softly.

'I'll miss you.'

'I'll miss you, too, but it might be good for us. As they say, abstinence makes the heart grow fonder.'

She felt her mouth twitch into a smile, and she reached out and cupped his jaw again, her fingers testing the slight roughness of the stubble coming through. 'Promise me something.'

'What?'

'Keep the stubble this time? It makes you look sexy and a teensy bit badass.'

'What?' he said with a laugh. 'Why would you want me to look like that?'

'You know what I mean.'

'Yeah. Your bit of rough,' he said self-mockingly, and she smacked his hand and laughed.

'You are so not my bit of rough. It just makes you look—'

'Badass,' he said on a chuckle. 'Good grief. I don't want to upset my patients.'

'Too late to worry about that. You heard what Judy said about me letting you go. *She* thinks you're hot.'

He frowned and stared down at her. 'Hot? Judy? You're kidding me.'

She rolled her eyes, and he laughed again.

'Seriously?'

'You just have no idea, do you?' she said, shaking her head slowly from side to side. 'Nick, you are *such* a hottie.'

He lifted his hand, fingering his jaw thoughtfully. 'Well, maybe I should get a stubble blade for my razor. You know—just to keep you interested.'

His eyes were sparkling with mischief, and he looked so like his old self that it made her want to cry—or hug him. She did that, as the safest option, and then let him go.

'Go on, go home.'

'I wish,' he said softly, and she felt like crying again.

'I meant back to Sam's. Quick, while I'll still let you.'

He got to his feet and pulled her up, then kissed her

again, his mouth lingering on hers for the longest moment before he took a step back out of reach.

'You go on up to bed. I'll put the dishwasher on and clear up before I leave. Shoo.'

She shooed, because she truly was exhausted, but she didn't sleep until she heard the front door close softly, and then the scrunch of tyres as he drove away. By the time the sound of his engine had faded, she was asleep...

He kept the stubble.

Not because of what she'd said, apparently, but because he had a call from the hospital about Judy Richards, so he'd thrown on his clothes and gone straight there.

By the time Liv went on duty at seven, he'd already been in the hospital for two hours and Judy had had another Doppler ultrasound scan of her placenta because the monitor had shown a slight dip in the baby's heart rate and it hadn't been moving quite as much as usual.

'Is she going to be all right?' she asked him, moving to stand next to him behind the nursing station desk, and he pursed his lips, his eyes still tracking over the scan images on the computer.

'I hope so. Her placenta's certainly not brilliant, but she's going to have another scan in two hours. If there's any change at all, I'm going to deliver it.'

'At thirty-two weeks?'

'Thirty-three today. And every day counts at this stage.'

He turned and gave her a tired smile. 'Talking of which, how are you?'

'Better. I slept like a log.'

'See? I told you you were tired,' he murmured.

'I'm not tired now,' she murmured, 'not looking at that badass stubble,' but he just laughed and stood up.

'No, you're at work,' he pointed out, but he winked at her as he turned away and her heart fluttered. Then he turned back.

'What are you doing this evening?'

'Eating with you?'

He smiled. 'Good. Want to come down to the cabin? I'll pick you and the food up, if you like.'

'Assuming Judy's OK, because I know you and I know she'll come first.'

'Are you jealous of a patient?'

She folded her arms. 'Absolutely.'

He laughed again and walked away, and she stood there staring after him like a moonstruck fool.

'You two seem to be getting on pretty well.'

She jumped and spun round.

'Ben! Do you have to sneak up on me like that? You scared the living daylights out of me!'

He raised his hands in apology. 'Sorry. I didn't mean to startle you, I just wanted your input on a patient,' he said, but his eyes were twinkling and she felt herself colour.

'No, you didn't, you were just fishing for gossip.'

'Not gossip. I'm actually very relieved to see you getting on, on several fronts.'

'Several?'

'Mmm. For a start you're alive, so after worrying us all to death on Friday that's a massive plus. And you're both friends of mine, so it's good to see you together again.'

'We're not "together" together, so don't get over-excited,' she cautioned. 'And anyway, that's only two fronts.'

'Well, he hasn't left yet, so we still have our locum. That's a very fat three.'

She chuckled. 'I can imagine. So, which patient did

you want to talk to me about?' she asked, but he frowned thoughtfully.

'Patient? Did I say something about a patient?' he murmured, and then wandered off, leaving her laughing softly under her breath. *Idiot*...

'Liv, we've got a new mum on the way in in an ambo. Are you involved in a delivery at the moment?'

'No, do you want me to take her?' she asked the duty line manager, and she nodded.

'Please. The baby's OP, and she was in too much pain to get in the car, apparently. It's only precautionary, so it should be pretty straightforward.'

Famous last words.

The back-to-back presentation was always potentially difficult, especially for a first-time mother, and the terrified young woman was in so much pain when she arrived that she refused to move, but without moving she was never going to get her baby out and it was ready to come.

'OK,' Liv said, 'I'll get you some pain relief, and then I'm going to get you up, because you're fully dilated and this baby needs you to push.'

'I can't—'

'Yes, you can, you'll see. I'll be back in a minute.'

She left the mother in the care of another midwife while she went to find Nick. 'Are you busy in the next half hour or so? I might need you.'

'Sounds promising,' he murmured, a lazy, sexy smile playing around his mouth, and she ignored the little shiver of need and rolled her eyes.

'I've got a primipara struggling with an OP labour and she might need a bit of assistance. I'm going to give her some Pethidine and then try and get her up, but I'm not holding out much hope. She's being pretty adamant about not moving.'

'OK. Page me if you need me. I've got a conference call with Ben's brother in an hour to talk about Judy's scans, but if I can help before then, give me a shout. Otherwise it'll be Ben.'

'OK.'

She didn't need him.

Between the painkiller, her partner's physical and emotional support and a bit of cajoling and encouragement from Liv, they got her up onto all fours which expanded her pelvis enough to allow the baby to pass through it, and no sooner was the mother lying down again with the squalling baby in her arms than there was a knock on the door and Nick stuck his head round.

'That answers that question, then,' he said with a crooked little smile. 'Everything OK?'

She smiled back, blinking away the tears that accompanied every delivery these days. 'Perfect, thank you, Mr Jarvis.'

'Good. Come and find me when you're done, please. I might need you.'

She raised an eyebrow, her back to the patient, and he winked and sent her blood pressure rocketing.

The door closed with a soft click, and she blinked again and turned back to the mother with what she hoped was a nice, professional smile firmly pinned on her face.

'You see?' she said. 'I told you you could do it. Well done.'

It was after seven before he finished work and came to pick her up. She didn't mind for herself, because she'd had a nap after she got home, but he'd been at the hospital for fourteen hours and he must be exhausted.

'How's Judy?'

'Fine. OK. Ben's brother Matt was pretty positive

about the baby, which was good. It's handy having a prenatal paediatrician on tap like that. What do you fancy for supper?'

'Something quick and easy. You must be really tired.'

He smiled and dropped a kiss on her hair, hugging her gently. 'I am, but I need to wind down. I'm not on call tonight so I shouldn't get called in unless Judy has a crisis, and I'm hoping we've averted that, so I should get eight straight hours in bed.

'Fancy fish and chips?'

'I thought you were on a health kick?'

He laughed. 'It's not a health kick, it's a lifestyle choice, and I can choose to have a treat if I want one. Or if you'd rather, I can knock up a salad. I've got roasted aubergine, braised artichoke hearts, hot-smoked salmon fillets—'

'That sounds gorgeous.'

'Good. Right, let's go because the evening's ebbing away and we're wasting it and we both need an early night.'

He raided the fridge and drove her down to the harbour, pulled up outside the back of Sam and Kate's house and took her into the cabin.

'Oh, it's lovely!' she said, looking round. 'Really nice. And to think I was feeling sorry for you.'

'Oh, don't feel sorry for me, I'm very happy here, it's perfect. Or it is now, now you're here.'

He put the bag down and pulled her into his arms, staring down into her eyes and searching them for answers.

'Can we do this, Liv?' he asked softly. 'Can we make it work? Even if in the end we can never have kids?'

'We can give it our best shot. My mum this morning didn't think she was going to be able to get her baby out without help, but she did it. Maybe that's the clue. Maybe we have to work at it instead of expecting it to look after itself. But you might have to feed me first,' she added with a smile as her stomach rumbled, and he laughed and let her go.

They had coffee after dinner with Sam and Kate, and they could see lights twinkling out on the water, and hear the clatter of the rigging from the boat yard, and she could see why Nick loved it so much.

Then Nick looked at his watch. 'Right, I need to get some sleep because until Judy's delivered I'm just waiting for the call.'

'You need to learn to delegate,' Sam said, which made her laugh.

'He doesn't delegate,' she told Sam. 'He doesn't trust anyone else—a little bit like you, really. I seem to remember you had to check up on me on Saturday morning after the accident.'

'Rumbled,' he said with a grin, and Nick pulled Liv to her feet.

'Come on, I need my bed. Thanks for the coffee, guys.'

'They're such nice people,' Liv said as he started the car. 'Have you told them about us?'

'No. I don't talk about us, you know that.'

'You talked to Suze.'

'Just once, and look where it got me.'

He gave her a fleeting smile, and even the moonlight picked up the sadness in his eyes.

He pulled up on the drive and cut the engine.

'Oh. Are you coming in?' she asked. 'I thought you were in a hurry to get to bed?'

That made him chuckle. 'Are they mutually exclusive?'

Her jaw dropped a fraction and he stopped teasing

her. 'If I kiss you goodnight out here in the car the way I want to kiss you goodnight, Bert and Gwen will probably have a stroke.'

She stifled a laugh and opened her door. 'Well, we can't have that.'

'Absolutely not.'

He followed her into the house, still chuckling, closed the door and leant back on it, pulling her into his arms.

'Oh, that's better.' His mouth found hers, and he felt the smile on it fade as need moved in and swamped them both.

She arched up and kissed him back, tunnelling her fingers through his hair as he plundered her mouth, his hands holding her head steady as he deepened the kiss, his tongue duelling with hers, his hips rocking against her body.

Then he lifted his head and rested his forehead against hers, his breath rasping in and out as if he'd been running.

'I want you,' he whispered roughly, nipping and nibbling over her throat as she arched her head back invitingly.

'So stay,' she murmured, and he wavered for a second then shook his head.

'No, I can't. I have to go. I'm dead beat and I'm on call tomorrow night, so this is my last chance at a good uninterrupted stretch. What time are you on tomorrow?'

'Seven, again.'

'Me, too. I'll pick you up at a quarter to, and we can have breakfast together when I've done my ward round if you're not involved in a delivery by then.'

He kissed her again, just a tender, lingering caress, and then he moved her gently out of his way before he surrendered to temptation. It would be so easy—

'I need to go.'

'I know you do. I love you.'

He groaned. 'Oh, Liv. I love you, too,' he murmured. He kissed her again, then opened the door, got into the car and drove away, wondering what the hell he was doing and why, when he could have been upstairs with her by now, buried in that beautiful, willing body.

He must be mad, but he was also wary and he didn't want to be hasty.

Yes, he loved her, and he needed her, and she clearly felt the same way, but there was so much left unresolved about their infertility, so many things they hadn't tried. They'd hardly got past first base, but their relationship had already crumbled under the strain and he wasn't sure he could face the emotional upheaval of trying to repair their marriage, just to watch it torn down again.

He just had to be sure when they took that next step that they were doing it for all the right reasons, and that meant going back to his own bed.

Alone—but hopefully not for much longer, because the waiting was killing him.

CHAPTER NINE

'YOU'VE GOT STUBBLE RASH.'

His finger traced her top lip, and she had to resist the temptation to draw it into her mouth and suck it. In the hospital café, right in front of everyone, that might not be smart.

'Stop frowning, you'll get wrinkles,' she told him.

'Good. It might stop the patients thinking I'm hot, of all things,' he said, sounding almost disgusted with himself. 'I can't believe I scraped your lip with my stubble.'

She chuckled. 'Well, if you will kiss me like that...'

'Then I'll have to shave. And I fully intend to kiss you like that. Every night. At least.'

She didn't even try to stop the smile. 'Good. How's Judy?'

'Fine. Stable. Her placenta seems to be holding its own and I'm going to get another ultrasound to check if the baby's grown at all. If not, I might have to reconsider leaving her any longer.'

He glanced at his phone. 'Right. I'd better get on.'

'Me, too.' She drained her coffee and walked back towards the maternity unit with him, parting at the lift.

'Lunch?' he asked.

'If I'm free. What are you doing now?'

'I've got my first stint in the fertility clinic.'

She felt her heart hitch in her chest.

'Have fun,' she said lightly, but just the word *fertility* was enough to bring all her fears home to roost. Were they really ready to go back to all that?

'Send me a text when you finish. Failing that, supper?'

'Sounds good. I'll catch you later.'

They fell into a routine from then on.

He picked her up from home if their shifts started at the same time, and if not she walked in, not because she shouldn't drive yet after her concussion, but just because the weather was warmer now and so beautiful and she enjoyed it.

If they could, they shared a break, and if their shifts allowed, they ate together in the evenings, and when they couldn't do either and they weren't working together, he sent her texts. Sometimes cheeky, sometimes funny, sometimes just simply, 'Miss you'.

And bit by bit, over the course of the next week, they started to relax with each other and have fun. And he kissed her. A lot.

And then he rang her at six on Thursday morning, nearly two weeks after her accident, to tell her that Amy Zacharelli was on her way in.

'I'd like you to be her midwife, if that's possible. I think you're on at seven, aren't you?'

'Yes, I am. That's fine, I'll come in now and sort it with my line manager. Don't worry, I'll be there.'

'Good. I'll see you shortly. I'll make sure she's in a side room in the labour ward.'

'OK. Thanks. See you.'

She had the fastest shower on record, grabbed a banana out of the fruit bowl and ate it on her walk in. No time to think about driving, or parking the car, so she walked briskly and arrived just as Leo pulled up at the entrance with Amy.

'Hi, Amy,' she said as Leo opened the door. 'Nick's here, we're all ready for you. Are you OK to walk?'

'I'll be fine, but Leo has to park the car.'

'That's OK, I'll stay with you and check you in. Leo, do you want to park and come back and find us? We'll be on the labour ward on the fourth floor.'

'Sure. Thanks.'

He got back in the car and drove off, and Amy grabbed her hand and held on. 'Oh. Contraction.'

'That's OK. Just relax and breathe through it, there's no hurry. You can lean on me if it helps.'

The next one was three minutes later, just as they arrived on the ward, and the third one came as Leo walked in through the door. She sent Nick a text, and he must have been in his office because there was a tap on the door and he was there just as Amy was undressing, so she slipped out to update him.

'How's it going?'

'Contractions every three minutes, dead on. I haven't had time to examine her yet so I don't know how dilated she is, but so far she's coping well. I don't know what you want to do about pain relief?'

He pulled a face. 'Nothing if she can manage without it, and I'd really rather she didn't have an epidural because she won't have any feedback if her uterus starts to tear along the scar, which she would feel otherwise. Has she asked for pain relief?'

'No, not yet. I just wanted all my ducks in a row.'

'Well, see how it goes. Don't let her struggle.'

'I won't. I'll put her on a monitor in a minute. Do you want to examine her yourself or do you want me to do it?'

'No, you do it, it's your labour. I'm just on standby,' he said. 'I'll come in and say hi, and then leave her with you.'

'Sure? That sounds like delegating,' she teased.

He laughed softly, checked the corridor and dropped a fleeting kiss on her lips. 'Of course I'm sure. I trust you.'

'OK. I'll leave her with you while I get rid of my stuff and tell them I'm here, then I'll be back.'

She was only two minutes, and she found Amy propped up on the bed, with Leo perched on the edge. Nick had put her on the monitor, and the baby's heart rate was nice and steady.

'Good, you're back,' he said, his eyes speaking volumes. 'She could do with a quick check, I think.'

AKA things are moving rapidly. She nodded and snapped on some gloves. 'If you hang on I'll give you a progress report,' she murmured and turned to Amy. 'Right, let's have a look. How are you doing?'

'OK, I think. I wasn't expecting it to hot up so quickly.'

'Everyone's different,' she said comfortingly. 'Still happy to give this a try?'

'Oh, yes. I don't want another C-section, not with two little ones to look after.'

'Well, we'll try and avoid it, but if you start getting any sharp or persistent pains around your scar area that aren't like the contractions, tell us straight away. I'll just examine you and see how far on you are.'

'OK—oh, it's another one.'

'Two minutes,' Nick murmured in her ear, and she nodded as her eyes flicked to the monitor. 'Right, try and relax, let your body do the work. That's it, you're doing really well.'

She watched the baby's heart rate dip a fraction, then recover as the contraction eased. 'OK now?'

Amy nodded and leant against Leo, who was sitting up beside her pillows, his arm around her shoulders.

'Right, Amy, can you just drop your knees out for me and relax as much as you can—that's lovely—wow, you're doing really well. You're nearly there. There's just a tiny anterior lip of your cervix left to pull up and you're ready to go.'

'Really? So fast?'

Liv pressed the call button to summon another midwife. 'Like I said, everyone's different and your baby's obviously in a hurry.'

'I need to push now!' she said, her eyes widening, grabbing Leo's hand.

'Well, that answers that,' she said with a smile. 'Just pant for me, Amy. Don't push until I'm sure that lip's gone.'

'Do you mind if I stay?' Nick asked, and she glanced over her shoulder at him, her smile slipping a fraction. He was such a sucker for a new baby.

'Be my guest,' she said softly. 'There should be two of us and nobody's come yet. Right, let's have a look—OK, it's gone, so on the next contraction I want you to take a deep breath and tuck your chin down and push for me.'

'Can I move? I sort of want to kneel, I think.'

'Sure. Turn round and lean on Leo, or the pillows, whatever's most comfortable.'

'Shall I glove up?' Nick murmured. 'They're pretty busy.'

'If you don't mind.'

His smile was crooked. 'When did I ever mind being present at a delivery?' he asked, and turned away before she could answer.

'Oh, I have to push!'

'OK. Deep breath, chin down, let your breath out

as you push into your bottom—that's lovely. Good girl. Well done.'

Two contractions later the baby's head was crowning, and Liv told Amy to pant as she carefully guided the baby's head out and round and checked for the cord.

'Right, little push for me—perfect, well done!'

Amy turned and sat down, and Liv stood back and let Nick lift the baby and pass him to Amy, the tiny slippery body safely cradled in those big, capable hands.

He looked so sure, so natural, so perfect...

He glanced up and met her eyes, and she had to turn away. He wanted this so much for them, needed it so much, and she realised in that moment that she'd go through anything to give him a child.

But what if it never happened for them? What if they went through all the intrusive and gruelling procedures that could be tried and still got nowhere? Would they be able to cope?

She heard the snap as he pulled off his gloves, then felt his arms come round her in a gentle hug.

'Well done, my love,' he murmured, and she knew they had to try, even if they failed, because not to try was to condemn them both to eternal regret.

Nick stayed just long enough to congratulate them and make sure all was well, then retreated to his office, shut the door and leant back against it with a shaky sigh.

Why did he do this job? He must be a masochist.

And Liv thought working in the fertility clinic was hard for him? He let out a humourless little laugh. Every time he saw a baby born, his heart tore a little more. Delivering babies, handing them to their delighted parents—that was far harder, knowing how out of reach it was to him and Liv.

Sure, it was a wonderful and joyous thing to do, but on a personal level it killed him a little bit more every single time—and watching Liv, he knew she felt it, too.

There was a tap on the door behind him, and he took a deep breath, blinked away the tears he hadn't even known were there and opened the door.

'Hi, Ben. What's up?'

'Nothing, I just saw that Amy Zacharelli's come in. I wondered if you knew.'

'Yes, she's had the baby, I was there,' he said, and turned away, flicking through a file on his desk because he wasn't sure his feelings weren't written all over his face. 'Straightforward easy delivery, mum and baby both doing well. I left them in Liv's hands. She knows where I am.'

'Good. Great.'

There was a pause, and Nick frowned and turned back to look at Ben. 'Was there something else?'

'How are you and Liv?'

He blinked. 'What's that got to do with the price of fish?'

'That's not a straight answer to a straight question.'

He shut the file and forced himself to meet Ben's eyes.

'I didn't think it was a straight question. I would say it was thoroughly loaded and probably none of your business.'

Ben studied him thoughtfully for a moment, then nodded slowly. 'OK, fair enough, but it's kind of relevant. Off the record, Simon's not coming back. Jen's doing OK, but he says it's going to be a long haul and whichever way it goes, they need to be near the family for support, so I'm going to have to advertise the post. I'm going to be blunt, I want you back but only if you and Liv are OK with it. You fit in well, you know your way around, you're a team player, you have additional skills which we need—we don't need to look any further, but I need to know that you're going to stick around if we appoint you. Assuming we do appoint you, which I think is pretty much a given, but we have to abide by the rules and advertise.'

His heart was thumping in his chest, because a part of him wanted this so much it was eating him alive. The other part was still wondering if he and Liv stood a prayer of making it work.

'Of course you have to advertise it. And you don't know what that'll throw up. You might get someone extraordinary apply.'

Ben shrugged. 'We might, although I doubt very much we'd get anyone better than you, but the bottom line is I can't even consider you for the post if you and Liv are going to find you can't hack it, because that's no good for either of you and it's no good for the department. I need to know that you're in it for the long haul.'

He couldn't give Ben an answer. Not yet, not without talking to Liv.

'You said it's off the record.'

'You can talk to Liv. She's the soul of discretion and anyway, her support is key. I realise that.'

He nodded. 'OK. Thanks for the heads up. I'll let you know. When's the closing date?'

Ben laughed. 'Realistically, until we get a suitable candidate, but probably a month at the outside? If you don't apply, we'll have to keep the advert open until we get someone. Talk to Liv, think it over. I don't want to put you under pressure.'

That made him laugh.

'Yeah, right,' he said drily, then shook his head slowly. 'Leave it with me, Ben. I knew it was a possibility, but

I hadn't really let myself consider it, so this is a bit of a game-changer.'

'No hurry. This needs to be the right decision.'

He nodded again, but didn't say any more because there wasn't really anything to say. Not until he'd spoken to Liv, and he wouldn't do that until they could talk about this properly, in private.

Leo, Amy and baby Rocco left the hospital at three, just at the end of Liv's shift.

To her surprise Nick came to say goodbye, and Leo put the baby carrier down and hugged them both.

'Thank you so much. I'm so, so grateful. So's Amy.'

'Absolutely,' Amy chipped in. 'I can't believe I didn't need a section, I really didn't think it was going to happen. I'm so glad you let me try, and that you were both there. It made me feel so safe, and that made a massive difference, and so has not having had a section. I couldn't have done it without you, either of you.'

Tears welled in her eyes, and Liv hugged her gently and told Leo to take her home. 'Go on. Go and show the girls their little brother. I'm sure they'll be thrilled to bits.'

'I'm sure they will,' Leo said, his smile a little crooked. 'I know we are. Look, I don't know if you like eating out, if it's your thing, but if you want to come down for dinner to the restaurant any time, just phone up and we'll find you a table. It would be great to see you again.'

'That's very kind of you, Leo, thank you.'

'It's nothing,' Leo said. 'Remember, any time.'

'That would be lovely,' Liv said, reaching up and kissing Leo on the cheek. 'Thank you. Now take your wife home, please, and spoil her a little. She's done really well today.'

They watched them go, Leo with one arm round Amy

and the other carrying their precious cargo, and Liv felt
Nick's hand on her shoulder, giving it a quick squeeze.

'You did well today, too,' he murmured. 'Thank you
for coming in early.'

'You don't need to thank me, Nick. I did it for Amy.
I knew she'd feel better with people she knew around
her, especially under the circumstances. That's all the
thanks I need.'

'I'm still thanking you. What are you doing later?'

'I don't know. Are you going to tell me?' she asked,
looking up and catching a fleeting glimpse of worry in
his eyes. 'Nick? What is it?'

His hand dropped from her shoulder and he shook
his head. 'Nothing. Nothing to worry about, but there's
something we need to discuss and we can't do it here.
Yours or mine?'

'Come to the house. I need to put some laundry on
and I could do with washing my hair. I didn't have time
this morning. What time do you finish?'

He laughed. 'How long is a piece of string? Hopefully
by seven anyway. Judy's OK, so I'm starting to relax on
that front, and I haven't got any other mums I need to
worry about at the moment—well nothing urgent anyway. I'll give you a call if I get held up but you should
probably eat without me to be on the safe side.'

'OK. I'll see you later.'

It was much later.

He rang at six to say that Judy's blood pressure had
risen suddenly and the Doppler scan of her placenta
showed marked deterioration.

'You weren't worried earlier. Famous last words?'
Liv said, knowing what was coming next, and he gave
a tight laugh.

'You could say that. Anyway, I'm going to have to deliver the baby and I know I'm not supposed to be here tonight but I promised her I'd look after her and after we've got her this far I'm not going to let her down.'

'Of course you're not, you old softie. Get something to eat before you take her into Theatre, and I'll see you later, maybe.'

'OK, but don't hold your breath. I might have to take a raincheck.'

'OK. That's fine. Just let me know.'

She put the phone down, examined the contents of the fridge and decided to make a Thai chicken curry with cauliflower rice. She knew he liked it, she had all the ingredients and he could reheat it when he got there or she could freeze it.

It didn't take long, and after she'd eaten hers the evening seemed to stretch out endlessly. There was nothing she wanted to watch on the TV, she still hadn't washed her hair, and she really fancied a nice, long, lazy bath.

Probably with a glass of wine, but there wasn't any in the house, so she made a fruit tea and took it up with her, ran the bath, added bubbles and found her book before climbing in.

Luxury.

She wallowed until the bubbles had all gone, the water was tepid and her book was all but finished, then pulled out the plug, washed her hair in the shower and dried it.

Did she bother to dress, or should she just put on her towelling robe and slippers and assume he wasn't coming? Probably a safe assumption. She could lie on the bed and finish her book while she waited.

By the time she'd turned the last page there was still no word from him, and it was after ten. She might as well just go to sleep.

* * *

The house was in darkness, apart from a light in the hall.

Should he go in? He really needed to talk to her, but she wasn't at work tomorrow so he wouldn't see her then, and Ben's words were gnawing at him.

And she'd given him keys.

He let himself in, and swore as the alarm started its entry countdown. He flipped down the cover on the control panel and punched in his old code on autopilot, but it carried on beeping, the seconds ticking down. 'Dammit, of course, she's changed the code—'

The alarm gave up waiting and wailed into life, and he frantically keyed in the new number and sighed with relief as it went quiet. Not before the light went on in Bert and Gwen's house, though. Damn. That was all he needed.

'It's only me,' he called, as their front door opened.

'Is everything all right?'

'Yes, it's fine, Bert. No problem. Sorry to disturb you.'

He shut the door as Liv appeared at the top of the stairs, hastily belting her robe, her hair tousled. 'I'm sorry, I shouldn't have set it but you didn't ring. Was Bert cross?'

'No, worried I think. I expect he thought I'd broken in to give you another black eye.'

She laughed and shook her head. 'No, they know I was knocked down by a car. I told them.'

'Well, thank God for that, I thought he was about to call the police. And I'm sorry I didn't ring you. I thought I'd left it too late, but I just needed to talk to you, and then I saw the hall light on and I thought you might still be awake.'

'Oh, that's my fault as well, I must have forgotten to turn it off.' She ran lightly down the stairs and kissed his cheek. 'Have you eaten? I made a Thai curry for us and there's some left.'

'That sounds amazing. I grabbed a piece of toast from the ward kitchen but that was hours ago.'

'Come and eat, then, and you can tell me all about Judy.'

'She's fine, and the baby's fine,' he said, following her into the kitchen. 'Small, but pretty well. She's in SCBU but she's over thirty-four weeks so it's not too much of a worry. She'll just need a bit of support.'

'Well, that's good. I bet they're really happy.' Liv took a bowl out of the fridge and put it in the microwave and turned to him with a concerned smile.

'So what was it you wanted to talk to me about?'

He hesitated, then went for it. 'Simon's not coming back,' he said, studying her face for her reaction. 'Ben wants me to apply for the job, but there was a sort of caveat that I'm not going to do another runner.'

'And are you?'

He sighed heavily. 'I don't know, Liv. It all depends on you and the baby thing. If we jump through all the available hoops, have every test, go through every procedure and still fail, will you be to deal with it?' he asked softly.

'Yes—because we love each other, and we'll be all right.'

'Sweetheart, you don't know that. I've seen level-headed, reasonable people take each other apart over this, and it's not because they don't love each other. Look what happened to us before.'

She hitched up onto the stool beside him. 'But we weren't talking. We'd stopped communicating with each other—you didn't even tell me you'd had semen analysis, for goodness sake! We should have shared that right at the beginning, when you had the first test, talked about the result and what it meant.'

'But I didn't *know* what it meant. I didn't know if it was bad enough to make a difference, so I tried to improve it, I changed my lifestyle—'

'And it still didn't work, so instead of talking to me and sharing your fears you shut me out. How much of an improvement was that?'

He stabbed a hand through his hair.

'It wasn't. I know that. But I felt guilty—'

'That's ridiculous, it wasn't your fault—'

'It was my fault, or it could have been. You're right, I should have talked to you about it when I had the first test, never mind the second. But I didn't, because I couldn't, because it was falling apart all around us and we weren't talking about anything by that point.'

'Oh, Nick. Come here...'

Her arms slid round him, and he turned on the stool and took her in his arms, resting his cheek against her hair. It smelt of sunshine and apples and Liv, and he buried his face in it and breathed deeply. He wanted her so much. Needed her so much.

'I just feel—this is a real chance for us, Liv, but I can't muck Ben around, so I have to tell him yes and stick with it or give up on us and get another job somewhere else.'

'You can't do that!' she said, her voice a desperate whisper. 'You can't walk out on us now, Nick. Please? I love you. I need you. And you said you needed me.'

His arms tightened round her. 'I do, more than anything else.'

'So apply for it. From the way Ben's talking, it's yours for the asking, so ask. We know we can work together. If we find we can't live together, then we'll deal with it.'

'You make it sound so easy, but it's not. It's the job I

always wanted, the job I'd just secured when we split up. I'm lucky he's even giving me a second chance at it, and I'm so, so tempted, but—he wants me to be able to commit to something I just don't know the answer to and I don't want us to feel trapped. We felt trapped before and it nearly killed us.'

She pushed herself away so she could look up at him, and he met her eyes, open, honest, and so revealing.

'We won't feel trapped,' she promised him. 'Not this time, because this time we'll be going into it with our eyes open. Have you told him about us? About the baby thing?'

'No. That's why I went private for the semen analysis. You know what the grapevine's like.'

'Don't you think you should tell him?'

He swallowed hard. 'They're just about to have their third child. His fourth.'

'So? It's not a competition.'

'It feels like it sometimes—and you know that. It's why you wouldn't come to the conference. Anyway, it's none of his business and it's not relevant to whether or not I can do the job, so he can't legally use it as a reason for not offering it to me.'

He sighed and rammed a hand through his hair.

'The trouble is I just feel I don't have a choice. There aren't any other decent jobs out there and that's taken away any choice over whether or not I apply for this one because I need a job, one way or the other, or I can't pay the mortgage and you'll be homeless. We'll be homeless. I can't do that to you.'

'You can't do this just for money, Nick, and I won't let you! I could pay the mortgage—or rent something, if it came to that. If we want to be together and can accept the fact that we might never have children, and I think we both feel like that, then we should be together, either here or somewhere else. Anywhere, so long as we were happy, but you can't take this job just because you need to earn a living. It has to be because it's what you really, truly want, and only you can decide that.'

He reached out a hand and rested it lightly against her cheek, over the faint yellow stain left by the bruise. He frowned and traced the stain tenderly with his thumb.

'It is what I really, truly want,' he said softly. 'That, and you, as a package. But you first. Always you, front and centre.'

A frown pleated her brow and her eyes were troubled. 'Then what's the problem? Life doesn't come with guarantees, and Ben knows that, but you're talking as if you're expecting it to go wrong between us. It can't work with that attitude. We both have to be behind it one hundred percent, or it won't work. It can't work.'

'I am behind it,' he said. 'I was behind it before, and look what happened.'

Her hand caressed his face, her fingertips gentle against his cheek. 'Yes, look what happened. We didn't talk, we didn't say "I love you", we didn't take care of each other. We just let everything between us grind to a halt because I didn't get pregnant. And we won't do that this time. We *can't* do that this time, because that's not what it's about. It's about the fact that we love each other and want to be together, and we can't let that fail, so why don't we just kick this baby thing into the long grass and concentrate on *us*? Because I miss you, Nick, I miss you *so* much.'

His fingers stroked her cheek tenderly, sliding down to cup her chin as he shifted towards her and touched his mouth to hers in a gentle, lingering kiss.

'I miss you, too,' he murmured gruffly. 'And you're

right, we can't let it fail this time. We'll give it everything we've got, no holding back. But on one condition. This baby thing—I don't want to think about it or worry about it until we're feeling confident and settled and we know we're strong enough to face it. I'm almost one hundred percent sure that we'll need help in some form or another, and I don't want to start down that road until we're both sure we're ready. If we ever are.'

She nodded slowly. 'I'll buy that. It's a good idea.'

He kissed her again, the caress tender and sensuous, the passion reined in. But it was there in her, too; he could feel it simmering just below the surface, ready to explode at the slightest provocation, so he drew back.

She curled her fingers over his jaw and let her fingers explore the texture. He could feel his stubble catching on her skin, grazing softly against it, and her pupils darkened.

'You didn't shave today,' she murmured.

He felt her smile against his lips and drew away again. 'No, I didn't have time, and anyway, you said you liked it.'

'I do.' She smiled back and leant in again, kissing him once more, her fingers still curled softly against his jaw. 'Stay with me,' she murmured, and he felt his pulse hammer in his throat. Could she feel it? Probably.

He turned his face into her palm and kissed it, then got to his feet. 'Not tonight. Not when I'm exhausted. I need some sleep, Liv, and so do you. I'll see you tomorrow and we'll talk then.'

'Stay anyway,' she said suddenly. 'You can use the spare room if you don't want to share ours. You've already slept in there, it's not like I've got to find clean sheets for you. I might even bring you early morning tea.'

'No, Liv, I'm going to Sam's. I'll ring you in the morning.'

He cradled her head in his hands and kissed her lightly on the lips, then forced himself to let her go. 'Sleep well. I'm sorry I woke you.'

'You, too. And, Nick? Don't worry. It'll be all right.'

CHAPTER TEN

HE KISSED HER AGAIN, then let himself out, and she listened as he started the car and drove away.

Would they really be all right? She could only hope, because that was all she had left, but at least she *had* hope now. It was more than she'd had for ages, that and determination, and she was going to do everything in her power to make this work.

If he applied for the job and didn't get it for some reason then they'd go elsewhere, because one thing she was sure of, she wasn't losing Nick again, come what may. She'd live in a hut delivering babies in some third-world country so long as she was with him.

She went back into the kitchen to turn off the lights and realised he hadn't had the curry. Poor Nick. He'd be eating toast again, but it was too late now. She threw it out, set the alarm again and went up to bed.

Nick made himself some toast—again—and went to bed alone, racked with frustration and buoyed up by hope.

He'd been so tempted to stay with her, so tempted to scoop her up in his arms and carry her up to bed, but he wanted it to be better than that, better than some random fumble when he was reeling with exhaustion and running on empty.

No. If they were going to make a success of it, they needed a clean slate, and that meant taking it all back to first principles.

A first date to remember…?

He could take her to Zacharelli's. Leo wouldn't have had time to speak to them by tomorrow, but he might get lucky with a cancellation—or, failing that, there'd be somewhere else he could take her to and spoil her.

And then he'd bring her back here.

Sam and Kate were away for the weekend, they'd have the place to themselves—and neither of them was working on Saturday, either, so they could get up when they wanted, or stay in bed all day. No prying neighbours, and even more importantly, no ghosts from their tortured past. No echoes of sadness, no blighted memories, just the two of them alone together with a clean slate.

Less than twenty-four hours and she'd be here with him, in his arms.

The wait was going to kill him.

'Do you have any plans for tonight?'

She cradled the phone in one hand and carried on sorting washing with the other. 'No—I thought you were coming over?'

'I am. I'm taking you out for dinner. We've got a table at seven-thirty. Wear something pretty.'

Her heart jiggled happily in her chest. 'Are you taking me on a date, Mr Jarvis?'

'I am, Mrs Jarvis. I most certainly am.'

'How posh?'

'Oh, nice but not that posh. Smart casual?'

She smiled. Nick did smart casual like no other man she'd ever met. 'Perfect.'

Except it wasn't, of course, because she didn't have

anything in her wardrobe that fitted any more that could come under the heading of smart casual. She hadn't had any need for it until now—unless...

She opened her wardrobe and pulled out a subtle blue-grey dress that hadn't seen the light of day for over two years. It had a soft metallic sheen, the fabric almost fluid, and she'd given up wearing it because it hung on her after all the running, but Nick had always loved it because it exactly matched the colour of her eyes.

And, she remembered, he could take it off easily.

A secret little smile on her face, she stripped and pulled it on, and it fitted perfectly again now she was a sensible weight. And she had some ridiculously high heels that were covered in tiny sparkly bits—nothing casual about them, but Nick was a sucker for high heels and she hadn't been able to resist them.

But he'd said they were going for it, holding nothing back, so—underwear? She tugged open the drawer and found nothing that was other than practical and utilitarian. She'd hadn't bought sexy underwear for ages, but she was going to today, and when she'd done that she'd see if she could get a manicure and pedicure. Nick always found painted toenails a turn-on.

Fizzing with excitement, she hung the dress up, pulled on her jeans and a jumper, and went shopping.

She was wearing that dress.

His pulse shot up, and he had to take a deep breath and count to ten. Twenty when he clocked the shoes.

'How do I look?'

'If we didn't have a table booked, I'd slam the front door and carry you upstairs and to hell with everything,' he said tightly, 'but we do, so let's not talk about how you look, eh?'

She smiled the smile he hadn't seen since the day after her accident, and he leant in and kissed her cheek. Her signature perfume wafted over him, and he sucked in his breath and pulled away.

'You look beautiful, Liv. Come on, let's go.'

'Is it far? Only the shoes aren't very practical to walk in.'

He laughed softly and shook his head as he settled her coat on her shoulders. 'No. No, it's not far, but we're taking the car anyway.'

'So where are we going?' she asked as he pulled off the drive and headed towards the sea front.

'On a need to know basis...'

'Nick, tell me!'

'No. It's a surprise.'

'We're not—no, we can't be...'

She trailed to a halt as he pulled up beside the prom, backed into a space and cut the engine.

'Yes, we can. I rang this morning, and Leo has already spoken to his staff.'

'But—it takes months to get a table! It's got two Michelin stars, Nick, for heaven's sake! It'll cost a fortune.'

'I know, and guess what? It's worth every penny just to have you beside me again. This is our first date, Liv. The first mark on our clean slate. Ready to rewrite history?'

The smile lit up her face. 'Absolutely. What a perfectly wonderful idea.'

She reached for the door handle.

'Uh-uh. Wait for me.'

He got out, went round and opened the door, and she stepped out onto the prom and the sea breeze caught her dress and flirted with the hem. She pressed it down with her hand, and for the first time he noticed she was wearing her wedding and engagement rings.

He slid his fingers through hers, lifted her hand and pressed his lips to the rings, then freed his hand and offered her his arm. 'Just so you don't fall over and snap the heel off those shoes before I get to take them off you,' he murmured, and smiled as colour seeped into her cheeks.

'Nick!' she said under her breath, but there was a thread of laughter in her voice and she tucked her hand into his arm, the diamonds sparkling in the evening sun, and he laid his other hand over hers and walked her to the door.

To their astonishment it was opened by Leo, with the baby propped up against his shoulder held securely by his father's hand.

'What are you doing here?' Liv asked, sounding astonished.

'Amy wanted to show him off, so her mother's babysitting the girls for a bit, and we heard you were coming down so it seemed like perfect timing. We've only popped down for a few minutes. Come and join us for a drink, if you're not in a hurry to eat? We've just opened some excellent Prosecco.'

'No, we're not in a hurry but we don't want to intrude—'

'Don't be ridiculous. Come on, Amy wants to see you.'

Leo handed round the glasses, and they all toasted the baby who seemed perfectly content snuggled down in his father's arms. Leo looked pretty happy, too, and so did Amy, but it wasn't long before the party broke up because little Rocco was beginning to stir and Amy wanted to take him home and feed and change him.

'You know what it's like when they're tiny and your milk's just come in and everything hurts—I just don't want to do that in public yet!' she murmured.

'I can understand that,' Liv said with a smile, and kissed Amy goodbye, trying desperately hard not to be jealous. 'Don't forget, any problems, any questions, either ask your community midwife or give me a ring—I don't mind, any time. Here—my number.' She jotted it on an old envelope in her bag and handed it over. 'Now go and enjoy him.'

'We will. And thanks again.'

'Yes, thank you, both of you,' Leo added. 'I hope you enjoy your meal.'

The maître d' appeared at their sides with a welcoming smile and showed them to their table, and after they were settled Liv looked up and met Nick's eyes.

'I can't believe we're here.'

'No, nor can I. We tried before once—do you remember? It was impossible.'

'I don't remember that. I thought this was our first date?'

His brows tweaked together, followed by a slow, lazy smile as he propped his elbows on the table and leant towards her. 'So it is.' He reached out and took her hand, his thumb stroking softly over the back of it. 'Did I tell you how beautiful you look tonight?'

She felt herself colour. 'You may have done, but I don't mind hearing it again. You don't look so shabby yourself, either, and I see you've shaved.'

'Well, you see, my mother told me that it was bad form for a chap to give a girl a rash on her lip from too much kissing—'

'Did she really?'

His sexy chuckle rippled over her and made her body quiver. 'No, of course not, but we should probably test the theory.'

'Sounds good.'

'I thought it sounded like a thoroughly *bad* idea,' he said softly, and she felt her pulse pick up a notch.

'Excuse me, are you ready to order or would you like a few more minutes?'

'Um—I think that would be a good idea,' Nick said, straightening up, and she had to bite her lip. 'Stop it and read the menu before we get chucked out,' he muttered, trying not to laugh, and she looked down and felt her eyes widen.

'Oh, my life, everything sounds amazing!'

'Doesn't it just? How many courses do you want?'

'Oh, two, max. I can't eat any more than that.'

'Main and dessert? I know you women like a pud.'

'Sounds lovely, and I wouldn't like to appear greedy on our first date,' she said, her lips twitching, but he didn't smile back.

'You can have anything you want tonight,' he said, 'anything at all,' but his eyes said far more than those apparently simple words, and it took her breath away.

'That was the most amazing meal of my life.'

'Mine, too. I can't believe they wouldn't let us pay. Do you fancy a stroll?'

Liv looked down ruefully. 'I do, I'd love to, but they're not really strolling shoes.'

'No, they're not, are they? Maybe on our next date.'

She tilted her head and smiled. 'You want to see more of me?' she asked mischievously, and his mouth twitched.

'Definitely. A lot more.'

'Mmm. I want to see more of you, too.'

The light from the streetlamps caught the beating pulse in the base of his throat, and his voice was low and promising. 'I'm sure that can be arranged. Shall we go?'

She tucked her hand into the crook of his elbow, and he led her to the car, opened the door for her and went

round to his side, starting the car in a silence screaming with tension.

Two minutes later they'd pulled up outside the cabin.

'There are no lights on in the house.'

'They're away,' he said, and she thought of the sig-
nificance of that—the utter solitude, the privacy, no one
to see or care what they did so they could be free to be
themselves—and a shiver of need ran over her.

The cabin was softly illuminated by a bedside light,
drawing her eyes to the bed. The curtains were closed,
the bedding crisp and smooth, but not for long. Her pulse
picked up and she turned towards him wordlessly.

His hands settled gently on her shoulders and he stared
down into her eyes, his own intent and focused solely
on her.

'I want you, Liv,' he said, his voice quiet but sure. 'I've
never wanted anyone as much as I want you now, but if
you're not ready for this, if you don't want it, then tell me.'

She met those serious, steady eyes, his gaze unwav-
ering, and knew she'd never wanted him or needed him
more. 'I want it. I want you, Nick. I always have, right
from the first moment I saw you, and I don't think I can
wait any longer. Make love to me—please?'

His eyes closed briefly, and when he opened them
again, passion burned bright in their depths. 'My pleasure,' he said, his voice little more than a breath that whispered over her skin, and taking her hand, he led her over
to the bed and slowly, inch by inch, he drew the dress up
over her legs, her body, her upstretched arms.

It fell to the floor in a shimmering puddle, and he
stood back and looked at her, those hot eyes raking over
her body and leaving a trail of invisible fire in their wake.

A fingertip followed, tracing the top edge of her bra,
following a strap down from her shoulder, over the swell

of her breast, dipping down into the hollow of her cleavage. It swept under the lace, trailing back up, his hand sliding in and following it until her breast was swallowed by his warm, clever hand.

His thumb flicked her nipple oh, so gently, and she gasped. So he did it again. And again, and all the time his eyes were locked with hers.

'Nick,' she breathed, her voice choppy, not knowing what she was asking, but he knew, and he bent his head, his eyes finally releasing hers as his hand pushed the lace out of the way and his mouth found her breast.

His tongue flicked over her nipple, then circled it before drawing it into his mouth, and her hands gripped his shoulders, her breath sobbing now, the ache in her body so intense she could barely stand.

'Nick…'

He lifted his head, tugged back the covers and pushed her gently back until her legs met the bed. She sat down abruptly and he tipped her back, ran his fingertips around the top of her new and barely there lace shorts and peeled them slowly, inch by inch, down her legs.

He reached her feet, eased them over the shoes and then picked up one foot and ran his tongue over the inside of her ankle, up over her calf, behind her knee, then up, along her inner thigh.

She knew what he was going to do, knew just how good he was, how exquisite it would be, and she felt her body liquefy for him.

At the first touch of his tongue she dug her fingers into the bedding, biting her lips to stifle the scream, but she couldn't silence it and she could hear as well as feel his breath as it sawed in and out of his chest.

'Don't hold it in, Liv,' he said, his voice rough with

need. 'There's no one to hear you except me, and I want to know exactly what I'm doing to you.'

'Nick, please...'

She felt the tug as he suckled, the flick of his tongue with its unerring accuracy, and she sobbed his name helplessly as her body peaked and everything shattered all around her like shards of light.

Then he was there, holding her in his arms, raining kisses on her face, his chest heaving against her.

'I need you,' he growled softly.

Her hands ran over him, finding silk and cotton where there should have been skin, and she plucked at his shirt. 'You've got too much on,' she wailed.

'So undress me,' he said, pulling her to her feet, but the buttons were too much for her so he hauled the shirt over his head himself. It landed on the floor near her dress, followed by her bra, their shoes, his trousers and socks and last, his jersey boxers. Her hand closed over his straining erection and a groan shuddered against her hair.

'Liv, no,' he begged, and she moved her hands to his shoulders, stepping back and meeting those fierce, white-hot eyes.

'I need you,' she said, her fingers curling into his shoulders. 'Please, Nick, I need you inside me—'

And at last—at last—he was there, thrusting deeply into her, taking her so close and yet not quite...

'Easy, Liv, easy. I won't last—'

'I don't want you to last. I want you to come with me this time, please, please...'

He drove into her then, every move of his body designed to wind her higher until she felt the starburst start again, spreading out and blinding her to everything but Nick.

He caught her scream in his mouth, his body stiffening as a ragged groan tore through him, and then as the contractions in her body died away he dropped his head against her shoulder, his cheek resting against hers as their breathing slowed and their heart rates came slowly back to normal.

Then he rolled to the side, taking her with him, their bodies still joined, and she opened her eyes and he was just there.

His lashes had clumped together, and she lifted a hand and brushed a tear from his cheek.

'Are you OK?' she asked softly, and he smiled, but it was a pretty sketchy smile and he couldn't stop the tears that leaked from his eyes and dribbled down onto her shoulder.

'I've missed you so, so much,' he said raggedly, and then she lost sight of him because her own tears flooded her vision, but she knew just where he was, and so she kissed him, and held him, and told him over and over that she loved him, until at last he fell asleep in her arms.

He woke in the night and made love to her again, but this time it was slow and lazy and tender, and they didn't wake again until the light filtering through a gap in the curtains cut a bright swathe across their pillows and dragged them out of sleep.

He propped himself up on one elbow and stared down into her eyes.

'Good morning.'

She smiled, a slow, contented smile that lit her eyes from within, and reached up a hand to touch his face. 'I couldn't agree more. It's a very good morning.'

'Mmm. I'm hoping it's going to get even better.' He lowered his head and kissed her gently, then swung his legs over the side of the bed and stood up, stretching hugely.

'Tea?' he asked, and she nodded.

'Lovely. Shall I just lie here while you wait on me?'

'You can. I was going to put the kettle on and then shower.'

'How big's your shower cubicle?' she asked, and he laughed and headed towards the bathroom.

'Not big enough for what you've got in mind.'

'You don't know what I've got in mind.'

'I'm sure I can have a fair stab at it. Just stay there a minute. I won't be long.'

He had the fastest shower on record, shaved—because he intended to kiss her a lot, lot more—then cleaned his teeth and left the bathroom to find her standing by the kettle humming softly to herself.

He walked up behind her, slid his arms around her and cupped her breasts with his hands.

'You're all damp,' she said.

'Because I was in a hurry. The bathroom's all yours. Don't be long.'

Long?

She didn't wash her hair, because she wasn't convinced the cabin had a hair dryer and anyway, she had much, much better things to do with the time, but she showered, borrowed his toothbrush and cleaned her teeth and went back out to find him propped up in the bed with two steaming mugs on the bedside table.

'What kept you?' he asked with a lazy smile, and she crawled across the bed to him and kissed the smile off his face.

'So what now?'

It was much, much later. The tea had grown stone cold,

and they'd showered again and put their clothes on, but although she might get away with the dress if they were to go out, the shoes were a bit of a giveaway.

'Well, if we're going to do anything other than lie in bed all day I probably need to go home and get a change of clothes. Shoes anyway.'

'We could go for a walk along the river wall.'

'We could. We used to love doing that.'

'We did. Right, let's go then, and see if you can get inside before Bert clocks you and asks what you were doing last night.'

She laughed at that. It was so unlikely she didn't even waste time worrying about it, but when they got to the house there was an ambulance outside Bert and Gwen's.

'What the hell's going on?' Nick said, and got out of the car. 'Liv, go and change and come back out. I'm going to see if they need help.'

He ran round the end of the hedge and in through their front door, and she let herself in, tugged on yesterday's jeans and jumper with a pair of flat pumps and went straight round to Bert and Gwen's.

She could hear them upstairs, and she ran up, calling Nick's name.

'In the front bedroom,' Nick called, and she went in and found Bert on the floor with a paramedic holding his head steady while Nick massaged his carotid sinus.

'He's in SVT,' he said over his shoulder. 'Can you look after Gwen and follow us to the hospital? I'm going in the ambulance with them but I'm just trying to get this to work first.' She went over to Gwen who was standing to one side, her hands pressed to her mouth, and gave her a hug.

'It's OK, Gwen. He's in good hands.'

'Is he going to die?' she asked, and Liv could feel her trembling violently.

'I don't think so. Let's see if Nick can get this to work.'

'What's wrong with him?'

'His heart's started beating very fast. What Nick's doing is stimulating the nerve beside his carotid artery, which sometimes gets the rhythm back to normal. It's not hurting him, and it often works.'

Just then Bert groaned, and Nick stopped and laid his fingers over the artery and nodded.

'That's got it. Hi, Bert, it's Nick,' he said calmly, taking the old man's hand. 'How are you feeling?'

'Tired. Chest feels really tight. Need my spray.'

'He's got angina,' Gwen said, and she handed a GTN spray to Nick and then started to cry. 'I thought he was dead,' she whispered brokenly, turning her face into Liv's shoulder for a moment until she'd recovered her composure.

Liv found a box of tissues on the bedside table and handed one to her. 'Here. Mop yourself up and give him a hug,' she said softly. 'He's looking a better colour now. I expect they'll take him to hospital soon and sort him out.'

Gwen crumpled the tissue into a ball and crouched awkwardly down beside her husband, clutching his hand as Nick got to his feet and came over to Liv.

'Well done, you,' she said with a smile, and he pulled a face.

'Thanks. I thought it was worth a shot.'

'Definitely. Hadn't they tried?'

He shook his head. 'They'd only just got here. Once I said I was a doctor they just stood back and let me get on with it.'

'I'm so glad we came back.'

'Me, too. Are you all right to drive?'

'Yes, I'm fine. My head's perfectly all right now, I just haven't bothered. I'll shut up the house with Gwen and follow you there.'

By the time they left the hospital it was almost one.

'Lunch?' Nick suggested, and she nodded.

'How about the pub on the river? We could go for a walk along the river wall afterwards.'

'Good idea. I'm starving.'

They went back to the house to swap cars and for her to change her pumps for trainers, and they ate lunch outside on the terrace overlooking the river, basking in the glorious spring sunshine and watching the boats swing lazily on their moorings.

'I could watch the river for ever.'

'Me, too. Shall we stroll?'

'Mmm. It might work off some of those gorgeous chips.'

'Don't work too many off. I rather like your new curves. It's like having the old you back again.'

'Well, ditto. You'd let yourself get flabby.'

'Flabby?' he said, sounding disgusted, and she laughed.

'Well, not flabby, that's going a bit far, but certainly not as toned and luscious as you are now.'

'Hmm. I like luscious better than flabby.'

'Me, too. I might have to check out your lusciousness again later.'

'Only if I can check out your curves.'

She gave him a cheeky grin. 'Be my guest. But maybe not here or now.'

CHAPTER ELEVEN

'SO WHERE ARE we spending the night?' he asked later when they were back at the house. 'Here, after we eat, or in the cabin?'

'I rather like the cabin,' she said, but then she frowned as they heard a car drive up, pause for a moment and then drive away after the door slammed, and she went to the window and saw Gwen letting herself in next door.

'Gwen's back. Should we offer her supper?'

Nick gave a wry smile. 'That would be nice—and if she's back, we really ought to be here. I don't like the thought of her on her own.'

Liv tipped her head on one side and stared at him. 'They drive you mad!'

He laughed ruefully and pulled her into his arms. 'I know, but they're harmless and he looked such a poor old boy, I just—they've been married for ever, Liv. What must it feel like to know you're getting near the end and one or other of you is going to go first? They'd be lost without each other.'

'I was lost without you,' she said, tipping her head back and meeting his eyes. 'So lost.'

'Me, too, but I'm back now, Liv, and I'm staying.'

'Good. And I know it won't necessarily be easy, but we can make this work, Nick.'

'Yeah. You're right. And if it gets tough, we'll just have to bite the bullet.'

'Wasn't that what people in the trenches used to do before their legs were amputated without anaesthetic?'

He laughed and drew her into his arms. 'I'm hoping it won't go that badly wrong,' he said, and then his mouth found hers and feathered a gentle kiss on her lips.

She looked up at him. 'So are you going to apply for the job?'

'Yes. Definitely. And I'll move back in here.'

'Sure?'

He kissed her again. 'Yes, I'm sure.'

'Even with Bert and Gwen watching our every move?'

'Even so.'

She felt the smile bloom in her heart and spread to her face. 'Good. Let's go and talk to Gwen and find out how he is.'

He moved back in the following day, while she was at work on a late shift, and when she got home that evening the light was on in his study.

It hadn't been on to welcome her home for so long, and her heart was filled with the sort of deep happiness and contentment that she'd only ever felt in their first years together.

There was only one thing missing, and she was used to that by now and it didn't dent her happiness.

He must have heard her car because he opened the front door, shut it behind her and pulled her into his arms.

'Welcome home, Mrs Jarvis,' he murmured, and it had never sounded so good.

He'd been working on his CV, he told her, and the next day he applied for the job, went through the formal interview process a fortnight later and found her in the ward office afterwards.

He pushed the door shut and let out a long, slow breath.

'God, that was tough. Ben really grilled me.'

'That was mean.'

'No, it was fair. They had a couple of very good candidates and the hospital seems to be able to attract them. This department's got a great reputation. I just hope I've done enough.'

She got up from the desk and hugged him. 'Of course you have. And if not, we'll go elsewhere. I don't care where I am so long as I'm with you.'

'What about our friends?'

She shrugged. 'We can make new friends. There's only one friend I'm really bothered about and that's you. Come on, let's go and get lunch, I'm starving. I've been waiting for you because we've got a lull, which means all hell's going to break loose later, so let's make the most of it.'

'There's a second interview round,' he told her the next day as he checked his phone over breakfast.

'Really?' Liv felt her stomach tighten, and she pushed away her cereal. 'Did you know that was on the cards?'

He shrugged and put his phone away. 'It was always a possibility. Oh, Liv, I hate this uncertainty.'

'It's only a job. There'll be others—and anyway, I'm still sure you'll get it,' she lied, her stomach in knots. 'I need to go, I'm due at work in a minute.'

'You haven't finished your breakfast.'

'No, I know. I'm not hungry yet, it's too early.' And she was way too stressed to worry about food. 'I'll see you later.'

The second interview was in three days, he told her later, and by the time it arrived they were both living on their nerves. The only thing that made it all go away was the time they spent together at night, when the lights were off and everything was quiet and she was in his arms.

Sometimes they talked, sometimes they made love, sometimes they just held each other, and in those times everything that was wrong seemed to right itself.

He got through the second interview, but that night he told her it was worse than the first and he was beginning to doubt Ben's friendship.

'Of course he's still a friend. He just has to be your boss, too—he's the clinical lead and he's way too ethical to do anything other than give everyone the same treatment. You can be sure he was every bit as mean to them.'

'He wasn't mean, he just asked some really tricky questions—what would you do in this or that circumstance, that kind of thing. Really tricky cases where there's no definitive answer, and your brain just goes to mush.'

'I'm sure yours didn't,' she told him comfortingly, but the tension was getting to her and she wasn't sure she could stand the wait much longer. 'When will they let you know?'

'Ben said a couple of days, perhaps? I got the feeling the board were divided.'

She was off the next day, and because Nick was at work and she had to do something to keep herself sane, she went into her little study upstairs—the nursery that had never been needed—and settled herself down at the desk to read up on hypnosis as a form of pain relief in labour, but she couldn't concentrate.

Stress? Or an after-effect of her concussion? She didn't know, but it wasn't working, so she went downstairs, put the kettle on and reached for the instant coffee, then pulled a face.

She just didn't fancy coffee. Or tea, come to that. Or

food. No, that wasn't true. There were some things she couldn't get enough of, like chocolate. And pasta. She could eat mountains of pasta and pesto. Maybe she was just hungry.

Or maybe she just needed to know what on earth was happening in their lives, and where their future lay?

She went for a walk, popped into the little local supermarket for some more bread and pasta and heading for the till she felt the blood drain from her head, and reached out and grabbed a nearby shelf. She'd walked down the aisle with personal products—feminine hygiene, condoms, pregnancy tests...

Pregnancy tests?

They were right there, in front of her. She'd bought countless numbers of them in that dreadful time, but she'd always done the test before her period was due, and if she'd only waited she would have had her answer for nothing.

But she'd lost track, between Nick coming back and her accident and the job thing. She'd had one period, but that had been weeks ago.

More than four?

Her fingers shaking, she reached for a packet, put it in her basket next to the bread and pasta and went to the till.

'Liv?'

She must be out, he thought, and ran upstairs to change—and stopped dead.

Lying on the bed was the open packet of a pregnancy test.

His mouth dried and he felt sick. God, no. Not back to this again.

He changed into jeans and a thin T-shirt and sat down

on the edge of the bed, staring at the open packet as if it was a bomb.

Why? They'd agreed on the rules—no trying, no thinking about it, no worrying, just accept that it wasn't going to happen for them without help and not until they were ready, but—no. She couldn't do that, and suddenly he wondered if she really loved him, really wanted him, or if it had just been a way of getting him back so she could use him as a stud, a sperm donor.

Jeez. He pressed his hand to his mouth, holding in the hurt, the rage, the overwhelming disappointment. The betrayal. And then he heard her call him.

He didn't want to answer. He'd promised they'd talk, promised they wouldn't let this destroy them again. Kick it into the long grass, she'd said, but there it was again, just when he'd burned his boats and taken the job, and he didn't know what to say to her because he didn't know if it was all a lie.

His heart in his mouth, he stood up and walked out of the bedroom.

'Where are you?' he asked, and followed the sound of her voice to the little room they'd never quite dared to call the nursery.

She was sitting at her desk, the test wand in her hand, and as he went in she turned her head and looked up at him and her face was streaked with tears.

'Why now?' he asked quietly. 'Just when everything was looking promising—why now, Liv? I thought we weren't going to do this?' he said, trying to keep a lid on his hurt, his anger. 'Dammit, you promised me we wouldn't do this!'

Her face froze, and she dropped the wand and stared at him. 'Nick—'

'No. I can't cope with it any more. I told you that, I warned you—'

He turned on his heel and walked out, and he was half-way down the stairs when something hit him on the head.

'What's *wrong* with you?' she sobbed. 'You can't cope with it when I'm not pregnant, and now, for God's sake, you can't cope with it when I *am*! What kind of a person *are* you?'

He slowed to a halt and turned and looked up at her. His heart was climbing out of his chest, his mouth was dry, and...

'I don't understand,' he said numbly. 'You can't be. I warned you my semen analysis was rubbish, we knew this wasn't going to happen—'

'No—no, Nick, you're wrong,' she said, shaking her head. 'Look at it! Look at the wand!'

He glanced down and saw it lying on the hall floor. His hand trembling, he bent and picked it up, and read the word in the little window.

Pregnant

He stared at it blindly, until the word blurred in front of his eyes. 'I don't understand.'

She came slowly down the stairs and sat just above him on the second step. 'I'm pregnant—we're having a baby, Nick. We're having a baby—'

Her voice cracked, and he looked up from the wand and met her eyes. 'How?'

She laughed then, the sound music to his ears. 'If you don't know that by now, Nick, you're *really* in the wrong job.'

He sat down next to her, his heart still pounding, and put his arm round her. 'But—why now and not then?'

She shrugged.

'Think about it. I was too thin, your diet was appalling, you were possibly drinking too much, having tons of coffee, not exercising, I was running every chance I had, we only made love when the techie runes told us to—and now we're healthy, we're relaxed, and we're making love every chance we have. It's not rocket science.'

She was pregnant. He felt the smile first, and then his eyes prickled and her face blurred, so he shut them and pulled her into his arms and held her, pressing his cheek against her hair.

'I thought you'd lied to me. I thought you didn't love me, you just wanted me back so you could keep on trying. I never dreamt...' He broke off to kiss her, then cupped her face in his hands and stared down into her eyes. 'I love you,' he said raggedly. 'I love you so, so much, and I can't believe it's finally happened for us.'

Her hand came up and stroked his cheek, wiping away the tears. 'Nor can I. Now if we could only hear about the job—'

'I have.'

Her mouth opened and she looked up at him, her eyes hopeful and fearful at the same time. 'And?'

'I got it. I got the job,' he told her, and she put her hand over her mouth and let out a sobbing laugh.

'Really? You got it? We can stay here in Yoxburgh, in this house, near all our friends, take our baby to the park...?'

'Yes. We can stay here. We sort of have to. I promised Ben we would.'

'Oh, Nick, that's amazing!' She flung her arms around him and hugged him so hard his ribs crunched.

'Ouch.' He laughed, and eased her away. 'I'm glad you're pleased. We can celebrate that later. Right now

I'm busy dealing with the fact that we're going to have a baby.'

Her eyes were soft, almost luminous, and her smile lit him up from the inside out.

'I know. I might have to share your study.'

'You might—if you have time for that when you're a mum. I still can't quite believe it's real.'

'I can't believe you've got the job, either. It's like we've reset the clock on our lives and gone back to where it all went wrong and put it right, and this is our reward.'

'Oh, Liv.' He hugged her again, then scrubbed his hands over his face and sniffed hard. 'I'm a mess.'

'You're a lovely mess. I was a very unlovely mess earlier, because I'd managed to convince myself that you hadn't got the job, and there we were pregnant and with nowhere to go and no visible means of support. It wasn't a good moment.'

'I'll bet. Poor you. How are you feeling now?'

'All right. I'm fine so long as I eat chocolate in industrial quantities,' she said, and he laughed again and hugged her.

'I'll add it to my regular internet shop,' he said drily, and then got to his feet and pulled her up. 'Come on, let's go and tell Bert and Gwen. Their grandchildren live hundreds of miles away, and I reckon they'll love having a baby next door.'

'Can you bear it?'

'What, them? They're fine, Liv.'

'Bert thinks you saved his life.'

'Well, he might be right. We'll let him think it. If he feels he came that close, he might let me take over the hedge cutting.'

She started to laugh, and once she'd started she

couldn't stop, so he turned her into his arms and they leant on each other and laughed until their sides ached.

'Better now?' he asked eventually, and she nodded.

'Never better than this. The job, the baby, you back in my life for keeps—what more could a woman want?'

'Diamonds?'

'No. Cold, hard—and they don't hug you. I wouldn't swap your hugs for anything. Come on.'

She took his hand and stood up, only instead of heading out of the door towards Bert and Gwen, she turned towards the stairs.

'Where are we going?' he asked, and she just smiled.

'Up here. We've got a nursery to plan...'

EPILOGUE

NICK CLOSED THE door behind the midwife and went back into the family room, where Liv was curled up on the sofa in her towelling robe with the baby asleep in her arms.

'Cup of tea?' he asked, but she shook her head.

'I'm going to drown if I drink any more tea. Come and sit here and admire your daughter.'

She shifted her feet out of the way, then plonked them back on his lap as he sat down.

'Happy?' she asked him, and he gave a tired laugh.

'Yes, my darling, I'm very happy. A teeny bit stressed, but I might have known you'd want to be different.'

'I didn't plan a home birth. She was just in a hurry.'

'And I was in a clinic. I only got here by the skin of my teeth. I'm an obstetrician, for goodness sake, and I didn't even realise you were going into labour.'

'I'm a midwife. It's all I deal with, and I didn't recognise the signs. We're both rubbish.'

'No, we're not. We're amazing. Look at her. How could two rubbish people create anything as amazing as that?'

'Want a cuddle?'

He reached over and took the baby from her, staring down into her dainty, screwed up little face with its tiny button nose and rosebud lips. 'She's so perfect—such a miracle.' He looked up and met Liv's eyes and tried to smile, but it was too hard so he gave up.

'Have I told you lately how much I love you?'

'Only a million or so times.' She sat up with a little wince and put her arms around him and kissed him. 'But don't stop. I'll never get tired of hearing it.'

'I love you,' he said softly, and then propped his feet up on the coffee table, right over the tiny mark that he'd wiped clean, and rested his head back against the sofa and smiled at her.

Life had never felt so good...

* * * * *

FROM MIDWIFE
TO MUMMY

DEANNE ANDERS

This book is dedicated to my parents, Rev and Mrs J. A. Atkison, who loved and supported me and made sure I always knew I belonged.

And to Lucretia Lee, R. N. The best Labour and Delivery nurse I ever had the privilege to work with. I can never thank you enough for the gift of your mentorship.

And to Theresa Lee. While you might not be my sister by blood or adoption, you will always be my sister of my heart.

CHAPTER ONE

DIM LIGHTS AND the sound of soft waves crashing against the shore had created an atmosphere of a calm retreat, but midwife Lana Sanders knew that her patient had long passed the point of caring.

"You're doing great," Lana said as she coached Kim through another contraction and watched the fetal monitor. She watched the fetal heart-rate accelerate, then come down to its baseline. So far this had been a perfect labor.

"You're going to be late," Jeannie whispered to Lana as she arranged the delivery table.

"It won't be long now," Lana said, as much to reassure the labor and delivery nurse as well as her patient.

"Push. *Now.*" Kim ground out.

"Wait, I've got to get the camera!" Kim's husband Tom called out as he turned his back and started going through a duffle bag laid upon the bedside table.

"Wait?" said Kim. Her voice rose an octave and took on that gravelly sound that only a woman in transition, or one possessed, could reach. "What have you been doing all this time?"

"It's okay, Tom, we have a couple minutes," Lana said.

A deep growl escaped from Kim.

"Okay, maybe we don't," Lana said as she watched a circle of dark wet curls crown.

She positioned the delivery table so that it would be within easy reach, then undraped it, letting the protective covering fall to the floor.

"Kim, we've done this before, right?" Lana waited till she had Kim's attention. "The baby's starting to crown so whenever you're ready go ahead and push."

"Now!" said Kim, then took a fast breath.

Tom rushed to his wife's side and helped her get into position as she curled her body and pushed down. Lana watched as the couple worked together for their child. Kim's face was flushed and glowing with color as she concentrated on nothing but this moment—the moment she would bring a new life into the world. It was both beautiful and heart-wrenching for Lana to watch this miracle.

"Take another breath," Lana said. "Is the contraction gone?"

"No," Kim said, before she took a deep breath then returned to pushing.

"Okay, Kim, I need you to listen to me," Lana said.

She waited as Kim looked up at her.

"Next push we're going to have a baby, okay?" Lana watched as both excitement and fear filled her patient's tired eyes. "You can do this. I promise."

Kim nodded her head and grabbed Tom's hand as she positioned herself again, then pushed.

Seconds later a screaming, squirming baby boy was delivered. Lana carefully suctioned the baby's mouth, then handed Kim her new baby and watched as the experienced mom caught him close against her body, putting him skin to skin to keep him warm while Jeannie dried him off with some fluffy towels. She clamped then cut the umbilical cord that had been the baby's lifeline. Seeing both mom and baby meeting for the first time, she was amazed, as always, by the miracle of life that she was blessed to witness.

"You did wonderfully," Lana told Kim.

Lana delivered the placenta, then made sure her patient's bleeding was controlled. A quick glance at the clock above the bed had her suddenly feeling a sense of panic. She had to get out of the hospital in the next twenty minutes or she was never going to make it to court on time.

She gave the new mom a hug, then posed for a picture with the rest of the Callahan family once they were allowed in the room. She headed to the nurses' lounge for a quick change of clothes, then headed out of the hospital. This was going to be one of the most important days of her life. Today she would officially become a new mom herself—something that until a year and a half ago she had thought would never happen.

There was no way she was going to be late.

Lana white-knuckled her way through the nightmare of Miami traffic. The multiple lanes all seemed to be going nowhere, and Lana was short on both time and patience. For the first time she was scared she really was going to miss her appointment with the judge who would be finalizing Maggie's adoption.

The thought of her sweet, adorable little toddler had her taking a deep breath and relaxing. It would be okay. She was cutting it close, but she would make it. After over twelve months of social workers' visits and court appearances, there was no way fate would fail her now.

It had been fate that had brought the little girl into her life, after Lana had just happened to take on her young mother as a patient. When Chloe had later decided she couldn't handle the responsibility of a new baby and showed up on her doorstep, handing Lana the child along with a notarized letter saying she wanted Lana to adopt her, it had been nothing short of a miracle.

A lane opened up to her right and she swung into it and followed it to the next exit. Fifteen minutes later she made it to the judge's chamber where her appearance was scheduled to be. She was surprised to see that neither her lawyer nor her babysitter and Maggie were outside the room, waiting for her. She had texted both of them to let them know she was going to cut it close.

A note on the door explained that there had been a change in where the session would be held. Lana rushed down the hall to the courtroom. As she reached for the handle of the door a large hand reached around her.

"Let me," said a male voice in a slow drawl that almost curled her toes.

Lana turned and followed the outstretched arm up to the man behind it. The sight of coal-black hair curling around an angular face with a pair of deep blue eyes was startling. Forgetting that she was blocking the door, she let her gaze continue down the tailored black suit to the pointed toes of black leather cowboy boots peeking from beneath his pants leg.

A cowboy in Miami?

The thought had Lana smiling as she looked up at the handsome man and with a quick "Thank you" continued into the courtroom.

A frantic Amanda waved at her from the front of the courtroom, where she and Lana's lawyer Nathan had taken their seats. As soon as Maggie got a look at Lana the toddler started protesting. She wanted to get down and see her "mama" right then.

Amanda had dressed her in the new pink sundress Lana had recently bought, and with her dark curls and big deep blue eyes she looked like a china doll come to life. Lana reached over and took her little girl. She gave her a big tight hug that had Maggie giggling and squirming in her lap.

"Why the change to the courtroom?" she asked Nathan as she scooted into the seat next to him.

"Shh…" Nathan whispered back as he studied some of the papers in his hand.

Amanda looked at the two of them, then shrugged her shoulders, letting Lana know that she didn't have a clue about what was going on.

Nathan was always a little uptight-looking, which Lana put down to his job in family law. She knew that sometimes his cases were very stressful, with emotions riding high, but there was something about the way he was studying the papers in his hands that told her something was wrong.

Suddenly her heart kicked into panic mode. It was the same feeling she had when she woke up in the middle of her repeated nightmare about Chloe showing up at her door and telling her that she had changed her mind. That she didn't think Lana would be a good enough mother for Maggie and she was taking her away. Taking the little girl Lana had fostered since she was six weeks old. Taking her far away to somewhere Lana would never see her again.

It was the same nightmare she'd had for months now, but after today it would surely go away. Once the adoption was final Lana would be Maggie's mother, just as if she had given birth to her. There would be no way anyone would be able to take her away then.

As Judge Hamilton entered the courtroom everyone rose, then sat when the bailiff indicated. Taking a second to look around the courtroom, Lana noted that the social worker, Ms. Nelson from the Florida Department of Children and Families, who had been handling her case, was seated on the right at the front of the courtroom. She watched as the older woman handed the bailiff some papers that were then given to the judge.

Apprehension sent a shiver down her back. Lana looked

at her lawyer again, to see his attention glued to the judge, who was now reading over the documents the social worker had presented to him.

"This is the hearing for the final placement of the child known here as Maggie. I know that Maggie has been fostered with Ms. Sanders since…" Judge Hamilton paused as he read the documents in front of him "…since she was six weeks old, and that the child's biological mother personally requested that Ms. Sanders be allowed to adopt her daughter."

The judge looked up and gave Lana a smile. Lana felt the tension ease and relaxed back into her seat. Judge Hamilton had always been encouraging in her quest to adopt Maggie. She knew her case was in good hands as long as he was on the bench.

"Ms. Sanders has been forthcoming in all the demands the court has placed on her, and she has met every requirement that the Department of Children and Families demands."

Judge Hamilton once more picked up the documents. This was it—finally he would say the words she had been waiting for and Maggie would be all hers.

"To be clear, this was to have been the last hearing and the adoption was to have become final today."

Was to have become final? Were they going to make her jump through another hoop today?

"Ms. Nelson, you have indicated in your request to postpone the adoption that you have some new information that needs to be considered. Is that correct?"

Lana watched the social worker as she rose and walked to the front of the court room. Glancing at her lawyer for some sign as to what was happening, she noted that there was no look of surprise in his eyes as he watched the judge and the social worker quietly discussing the new documents she had handed him. When Nathan turned and took Lana's hands his look of concern pierced her heart.

Only something truly wrong would cause that kind of reaction in Nathan.

Amanda reached for her other hand and, looking at her, Lana saw the fear that she knew mirrored her own. Maggie, thinking this was a game in which she was not included, pulled at the adults' hands and started babbling in her sweet baby voice.

Lana released her hold on the others and wrapped her arms around her little girl. Okay, so there was another delay. There had been several over the last year. They had managed to clear each hurdle to get to this point, and if there was something else the court wanted from her she could handle it.

"It has come to the court's attention that there is a new petition to stop this adoption by someone who claims to be a family member—a brother of the biological father," Judge Hamilton stated.

Lana's heart stuttered for a moment, then raced forward at a speed that had a gasp escaping into the quiet court room. She pressed Maggie closer to her chest as she felt the adrenaline rush hit her, telling her either to run or prepare to fight. She clasped Maggie tightly, needing to feel the reassurance that only physically holding her child in her arms could give her.

"Is the person petitioning the court present?" the judge asked.

Lana watched her nightmare play out in front of her as the cowboy she'd seen earlier rose to his feet.

"I'm Trent Montgomery, Judge Hamilton, and I have reason to believe that I'm Maggie's uncle."

Trent walked into the small room at the side of the courtroom and took a seat at the small rickety table. Across the table sat the young woman he had met going into the courtroom—the woman he now knew as Lana Sanders.

He was surprised he hadn't recognized her from the picture he had found among the items his brother had had when he was taken to the hospital. Of course the young woman pictured smiling at the toddler whose hand she held looked young and carefree, with her hair flying all around her face as a breeze blew through the blond strands, while the woman he had opened the door for was all business, in her tailored skirt and blouse and her hair pulled back in some sort of clip.

Now the woman had let her hair down in more than one way, and her bright green eyes shot daggers at him as she talked with an older woman with steel-gray hair and eyes to match. He had no doubt that at that moment she wanted nothing more than to come over to the table where he sat.

Not that he didn't understand the kind of anger she was feeling. When his brother's lawyer had contacted him about the child he had wanted to hit something—anything—just to be able to take out the anger he'd felt at his brother. How could his brother have kept it from him that he had a little girl?

The lawyer had stated that Michael hadn't believed the contents of the letter he had received from his ex-girlfriend. But when the private detective he had hired had brought back pictures of a smiling toddler with coal-black ringlets and bright blue eyes, he'd known that the child was his.

After the lawyer had read Michael's will, and left some pictures of the child, Trent had come to the same conclusion as his brother. The child could only be a Montgomery. Another Montgomery child that had been abandoned.

He'd looked at those pictures a lot during the last two weeks, as he had tried to decide what to do about the child. She looked happy, smiling at the pretty blond woman, who smiled back with a love that seemed to pour out of the picture.

Why would he want to take this child away from this woman who appeared to love her? And what did he know about raising a little girl? Sitting there across from a woman who plainly wished a hole would open up and swallow him, he wondered for the hundredth time why he'd uprooted his life to come somewhere he didn't want to be and where he certainly didn't have a clue about what he was doing.

But he would go through with it. Because his brother had asked him to take care of this child if something happened to him. And because the little girl was a Montgomery, and that made her his responsibility.

He had failed to keep his brother safe from his father's destructive influence, but he wouldn't fail this child. On paper, Lana Sanders looked like the perfect mom, but Trent knew better than to believe everything he read. He would protect Michael's child as he should have protected Michael.

Once the court awarded him custody of his niece he would pack up and head back to Houston, where he belonged. Somehow he would have to find a way to make things work till then.

"Lana, I want to tell you first that I know this isn't going to be easy for you. You've been taking care of Maggie for months now, and I know you love her very much. Second, you need to know that the court has to consider any interest the biological family has in Maggie." Ms. Nelson the social worker stated. "I've seen the letter they have from Chloe, telling Mr. Montgomery's brother about her pregnancy. And then, of course, there's the resemblance that none of us can deny."

"And where was this biological family when she was six weeks old with no one to take care of her?" Lana spat out.

She looked across the table at the man who had been sitting quietly as she had questioned the social worker. Those blue eyes that she had found so appealing earlier now seemed ice-cold as they followed her every movement. He might as well just be an onlooker into this catastrophe he had orchestrated. Her life had suddenly been turned upside down, and he acted as if this was just another meeting for him to attend. As if he had no interest at all in the outcome.

But then he shouldn't have any interest in her and Maggie's life. He shouldn't even be here.

The pain of her nails biting into her hands had her uncurling her fingers. So far she had managed to rein in her temper. Now, running her hands through her hair, she pushed it back from her face and wished she had left it up in the clip. She could feel the heat of anger in her face and she knew the sight of her reddened face and scattered hair couldn't be a pretty picture.

She would have to get herself under control before she reached panic mode. That was not something she wanted either of these two people in the room to see. Taking a deep, steady breath, she willed her body to relax. Turning back toward the social worker, she pleaded her case once more.

"What about when she was just born and she was going through withdrawal? Was there anybody from this so-called family interested in Maggie then?" Lana said, glad that she no longer heard a tremor in her voice.

"I'm sorry," Trent said. "I wasn't aware of the child until a couple of weeks ago. If I had known I would have seen to it that my brother was here when she was born."

"And where is this brother of yours, huh? Why is it that

you're here without him?" Lana asked. "If he's Maggie's father why isn't he here?"

Lana watched the man she had earlier thought of as cold turn glacial.

"My brother passed away three weeks ago."

The shock of the statement stunned her into silence. The man who was supposed to be Maggie's biological father was *dead*? She stared at the man sitting across from her, who had shown no emotion while discussing his brother's death. He was just full of bombshells, wasn't he?

"So why are you here? Why are you so interested in Maggie's life when apparently your brother had no interest at all?" Lana asked.

Turning toward the social worker, she noticed that the older woman had shown no reaction to this new information. Realizing that Ms. Nelson must already know about the death of the supposed biological father, she felt the relief of earlier fade.

"There is no way you can expect me to give Maggie up to a man who isn't even her father. It's one thing to consider the father's rights, but this man is a stranger to Maggie. You have to see that Maggie is better off in a home where she feels safe and loved. That's why Chloe didn't take her. Why she left her with me. She wanted to make sure Maggie would always be in a stable home. She didn't want to ever have to worry that her baby was not being properly taken care of," she said as tears spilled from her eyes.

No way. No way would she let them take Maggie.

"We're not making any changes as far as Maggie is concerned until we investigate the situation, Lana," the social worker said as she took Lana's hand and squeezed. "The first thing we'll do is have a DNA test done on both Maggie and Mr. Montgomery."

"I'll give you the information you need to contact me," Trent volunteered.

"Thank you," the social worker responded. "And your lawyer has given us the information you have in relation to your brother's alleged paternity."

"And, having given you that information, I would like you to consider allowing me some visitation with the child," Trent said.

"'The child' has a name. It's Maggie. And why should I let you anywhere near her?" Lana asked.

"It's your decision at this time, Lana, but we do have good reason to think that Mr. Montgomery's brother was Maggie's father," said Ms. Nelson. "And if the DNA tests come back to show Mr. Montgomery as being her uncle, he will be able to ask for visitation while the court decides on custody."

Lana looked at the man across from her. Cool blue eyes watched her from beneath thick dark lashes. She'd seen that calculating look before, only then it had been on the face of a toddler trying to figure out how to get another cookie after she had eaten her limit.

There was no denying the similarities this man shared with Maggie. And she feared that the DNA test would only confirm what her eyes were telling her now. Chloe had never said much about Maggie's father, but she had said she'd written him a letter telling him she was pregnant when she hadn't been able to get him to answer her calls. She had listed Maggie's father as "unknown" on the birth certificate when she hadn't heard anything from him, and she had refused to discuss him any further with Lana.

Lana rubbed at the tight knot she felt forming at the back of her neck. How could this day have gone so wrong? She was suddenly bone-tired. She knew she had to accept the fact that this fight wouldn't be won here today.

"I'll consider it," Lana said. "But if I agree, I will be present at all times."

"Thank you," Trent said.

"About the DNA, Mr. Montgomery… I'm sure your lawyer has made you aware that the results when testing for an aunt or uncle of a child will not be definitive. It will give us more of a likely match than proof of a biological relationship."

"Actually, it's *Dr.* Montgomery, Ms. Nelson. But please call me Trent."

For a moment Lana thought her brain would explode at this new piece of information. While she knew the court wouldn't show any prejudice as far as financial circumstances were concerned, it would surely still consider if a child's needs could be met. What if they felt that this Dr. Montgomery could provide better for Maggie?

"I'll contact you both after we receive the DNA results and set up another appointment," Ms. Nelson continued as she stood, letting Lana know that there wasn't anything else to be said today.

Lana stepped out of the room and drew her keys out of her purse with trembling hands. She was glad she had sent Maggie home with Amanda instead of having them wait for her. She would have to use the time it would take her to get home to get herself together.

Thank goodness she had found Amanda, a medical student, while she had been looking for a roommate. With Amanda able to fill in as babysitter in exchange for rent, she had the extra help that a single parent needed.

She'd go home and get Maggie into bed, call Nathan to see what her options were, and then she would come up with a plan. Dr. Trent Montgomery might think that he had everything going his way, but they said possession was nine-tenths of the law and right now Maggie was hers.

Lana had only been fifteen when she had beaten the cancer that had been growing in her body. She'd lived through chemo and radiation treatment. She'd stumbled a bit when she had learned that the treatments that had saved her life had destroyed her dreams of having children, but she had managed to keep going even though she'd been hurting.

She was a fighter and she didn't give up. And she was about to make a certain cowboy wish he had never left Texas.

CHAPTER TWO

LANA WALKED OUT of LDR Four and headed for the OB nurses' lounge. The delivery had been complicated, due to the size of the baby boy, and the new mom had needed extra reassurance that everything was fine with both her and her baby. Now she would have to hurry back to the office as soon as she'd finished signing off on her orders.

She could hear the whispers and laughter of the nurses as she turned the corner of the nurses' station. There had to be some new rumor spreading through the hospital, because she noted that everyone was gathered around Kat, the queen of hospital gossip. Usually she would have paused to hear what the newest bit of gossip was, but today she didn't have time.

As soon as her paperwork was completed she changed out of her scrubs and headed back to her office. She didn't want to leave her patients waiting any longer. Irate pregnant women could be downright scary, and her staff could only appease them with promises of her return for so long.

John Lincoln, one of the pediatricians employed by the hospital working the obstetric hall, waved from the nursery hallway as she passed. A few seconds later she heard her name called and turned to find John was following her, with another man dressed in the hospital's light blue scrubs beside him.

Lana stopped and stared at the two men even as she shook her head in denial. There was no way this could be happening to her.

"Hey, Lana," John said as he approached. "This is Dr. Trent Montgomery. He's taken the *locum tenen* position we've had open since Dr. Lee left."

"We've met," Lana said as she turned toward Trent. "What are *you* doing here?"

"As John just told you, Ms. Sanders, I've accepted a temporary job with the pediatric department," Trent said. "I'm looking forward to the two of us working together."

Work with the person who was trying to take Maggie away from her? No way was *that* going to happen.

"But why? Why are you here?" Lana asked.

John looked at Lana, then back at Trent with a frown. "I take it you two know each other?" John asked.

"We've met." Lana said as she moved to one side of the hall to let a nurse pushing a patient in a wheelchair pass.

She noticed the look the nurse gave this new doctor in town. Yeah, she hated to admit it, but he was something to look at. Even with his high-dollar suit and cowboy boots gone he looked good. The pastel color of the cotton scrubs should have dimmed some of that masculine power that he threw off, but instead it seemed to amplify the hardness of the body they covered.

There would be a swarm of women circling around him as if he was roadkill as soon as they got a good look at him. And she would just leave them to it. Because no matter how good he looked she didn't want him anywhere near her and Maggie. Why was he doing this to her? Her life was stressful enough without him in *her* hospital, where she would be running into him all the time.

Crossing her arms, she leaned against the wall. There was no way she was going to let him know how rattled he made her. She didn't care how sexy he looked standing there, she was going to let him know exactly how she felt about this ploy of his. Because that had to be what this was—just one more way to intimidate her into giving up Maggie.

But it wouldn't work, she was tougher than that. She would not let him get to her. There was too much at stake here. She had too much to lose to let a hard-bodied, hardheaded man get the best of her. She'd play his game if that was what it took to beat him.

"I'll catch up with you in the lounge," Trent said to John.

Lana waited till John was out of hearing range before asking the question that was burning her tongue. "What do you think you're doing here, Dr. Montgomery?" she asked. "Why aren't you back in Houston?"

Lana watched him take in her knowledge of that piece of information. Yeah, she'd done a little online stalking and it had paid off.

She'd found out that he worked in one of the largest women and children's hospitals in Houston as a pediatrician, for Pete's sake. Why he worked as a doctor at all, when he came from a family loaded with oil money, she didn't understand.

After seeing several pictures of him at different social affairs, all with a different beautiful woman on his arm, she had thought her heart would stop when she'd found an article that listed him as one of Houston's most eligible bachelors and had seen what was listed as his estimated net worth.

After that she had read everything the internet had on him, looking for something—anything—to use against him. But she hadn't found anything, and with every article her fear of losing Maggie had increased.

And apparently all the while she had been checking

him out, he had been checking her out too. Because even if he had a good reason for leaving the hospital in Houston, the fact that he'd shown up at the hospital where she practiced out of all the hospitals in Miami meant he'd done his research. Or paid someone else to do it.

Wasn't that what the rich did? Hired someone else to do all the dirty work for them? There were no coincidences with men like Trent Montgomery. No, he had an agenda in coming here, and she would find out what it was one way or the other.

"After my lawyer informed me that the courts would look favorably on me being within their district, I took leave from my job in Houston. Also, it made sense that it would be easier to work with you as far as visitation goes if I was living in the area. A temporary position opened up here, so I inquired and was offered the position."

As if the pediatric department was going to turn down a qualified pediatrician who had graduated from Emory and done a residency in neonatology when they were so short on staff.

"Besides, Miami is a beautiful city," he said as he moved closer, leaning in toward her as a group of staff members came down the hall. "Who *wouldn't* want to live here?"

She knew better than to let his look of innocence fool her, and she certainly wasn't going to let the fact that his body was now only inches away affect her.

"What did you tell the interviewers?" she continued, as she tried to ignore her speeding heartbeat. She hadn't discussed her court appearance with anyone at work—had just told those who'd asked that there had been a small delay in the paperwork at the court.

"I told them I had an interest in the position due to some business I had here in Miami," Trent said as he moved back a few inches. "I don't see why the hospital should have any concern for our private affairs."

Realizing she had been holding her breath, Lana let her lungs expand fully. The racing of her heart let her know she was allowing this man to get to her, and that wasn't acceptable. She would have to stop letting him intimidate her.

"And I'm supposed to believe that you just happened to end up at the same hospital where I work?"

Trent shrugged a shoulder, then gave her a smile that set her teeth on edge. This was a man who not only knew he was charming, but also knew how to use it to his advantage.

"That's what I thought," Lana said as she moved once more to let one of the unit nurses pass.

The fact that it was the same brunette nurse who had walked by earlier didn't surprise her. Word had clearly already gotten out that there was a new male doctor on the unit, and the fact that he was sexy as hell meant that he would be getting even more attention than usual.

Soon the fact that she knew the new doc would come to the attention of the staff. And that was something that she didn't want to deal with right now.

Trent watched Lana as she stomped off, then stopped to pull a ringing phone from her pocket and answer it. He'd known she'd be angry when she found out he'd obtained a job at the hospital she worked at, and he couldn't blame her. What had surprised him was his reaction to her anger. The woman was as feisty as a wild filly, and reluctantly he had to admit that he'd found it entertaining and even a little arousing to watch her spit and sputter as she reached her boiling point with him.

And that was the strangest thing. Normally the sight of a woman's anger sent him running in the opposite direction.

He'd seen enough of his mother's tantrums with his father to know he didn't want any part of that in his life. But this woman's anger was different. It was hot and furious, but at the same time it was controlled and non-threatening.

And she was sure something to see when her green eyes started to spark lightning strikes at him.

The woman would have his head if she knew that while she'd been doing all that ranting and raving he'd been thinking about how cute she was, trying to intimidate him with her five and a half feet against his six-feet-two-inch self.

The insistent screech of the beeper attached to his scrub bottoms went off and he read a message from the ER, concerning a preterm imminent delivery coming in.

"Which way to the ER?" he asked Lana as she ended her call.

For a second she just stared at him. Then, shaking her head, she turned down another hallway. "Come on, I'll show you," she said, not looking back to see if he was following her.

"There's a thirty-three-week antepartum coming in by ambulance," he said when he caught up with her.

"She's thirty-four weeks and six days. That was her husband on the phone," she said.

He knew those six days could make a big difference in the outcome of the delivery.

"Your patient?" he asked as they boarded an empty elevator to the bottom floor.

"Her name is Taylor. Her husband Dean says that her water suddenly broke and contractions started immediately. She has a history of preterm delivery and was on bedrest."

"How early were her other deliveries?"

"She's only had one. Her son Phillip was born at thirty-six weeks."

Trent waited for Lana to leave the elevator, then followed her through the double doors leading into the emergency room. Multiple glass-doored rooms opened up from what looked like the hub of the department, where nurses and doctors could be seen in front of monitors and answering phones.

"This way," Lana said as she turned left. "The department is basically set up with the trauma rooms on this end and the less urgent patients on the other."

She stopped in front of a large monitor set up at the end of the hallway then preceded into a room labeled Trauma Four.

As he entered the large room he noted the baby-warming unit set up in the corner, and the nurses around them opening up the delivery set on a stand near an empty stretcher.

He grabbed Lana's arm and moved her back as a couple of emergency responders pushed a stretcher into the room, holding a pregnant woman panting and gripping the hands of the female responder.

As he gowned and gloved up he listened as the other responder gave his report to the room. "Spontaneous rupture of membranes twenty minutes ago with contractions starting immediately. Contractions now every two minutes. Vital signs with blood pressure elevated and heart-rate tachy at one-twenty."

He watched as Lana, also gowned and gloved, helped move the patient to the trauma bed then immediately did a vaginal exam, all the time talking to her patient in a calm voice.

"Is there time to move her upstairs?" he asked. He knew everyone would feel better if they could do the delivery on the obstetric unit.

"Nope," Lana said. "This one is coming right now."

A young nurse he was sure he had been introduced to earlier as belonging to the NICU team laid a blanket over his arms and he moved over to where Lana stood.

A breath later and Lana was holding out a small baby for the sobbing mother to see, then reaching for clamps and scissors as she made fast work of freeing the baby from its cord.

Rubbing its back to stimulate a cry, she turned toward him. Pausing for a second, she gave him an assessing look, then with a hesitant nod she handed the baby girl to him.

He took over from where Lana had stopped, and rubbed the baby's back as he did his assessment. A small cry started as he reached the warmer, and had turned into a howl by the time he laid her down.

The whole room broke out in cheers. He looked back to where Lana was comforting the new mom and saw big smiles on both their faces.

"Sounds like she has a good set of lungs to me," he said.

He waited for the nurses to bundle her up, then brought the squalling baby to its mother and introduced himself.

"She's a little early, so I'd like to take her up to the nursery to observe her a little closer, but I'll get her back to you as soon as possible."

"But she's going to be okay?" the new mother asked.

"Her color looks good…she's going to get a seven and an eight on her Apgar. She was a bit slow starting up, but she's got the hang of it now, I'd say."

"As soon as you're ready I'll take you up to her," Lana told Taylor.

Trent laid the baby in the transport crib—she had calmed down some once she had been swaddled into a striped pink blanket—and followed the assigned nurse up to the nursery.

Considering everything that might have happened, he and Lana had managed to keep their personal issues out their jobs, thought Trent. He'd consider that a win for now.

He had no explanation for the way he responded to this woman. Since their first meeting thoughts of her had filled his mind, along with a deep pang of guilt at being the one who would to separate her from the little girl he could see she loved very much. But his agenda was set and nothing could change it now. He'd take care of his niece, just as his brother had asked him to, and he'd find a way to work with this midwife without everything around them exploding, while at the same time using the opportunity to find out everything he might be able to use in the custody battle.

He had to stop this adoption from going through. He wouldn't let his father ruin his niece's life the way he had ruined his brother's and mother's. He would protect her from his father no matter what it took, and once he had custody of his niece his brother's will would make sure his old man never had the power to hurt anyone again.

Lana took her place at Ms. Nelson's desk and waited for the social worker to finish her phone call. For once she had made it early for an appointment, and she planned on taking advantage of the time she had before Trent arrived.

Why the social worker felt it necessary for the two of them to meet together with her she didn't understand. The man rubbed her the wrong way, and she had spent the last few days doing her best to avoid him at the hospital, but there had been no way to get out of this meeting.

She would have to keep control of her temper, no matter how hard it was to stay in control when Trent Montgomery was in the room. Making a good impression with the social worker was too important. And, while her lawyer had given her his opinion of Trent's case for custody, she knew that a lot of the custody decision would be based on the social worker's investigation.

"Sorry about that, Lana," said Karen Nelson as she hung up the phone. "It's been a busy day today. I know this might sound cold, with your situation, but I just wish every child had two adults like you and Mr. Montgomery wanting them."

"That bad?" Lana asked.

She knew that there were a lot of children in foster homes who would never be adopted. She had seen it in her practice as a midwife, when one of her patients might give birth to a child she couldn't take care of and the child would go into the system. Then the mother wouldn't agree to give up her rights to the child, making it impossible for the child to be adopted, so they just continued to stay in the foster system year after year.

Thankfully Chloe had made it clear in her notarized letter, and later in her correspondence with the court, that she wanted Maggie to be adopted. If only more mothers like her could see that they wouldn't be letting their children down but instead opening up a better option for them.

"Yeah," the social worker said as she finger-combed the back of her hair, took a deep breath and then seemed to reset herself back into work mode as she started going through the files on her desk.

Not for the first time Lana wondered why someone would ever go into social work—especially in Children and Families. The pressure to ensure the safety of all the children they were responsible for must be mind-boggling.

"While we wait for Dr. Montgomery to arrive let's talk about how *you're* doing. I know this isn't easy for you. Are you hanging in there okay?"

"I know you're right about Maggie being a lucky little girl. I get that," Lana said, "but how much harm will come to her if she's taken away from the only home she's ever known and placed with a stranger? She's been through so much already."

"I'm her uncle—not a stranger. And surely you can see the advantages of a child being raised among her biological family?" Trent said as he stared down at Lana.

"She's not even two. She's not really interested in your stock portfolio," Lana said.

How had she let him sneak up on her like that?

"Dr. Montgomery—" the social worker started.

"Ma'am," Trent said as he tipped his big cowboy hat before sitting down beside her. "Please, call me Trent."

Lana watched as he gave the woman what she had overheard one of the nurses call his "killer" smile. He was such a suck-up.

"Trent, please take a seat."

The social worker's smile beamed back at Trent, causing Lana to knot her hands into fists in her lap when what she really wanted to do was wrap them around the man's neck.

"I was just telling Lana that I know this is not easy for her. It must be hard for you too, having just lost your brother and now moving to Miami on such short notice. I was surprised when your lawyer notified me that you were relocating temporarily. I'm sure this has disrupted your life. You must have been very close to your brother to be willing to make these changes."

Lana saw the smile on his face tighten. She didn't have any doubt that there was a story there. Had there been trouble between the brothers? Was there something she could use?

"With my brother gone, I feel that it is my responsibility to make sure his daughter is taken care of," Trent said, and then he turned in his chair toward Lana. "That's what families are for. Wouldn't you agree, Lana?"

Lana looked into Trent's eyes. Somehow he had managed to turn the tables on her, making any protest she might come up with seem heartless and uncaring. Well, two could play that game.

"Yes, families *are* important. That's why I've decided to agree to you spending some time with Maggie," Lana said, and she watched Trent to see his reaction to this piece of news.

She'd thought her lawyer crazy when he'd advised her to consider the visitation, but after he had explained that it would be a way to show the courts that she was willing to allow Maggie to see her biological family after the adoption it had made sense. She was willing to do whatever was necessary to keep her little girl—even if it meant spending time with an irritating cowboy.

"That sounds great, Lana. I'm so glad that the two of you are working together so well," Ms. Nelson said. "The reason I asked for this meeting was so that we could discuss where we go from here. I know the two of you are on different sides in this case, but I want you both to remember the most important thing to consider here is Maggie and her wellbeing."

"Of course," Lana said, and then looked over at Trent.

"Certainly, Ms. Nelson," Trent said.

Lana watched the corners of Trent's mouth twitch, as if trying to hold back a smile. Why did she suddenly feel she had fallen into a trap? A trap with a big, bad smiling wolf in it, waiting to devour her.

"Good," said Ms. Nelson. "I take it you two will come to terms with the visitation arrangements, so unless there is anything else that comes up I won't need to see either of you again till the DNA test results come back."

"That's fine," Trent said. "I feel sure me and Lana will be able to come to an agreement."

"I'm sure we will," Lana said. *An agreement?* She'd have to remind him that she would be the person in control of their meetings.

"Thank you for your time, Ms. Nelson," Trent said, blessing the social worker with another one of his smiles as they rose to leave.

Lana walked beside Trent as they left the office building. He'd been quiet as they had ridden down on an overcrowded elevator. It had been uncomfortable, being squeezed next to him. It seemed that no matter how much she tried, she couldn't get away from the man.

They could play nice together in front of the social worker, but that was as far as she could go with it. Just standing next to him was enough to fire up her defenses. This man was a threat to her and she knew she had to stay alert.

Of course there was that saying about keeping your enemies closer than your friends. Was that what Trent was doing by coming to work where he knew he'd be able to observe her? Not that there was any dirt he could dig up on her. She had never lived much of an exciting life. She had even started to think lately that she was getting to be just plain old boring.

Maybe after Maggie's adoption had taken place she'd take up a hobby, or get back in the dating pool. *Maybe.*

Thoughts of Joe and the way their relationship had ended left her shaking her head. Even though the man had professed that he loved her, it hadn't been enough. Not enough to make him want a future with a woman who couldn't give him children.

Her dream of a forever marriage—a marriage filled with love and support like her parents'—had been destroyed the day they'd broken up and she'd had to accept that she would probably never be able to find a man who would accept her as she was, damaged and broken.

No, she wasn't going anywhere near heartache any time soon. She had created her own little family with Maggie and that was enough. Now she just had to find a way to keep her family intact and get this cowboy back to Texas. And, as much as it was going to kill her, it was going to mean spending some time with him.

"Look, we need to talk about this visitation. There will have to be some rules. Are you hungry?" Lana asked.

"Yeah, I skipped lunch so that I could get off on time," Trent said.

"There's a little Cuban deli I usually stop by when I'm down here," Lana said. "The food's good and the people are friendly."

Lana watched as Trent's lips twitched, as if he was unable to decide how to take her invitation, and then they parted. Something about his bright smile caused her warning bells to go off. *Danger, danger*, they said, but it was too late. For the second time that day she felt as if she was the fly that was getting caught up in Trent's web.

Maybe from now on they should discuss these visitations over the phone.

"Sounds good," Trent said. "Do we walk or drive?"

"Walk," Lana said.

She found herself about to smile back at him before she caught herself. She couldn't let herself be influenced by this man's charms. They would discuss the necessary arrangements and maybe she'd also try to pry a little information out of him. This was about Maggie—not the stupid way his smile made her legs wobble as she started walking up the street.

She had found Café MaRita on one of her visits to the Children and Families Department office, and she was glad to see the two sisters who owned the deli were work-ing when she arrived at the walk-up window.

"Hey, Rita," Lana said, then waved to Mary in the back, where she was putting together the spicy sandwiches they were known for. "Can I get two Cubanos, an iced tea and…?" Lana turned to Trent questioning.

"A coffee, please," Trent said. "A *cafecito*?"

The small Cuban woman smiled at his pronunciation of the word for a coffee topped with sugary foam.

"I like this one," Rita said, and she winked at Trent. "He's dark and hot. Like my coffee. If you decide to get rid of him let me know."

"Oh, no," Lana said as she felt heat spread up her face, "it's not like that—"

"I'll make it a point to look you up when she's finished with me," Trent said, interrupting Lana.

Did the man have to flirt with every woman he met? Taking the sandwiches, she found an empty picnic table set out in the front of the deli and started dividing the food while she waited for Trent.

Watching him as he talked to the older Cuban woman while she prepared their drinks, Lana was impressed at how at ease he seemed with people. He had the ability to charm everyone he met—well, everyone except for her. The only thing *she* would find charming about him would be his backside headed out of town.

Trent watched Lana as she bit into her sandwich. He could see she was concentrating on something, and he didn't think it was just the sandwich she was eating—though she did seem to be enjoying it. It was nice to see a woman eat her food without any posturing about diets and calories.

He watched as the pink tip of her tongue slipped out and caught some of the juice running down the side of her mouth. From nowhere a burst of desire filled him, and he felt a jolt of arousal as it spread down his groin. Another swipe of her tongue along the crease of her mouth had his pants becoming uncomfortably tight.

He shifted in his seat, causing Lana to suddenly look up from her meal, and he knew the second their eyes connected that he wasn't hiding the hunger that had hit him. The surprise came when her eyes changed and she lifted her eyebrows, silently questioning him. If this was any other woman he might have thought she was purposely playing with him, but that just didn't seem like Lana's style.

"Sorry, I haven't found a way to eat these without making a mess," Lana said.

"That's okay. I'm actually enjoying watching you." Trent said, then watched spots of color flush her cheeks.

"Tell me why you decided to go into medicine instead of staying in the family business," Lana said, changing the subject.

His gut tightened as he thought of the decision he had made to follow his dreams. Would his brother still be here if he hadn't left him behind with his father? He had let Michael down when he'd walked away from his father's expectations for him. In saving himself from becoming the heir apparent to the Montgomery empire he had left his brother to deal with their father's unreasonable demands and bouts of temper.

No one had ever been good enough for their father. No one had been able to stand up to the old man's expectations. Not him, not their mother, and certainly not his brother. He had urged his brother to follow after him and get away from his father's influence, but Michael hadn't been strong enough. He'd even tried to talk his brother into the two of them joining together and using their share of the company stocks to oust their father from his position as head of the company, but Michael had refused.

Instead, Michael had continually tried to earn their father's approval, and when that hadn't happened he had turned to the same thing their mother had used to escape their father: alcohol. And when that hadn't been enough he had turned to drugs, until finally the two had killed him.

"You could say I did follow in one of my family's footsteps. My Uncle Jim was a surgeon. He had a lot of influence on my decision," Trent answered. She didn't need to know the turmoil his decision had caused to his family.

"Any regrets?" Lana asked.

"What?" Trent asked, startled by the question.

Did she know about the division in his family? Had she somehow learned about the threats and bribes his father constantly sent him, trying to get him to come back to the family-run business?

"I don't know much about the oil business, but I do know about all the demands and sacrifices a medical career requires. It just seems you could have had a pretty good thing going for you, working in your own company," Lana said.

"I find being a pediatrician very satisfying and challenging. And I can make far more of a difference as a pediatrician than as a businessman, don't you think?" Trent said.

He stood and started gathering up items from the table to throw out. For now, the less this woman knew about his business, the better.

"You said you wanted to discuss the visitations?" Trent said.

"Yes, I do. I hope you understand that just because I'm letting you spend time with Maggie it doesn't mean I've changed my mind about keeping her?"

"I think you've made that plain," Trent said.

The only way she could have made her intentions any plainer would have been for her to tattoo them on her body. He had no doubt this woman was going to fight him all the way.

"Okay, then. I'm willing to allow visitations as long as it's understood that I'm in charge of everything that concerns her. I'll always be present and I'll have the final word on when and where."

After the short walk back, Trent watched as Lana's car pulled out of the parking garage. Nothing he had learned so far, today or at the hospital, indicated that she was anything other than a young woman working as a midwife and raising a child she loved as her own. He couldn't help but like her, and he hated that she was being pulled into this mess with his father, but he didn't see any way out of it. And it was better that she had to deal with him instead of the old man. At least he fought fair. He couldn't say that about his father.

They had arranged a time for him to visit Maggie during their walk back to their cars and Lana had been more than fair with him. Everything he had heard around the hospital about Lana had been positive. He even felt a little guilty that he had taken a job here to see what he could dig up on her. From what he had seen so far there wasn't anything in her character that made him think he needed to be worried about his niece not being cared for, or that there was anything he could use against her in the court case.

But he knew how appearances could be deceptive. Hadn't his mom had everyone fooled until it was too late? No one had ever known about the fights between his parents. or the times when his mother had never even got out of the bed in the mornings, leaving two little boys to care for themselves.

He knew first-hand that no one ever really knew what went on behind the closed doors of a home. No matter how much Lana Sanders looked like the perfect mother, he would be sticking to the woman like glue until he had custody of his niece and knew without a doubt that she was safe.

CHAPTER THREE

TRENT STOOD ON the sidewalk outside Lana's home. He had seen a lot of these small block houses since he had arrived in Miami and though they were older buildings, he liked them.

The neat bungalows reminded him of the difference between his life in Houston and Maggie and Lana's here. While his condo in the busy metropolis area was modern, with all the amenities available, Lana's front yard was full of pink and yellow blooms and looked friendly and inviting. And whereas a doorman met visitors on arrival in his building, a colorful gnome sat on Lana's small porch, holding a "Welcome" sign which made even Trent feel as if he would be greeted warmly.

Of course neither of the two places compared to his father's ranch, where he had grown up. Even with the chaos that had made up his parents' relationship he had always felt at home there, with its sprawling acres of pastures. He had been able to escape for long rides on one of his horses and he'd come back feeling better every time. He had to admit he missed that feeling of being at home, of belonging somewhere.

Lana answered the door looking every bit the suburban mom in her tee shirt and jeans. While he might have thought the "mom look" would put him off, he was surprised to find that he liked it on her. She looked comfortable in the mommy role.

"Hey," Lana said as she held the door open.

There was a nervousness about her today that had him thinking she was having second thoughts about letting him into her home.

"Is everything okay?" Trent asked. "If you've changed you mind and want to…?"

"No," Lana said. "I'm sorry. Come in. Maggie's in her room, playing."

Lana directed Trent down the hall, where he found a room decorated in light pinks and purples. Sitting in the middle of the floor was a little girl, pouring what had to be pretend tea into a group of small cups. The table where she sat was surrounded by tiny chairs, upon one of which a rabbit was waiting to be served.

"Maggie?" Lana called the toddler's attention to her. "This is the man I told you was coming to see you. His name is Trent."

The raven-haired child looked up at Trent and a long-forgotten memory hit him as if it were a physical blow. While Maggie's eyes were blue, like both his and his brother's, the shade was slightly different. He had only seen that shade of clear cerulean blue once and, though his memories of his mother after all these years were few, he could still remember her eyes. The same eyes that now stared back at him from the face of the small girl who was studying him with a seriousness he was surprised to see in one so young.

"Maggie, will you let Trent play with you while I get your snack?" Lana asked.

"Cookie?" the child said as she looked back at her.

Trent watched as the toddler turned her smile on Lana. It was easy to see that Maggie had already begun developing the Montgomery negotiation skills.

"You can have two," Lana said as she held up two fingers, "with your juice."

Maggie smiled back at Lana, then got up and walked over to him. "Play?" she asked as she looked up at him.

"Ah...okay..." Trent said, surprised by the nervousness that suddenly hit him.

He was a pediatrician, for heaven's sake. He cared for kids of all ages in his practice. There was no reason for this one little girl to scare him, but inside his heart he knew there *was* a difference between this child and his patients. This was his brother's little girl. She was *family*.

Before the panic had time to overwhelm him, the child said something in an unknown language, then pulled on his hand. He shot a look back at Lana, who just smiled at them, then turned and left the room.

Lana stood and looked out the kitchen window. She couldn't help the smile she saw reflected in the window pane. The look on Trent's face had been priceless. How could a man who took care of sick children every day at work be scared of one little girl?

Just knowing that he was as uneasy about this meeting as she was made her feel a little better. She had been nervous about having Trent in her home. She knew her home was old and small, but she had made a comfortable place there for herself and Maggie. Would a man like Trent be able to appreciate the small house for what it was? A home where she and Maggie had become a family?

She watched as the smile that had been reflected just moments earlier disappeared.

A family—everything a little girl dreamed of. But when you were fifteen years old, and adults were telling you that you had cancer, the last thing you thought of was your infertility. She had just wanted to know if she would live long enough to make it to junior prom. But while she had worried about the chemo and the radiation causing her hair to fall out, she should have been worried about what the treatments were doing to the inside of her body instead.

Being told that you would not be able to have children at any age was a horrible thing. Being a teenager and learning that you would never be able to give birth to a child had been devastating.

She had given up on her dream of having a family and instead had thrown herself into high school and later her college education. Once she had gotten her degree in nursing she had found her calling in labor and delivery. If she could not have a child herself, at least she could help bring children into the world.

Then during her last year at midwifery school her Prince Charming had come and she had thought her life would be perfect from then on out. When a year later she had discovered that her prince, Joe, was really a frog, warts and all, it had been too late.

When the man she'd loved had told her that he just couldn't settle for a woman who wasn't able to give him children she had hit the lowest point in her life. But then Maggie had come along and everything had felt right. She *knew* she was meant to have Maggie, but how could she convince the man in the next room?

She finished fixing the drinks—two iced teas for them and one sippy cup of juice for Maggie—and then stacked some of the cookies she had made earlier that morning on a tray. She stopped at the door, then covered her mouth to hold a laugh inside as she watched her daughter initiate Trent the manly cowboy into the world of playing pretend with a little girl.

He sat on the floor cross-legged, in front of the small

table, with a pink polka dot hat on top of his head, and pretended to drink from a small plastic cup.

"Would you like some real tea?" Lana asked. "Sorry, I don't have any coffee."

"Tea's fine," Trent said. "But it will have to be some brew to compete with Maggie's. Isn't that right, Maggie?"

Maggie gave Trent a beaming smile. Somehow in the few minutes Lana had been gone Trent had managed to charm her little girl—not that she could blame her. There wasn't a female around who could withstand this man when he was smiling like he was right then.

She had heard all the rumors about the hospital nurses making fools of themselves around him, and if she was honest with herself she had to admit that being around him made her feel just as enchanted as the rest of womankind.

That was just what the man *wanted* her to feel, but she wasn't stupid enough to let a little bit of physical attraction muddle her brain. If he thought that he could charm her into letting her guard down around him, he was wrong.

Getting Maggie to settle down for a nap after finishing her snack had been a chore, but finally the toddler had tearfully waved goodbye to Trent and Lana had carried the worn-out baby to her room and put her in her crib.

She shut the door quietly and found Trent standing behind her.

"She's beautiful," Trent said, with a reverence that touched something deep down inside her.

Lana felt the same way every day she spent with Maggie. She was surprised at how sharing this feeling of caring for a child made her suddenly feel so close to him. Was this another ploy on his part?

"Thanks for letting me see her," Trent said softly.

Lana pushed her hair out of her face and looked up at

him. It was easy to see that he had been moved by the time he had spent with Maggie. It had to be hard for him after the loss of his brother—to see this reminder of him.

"Are you okay?" she asked.

"It shouldn't be me standing here," he said. "It should be my brother."

"What happened to him, Trent?"

"Michael had the same problems as Chloe. His addiction of choice was alcohol, though recently he had begun combining it with drugs. One night he just took too many…"

Michael's voice cracked for a second, and then he cleared his throat.

"And now he's not here to enjoy that beautiful little girl," he said.

Suddenly she was aware of the closeness caused by the small hallway, and for a moment she felt the need to reach out and touch him, to smooth away the pain she saw in his face. And then she remembered the reason he was standing here in her house. He had come to establish a relationship with her daughter—a relationship that he intended to continue by taking Maggie away from her.

"I won't let you take her without a fight," Lana said.

Her body was relaxed, more comfortable with the anger inside her than with the attraction that had wound so tightly inside her body just seconds earlier.

"I know," Trent said.

His whisper seemed to bounce off the walls of the hallway. He reached up and pushed a stray hair behind her ear, his touch leaving a soft tingle behind. Then he turned and walked out of her house, leaving her alone with her young daughter, and for the first time since she had moved in it felt empty.

She'd worked hard to make her home a safe place, her retreat from the world after a hard day. She had accepted that she might never meet a man who could give her the forever love that she longed for—the type of love she'd witnessed between her parents—but she had made a home here for her little family and she would not let anyone take that away from her.

"You are doing *great*, Jaden," Lana said as she watched her patient breathe through another contraction.

The fetal heart tones were reassuring, but the labor process had slowed down. If there wasn't a change soon, the OB on call would start questioning if Jaden was going to be able to have a vaginal birth. The baby's posterior position was just not allowing it to come farther down into the birth canal.

"We can try moving you back onto your knees and see if we can get the baby to turn, if you'd like," Lana said.

"It didn't help last time," Jaden said as she took a deep breath and prepared for the next contraction.

"I know you wanted to do this without any type of pain control—" Lana started.

"She went through all the classes," Jaden's sister said.

"I know, and she's doing great. But the labor has gotten long now, and I really think we need to consider all our options. That includes an epidural," Lana said as she took the cool washcloth a nurse handed her and wiped Jaden's face.

"They said it would slow down labor," Jaden said.

"Sometimes it can, but right now your labor is not progressing at all," Lana said.

"I'll think about it," Jaden said.

The phone clipped to Lana's green scrubs pocket vibrated. She knew it had to be the office again.

"I'm going to step out for a moment," Lana said. "Why don't you think about whether getting an epidural is something you want to do while I take this call?"

Lana nodded to the nurse and walked out of the room. A call to her office told her that the department was packed with patients waiting to see her. The crowd was getting restless and her staff needed to know what to tell the women who were waiting.

Some days Lana needed to be cloned. Today was one of those days.

After talking with her office nurse, and catching up on Jaden's progress notes, she returned to the labor room. The sight of the anesthesiologist standing at the bottom of the bed and talking to her patient told her Jaden had decided to opt for the epidural.

"They decided on the epidural," the nurse, Shelley, whispered as she leaned toward Lana.

The door opened and Trent walked in, carrying a clipboard. He nodded to her, then moved over to Jaden as the anesthesiologist started setting up his tray.

"Trent is so good with the patients," the nurse said. "He makes a point to come and see them before they deliver, and they love him."

"His name is Dr. Montgomery," Lana said, and then regretted it as soon as she saw the questioning look on Shelley's face.

It wasn't any of her business if Trent got friendly with the nurses. She couldn't even blame them for wanting to get his attention. The man appeared to be a sexual magnet for women. Didn't she know it herself? She couldn't keep her own traitorous body from responding to the sexual pull of him, but that didn't mean she had to like it.

She moved over to the bed and helped the nurse position Jaden for her epidural. Trent stood to one side while she answered some of Jaden's sister's questions.

She thought about that moment in her hallway, when for a second she had felt a connection with him, When he'd touched her she had been sure he had felt it too. Had that moment been real or had she just imagined it? And why was she standing in the middle of a labor room thinking about Trent instead of her patient?

Forcing her attention back to where it should have stayed, Lana took her place to help her patient concentrate on her breathing and remain in the proper position. Just as they were ready, her phone rang.

"If you need to get that I can help," Trent said. "Unless you want to?" He addressed the patient's sister.

"Oh, no, I hate needles," the sister said, and she moved across the room as far away as she could.

As her phone went to voicemail Lana relaxed. Then it immediately rang again. Someone was certainly being persistent.

"Have you ever helped with an epidural before?" she asked.

"I can't say I have, but I'm willing to learn," Trent said.

"Okay, come over here and help support her," Lana said as her phone continued to ring.

She traded places with Trent, then left the room to take the call.

When she stepped back into the room she was hit with a picture of Trent bent over Jaden, talking quietly as he assured her that they were almost finished. Anyone else walking in might easily have thought he was just another father helping his wife get through her labor.

The thought caused a small pain in her heart.

Fifteen minutes later Jaden was lying down and tilted onto her left side. While it would take several minutes for the medication to reach its full effect, Lana could tell by the way Jaden was starting to relax into the bed that she was already starting to feel some relief.

Lana checked the fetal monitor, then suggested a nap for both Jaden and her sister.

"Since you seem to always be feeding me, I thought I'd buy you lunch this time," Trent said as they stepped out of the labor room.

Lana glanced down the hallway and saw that two of the labor nurses had stopped and were looking their way. While she and Trent were standing outside one of the hospital rooms it would look as if they were discussing a patient's care, and no one would make any comments. But if they were sitting together at a table in the hospital café…?

That would definitely stir up the rumor mill.

"It might not be a good idea," Lana said.

"I promise I won't discuss the court case," Trent said, and then leaned against the wall looking at her expectantly. "I heard they're serving fried potato casserole today. You wouldn't want to miss *that*, would you?"

"So I treat you to the city's best *cubano* and my famous chocolate chip cookies and the best you can do is that? Besides, I need to get back to my office."

"I'd be happy to do better," Trent said. "How about dinner Saturday night?"

Lana felt her senses go on alert. The teasing tone in his voice was gone now. Was this another one of his tricks to get to her?

"I thought we had agreed to a visitation with Maggie on Saturday at the beach?" Lana asked.

"I'm talking about after our day at the beach," Trent said.

Lana watched as Trent pushed off the wall and took a step closer. That flirty smile he had flashed earlier was gone, leaving her in no doubt that he was serious in his invitation.

"What do you want from me?" she asked, unable to keep the stress from her voice.

Was this another ploy to get her to cave in to the Montgomery demands for custody of Maggie?

"Look, Lana, whether we like it or not, until the court makes its decision we're going to have to get along. It just seems like it would be easier if we got to know each other better."

And then his smile was back with all its magical appeal. "I'm really not a bad guy, you know."

Maybe he wasn't a bad guy, but he was still the enemy. "Okay," Lana said.

If he wanted to get to know her better—fine. It wasn't as if that was going to change her mind about keeping Maggie. Besides, maybe if he got to know her better he'd see that Maggie was where she needed to be. It would definitely be harder for him to take her daughter away from someone he'd come to know instead of a stranger.

It was a long shot, but she would take any chances she could get to keep her daughter.

"But don't say I didn't warn you about the fried potato casserole. You'll need to get your cholesterol checked as soon as lunch is over."

She arrived back on the labor and delivery unit to find Jaden almost ready for delivery. After less than an hour of pushing she delivered a healthy eight-pound baby boy. As Trent handed the new mom her baby her patient thanked him for all his help, and as Lana left the unit she thought about how Trent had been so good with her.

The quick lunch they had shared had been relaxing. They had discussed some of the differences between his job on the pediatric floor at his Houston hospital and the neonatal unit he was working in here. She'd been able to tell he had a true love for his job in Houston, and she couldn't help but wonder again at his choice to leave it to pursue his court case.

Neither one of them had brought up the custody case, and for the first time there hadn't been any conflict between them. Was it possible that they could work together without letting their outside problems get in the way? It looked as if they might be able to, but she knew she was walking on thin ice when it came to any type of relationship between the two of them.

It would be a very easy man to let her guard down around a man like Trent, and no matter how at ease she might feel around him she needed to remember they were on opposite sides when it came to Maggie. That was truly all that counted.

CHAPTER FOUR

AS SHE DRAGGED HERSELF through the front door, the quiet house told Lana that Amanda had already put Maggie to bed. She hated to miss that time of day, when Maggie, with damp curls and smelling of baby wash, would climb up into her lap and snuggle while they read a book together, but as hard as she'd tried she hadn't been able to catch up at the office without staying late.

As soon as she shut the door Amanda stepped out of the kitchen carrying two glasses of some kind of pink fruity-looking drink.

"Energy smoothie," she said as she handed one of the drinks to Lana. "You sounded like you could use a pick-me-up when you called."

"Thanks," Lana said.

The refreshing liquid slid down easily, bringing a soothing feeling through her body. She took a quick peek into Maggie's room and found her sleeping like an angel, then headed back into the living room. She let herself slump down on her couch and found herself relaxing for the first time all day.

She toed her shoes off and wiggled her tired feet. Dorothy in *The Wizard of Oz* was so right. There was no place like home.

"I left some pasta on the stove. You want me to fix you a plate?" Amanda asked.

"No, thanks. I'll get it later."

"Bad day, huh?" the young woman asked.

Amanda had been Maggie's live-in babysitter since Maggie was two months old. She had been there on those days when Lana had come home thrilled with the experience of having been a part of bringing a new baby into the world, and she had been there when Lana had come home emotionally torn up after giving an expectant mom news that had destroyed their hopes and dreams.

Today had been neither of those. It had just been very long.

She played over the events of the day, remembering the delivery she had done and the part Trent had played in it.

She hadn't been able to get his invitation to dinner off her mind. She would have to decide what she wanted to do about it. It should be an easy decision. She had told herself not to let their relationship become any more personal, but after their lunch together she was finding it hard to ignore her desire to see him some more.

"Lana…?"

"Oh, sorry. I zoned out for a minute," she answered. "Not really bad. I just ran late all day after a long delivery."

She sipped her drink and considered her options. She could try to ignore Trent, with the hope that he would soon go away, or she could let him get to know her better, with the hope that she would make him see that she was the perfect mother for Maggie.

The question of why he was pushing to spend more time with her kept circling in her mind, reminding her to beware of good-looking men with possible hidden agendas…reminding her of the need to stay on alert. What was he up to?

"What do you think about Trent Montgomery?" she asked.

Amanda studied her over the rim of her glass, then finally asked, "As an uncle to Maggie?"

"No. Not in relationship to Maggie."

Lana sat up straight and adjusted the pillows on the couch. Grabbing one, she hugged it close to her body, then combed her fingers through the satin cord tassels.

"So you mean as a man?" Amanda asked.

Lana nodded at Amanda. While she knew the babysitter was very protective of both her and Maggie, she also knew that she'd be honest and fair in her opinion.

"Well…" A big smile spread across Amanda's face. "If it wasn't for his involvement in stopping the adoption, I'd probably be thinking about jumping his bones—just like you."

"Amanda!" she said, feigning shock and throwing the pillow she'd been holding at her friend's laughing face. "I haven't—"

"Well, maybe you should." Amanda laughed again as Lana grabbed another pillow and shot it toward her.

She could feel the heat of embarrassment spreading up her face. Okay, maybe since they'd had that moment in her hallway she *had* been having dreams which included getting Trent out of his scrubs. Or his suit. Or whatever he had been wearing the last time she saw him. But she wasn't going to admit it.

"He asked me out."

"Like on a date?"

"More of a let's-get-to-know-each-other-better kind of thing, I think," Lana said.

"Wow," Amanda said. "Are you going?"

"I'm thinking about it," she answered.

The look of surprise on Amanda's face mirrored her

own. Was she seriously thinking about spending time alone with Trent? Was she crazy?

"I don't know if I should be more shocked by the fact that you're even considering going out or by who you're considering going out *with*," Amanda said.

"Trent wants Maggie, Amanda—nothing else."

"What about you? What do *you* want?" Amanda asked.

And that was the problem. One moment the man was irritating her, with his *I'm Maggie's uncle and I know what's best for her* attitude, and the next he was charming her with that Texas drawl and that sexy smile of his. And then there was that irritating tingling she felt whenever he was near—a physical awareness of him that made her want to run far away but at the same time want to seek him out.

None of it made sense, and spending more time with him would be like playing with fire. No matter how safe you thought you were, there was still a possibility that you'd get burnt.

Of course the good thing was that he'd be leaving as soon as the court came up with a ruling on Maggie's custody. A ruling that could result in her losing Maggie.

That thought sobered her out of her daydream. Making sure that didn't happen was what she needed to concentrate on. As soon as the adoption was finalized she would think about getting back out in the dating jungle. The attraction she was feeling for Trent was just another sign that she'd been too long without a man in her life. She'd thought after what she'd gone through with Joe that she had accepted she had no need for a man in her life. Apparently she had been wrong.

"I just want life to go back to the way it was before he showed up," Lana said. "But I need to keep an eye on him. Hopefully he'll be leaving soon."

"And without Maggie," Amanda said, with a confidence that Lana wished she felt.

"Without Maggie," Lana seconded, and the two of them clinked their glasses together.

As the bikini clad blond roller-skated around them Lana considered her choice of beach once again. While she was usually comfortable with her body, now, seeing all the perfectly tanned beauties who flocked to the South Beach location. she felt self-conscious, knowing her body was not like the thin, willowy specimens out on display today.

She had what her mother had always referred to as "a curvy figure." She had never been lacking in the breast department, and her hips and thighs were definitely wider than those belonging to the women on all the magazine covers that tried to tell you what you should look like.

Her body was basically just like the rest of her—nothing above average—and up until now she had always been okay with that. She knew the only reason she felt inadequate now was because she had seen the women Trent was normally photographed with. But she wasn't one of those women. She was just herself and she needed to accept it.

"Here?" Trent motioned toward the crosswalk over to the beach.

He had insisted on carrying Maggie through the crowd, instead of using the stroller she kept in the car to help with carrying both baby and all the items that were needed when traveling with a toddler.

"Let's wait till the next one," Lana said, not wanting to mention that she was trying to avoid the topless section of the beach.

"You know, we have beaches in Texas, but they're not nearly as entertaining as this," Trent said as a second barely clad woman skated past.

A sleek cherry-red muscle car drove by, blaring music out the windows, making it impossible to talk. It was still quite early for the weekend crowd, but it appeared they were all ready to party even at this hour.

Lana had chosen to go early so that she could get Maggie back home in time for a nap, but she was also hoping to escape before the afternoon crowd showed up, making it impossible to get through on the small streets crowded with shops and restaurants.

"We can take the next crossover."

Lana moved in close, trying to avoid a group of tourists standing outside the old-fashioned soda shop. She felt the warm heat of Trent's hand when he reached around her waist and guided her through the crowd. They crossed the street to the entrance for the beach. When they reached the thick sand he moved his hand to grip her elbow, helping her as she plodded down to the shore.

They found a space with room to stretch out a blanket and Trent let the toddler down, but kept hold of her hand as she pulled him closer to the waves.

Grabbing some sunscreen, Lana joined them and began to slather lotion over Maggie as she giggled and stomped her feet in the water.

"Be still, you little wiggle-worm!" Lana laughed as she fought to make sure there weren't any areas not covered.

Maggie, deciding it was a game, squirmed around Trent's leg, causing Lana to miss the intended cheek and smear lotion across Trent's leg. At the feel of the coarse hair on this intimate part of Trent's thigh Lana's face flushed with redness. This had been such a bad idea.

"I'm so sorry..." Lana said, and she scooted back fast, almost tripping over Maggie.

"No problem—thanks for helping me with the sunscreen," Trent said.

She watched a smile curve across his lips that let her know he found her embarrassment amusing.

He picked up Maggie and held her out at arm's length. "I'll hold her for you."

Lana quickly finished with the lotion and then grabbed the little hand Maggie held out to her after Trent put her back down on the sand.

"Me play. *Now*," Maggie demanded, and she pulled down on both the adult hands holding her back from the waves.

They walked out a couple feet until Maggie could feel the cool water lap against her legs. Again she pulled down on Lana and Trent's arms, and she started swinging back and forth while dragging her feet through the water and giggling.

All around them people were wading out into the water or stretching out on the coarse sand. It was a great place for Maggie to play, and in minutes all three of them were laughing. with water soaking through their clothes.

They walked back to their blanket, where Trent set Maggie up with her pail and shovel. Lana started to peel her wet shirt off, then turned just in time to see Trent lift his own shirt over his head. For a second she had a full view of a firm, toned chest with a small strip of hair. She followed the dark line down to where it disappeared into a water-soaked bathing suit that molded around his groin, leaving very little to her imagination.

Realizing she had been guilty of staring, she looked up to find Trent's eyes glued to her face. She had definitely been caught. Where was a Florida sink hole when you needed one?

She jerked her tee shirt up over her face and then peeked through the armhole to see him still staring at her. The stupidity of hiding there, with her shirt over her head, just increased her embarrassment. Acting like a sex-starved female was bad enough—not having the courage to own up to it was worse.

She finished pulling off her shirt, moving slowly to disguise her nervousness. One look at Trent had her wishing her shirt was back in place. A smile still filled his face, but the heat now in his eyes out-burned the Florida sun.

A warm stream of desire began in her chest and then flowed down to pool deep into her core. How did he *do* that? It was as if he was touching her with those beautiful eyes, melting her with the heat she saw in them. As if reading her mind, he swept her body with one more appreciative look, causing her body to respond with a need she had long forgotten and didn't want to remember.

"Me, me!" Maggie cried as she pulled down on Trent's bathing suit, not happy that she had lost her new friend's attention.

"What a beautiful child—you must be very proud."

The voice cut through her thoughts and Lana looked over to where an older couple had stopped to admire Maggie. She was used to being stopped by strangers, commenting on her little girl.

"Thank you," Lana said.

"It's so nice to see a young family spending time together," the elderly woman continued.

"Oh, we're not—" Lana started to correct her.

"You're a lucky man," the white-headed man complimented Trent.

"Yes, I am," Trent said as he placed his arm around Lana's shoulders and pulled her close to his side. "Thank you."

The couple waved goodbye to Maggie, then continued their walk down the beach hand in hand.

"Okay. Let's make us a big castle," Trent said as he

let go of Lana and knelt down to help fill the pail full of wet sand.

"Why did you do that?" Lana sputtered.

"Did you *really* want to try to explain our unique relationship to them?"

Unique? Yeah, that would be a good description for them.

No one seeing the two of them together with Maggie would think there was a battle going on between the two of them. For a minute while they had played together in the water she had forgotten herself. It had just seemed so natural and right for the two of them to be enjoying time with this beautiful child.

She knew she needed to take a step back from Trent and see what was really happening here. She had no doubt that there were ulterior motives behind all the attention he had been giving her lately.

Playing "Mommy and Daddy" with Trent would only get her hurt. It was too close to the happily-ever-after dream she'd carried with her for years—the dream that had died when Joe had walked out on her.

She and Maggie made a great family. They didn't need anyone else in their life.

"I think I'll stretch out and catch some sun, if you don't mind watching her," Lana said as she stepped away.

"Sure. Relax. I've got Maggie," he said as he looked across at her.

Knowing he hadn't meant that in any way except to say that he was watching over her little girl, Lana tried to make herself think of nothing except enjoying the salty breeze and Maggie's laughter as her little girl played with Trent.

Sometimes you just had to pull a Scarlett O'Hara and save your worrying for tomorrow, so you didn't waste the day you'd been given. That was a lesson that cancer had taught her very early in life.

Trent hung up the phone after listening to his father's message right before he turned into Lana's drive. He had known his father would be curious about his missing the latest board meeting of Montgomery and Lord, and that it was just a matter of time before his father started to make inquiries into his absence.

He had to make a decision about whether to continue with his plans or to trust Lana with the information that as of now was only known by him and his lawyer.

It had seemed so simple when he had first decided to come to Florida and get custody of his niece. First he would hire a nanny and make sure the child was taken care of. Then he'd approach his father with his brother's will and make sure the old man knew that he no longer had any power to manipulate others the way he had his wife and younger son.

Trent got out of the car and smoothed his dark dress pants as he tried to clear his mind of all the pain and anger that immediately consumed him when he thought of his father. The old man had a lot to answer for, and for the first time in his life Trent might have the means of making him pay for his sins.

But first he had to decide what to do about Lana. Could he trust her to understand the danger his father was to Maggie? More importantly, would she trust *him* if she learned about the stipulations in Michael's will?

He had no explanation for the intimate tug he felt drawing them closer together, but it was easy to see that the physical attraction between them made Lana uncomfortable. With the little he had learned about her he knew she was as much out of her comfort zone with him as he was with her.

He had felt her pull away from him as soon as they had left the beach and he hadn't liked it. After Maggie had fallen asleep in her car seat Lana had been quiet until they had arrived back at her place, where she had very curtly thanked him for the trip to the beach. Then she had stated that she didn't think it was a good idea for them to go out to dinner together.

He'd somehow managed to turn the conversation around, though, so that she had agreed to go out with him tonight to "discuss their options" in relation to Maggie. He couldn't help but smile when he thought of that clipped tone her voice took on when she turned all Momma Bear on him.

He ran his hands through his hair and let out a heartfelt groan. Why was he rethinking all his carefully laid plans *now*? It had been a lot easier to think of taking his niece away from some stranger than it was to execute that plan now. The more time he spent with Lana the harder it was going to be to take Maggie away from her.

It seemed as if his plan to stick close to Lana and Maggie was starting to backfire on him and he only had himself to blame.

Maggie checked the mirror one last time, turning to get a view of the way the black dress followed the curve of her hips, stopping a few inches before reaching the back of her knees. Turning back around, she admired the way the jeweled neckline that circled her neck sparkled. It had been a long time since she had dressed up for a date. Okay, so maybe it wasn't really a date, but she still deserved a little mirror-time.

"You look hot," Amanda said from where she sat on the edge of the bed. "Doesn't Mommy look hot, Maggie?"

"Hot?" Maggie asked, giving Lana a questioning look.

"No, Mommy's not hot," Lana said as she picked up the sweet-smelling toddler and snuggled her close. Nothing could be as angelic as a freshly bathed toddler all ready for bed.

"See?" Lana told Maggie as she tickled her belly. "Not hot."

"I'll have to ask Trent his opinion when he arrives," Amanda said, reaching over to take the toddler.

"You do and I'll tell that resident on the oncology floor that you were ogling his backside the other day when I stopped by."

"I was not... Okay, maybe I was." Amanda giggled. "But have you seen how cute he is in those scrubs?"

"Yeah," Lana said "it was all the nurses could talk about until..."

"Until the cowboy doctor showed up?" Amanda teased. "Too bad for them that the only person he seems to be looking back at is you."

"He just wants to get to know his niece," Lana said. "That's all it is," she insisted as she saw Amanda's expression in the mirror. "The only reason I agreed to go tonight was to see if I could find out more about him," she said. "I need all the ammunition I can get in this fight."

"Are you trying to convince me or yourself?" Amanda said as she hurried off to answer the door.

"Behave!" Lana called after her friend.

The last thing she needed was for Amanda to insinuate that there was something romantic going on between them. There was too much tension between them as it was. She didn't need Trent thinking that she was like all the other nurses in the hospital, who had joined the Team Trent fan club.

She would go out tonight and listen to what he had to say, and then she would get her turn to explain to the man why her daughter needed to stay with *her*.

CHAPTER FIVE

TRENT HAD KNOWN he was in trouble the minute Lana had stepped into the tiny living room wearing that sexy as hell black dress. His hands had clenched with the need to explore the body wrapped up in all that slinky black material and the woman dressed in the package hadn't had a clue what she was doing to him.

She had stood there in her living room, with that same sweet smile of hers that screamed innocence, while every delicious curve of her had sent him into sexual overdrive. Then there were those ridiculously high gold heels that had her almost coming up to stand eye to eye to him. Did she have *any* idea what having her lips that much closer to his was doing to him?

If it had been one of his usual dating partners he'd have had no doubt that this was a calculated move to reel him in—but this woman? No, one of the things he found so surprising about her was her honesty. She said what she thought and expected the same of others. She didn't play crazy games that ended up causing hurt feelings and resentment.

As a young man he'd learned quickly that there were women in the world who would use their bodies to manipulate you if you gave them a chance. It was something he did not put up with. He'd seen enough drama in his life as a child with his parents; he didn't need any in his adult life.

It was going to be a long night, he decided as he joined Lana in the car and headed for the restaurant.

As they drove he kept the conversation to common small talk as he tried to get his body under control—something he found almost impossible with her sitting close beside him. Keeping his eyes on the road, he reminded his overheated body of all the complications getting involved with her would cause.

He was relieved to find that by the time they drove up to the entrance and he handed his keys over to the valet the self-control he depended on had taken over once more. He couldn't afford to show any sign of weakness to Lana.

Lana took her seat at the linen-draped table. Except for discussing his choice of the newest Brazilian steak house in town, they'd kept their conversation to discussions of work and weather. She waited until the waiter had taken their orders and moved away before trying to turn the conversation to a more personal topic.

"So, are you missing Houston yet?" she asked.

Maybe if she could get him talking about his home he'd open up more about his brother. She had to figure out if there was more to his seeking out Maggie and moving to Miami. She could understand he would have an interest in seeing that his niece was being taken care of, but most unmarried men would have made a fast check on the child then flown out of town as soon as possible.

But not Trent. No, he had dug in with both feet in this custody battle. Somehow she just knew there was more going on than she was aware of. Just the mention of his brother and he turned to stone. Was he grieving? Yes, she was sure there was pain in his eyes when the subject came up, but there was much more that he was keeping to himself. It was the key to his being here in Miami and she wanted to know just what he was holding back from her.

"I miss my colleagues, and of course I miss Tanglefoot," Trent answered.

"Tanglefoot?" Lana asked. "Is that the name of some sort of animal or do you have a very clumsy friend?"

"She's a very stubborn horse," Trent said, "but I love her."

Lana watched the smile that lit his face as some unshared memory seemed to come to his mind. It was nice to see the man truly relax and lower those shields he kept up between himself and others. Or was it just *her* that he was trying to keep out?

They each chose a selection of meat from the platter one of the gauchos was serving from and then continued.

"So, where does Tanglefoot stay?" Lana asked. Maybe if she kept him on what seemed like a safe subject he would finally open up to her.

"She's at my family's ranch," Trent said.

"But you live in the city, right?" Lana asked between bites of thinly sliced beef.

"I have a place in the city, but I try to get away at least once a week," Trent answered. "I spend as much of my off-time helping around the ranch as possible"

"Like what? Riding fences and looking for stray cattle?" Lana asked.

"Yeah, some..." Trent answered.

"Really?" Lana asked.

Trent gave one of his killer smiles that had her imagining him in his jeans and boots. She had no problem envisioning him on his horse, waving his hat as he rode off into the sunset.

"There's only a few hundred head of cattle left now. My

father is more interested in the oil industry. But the ranch has been in my mother's family for a long time, so I try to keep an eye on the place. I like to spend time with the horses and do some of the necessary maintenance around the place."

"I can't really see you as a handyman," Lana said. No, she definitely saw him more as a cowboy.

"I might surprise you," Trent said, and flashed her another one of his potent smiles. "I'm pretty good with my hands."

Lana looked down at her plate, trying to ignore his intended innuendo. She wasn't stupid, and she had noticed that any time she started making headway into his personal life he turned on that flirty charm of his. It might work with some women, but she wasn't about to fall for it.

Not that she was unaffected by the thought of his hands. She had no doubt that those hands were very talented, and she'd seen how gentle they could be when he held tiny newborn babies…

"What?" she asked when she allowed herself to look up from her plate and caught his amused look.

"I like that flustered look you get whenever you're embarrassed," Trent said. "And then there's the blush…"

She had felt warmth spread through her cheeks barely a second before his comment. How did he *do* that? It was if he had been studying her and knew her responses even before she did. Was she that transparent?

"Sorry," Trent said. "I really didn't mean to embarrass you."

"I was asking you about the ranch," Lana said.

"Yes, you were."

"You mentioned your dad…what about your mom?"

Lana noted the change in Trent immediately. All joking was gone now and sadness touched his eyes.

"She passed away when me and Michael were still kids," Trent answered.

"I'm sorry," Lana said.

Reaching over, she covered his hand with hers. Though it had been a long time since his mother's death, she could tell he was still grieving. Some deaths were like that. They touched you forever. She had seen it in patients who had lost a child many years earlier.

For a second the thought of losing Maggie crossed her mind. She closed the door on those thoughts quickly. She wouldn't go there tonight.

"Thanks, but it was a long time ago."

"It had to have been hard on the two of you," she said.

"Especially Michael—he was so young that I don't think he even had many memories of her," Trent said.

"But you do. I'd think it would have been harder on you, really knowing what was missing from your life," she said as she removed her hand and went back to her meal. Even with his mother's death, Trent was determined to put his brother before himself.

"Maybe, but then again I have memories. He didn't."

"So who took care of you when the two of you were growing up?"

"My great-aunt Flo came to live with us. My mother's aunt. She still lives there."

Trent watched as Lana pushed back her plate so that the restaurant staff would stop the continuous flow of food to their table. He ordered a coffee for himself when she turned down dessert, then leaned back in his chair. The tension that had been with him when they had started the evening had drained to only a tinge of discomfort now centered in his upper shoulders.

He rolled his head to ease the pulling on his muscles.

He had been worried when Lana had started with the questions about his brother, but though he usually didn't discuss much of his personal life with others, talking with Lana hadn't been the uncomfortable conversation he might have thought it would be. Not that he hadn't recognized all this interest in his life for what it was: Lana was fishing for anything she could use against him.

"You look tired," Lana commented. "Are we working you too hard?"

Was that concern in her voice? How could she possibly care about how he was doing when he had brought all kinds of trouble into her life?

"I'm fine," Trent said.

He was about to leave it at that when he saw a flicker of distress flash through her eyes. Taking a slow, deep breath, to prepare himself to be hit with all her accusations, he continued.

"I'm sorry, Lana. I know my coming into your life like this has to be a nightmare," Trent said. "I bet you wish I'd get on the first plane out of town."

"I was thinking more like you would ride off into the sunset, Cowboy."

He watched as a small twitch played at the corner of her mouth, then she looked down at her hands, which were tangled in the napkin in her lap.

"I can't say what I would do if I found out my brother had a kid out there I hadn't been told about, but that doesn't make the position you've put me in any easier. Haven't you wondered why Chloe picked me to give Maggie to?" Lana asked. "She could have gone with any one of a dozen private adoption lawyers in town, but she came to *me*."

"I know you were her midwife," Trent answered.

"I was." Lana said. "And you must know how sometimes you just develop a bond with your patient? When they just seem to touch something inside of you? That part of you that you feel you have to protect, because you know if you let it the heartbreak you see every day will cause you to burn out, and then you wouldn't be able to help anyone anymore?"

Trent nodded his head toward her. He'd learned at an early age that you had to keep those feelings that left you vulnerable to the outside world locked up inside, where they couldn't be used against you, and during his clinical rotations he had been able to put up the walls that protected him. Until he had started his pediatric rotation. It had been the young ones, the innocent ones so filled with hope and trust, that he hadn't been able to help but feel his heart soften toward.

And wasn't that what was happening with the woman sitting across from him? Somehow, no matter how he built up those walls he knew he needed to keep erected between them, she could find a way over, around or through them. And that made her a weakness he couldn't afford.

"I knew Chloe was all alone in town—she told me when I first saw her in the office. And she had been very open about her addiction problem with prescription drugs, and about her rehab and methadone treatment. But it really wasn't until after Maggie was born that I got to know her."

"Ms. Nelson at Children and Families told me about Maggie's withdrawal," Trent said.

"You know how that is. It's like going through hell when someone goes through withdrawal. Watching an adult patient go through it is hard enough, but watching a baby… Maggie…" Lana stopped and reached for her glass.

The tremble in her hand as she raised her glass to her mouth told him that Maggie had to have been really sick. He'd seen infants go through withdrawal many times, and it was a horror for the staff as well as the parents. He could only imagine how hard it had been for Lana to watch Maggie experiencing the pain and agitation her withdrawal would have caused. The thought of it had him clenching his fists.

Why were children always the ones who had to pay for the mistakes of their parents? It was a question that had haunted him for years as he had watched his brother's drinking spiral out of control.

"I'd find Chloe sitting beside Maggie's crib in the neonatal unit, just staring at her baby. She looked so lost and alone that I found myself sitting with her there, talking to her for longer and longer each day."

Lana looked up at Trent, capturing his eyes with hers until he felt himself drawn into her sorrow.

"I'm not trying to make excuses for her. But after Maggie got out of withdrawal, when Chloe decided she couldn't take the stress of caring for her, she did the most unselfish thing she could do. She put the care and wellbeing of her baby first. I can't imagine what it took for her to come to my house the night she brought Maggie to me," Lana continued. "And I'll admit I'm not nearly as brave. I can't give Maggie up. I *won't* give her up," Lana said as she rose from her chair.

Trent could see the pleading in her eyes, the innocent hope that shone out of them, asking for his help. She could have asked him for anything right then. Anything except for what she needed—his assurance that everything would be all right. Of course it wouldn't. They both knew that. Only one of them could win custody of Maggie, and right now he wasn't sure who he was hoping that would be.

It was only knowing the harm that his father could do to both Maggie *and* Lana that assured him he was doing the right thing.

* * *

"I saw them myself!"

"Saw who?" Lana asked as she walked into the nurses' break room.

She watched as two of the nurses who had been in there excused themselves. The other four nurses were either looking down at the floor or at Kat, the department's queen of gossip.

"We were just talking about what we did on our time off," said Laurie, the charge nurse.

"Did *you* do anything exciting this weekend?" Kat asked, and leaned toward Lana.

The room suddenly became quiet and everyone in turned toward her expectantly. It was becoming very obvious that there was some piece of information they were all waiting for her to share. And by the way they all seemed to be anticipating her answer she knew this wasn't a casual question.

And then it hit her. Someone had seen her out with Trent. And that someone was apparently Kat, who she could see had been only too happy to run back and share the news with her colleagues.

She couldn't blame them for their interest. While the hospital was quite large, they were still a tight-knit group who seemed to share everything with each other—even things that were really none of their business. But that didn't mean she was prepared to go into details about her and Trent's relationship.

She had enough problems keeping Trent and her court case from interfering with their work relationship. So far her explanation that a last-minute complication had temporarily postponed Maggie's adoption had been all the reason she had needed. No one knew that the "complication" was Trent—or at least if they did she hadn't heard any talk about it. If it got out there that they were seeing each other socially, the gossip fire would be raging out of control. There was no way she was going to give it any more fuel.

"Nothing special. I just took Maggie to the beach Saturday. She loved it, of course. Besides that it was just a normal weekend."

Lana almost laughed at the look of disappointment on the group's faces. There would be more talk when she left the room, she was sure. And if Kat ws being her imaginative self by the end of the day she was also sure the hospital would be full of gossip about her and Trent's torrid affair. She'd have to warn him, but besides that she decided just to ignore it.

"Laurie—Hannah Bowers has texted me that she is on her way," Lana told the charge nurse. "Hopefully she's just having Braxton Hicks contractions."

"How many weeks is she now?" Laurie asked as she got up and began to clear the space where she had been eating.

"She was thirty-six last Friday, when I saw her," Lana answered. "I checked her cervix and she was thinning out, but not dilated yet."

"Thirty-six is pretty good for twins," Kat commented.

"We won't stop her if she's in labor," Lana said. "Just call me when she comes in and I'll come over and do an exam."

Hoping that the excitement of possibly having a twin delivery would give the staff something to talk about besides her love-life, Lana headed back to her office to catch up on her daily appointments.

The prospect of a twin delivery thrilled her too, but she'd have to use some good time management or things would back up fast in the office.

Lana had only managed to see a couple of patients before Laurie called to say that Hannah had arrived with her mother and was having contractions.

After signing out with the office she made the quick walk over to the labor unit. Looking at the contraction pattern of two minutes apart, Lana wasn't surprised to find Hannah's cervical exam showing that she was definitely in labor.

"Ready to meet these two?" Lana asked as she motioned toward Hannah's stretched belly.

"Really?" Hannah asked. "I've got to call Jimmy. Momma—you call him. I've had so many false alarms that he'll never believe me."

"Probably would be a good idea to go ahead and make that call," Lana said. "You're progressing pretty well. When did the contractions start?"

"Just before Jimmy left for work. I didn't want to tell him. He'd have insisted on staying home and I didn't want him to miss work. Are they okay?" Hannah asked as she indicated the monitor screen, where four different lines graphed out, each in a different color.

"Their heart-rates look great," Lana answered. "They're early, but it's not unusual for twins to come early."

"Probably because they've run out of room in there," Hannah said as she rubbed her large belly.

"I'm going to order an ultrasound. I can tell that Baby Anna is presenting with her head down, but I need to check on James Junior," Lana said. "I know we discussed you trying for a vaginal delivery…"

"If I can," Hannah said.

"Is that safe?" asked Hannah's mother. "When my sister had her twins they just cut her and took them out."

The middle-aged woman came to stand near her daughter and Lana could see the concern in the woman's eyes.

"Things have changed since then, Momma," Hannah said as she reached over and took her mother's hand. "Remember one of the girls at your church delivered her twins vaginally?"

"I'll wait for the ultrasound results and then I'll talk with the obstetrician on call. If both twins are positioned correctly it will be okay to let the labor continue to progress," Lana said. "But don't forget—if the second baby decides to change position after we deliver the first, you probably will end up with a Cesarean section."

"You mean she could have *both*?" Hannah's mother asked as she got up from her chair and walked over to the monitors to study the readings.

"Momma worries," Hannah explained.

"And I don't blame her one bit," Lana said as she headed for the door. "I'm going to go get that ultrasound ordered now. You just get Jimmy on his way here, and after the ultrasound we'll all get together to decide how we're going to go from here. I also think you should consider going ahead and getting an epidural."

"This soon?" Hannah asked as she shifted in the bed.

Lana watched as the contraction that was tracing on the monitor peaked, then slowly went down. She had noticed Hannah instinctively take deeper breaths as the contractions had come and gone.

"You're going to need one soon. We can get some IV fluids going too, so that you'll be ready when Anesthesia gets here."

"Thanks, Lana," Hannah said.

"And just remember," Lana said when she reached the door. "The most important thing today isn't *how* you deliver—it's that we end up with two healthy babies and a healthy momma."

As she shut the door she heard Hannah's nervous mother say, "Amen." She couldn't blame her for having concerns about her daughter. Even knowing everything she knew about childbirth, Lana still knew that if it were her Maggie in there she would be a nervous wreck.

But what if she wasn't around when Maggie grew up and had children of her own?

That thought had her stopping to lean against the nearest wall. She took a deep breath that would have made any labor doula proud, and let it out slowly as she tried to calm herself. She was starting to have more and more periods of anxiety over the custody case, and was afraid that one day she was going to find herself in a full-blown panic attack.

And how would *that* look to the court? And to Trent? He was always so in control of his emotions. He would never understand what she was going through. There had to be something she could do to help ease the anxiety she was feeling.

Of course the only thing that would really help would be Trent dropping his petition with the court and returning to Texas, so that she and Maggie could get back to their life together.

Yes, Trent leaving would be the answer to all her troubles—but what could she do to make that happen? She'd shown him that Maggie was happy and safe with her. He had to be able to see how much she loved her little girl. What more did he want?

And to top everything off she *didn't* need the complication of her hormones going crazy every time she was around the man. There had never been a man she was so sexually aware of in her life, and it made her feel self-conscious and unsure of herself at a time when she needed to be portraying someone who was totally confident in her life.

She took another deep breath to help cleanse her thoughts, then continued down the hall. She'd call her mother tonight. Between sharing her heartache with her momma and a pint of chocolate ice cream she would surely come up with some strategy to get her through the next couple of weeks.

Trent entered the labor and delivery unit and went in search of Lana. He was telling himself he needed to get an update on her patient's condition so he'd know how soon he and the nursery team would be needed, but he knew it was just an excuse to go and see the midwife. He hadn't seen her since their night out, and he had already planned to hunt her down later that day to make more arrangements to see Maggie.

Of course he could have just called to set that up, but that wasn't what he wanted.

What was it about her that had caught his interest and refused to let it go? She was certainly a beautiful woman, with her seductive curves and that thick blond mane of hers, and those green eyes that filled with love when she talked about Maggie. But he had dated plenty of beautiful women who hadn't affected him like she did. Even Maria hadn't captivated him the way Lana did, and Maria had been the perfect woman.

Maria had been everything he had wanted in a woman—beautiful, smart, and most importantly independent. He'd never had to worry about her throwing a fit if he got called into work, or complaining about him not spending enough time with her. If he'd been late for a social function due to a case going long she'd never been angry with him.

It had been the perfect relationship and he had been surprised when, after dating him for several months, she had called him one day to tell him she wouldn't be seeing him anymore—that she wanted to see other people and didn't feel that he could give her what she needed out of a relationship.

While he couldn't say that she had broken his heart, he *had* been hurt. No, he'd never felt that all-consuming love everyone talked about, but he had cared about her.

He'd seen her a few weeks later in a corner of the hospital cafeteria, holding the hand of one of the residents. Stopping to study them for a moment, he'd noted the flush of Maria's face and the way those deep brown eyes of hers had never left the young man. He had waited for jealousy to fill him, but he'd felt nothing.

It was then he'd realized that, no matter how intimate they had been, what they'd had was just a close friendship and nothing more. Maria had realized that too and wanted more. He hadn't.

And that brought him back to Lana. The two of them had managed to create a good working relationship and, even with everything between them, if not a friendship at least they'd managed a truce. He didn't want to endanger that because of some misplaced attraction between the two of them. Maybe if she was another woman they'd be able to scratch the itch and move on, but everything he'd learned about Lana told him that wasn't her way.

Lana was the kind of woman who would want roses and candles before she became in any way involved with someone, and then she'd be wanting the house with the white picket fence. She had quickly shown him that she was all about family, which put her at the top of his list of women to stay away from.

He'd learned a long time ago that he didn't have anything to give a woman other than his friendship and sex, and that was enough for him. He had no desire to be responsible for someone else's happiness. He'd heard his mother's claims of love for his father and it had destroyed not only her but the rest of their family. He never wanted to get caught in that trap, where everything depended on someone's feeling for you or your feelings for them.

He owed Lana a lot for taking care of his niece, and he wouldn't repay her by letting her think there could be more between them than there was. He was already trying to take the baby she loved away from her, and he knew that already made him just as much of a cold bastard as his father.

He'd found himself wrestling with that fact each night when he lay in his bed. On one hand he wanted to leave Maggie with Lana, knowing that she would always be loved and taken care of. But on the other hand Michael had asked him in his will to take care of the little girl. Couldn't Lana understand that he had to honor his brother's request?

And then there was Maggie's inheritance... So far Michael's lawyer had been able to stall his father concerning the contents of his brother's will, but he knew his father would have his own lawyers looking into it soon.

No one except for him and his brother's lawyers knew that upon gaining custody of Maggie he, Trent, would have control of the majority of the shares to Montgomery and Lord, but if his father found out that little tidbit before the custody case was settled he knew Maggie would be in danger of being used like everyone else Calvin Montgomery touched, and he couldn't let that happen to another person he cared about.

It was up to him to protect his niece and he was going to have to find a way to make Lana understand—even if it meant airing some of his family's dirty laundry. And there was plenty of that.

Trent was about to give up on finding Lana when he saw her in the nurses' break room. For a moment he just watched as she laughed with the two labor nurses she was sharing her lunch with. It was nice to see her laughing with her friends. With all the stress he had added to her life, it was amazing that she could still relax for a moment. And no matter how much he told himself the woman was dangerous, he had to admit he enjoyed looking at her.

"Excuse me," Trent said as he interrupted the three of them in their meal. "I was wondering if I could see you for just a minute, Lana?"

He stepped out through the door to let her pass, and was surprised when she grabbed his arm and pulled him down the hall to one of the empty exam rooms.

"What are you *doing*?" she asked him in a voice not much over a whisper.

"I'm not sure," he whispered back as he looked down to where Lana was still gripping his arm. "And why are we whispering?"

Lana dropped his arm. "Do you know who that was I was eating with?"

"Well, I know Kat…" Trent said.

"Of *course* you do," Lana said, then walked across the room away from him.

"What does that mean?" he said as he followed her.

"Nothing," she said.

Trent watched her as she stood there with her arms crossed, glaring at him while she chewed at her bottom lip. Then, as if coming to some conclusion—although on what he had no clue—she marched up to him.

"Kat is the biggest gossiper in the unit—probably in the whole hospital, for that matter," Lana said.

"And I should be concerned about that…why?" Trent asked.

Was the man dense? Lana had been tiptoeing around questions about her weekend all day, and then he'd walked right into the break room and asked to speak to her. By now everybody on the floor would be speculating about what was going on between the two of them.

"Because somebody saw us out together the other night, and now everyone has got it into their head that there's something going on between us."

Lana watched as that information hit him. And then the stupid man smiled.

"It's not funny!" she said as she punched him in the arm.

"Ouch," he said, rubbing his arm.

"Will you just be serious for a moment?" Lana asked. "The last thing I want is for everyone to find out that there's something going on between us."

Lana watched as Trent sobered. He leaned back and then sat on the tightly made hospital bed.

"And what exactly *is* going on between us?" Trent asked.

"They don't know about your brother, or the reason my adoption of Maggie has been put on hold," she said. "I don't want to have to walk around this hospital with everybody talking about it."

She'd had enough of those pity-filled stares when she was a bald-headed teenager after her chemo and radiation treatments. She didn't want to live through that again.

"Sorry," he said. "I just wanted to ask you about this weekend—about me seeing Maggie."

Lana stopped and looked at him. He hadn't meant to cause trouble. It wasn't his fault that tongues were wagging.

"No, *I'm* sorry," she said. "I shouldn't be so sensitive."

Walking across the room she took a seat beside him, and for a few seconds they sat there together in silence. She was starting to realize that in some ways Trent was just as much a victim in this nightmare of a court case as she was.

He hadn't left Maggie's mother when she was pregnant. He hadn't come to Miami to stop her adopting Maggie for himself. Everything he was doing was for his brother.

While it was easy for her to see that taking Maggie away from the only home she had ever known was not the right thing for the child, she knew he was just trying to do what he thought was best for his niece—even though she knew he was wrong.

"Let me check my call schedule for the weekend…"

"Oh, *there* you two are," Kat said as she stuck her head in the door. "Dr. Miller called for an update on Hannah's progress. I told him I couldn't find you, but that I'd be glad to have you call him back."

Lana looked at Trent before jumping down off the bed. By the silly smile he gave her as she left the room she knew he was aware of just what the next set of rumors would be. She'd have some explaining to do to the people she worked with if they got wind of the fact that the two of them had been caught together on one of the hospital beds.

Because one look at Trent and no one would believe they were innocent. At least no female would.

CHAPTER SIX

WITH HANNAH'S TWINS in the right position, they decided
to go through with a vaginal delivery. As soon as Hannah was fully dilated and ready to push, they moved her
to an operating room to deliver in case there were any
complications.

Lana saw Trent dressed in his scrubs helping the nursery team set up when she entered after scrubbing up.

"Twins, huh?" Trent said.

"You don't do vaginal delivery of twins in Texas?" she
asked.

"We do. Just most of ours are delivered by doctors,"
he said.

"I've done several, and Dr. Miller is on standby in the
unit in case the second baby decides to misbehave. Trust
me—I've got this," she said with a smile, then winked at
him.

She knew the adrenaline rush was making her cocky
and hoped she didn't regret the words later.

Trent watched as Lana moved over to her patient and
couldn't help but smile back. If the look on her face was
any indication, Lana had certainly found her calling in
midwifery. While she was definitely full of confidence,
he saw that she checked through the instruments arranged

for the double vaginal delivery, as well as checking that she had everything they'd need if things changed and they had to do a C-section.

After having one of the nurses confirm that Dr. Miller, the obstetrician, was on the unit and available, she had Hannah start to push.

Several minutes later the first twin started to crown and Trent gowned and prepared for the delivery. when Lana handed the crying little girl to him, he carried her over to the warmer and checked her out from head to toe. She was a bit small for her gestation, but nothing that wouldn't be expected in a twin.

One of the nurses name-banded and bundled the baby, then carried it over to the waiting father.

Lana was busy doing an ultrasound on her patient. "Okay, Hannah and Jimmy—you ready to meet James Junior?"

Hannah nodded her head excitedly, then started to push again. Trent had to give it to the woman—and to women in general. He didn't know a man alive who would be able to go through what these mothers did.

With the top of a second little head crowning after a few pushes, he watched as Lana carefully delivered the head, then the shoulders.

"James Junior's been stealing the food from his sister," she said as she held the much larger baby boy up for them to see.

She cut the cord, then handed the newest member of the family to Trent. Within seconds of stimulating him with a firm rub on his back he had the baby boy as pink and as loud as his sister.

"Congratulations!" Trent said later, as Lana took a seat on one of the benches across from him in the locker room.

"Thanks. How are the babies?" Lana asked.

"They're doing good. They're both with their parents. We're watching their sugars, but besides the extreme difference in size they're perfect," he said. "The nurses are all talking about how good you did. And I didn't hear a word about us being caught in bed together."

Lana made a face at him and then broke down in giggles. She knew she was still on an adrenaline high from the delivery, but it felt good to just relax and enjoy it for a minute. Today was a day to celebrate the two new lives that had come into the world. Nothing could be better for renewing a person's hope in life than seeing a baby starting out it's life.

Trent watched her as she talked about what a privilege it was to be a part of the twins delivery. Joy seemed to flow out of her as she described the two babies who had just come into the world.

It was as if the beauty that he had learned was inside her was blooming out into her sparkling green eyes. Her cheeks glowed bright with color from her excitement and he had never been so turned on by just watching a woman talk.

He felt something in him thaw as the beautiful sound of her laughter touched him in a place he had closed up inside himself years ago. Her laughter warmed him and her smile teased him into wanting more. Would it be so bad just to enjoy this moment without worrying about all the complications that could follow?

Realizing she was on the point of blabbering, Lana stopped and looked up to see Trent had come to stand in front of her. Gone was the man who had earlier in the day joked with her about her concerns over gossiping nurses. The playful teasing she had become accustomed to had been replaced by a dangerous intensity that seemed to fill him, leaving his body taut with tension and reminding her of a wild cat preparing to pounce.

Everything about him had become hard now—everything except for his eyes.

Lana stood and moved closer, as if drawn into them. They seemed a deeper blue today. A blue she knew she would drown in if she wasn't careful. Then Trent took a step forward and his eyes went from calm sea to hungry storm—a storm that had the power either to pull her in or toss her away.

Fear about which he would choose, and what she herself wanted, had her taking a step back and moving around the wooden bench that penned her into the tight space.

"Trent?" she heard herself say, the sound barely audible as if it came from far away.

When he ignored her plea and took a second and then another step toward her, instinct had her continuing her retreat until she felt the door against her back.

She held herself still as he reached around her and locked the door. The warmth of his breath fanned her face, and when she glanced up at his lips she was surprised to find them so close to hers. So close that she could feel the warmth of them.

No longer willing to wait for his advance, she pushed up on her toes and met his mouth with hers. A white heat scorched her as it rushed through her body, then puddled in her core. The excitement of the twin delivery was scattered away as a new, more dangerous thrill filled her. Soon hard lips were meeting soft tongues as they battled, both of them advancing and retreating.

She felt Trent's hands as they skimmed over her back, then came to rest on her hips. He pulled her body closer until she felt the length of his erection as it rested between her legs. When he pushed himself against her, pinning her against the door, she was left with no doubt as to what he wanted. What they both wanted.

As their mouths continued to war she felt herself surrender to him. He was hard for her and she was aching to let him take her. Right then. Right there. Against the locker room door.

The memory of where they were suddenly broke through her clouded mind. She was about to have sex in a locker room. In the middle of the day. With the man who was trying to take her daughter away from her.

For a second Trent ignored her when she tried to pull away.

"Trent," she said when she managed to free her mouth, "we've got to stop."

She felt his fingers relax on her hips, but still he didn't move.

"I guess we were about to give the staff something to *really* talk about," Trent said as he rested his chin on the top of her head, so that her face was cradled against his chest.

Lana took a deep breath in, enjoying the tangy scent of hot and bothered male. She would take that smell with her. But it was *all* she could take of him. She had never been a woman who could handle a sex-only relationship. She needed more from a man. But with her body still aching for his she knew she had to get away from him.

"I've got to go," Lana said as she shifted against him.

"You never answered my question," Trent said.

She pulled back and looked up at him.

"What *is* going on between the two of us?" he asked.

"Nothing," she answered, then looked away, afraid that

her eyes would show a longing for something more that she knew she couldn't have.

"If that was nothing, I don't know if I could live through your something," he said, with a touch of humor that surprised her.

He held her to him for just a second longer before he released her and moved away.

"I got a call earlier from Ms. Nelson," he said.

With the mention of the social worker's name the warmth that had been between them faded. *This* was why she knew the right thing to do was to step back from Trent. Anything that they could possibly have would never survive the battle they would soon find themselves in.

"What did she say?" Lana said as she tried to stomp down on the panic that wanted to rise up and take control.

"Nothing that we weren't expecting. The DNA testing came back. I'm Maggie's uncle, Lana," Trent said. "Maggie's a Montgomery."

She watched him reach down and lift his duffle bag onto his shoulder. She walked across the room and kicked off her shoes. Feeling a bit shaky, she sat on the bench in front of her locker. She took her time changing into her street shoes and storing her work pair, and by the time she looked up the door was shutting, leaving her alone with even more questions than she'd had before.

Lana walked into the social worker's office knowing she was a coward. She had spent the week avoiding Trent as much as possible. The few times they had ended up on the labor unit at the same time she had made a fast retreat to her office.

If only it was that easy to run away from the dreams that haunted her nights, leaving her in tangled sheets with an unsatisfied need that filled her days.

She could deny that there was anything between them to Trent, but she wasn't able to lie to herself. She was letting herself get too close to him and that was dangerous. She couldn't allow herself to put anything before her family right now. She had to be totally professional from now on, and that meant no nights out with Trent and no moments alone together.

Then he walked into the room, and all her determination to keep things strictly business between them fled. How was she supposed to ignore this man who could turn her libido into a hormonal teenager's just by entering the room?

Dressed in soft gray dress pants and a black polo shirt, he had the look of a wealthy oil tycoon, with his charcoal cowboy boots and the black Stetson hat he held in his hands. She remembered the night at the restaurant, when he had told her about working on the family ranch and joked about how good he was with his hands.

The room suddenly heated up with her memories of those hands holding her in place while he pressed himself tight against her, his lips hot against hers. His hands were not the only things he was good with...

"Ms. Nelson... Lana," he said as he took the seat next to her.

"Thanks for coming down," the social worker said. "I think the two of you have gotten the information on the DNA testing from your lawyers?"

She continued when they each nodded their heads.

"I just wanted to get the two of you together to discuss how the visitations are going and to let you know what our plans are from here forward. I've talked with Nathan, Lana, and he has told me you're planning on continuing with the adoption."

"Yes, I plan on continuing with my plans for custody

of Maggie," Lana said, hoping she had managed to keep the tremble she felt out of her voice.

"And I will need to continue with my petition also," Trent said.

"And your visitations with Maggie?" asked Ms. Nelson.

"We've done very well together," Trent commented, then looked over at Lana. "At least I think so."

"Trent is very good with Maggie," Lana answered. "He had no problem winning Maggie over. I think he's a natural in the uncle department."

"Well, thank you, ma'am," Trent said in his deepest Texan drawl.

Lana tried to stop the smile that always came when he was in this cute flirty mood.

"I think he just can't help charming every female he meets," she said.

"What?" Trent said. "I want you to know I take my wooing of a woman very seriously."

"*Wooing?* Who uses a word like 'wooing?'" she said as she turned back to Trent. "What does that even mean?"

"Well, I can tell you that any woman I woo will definitely know what it means."

Ms. Nelson cleared her throat and they both turned toward the social worker, who was looking at them as if they had lost their minds.

"The visitations are going well," Lana said, and she sat back in her seat, then looked down at her hands.

"So I see," the social worker said, and gave them a friendly smile.

Lana took a deep breath and decided to dive into the speech she had prepared on her way to the office. She made sure that when she looked up she avoided looking at Trent. She locked her eyes on the older woman and hoped to see some understanding in the gray eyes that met hers.

"Trent can come to visit Maggie as often as he wants—" Lana started.

"Thanks," Trent said.

"Let me finish," Lana said. "But while I plan on continuing Trent's visits with Maggie…"

From her seat beside him Lana felt the tension as it coiled through him and he visibly straightened in his chair. This wasn't going to be easy, but she had to have her say. Squaring her shoulders, she moved up to the edge of her seat and began again. She had practiced, she had memorized, and she *would* get through this.

"Trent will always be Maggie's uncle, and I will always allow him to see his niece," said Lana. She let the breath she had been holding out and took in another one, this one deeper, as she tried to get her thoughts together. "But with all the things Trent can provide for her, the one thing he can't provide is something every little girl needs. A mother."

"Are you saying a single father can't raise a child?" Trent asked. "Aren't fathers important too?"

"No. I mean, yes." Lana fumbled over the words as she tried to ignore the anger she could hear rising in Trent's voice. "Yes. Fathers are important. But Maggie's being raised with a mother figure. I'm all she's ever known. What happens when you take that away from her? What happens when she wakes up in the middle of the night crying and I'm not there, Trent?"

"It sounds to me like what she really needs is the both of you," Ms. Nelson interrupted, and then continued before either of them could comment. "Trent, I need to discuss a few matters with you, if you have a few more minutes? I appreciate you coming down to see me, Lana, and I understand your concerns. If you need anything, or have any questions, you know you can give me a call."

Lana stood and thanked the social worker before leaving the office. She had been dismissed.

Turning back, she saw the woman get up and shut her office door. She couldn't help feeling as if she was being shut out of something that might have a big impact on her little girl. She turned and headed for the elevators, trying to decide how she would get through the next few days while she waited to see what step the courts would take next.

"I think you can understand Lana's concerns," Ms. Nelson said.

Trent took a long look at the social worker. She wore a friendly concerned look that he knew must put her clients at ease, but she was shrewd too. She knew how to get information when she needed it to get her job done.

"I do understand where Lana is coming from," Trent said.

"What we need to remember here is that a little girl's future is about to be determined and it is our responsibility to make the best decision we can in her interests. Anything besides honesty between the three of us would be going against what is best for Maggie."

Trent nodded his head in agreement, then waited for the social worker to continue. He had agreed to be honest with her. He tried to push back the guilt he felt about keeping information about his brother's will from both the social worker and from Lana. It was something he would eventually have to deal with, but now was not the time.

"I like Lana, and I know that Maggie couldn't be any more loved or cared for then she is with her." The social worker removed her glasses and rubbed at her eyes. "But it's my job and the judge's job to make sure that everyone's interest in the child is explored and taken into consideration. Having said that, I'm going to admit that right now I feel the best place for Maggie is still with Lana."

Well, she couldn't be any more honest than that, thought Trent. And what kind of argument did he have to use against her?

"That doesn't mean you won't win custody," she continued. "As a family member, you have a strong case. Your biggest job is going to be to prepare yourself to take on everything raising your niece will require, and it's not going to be easy. I'm not sure you're ready for this change in your life. As a pediatrician, I'm sure you know there's more to raising a child than just providing for their needs."

Was she right? Was he fooling himself, thinking he could take on the job of raising a toddler? And this was adorable little Maggie, who had already been through so much in her short life. The last thing she needed was for him to do something that could screw her up.

Just look what had happened to Michael. He had been supposed to take care of him. He had been the oldest and he'd known his mother expected him to look out for his little brother. He had failed Michael and he didn't want to fail his niece too. But no matter what Lana and the social worker thought Maggie needed him. He was the only one who would be able to protect her from his father's control.

Trent quickly agreed to the home visit the state required before leaving the social worker's office. He had a lot to think about after this meeting.

Lana should have felt at least a little bit of guilt about what she was about to do to Trent, but she didn't. The idea had come to her in the middle of the night, when thoughts of losing Maggie had kept her awake.

While Trent talked a good game as far as wanting to be a responsible uncle and taking on the duty of caring for his niece went, in truth he had no idea of what taking care of Maggie would entail. Sure, he was qualified as a pediatrician to give proper medical care to a child, but she was pretty sure he wasn't really prepared for the day-to-day care a toddler needed.

An early call to Emily, the midwife covering deliveries this weekend, and everything had been set up. The fact that Maggie had woken up cranky from the teeth she was cutting was just the icing on the cake.

"I'm so sorry about this," she said to Trent now, trying to keep the evil laugh inside her from exploding, "but I didn't know I was going to have to cover the hospital today, and Amanda is out of town visiting with her parents."

"So, what exactly do I need to do?" Trent asked as he looked down at Maggie, who was still in her sleeper, with a good amount of oatmeal smeared on her face, her nose crusty with the mucus caused by her teething.

"You'll be fine," she said. "I've laid her clothes out in her room, and her lunch and her supper are in the fridge."

"Supper?" he asked.

"You know how deliveries are—some of them take hours, and there's no way for me to know when I'll get off. But don't worry—I'll be relieved early enough in the morning that you can make your shift tomorrow. You did say you were working Sunday, didn't you?"

"Uh, yeah… Sunday," Trent said.

Had the man's skin paled, or was that just wishful thinking?

"You'll be fine, Trent," she said.

Reaching down to hug her little girl, she took a second to make sure she didn't have a temperature. Maggie had never been one to run a fever while teething, but there was always a first time. She had no doubt that her daughter would be safe with Trent—she just wasn't sure if Trent would survive the day with the cranky toddler.

* * *

Trent looked down at the little girl holding on to his leg. Had she just wiped her nose on his jeans? This child, dressed in some kind of one-piece jumper, with food caked on her mouth, looked nothing like the Maggie he knew. Picking her up in his arms, he made another discovery: she smelled worse than she looked. The first order of business would have to be cleaning her up.

After fighting with her to get her face washed, taking off her dirty sleep outfit seemed a breeze. Putting new clothes on his niece was another matter. He tried all the tricks he knew from his practice. The tickle move he used before giving shots, his funny faces for after the shots, the calm voice he had learned to use with stressed-out kids.

Nothing in his box of tricks worked. It seemed the child was a nudist at heart and had no desire to wear any clothes. By the time he'd managed to get a clean diaper and a shirt on her, he gave up the battle. If running around half dressed made the child happy, so be it.

"I surrender to Princess Maggie," he said, then bowed his head to the toddler.

Maggie giggled at him, then ran to get a little plastic and crystal crown that was sitting on a small bookcase. She stopped and looked through the books stacked in piles, then pulled one out, sending the rest of them tumbling to the ground. Walking over to where he sat on the floor, she sat down on his lap and handed him a book.

He looked at the title. "A princess book for a princess?" he said. "I can do this."

Opening the pink sparkly book, he wasn't surprised to see a young girl dressed all in pink wearing a crown. He started to read.

Four books later he noticed Maggie's eyes drooping. Closing the book, he carefully got off the floor, trying not to disturb the sleepy baby. Laying her down in her crib, he tiptoed out of the room and smiled. What had he been so afraid of? Taking care of Maggie was nothing he couldn't handle.

He had just shut the door when the crying began.

Lana opened the door and stared at the chaos of her living room. Every toy Maggie owned had to be in that room—plus what looked like half the clothes from her dresser. She leaned down to pick up a large stuffed elephant that was in her way, then froze.

Stretched out on her couch was Trent—a sound asleep Trent. He held her sleeping daughter on top of him, with one of his arms laid protectively around her.

While wide-awake Trent, with his powerful frame and those mesmerizing blue eyes of his, was a seductive temptation even to her, this version of the man took her breath away. Thick, dark lashes lay resting on copper-toned skin, while lips usually turned up in a smile were relaxed in soft invitation.

She'd felt those lips against hers. She bent down closer. Had they really been that warm? That firm?

Bright blue eyes stared up at her and she jerked away from him. Heaven help her—had she really been about to kiss him? No, of course not. She'd never do anything like that.

"I need to put Maggie down in her crib," she said, trying to keep her voice even while her heart tried to come out of her chest.

Lifting Maggie up into her arms, she held her tight against her racing heart as she carried her into her room and laid her in her crib. She took a minute to catch her breath, then walked back into the living room where she found Trent sitting up and rubbing the back of his neck.

"I can't believe you did that," he said.

"What?" she said. Her heart sped up. Had he caught her?

"You got her to stay in her crib," he said.

She watched him walk toward the door, shoulders slumped and feet all but dragging, and said a silent thank-you to the sleeping Maggie.

"Just one of those tricks you learn when you're a mother," she said.

"You're a good mother, Lana," he said. "I just want you to know that. This isn't about me not thinking you can take care of Maggie."

"Then *what*, Trent? What *is* it about if not what's best for Maggie?"

She stilled as Trent's hand came up to her face. He ran the back of his hand down one cheek, then cupped her chin. He pulled her to him and laid on her lips a kiss so soft that she wondered if she'd imagined it.

He pulled away, a half-smile on his lips, and walked out the door.

As the door shut behind him she took a deep breath and let her body relax. From what she had seen she'd have to say that operation Teach Trent a Lesson about Parenthood had been a success—but would it be enough?

She still had so many unanswered questions. She knew that Trent's guilt concerning his brother's death was part of what was driving him to seek custody of Maggie, but she couldn't help but think there was something he was keeping from her—something important that would explain everything.

Trent sat in his car and watched as other employees came and went from the staff entrance to the hospital. So it all was about to hit the fan. The text he'd received from his lawyer that morning had been short, but to the point.

He looked down to read it one more time.

Time running out. Getting pressure. Must address other parts of your brother's will which includes your father. Will is set to go into probate this week.

His plan had been so simple. Go to Florida. Get child. Protect child from his father. Show the old man that he didn't have the power to control everyone's life anymore. So simple—and yet it had turned so complicated. And that complication was named Lana. Watching her interact with his niece had changed everything.

He never should have come here. He should have stayed far away from both Maggie and Lana and had his lawyer handle everything. But it was too late. He had got involved and now he had to take control of the situation.

He knew his next move should be to have his lawyer start applying pressure to the courts to get this thing done, but he had been dragging his feet. He was normally a very decisive man, but suddenly he couldn't determine a plan of action that he felt comfortable with.

His knew his father would be on this before he even left the probate hearing. He needed to come up with a new plan. One that was sure to protect his niece. And although he had ignored the social worker's earlier comment, about Maggie needing both him *and* Lana, after Ms. Nelson had shared her concerns with him he had caught himself considering her observation.

After taking care of Maggie all by himself, he had to admit that caring for a toddler was going to be harder than he had first considered. Oh, he could hire a nanny to take care of Maggie, but that didn't sit right with him. That wasn't what he wanted for his niece.

Possibilities entered his thoughts and he mentally made

notes. Maybe instead of fighting Lana he could find a way for them to work together. With all the force of his father's lawyers about to descend on them, he had to come up with a plan soon. He didn't have just Maggie to consider—he had to protect Lana too.

Getting out of the car and heading in to work, he willed himself to put everything behind him as he walked into the cool air of the hospital. He prided himself in being able to give his patients his complete attention and he wouldn't let anything get in the way of their care and safety. He'd deal with everything else after his shift.

CHAPTER SEVEN

"I WASN'T EXPECTING YOU," Lana said as she entered her office to find her lawyer, Nathan, sitting in one of the three chairs that circled her desk.

It had only been a few days since she and Trent had met with the social worker and she really hadn't expected to hear any news for at least another week.

"Thought I'd stop and see if you wanted to go out to lunch," Nathan said, and then he saw the sandwich she had laid out on her desk. "But I guess you have that covered."

She had planned a quick lunch and then to use an afternoon free of appointments to catch up on her charting. She had been leaving the office as early as possible the last few days, in order to spend every minute possible with Maggie. The number of file entries she needed to make were beginning to pile up and she had to get caught up. Being behind at work was just one more thing to stress over and she had all the stress she needed right now.

"I have a feeling that I'm not going to feel like eating after all," she said, after taking a seat behind her desk.

Nathan's wife had been one of her first patients when she'd begun her midwifery career. But that didn't explain why he'd shown up here instead of calling. Warning bells started going off in her head, making it almost impossible for her to remain in her seat.

"There's no way you came down here just on the off-chance that you might catch me for lunch," she said. "Especially with having to fight through the noon traffic."

Lana forced her hands to relax on her chair and tried to practice the deep breathing from the labor classes she taught. She had found in the last few days that it helped her get through those times when thoughts of losing Maggie started to overwhelm her.

"So, either you have some really good news that you couldn't wait to share with me or you have some really bad news you didn't want to give me over the phone."

"I got a call from Karen Nelson today that I wanted to talk to you about," Nathan said.

"And here comes the really bad news, I take it?" She sat up straight and braced herself for the blow. "Go ahead. I can take it."

"She's received a call from a lawyer in Houston about Maggie," Nathan said.

She had been wrong. She hadn't been ready for that bombshell at all.

"Trent has hired a new lawyer?" Lana asked.

"No, this one represents Trent's father," Nathan said.

Lana felt the pain of prickling needles shoot through her body as the shock of Nathan's statement hit her. *Maggie's grandfather.* Why hadn't she considered this? Of course the power of two Montgomerys would be stronger than just one. It was taking all she had to fight against one of them—what chance did she have against two of them? How could Trent do this to her?

"Karen Nelson just wanted to give us a heads-up," Nathan said. Leaning over her, he gave Lana a look that would have had her running if she hadn't known he was on her side. "We are going to *fight* this, Lana. I know I told you that we would have a hard time because of Trent's biological relationship, but we still have your history with Maggie. And the fact that the biological mother wanted you to adopt Maggie will play heavily on our side."

"But you know that when one of the biological family requests custody the court usually sides with them. Now there will be two. Two to one, Nathan."

Lana looked down to where her hands now gripped the armrests of her chair. So much for learning to deal with her stress. There was no way she was going to be able to ignore this hit. But Trent should have told her he was going to do this. They had agreed to be honest with each other, hadn't they? Even if there hadn't been any way to talk him out of it, he could have warned her. The fact that he hadn't told her caused an ache deep down inside her chest.

Suddenly, the butterflies that had been in her stomach for the last couple of weeks stopped doing jumping jacks. Now they seemed to have picked up pitchforks and were trying to fight their way out. A wave of nausea rolled over her and she made herself take a deep breath to calm her stomach.

Then a new emotion hit her. A burning anger boiled up from a stomach that only minutes ago had been ready to spew. How *dared* the man worm his way into her life and then blindside her this way?

The more she thought about it, the madder she got. Maybe it was time for her to show Trent that she was ready for a fight too.

When Nathan had finally quit trying to talk her out of rushing over to Trent's, he called his office and got the address for her. She wouldn't approach him at work, but if she had to hunt him down at his place she would do it.

After promising that she wasn't going to commit murder, she talked her lawyer into leaving the office. She hated it that the poor man would be worrying about needing to have bail posted for her for the rest of the day, but she knew that this was something she had to do.

Even if confronting Trent didn't get her anywhere, at least she'd feel better. She was tired of just sitting back and letting everybody else have a part in deciding her daughter's future. Maggie was *hers* and she wasn't going to just lie down and let somebody come down from Texas and take her child away from her.

She called the hospital and asked for Trent's schedule. Marty, the prenatal technician on duty, seemed suspicious about her needing the information, but with some sweet talk she managed to find out that Trent had gotten called in during the night and had been given the day off in exchange.

Marty was one of the quieter techs in the department, who normally just went about his business, but she would still be surprised if he didn't leak details of her call to the other techs in the department. She could expect a resurgence of gossip by the next time she was on the labor unit, but that was the least of her problems.

She had trusted Trent and he had let her down by pulling this last strategy on her. He needed to know that she wasn't going to be scared off by him and his father. If the Montgomerys wanted a fight she would give them one. What did she have to lose?

Just the most important person in her life—her daughter.

The ride over through bumper-to-bumper traffic just got her more ready for a fight. By the time she pulled up into the driveway of a two-story townhouse she was prepared to confront Trent.

She couldn't believe she had fallen for that sweet Texas

drawl of his and let down her guard. Okay, it hadn't been just that sexy accent he had. No, Trent had been blessed with the whole package. From his hard body to his sweet smile. She hadn't had a chance. Had that been the plan all the time? Was he just the front man for his father?

Yeah, the gloves were coming off now and she wasn't going to leave till she got some answers.

When ringing the doorbell didn't get a response she began pounding the decorative knocker on the front door. It didn't get any better results, but it sure did make her feel better. She had become a fountain of adrenaline, and she was about to spill over if she didn't get to burn it off soon.

Finally, she heard the door being unlocked and saw the knob turn. She was ready to blast Trent with everything she had when the door opened.

One look at the man standing in the foyer had her swallowing her words and forgetting her name. His inky dark hair was bed-tousled and his eyes, heavy with sleep, were seductive and inviting. His chest was bare and she followed the fine line of dark hair down his taut abs until it disappeared under a pair of silk sleeper pants that rode low on his hips and made no secret of the fact that he wore nothing under them.

He could have been born of any of the thousand fantasies that had filled her nights since meeting him. For a second she just stopped and drank him in as she thanked the fates that had seen fit to give her at least this moment of pleasure. How was she supposed to fight with this man when her whole body had suddenly melted into a puddle of need that had to be steaming up his front porch with its heat?

And then she remembered Maggie—sweet little Maggie who needed her so much.

She watched Trent scrub at his jaw as he tried to shake

off the remnants of sleep that seemed to be holding him captive. She could almost feel the rough sensation of the bristly stubble as it nuzzled her neck and tickled her chin.

Dreams, she reminded herself, those had just been dreams.

"Lana?" Trent said as he rubbed at his eyes, as if he was trying to get everything awake and operable. "Did I oversleep and miss something?"

"What…?" she said.

"Come in. Let me go change. I'll be right back." Trent said, and then turned to walk into his house.

Lana felt cool air hit her as she walked into the foyer. And after a couple steps into the room she felt herself surface from her lust-induced fog. This would never do. She couldn't keep letting him do this to her.

"Wait," she said as she caught up to him in a large room that opened into a modern stainless steel kitchen and a formal dining and living room. "Nathan told me about your father."

Trent stopped and turned back toward her. Was that remorse she saw in the pained expression on his face? For her? Or was it for himself? Did he regret that she had found out his plan? She wouldn't have known anything about his father's lawyer if the social worker hadn't informed Nathan. Maybe he had planned to throw her off by waiting till the court date to hit her with this news.

"Let me get some clothes on," Trent said, then turned to walk away.

Yeah, clothes. Clothes would be good. Maybe if the man covered up some of that inviting skin of his she would be able to think.

A glance around at the cool white-upholstered couches and off-white carpeting and walls had her imagining the damage one little toddler could do to a room like this. Images of Trent playing tea party with Maggie came to mind, and for a second she imagined a future with the three of them together, sharing lazy Sundays and evenings curled up together on the couch.

She shook her head, forcing the fantasies from her mind. She was happy with her daughter and their little block bungalow with its toy-strewn rooms. They had become a family. *Her* family. She wasn't going to let anyone destroy that. Not Trent and not his father.

But would the court see it the same way? She couldn't compete with all the things Trent and his family could give Maggie. She did okay in her midwife practice, and could certainly provide for Maggie, but looking around the expensively furnished room reminded her of the difference between her life and the Montgomerys'. It was just another thing where the judge could find her lacking.

"Ready to talk?" Trent asked as he walked into the room.

He had changed into a pair of worn jeans and a pale blue tee shirt but he'd left his feet bare, which gave him a casual look that did nothing to squash the desire she had felt for him earlier. She stared down at the long toes peeking out from the hem of his jeans. Who knew bare feet could be so sexy?

Lana shook her head. She was lusting after his toes? *Toes?* Someone really needed to come up with a vaccine she could take to keep her safe from this man. She had to snap out of it. She had to get back in control of herself. She had to get some answers.

"So what was the plan, Trent? Come to Florida and play nice with the little midwife while your father was back home putting together a legal team to fight me?" Lana asked.

The anger that had spurred her into hunting down Trent

had died somewhere between his opening the door and her walking into the house. She was so tired of playing games with him. Why couldn't he just be up-front with her? Didn't she deserve that?

He dropped his eyes for a minute, and then looked up as he rubbed the back of his neck. He looked more like a sheepish kid who had gotten caught with his hand in the cookie jar then a man who was trying to tear her world apart. How did he break her heart one minute and then rev it up the next? She felt as if she was being pulled in two when she was around him and she just couldn't keep going like this. Something had to give—and soon.

"I was going to call you and explain to you today…" Trent started. He ran his hands through his hair, then held them out to her. "Look… It's not what you think. I've tried to keep my father out of this. If anything, I've been trying to keep him out of Maggie's life—and yours."

"I don't understand," Lana said.

"Come sit down," Trent said as he reached for her hand.

She looked at the hand he held out to her. Another ploy? But one look at him had her doubting her earlier suspicions. He was pulling off the performance of his life if the pain she saw in his eyes was just an act. She knew better than to trust him, but still…

Trent sat, then pulled Lana down next to him. The warmth of her body eased the coldness that seeped into him whenever he had to deal with his old man. Her rigid posture told him she still didn't trust him. And could he blame her?

How much to tell her? He had to gain back her trust if there was any way for them to move on and do the right thing for his niece. She would need to be prepared for the force of his father's influence.

He had no doubt his father would be pulling out all the

stops now that he knew the conditions of Michael's will. Would she even understand what his father was like when it came to the family company? Of course it was more of an empire now. He had to give that to his father. The man had taken the small-time oil company his mother had inherited and made a multi-billion-dollar business out of it.

But how did he explain the dysfunction his father's obsession with the company had caused? He would have to start at the beginning. Digging into his past would be painful, but he had to make her understand what she was up against. What the two of them were up against.

"My parents came from totally different backgrounds. My mother was an only child and, while my grandparents weren't nearly as successful as my father has been with the oil company my Grandfather Lord started, she was well provided for. She went to all the right schools and had everything she wanted."

He felt Lana relax against him and some of the tension in his own body eased. Maybe he would be able to win her trust back. Maybe she would realize he hadn't had any choice other than to try to protect his niece.

"But my dad was a different story. Grandpa Montgomery worked for Grandfather Lord out on the ranch. He worked hard, and he had a wife and four kids. From what I've been told, my dad grew up helping his dad out with ranch chores," he said.

"So your parents grew up together?" Lana asked.

She was so close now that he could feel the vibration when she spoke. It was nice. He wasn't a man usually comfortable with someone in his personal space, but this felt good. Safe.

"Yeah, they did. Eventually they grew up, and I guess they fell in love and married."

"You *guess*?" she asked.

"I don't know. I think they loved each other at first. I do remember some times when I was young when they seemed happy together, but in the end all I remember is their fighting."

And his mother crying. He remembered his mother crying and his dad storming out of the house.

"My uncle has told me that my father buried himself in the business because he needed to prove to himself and the company that he could handle it."

"It couldn't have been easy for him to come into the company that way," said Lana.

"No—knowing where my father came from, I'm sure there were often people making comments about him marrying into the company."

His uncle had said as much on the many times he had taken sides with his brother when Trent had complained about his father ignoring Michael's problems.

"I'm sure it was hard at first, but by the time my mother died he had doubled the company's size and he should have been able to spare some time for Michael."

"You say Michael—what about you? You were just a boy yourself when your mother passed. Didn't you need a father too?"

"Michael was the youngest. He needed him more."

Trent looked away when Lana responded with a snort.

"You've got to understand… Michael was the baby of the family."

"What you're saying is that he was left to do whatever he wanted and there was no adult there to hold him accountable," she said.

"Unfortunately, yes," Trent agreed. "And it just got worse as he got older. I tried to help him, but he wouldn't listen to me. By the time my father decided to take an interest in him he was already in trouble. That's when things got really bad at home."

"Why?" she asked.

Trent felt his body tense. Talking about his brother was difficult, but it had to be done.

"Michael got into some trouble with the law and suddenly my father decided he needed to take control of the situation." He hated the bitterness he could hear in his voice. "By that time I had gone off to college and made it plain that I wasn't going to follow in the old man's footsteps. I guess my father knew that his only chance to pass on the company was through Michael."

"And Michael wasn't interested?"

"No, actually, just the opposite. For a while it looked like he was going to straighten out his life. But it seemed the harder he tried the more my father wanted from him. I think eventually he just gave up."

"What happened to Michael, Trent?"

"It was just too much for him. He started playing around with drugs. Street drugs, prescription drugs… I think he tried them all. Before I knew it he was hooked. We sent him to the best rehabs in the country, but in the end the drugs won. One night he just took too many and that was the end."

"Was it an accident or…?" Lana reached over and wrapped her arms around him.

"I don't know." But, God, how he hoped it had been an accident. Losing his brother to drugs had torn him up inside. Thinking that his brother had ended his own life was more than he could bear.

"I'm so sorry that you lost Michael, but what does this have to do with me and Maggie?"

"My father likes to take control of situations. It's what he did with my brother—what he tried to do with my mother. He'll want to take over Maggie's life too. He's powerful, Lana. He has the means to take Maggie away from you and I'm afraid he won't be satisfied until he does."

Trent felt tears on his shoulder where she had laid her head. He knew the tears were as much for him as they were for her. That was his Lana. She had a big heart. One that she had opened up to a young mother and a little baby. And now he was tearing her heart out when he should be thanking her for taking that little baby in and giving her a home.

Turning, he hugged her close to him, then slipped his hand under her chin. He began wiping his thumb across the smoothness of her wet cheek and then replaced her tears with soft kisses that led down to her mouth. Taking small sips of her lips, he worked to draw her out of her sorrow. It tore him apart to see her hurting.

"I'm sorry too," he whispered into her mouth. "I'm so sorry."

"Then show me," she whispered as she began kissing him back. "Take away the pain…make it all go away."

Lana let go of the hurt and the worry and gave in to her body's demands. Somehow it had separated her desire for Trent from her fear. She needed to forget all the pain, all the fear that haunted her every second of every day. She needed him to satisfy this ache, this itch, this all-consuming desire he made her feel that left her waking each night tangled in her sheets, frustrated and hurting.

She always did the right thing, the safe thing. Just for once she wanted to be able to do what she wanted without worrying about the consequences. To let go of all the reasons this was wrong and allow herself the freedom to just enjoy the moment.

She plunged into him.

Pleasure coursed through her at the feel of his hot, wet mouth. He tasted of spicy mint, and as his tongue circled hers she let the last remnants of anger leave her body. There was nothing to hold her back now. She combed her hands through his thick curls, then tightened her grip to anchor his lips against hers.

His hands stroked up and down her back in a rhythm that matched the mating of their tongues. He deepened his kiss, then ran his hands lower until they cupped her butt and lifted her up over him. She felt him long and hard against her belly and her body answered his with a wet need that pooled between her legs.

"Ah, Lana…" he groaned as he pulled back.

She reached for the bottom of his shirt, then ran her hands up inside till she found his nipples. She let her thumbs caress the twin nubs till they puckered for her. She felt his hands undo the clasp of her bra, then circle back around to her freed breasts. Her breath caught inside her when she felt him cup their weight. The feel of his coarse hands against her nipples had her arching into him. She'd wanted this—no, *needed* this since that first kiss in the locker room.

She let her hands trail lower as they followed the soft line of hair down his chest. The feel of his abs tightening at her touch urged her on to her target. She felt him tense, heard him moan as she teased the skin along his waistband. For the first time in her life she felt power in lovemaking and it was exhilarating. Trent made her feel like a real, whole woman—not broken like Joe had made her feel.

Yes, Trent had been with more experienced women then her—women who would have known how to attract and satisfy him—but there wasn't any way that a woman had ever wanted him more than she did at that moment. Maybe she had never learned the art of seduction, but she wasn't going to let her old insecurities stop her. She was too far gone now. No way was she going to let her feelings of inadequacy spoil this. No more waiting for what she wanted. She would take it this time.

Surprising herself, she let her hand wander down to his fly, where she let her nails run up and down over the teeth of the zipper. Feeling the hard ridge beneath the clothing, she teased herself as much as him—until she could no longer stand the thought of being this close yet still not touching him. She undid the button of his jeans and eased the zipper down.

Feeling the pressure ease as Lana lowered the zipper of his jeans, Trent fought for control. Backing away, he grabbed her hand, stilling its motion while at the same time pressing it against the length of him. Resting his head against her forehead, he took a deep breath…and then another. He needed to gain control or he would end up taking her on the floor where they stood.

What was it about her that heated his blood so hot that he couldn't think when she was around? As she closed her hand around him his whole body tensed with a need he had never known before. This woman, with her pure heart and sweet curvaceous body, undid him. If he didn't get her hands off him right then it would all be over. His body was going to go up in flames any minute.

He removed her hand and held it tightly in his own. They had to slow down. He needed to think.

Looking down into her wild green eyes, he was amazed by the trust he saw there. She was amazing in her capacity to love and nurture. It was unlike anything he had ever seen or known. The thought of being the one who was able to gift her with what she needed right then humbled him. He felt his own need as it pounded into his heart. He knew he wasn't worthy of the honor, but he felt no shame in his desire for her. Maybe in this one thing they could come together and give each other the comfort they both needed right now.

Keeping his eyes connected with hers, he threaded his fingers through hers and drew her up from the couch. He led her down the hall into his bedroom, where there would be no one but him and her, choosing to grab this precious time for themselves. He had to do this right. Things were so complicated between them now and he couldn't mess this up.

He shut the door behind them and turned to her.

"We leave everything, everybody, on the other side of that door. Can you do that, Lana?" he asked as he closed the space between them.

Lana forced herself to concentrate on his words. There would be no going back from here.

Sex had never been something she took lightly, but she had spent the last two years feeling like only half a woman, and she didn't want to feel like that anymore. She knew the intimacy of this moment would change her, touch her deep down in places she had kept guarded since Joe, but she knew it would be worth it.

Sometimes you just had to trust blindly. There could be no love without trust.

Love? Was she that far gone?

Fear suddenly flamed inside her at the thought of loving Trent, but then she remembered his words. He had told her to leave everything outside the door for just these few moments they had together. Could she? Should she?

"Yes," she heard herself say.

No matter how much her brain questioned the insanity

of this, there was no other option for her. Both her body and her heart needed him. Right then, right there.

He led her over to his rumpled bed and she watched his face as she released his hand and backed up toward the bed, removing her shirt and letting it fall to the floor, following it with her bra and skirt.

As the afternoon sunlight filtered through the closed blinds she stood there in only a white cotton thong. She should have felt cold and exposed, but as Trent walked towards her she felt the warmth of his eyes as they covered her body. She reached for his hand and led him with her to the bed.

When his arms circled her she let all her misgivings go. She pulled him down and then his hands were everywhere as they stroked and kissed. She let herself explore his arms and chest as she returned his burning kisses, reaching lower until she was circling him with her hands. She thrilled at the hard length that proved his desire for her.

His hands came between them and he began stroking her. She spread her legs to welcome him. Sensations flooded through her as her hips rocked against the thick hard length of him. And then he was there, thrusting inside her with a rhythm she fought to match until she was drenched with sweat.

He arched and stiffened inside her as his body rushed to its climax. Then he reached between them once again and with one shattering stroke she joined him.

Everything around them flew away as they held on to each other. For a brief second she felt them suspended in time, where nothing existed except for the two of them. And then they were crashing back down—together.

Lana glanced at the alarm clock sitting on the nightstand. She would have to leave soon. Amanda had a night class so she would have to pick up Maggie at daycare. She looked across the room, taking in the same simple white color scheme that had been present in what she had seen of the rest of the house.

There was nothing in the room that hinted of Trent's personal taste. White walls, off-white carpet, even shabby-chic white furniture throughout the room. The only thing with any color was the natural oak window trim and the door. The door that kept the world away…the door that allowed them to escape from all the reasons why they shouldn't be here, together, right now.

Wasn't that what everyone had to do sometimes? Just shut everything out and escape into a world where they felt secure and safe, away from all their troubles and free of all their responsibilities, even if it was just for a short time? Was it so bad that they had grabbed this little bit of time for themselves?

She thought of her agreement with Trent. *Leave everything, everybody, on the other side of that door.* But what happened when the door opened? When once again they found themselves in the heated fight that was turning them both inside out? What happened when they both had to face the fact that they were on opposite sides in a battle that had the highest stakes possible and that only one of them could win?

"Shh…" Trent said, and he shifted and drew her closer, trailing his hands through her hair, soothing her with his touch.

Letting go of a breath she hadn't known she was holding, she snuggled down into him. Resting her head on his chest and listening to the steady beat of his heart, she let her body recede into that calm place where Trent had taken her.

She just needed a few more minutes to enjoy the feel

of him. Enough time for her to capture this memory. She would wrap it up and take it with her. And when things got bad she would take it out and it would remind her that at least she'd had this moment. This little bit of time when life had been right between the two of them.

Trent combed his hands through the thick blond mass of hair that lay across his chest, then bent his head and took a deep breath. The soft scent of honeysuckle filled him, making him smile. It was a scent that he had come to recognize as Lana. It was fresh and feminine, with a touch of sweetness that was guileless in its simplicity and so like Lana, who had no desire to be anything but herself.

He had always enjoyed the smell of the little yellow flowers that grew wild on the rickety old fence that lined the entrance to the ranch. Though he could remember many an argument between his dad and mom about the trailing plants, with his dad calling them weeds and fussing about having to clear them every year after they'd died out. But his mom would always just ignore his dad and go right on picking the vines and sticking them into the old Mason jar that she'd kept sitting on the kitchen window sill.

Things were different around the ranch now, but the same old fence still stood, and every year the honeysuckle would grow back. He'd caught his dad staring out the window and looking at the fragrant yellow flowers once, and wondered if possibly the old man was thinking about the wife he had lost.

"I was eight and Michael only four when my mother left and never came back."

He felt Lana turn to him, but he knew he couldn't look down at her. He had promised her that they would keep everything out of the bedroom, but he could fill the world creeping in and knew they would soon have to return to their separate lives.

"She just walked out on you?"

"No. Well, not exactly," he said.

Once more he pulled her up close to him and turned her so that he could rest his chin on the top of her head. He let the scent of her soothe the raw hurt he felt every time he thought of that night twenty-four years ago.

"Mom and Dad had had a bad fight that day. He'd found where she'd hidden her whiskey bottle and had thrown it out the back door. She'd screamed at him about going through her things and he'd hollered back that she had promised to quit drinking. That she had promised there wouldn't be any more alcohol around the house. Then she started crying and telling him that he didn't understand. It was the same argument that they had almost daily. They argued about him always being at work and her always being left alone, but this time it was worse.

"Dad told Mom he'd have her put in a rehab clinic if she didn't stop drinking, and that's when my mom threatened to take the company away from him. My dad finally walked out and I thought things would be okay. That he'd come back in a little while and Momma would tell him that she was sorry and beg him to forgive her. Say that she'd try harder. It was how all their fights ended. They'd hug and kiss and everything would go on just fine."

Trent stopped. He had forgotten about those times when they had made up—the times when they had disappeared for an hour or two alone. Had they been happy together then?

"Your mother was an alcoholic," Lana stated.

"Yes. Looking back now, I can see all the signs. All the times she slept through the day, never getting up to check on either me or Michael. Then there were the times when I would find her hugging the toilet, too sick to hold her head up."

"But you couldn't have known what was wrong with her then. You were just a child," Lana said.

Trent clasped the hand she'd entangled with his. He hadn't really ever talked about that night with anyone. Not even Michael, who had been way too young to understand what was happening at the time.

"No, I didn't know what was wrong—but I did know something wasn't right," he said. "And that day when Momma left us home alone I knew she shouldn't have gone. I knew that moms didn't go off and leave their kids all alone like that. And when it got to be dark and she still hadn't come home, and Michael started crying that he was scared and wanted his momma, I got real mad. I got mad at the both of them."

He'd been scared too. Scared that his parents had both gone off and forgotten about them. But he hadn't told Michael he was scared. He'd had to be strong and take care of Michael.

"Momma said she'd be right back. She was going to run to the store and then she'd be right back. She said that I needed to take care of my little brother because I was the oldest, but that she wouldn't be long. Just a few minutes… that's all it would take her."

Trent remembered how relieved he'd been when he'd seen the lights from his dad's rusted old pick-up pull into the drive. But then his dad had found out that their mom wasn't home and that she'd left them all alone. He'd never seen his dad so mad. He'd been scared all over again. He'd tried to tell his dad that Momma had just gone to the store and that she'd be right back.

Then Harry from the sheriff's office had driven up.

He'd seen his daddy shake his head as tears ran down his weathered face.

That was the last time he'd seen his dad show any type of emotion for anything except his damn oil company. His father hadn't even cried at Michael's funeral—but then neither had he. Just how much like his father *was* he?

"Something happened to her, didn't it?" Lana asked in a voice that could barely be called a whisper.

"They found her car where she hit a tree, but I found out later—when I was older—that she had been thrown out of it," Trent said. "The accident report said that they found an open bottle of Jack Daniels on the seat."

For a few minutes they just lay there in silence as they held each other. Lana couldn't imagine what it had been like for the two little boys, all alone and scared one minute, while they waited for their momma to come home, and then the next to be told she was never coming back.

They'd both been so young, and there was no doubt that they'd been affected by the events of that night. Even Michael, at four, had to have known that their mom was supposed to *be* there. That she was supposed to take care of them. And her asking Trent to watch his brother so that she could go out and buy alcohol had been so irresponsible that it made her wonder if there had been other times when she had put the bottle before her two little boys.

"After my mom died and my great-aunt came to live with us my father devoted all his time to the oil company. Before long it had grown to one of the largest in the state," he said. "That's when he really changed."

Lana felt his hand under her chin, strong but tender as he raised her head up to his.

"The company was the center of his life. It became impossible to please him. No matter what Michael or I did, it was never good enough. By the time I started applying to colleges I knew that I didn't want to be involved with the family business, so I decided to go into medicine. My father has never forgiven me for that decision. He doesn't like it when things don't go his way."

He was *warning* her about his father. "You're not involved with him against me in the custody battle, are you?" she asked.

"No, I'm not," he said. "And now you know all my family's dirty secrets."

A chill washed over her. "We all have secrets," she said, pulling the sheet up higher.

"And you, Lana? Do you have secrets?" he asked.

The outside world was starting to seep into the room and none of it was pretty. He had shared so much with her. Was it not right that she did the same with him? Where things would go between them after this she didn't know, but she knew she needed to be honest about everything with him.

"I need to tell you something," she said, then swallowed.

She felt the slightest tightening of his muscles against her skin.

"Okay," he said.

He settled back in the bed, curling himself around her and pulling her against him, as if protecting her. If only he could... But there were some hurts that even Prince Charming, or in this case a sexy cowboy doctor, couldn't fix.

"When I was sixteen I went to my pediatrician for a school physical and he found a cancerous mass in my abdomen. I was lucky they found it early, but the chemo and radiation..." She took a deep breath, reaching for the strength she needed. "They damaged my ovaries. I can never have children, Trent."

They lay there with nothing but silence between them for a minute, Trent still wrapped around her.

"I'm so sorry, Lana," Trent said. "Cancer is such a harsh disease, and you were so young."

She shrugged her shoulders and pushed herself up, pulling herself away from him. The last thing she wanted Trent to feel for her was pity.

"It was a long time ago. I just thought you should know."

She needed to leave.

She wiped the tears away from her face and reached for the alarm clock to bring it closer to her. Propped up against a crystal lamp was a small picture of her and Maggie as they played in the sand on their trip to the beach. She hadn't known he was taking it—which was a good thing. With her hair soaking wet from their dip in the cold salt water and her face bare of everything except the red hint of sun on the tip of her nose, it was not a good picture of her.

Of course he had been taking pictures of Maggie that day—she had probably just happened to be in this one. But the fact that he had it there, where he would see it every night before he went to sleep, helped ease the pain of knowing that she would never be in this bedroom, behind this door, again.

"I've got to go pick up Maggie," she said as she climbed out of the bed.

Her body immediately felt cold, and she knew it had nothing to do with the air-conditioning in the house. All the warmth that had comforted her earlier was now gone.

She picked up her clothes from where they had been dropped earlier and told herself that everything would be okay between them. They were adults. They had both agreed to keep this time separate from everything else in their life and they would do it. Knowing what she did now about Trent and his father's relationship, there was no doubt that the two of them weren't working together against her, but that still didn't make him an ally. They were still on opposite sides of what was best for Maggie.

"Lana, I'm sorry. About everything. I'm *so* sorry."

Looking back at him, she saw pain in his eyes. And as she left to go back into the world outside she knew that somehow nothing and yet everything had changed since she had walked inside that bedroom.

Trent watched as Lana left the room. His heart went out to the sixteen-year-old girl who had been through so much and then had so much taken away from her after surviving cancer. He had seen the pain that still haunted her eyes when she'd talked about not being able to have children.

Looking over at the picture he had placed on the nightstand, he was hit with how unfair it was that the beautiful woman in the photo, who had so much love to give, and who had helped so many women as they labored to bring their children into the world, would never know what it was like to bring her own child into the world.

And as he turned over in his bed he was hit with the realization that his bed felt cold and empty without her.

CHAPTER EIGHT

IT HAD BEEN two days and thirteen hours since she had walked out of Trent's home. She had been waiting for him to contact her. She'd believed him when he'd said he wasn't involved with his father's plans, but she knew there was something going on between him and his father that he was holding back from her. There was a bitterness in Trent's voice whenever he spoke of his father that was inconsistent with everything else she thought she knew about him.

She decided to stop by Labor and Delivery after rounding on her patients on the recovery floor, hoping not only to see him, but also to talk to the charge nurse about the gossip Amanda had heard earlier that week, concerning her and Trent. She needed to address some of the tongue-wagging that was going around the hospital. She could have approached the people she thought were spreading the stories around, but she felt it would be better to have the charge nurse remind them to watch what they were saying.

Arriving on the unit, she found the nurses' station empty, which was never a good sign. Recognizing the flashing emergency light that was going off over Labor Room Five, she sprinted down the hall.

"Lana, we need some help," said Laurie, who was the day charge, as soon as she saw Lana enter the room.

Lana recognized the two nurses who were trying to

strip the clothes off a pale woman whose rounded belly indicated that she was due at any time.

"What do you need me to do?" Lana offered as she approached the bed.

The metallic smell hit her before she saw the blood that pooled between the patient's legs. The young woman looked to be of Asian descent and she seemed to be pleading in a language that Lana couldn't understand.

"What's she saying?" she asked as she grabbed the heart monitor and applied it to the swollen belly.

"Save my baby," said the man standing at the other side of the bed, holding her hand. "She doesn't want to lose our baby."

Lana touched the woman's abdomen and felt the hard tone of the uterus. Looking further down, she saw the outline of a faded scar. "Did she have surgery when she had another baby?" she asked the man.

"Yes—with our three sons. She was supposed to have another C-section."

"Ruptured uterus?" Laurie asked as she passed her a small hand-held ultrasound.

"No, I think her placenta is abrupting," Lana said as she looked at the black and white screen.

The labor monitors started to beep and the fetal heartbeat began tracing across the screen. It was lower than normal, but if they got the baby out fast it would have a chance.

The blood pressure machine went off too, and the cuff on one of the patient's arms began to tighten.

"Who's the doctor on call?" Lana asked as they worked to turn the patient and remove the rest of her clothes.

"Dr. Bradley and he's on his way," Laurie said. "We've already called the nursery and Dr. Montgomery is on his way over too."

The charge nurse finished inserting an intravenous needle and hung a large bag of fluids to help replace some of the volume of blood the patient was losing.

"We need to get her to the operating room *now*," Lana said as she looked at the low blood pressure reading that flashed up on the monitor. "I'll assist. Where's anesthesia?"

"Right here," said Debra, the nurse anesthetist, as she walked into the room. She grabbed a pair of gloves on her way to the bed when she saw the blood that was quickly filling the clean pads they'd just applied.

"Okay, let's roll," the charge nurse ordered her staff.

While Debra rushed to get her equipment ready, Lana stopped to put her arm around the father of the baby. She walked him out to the small waiting room outside the operating theater. The man had begun to tremble the minute he had left his wife's side and she knew he needed to sit down.

Lana was very familiar with the feeling of helplessness that the man had to be feeling, with both his wife and his child's life in danger. Bending down so that they were on eye level, she took his hand and gave it a squeeze. "What's her name?" Lana asked.

"Joy. Her name is Joy," he said.

"Is she allergic to anything that you know of?" she asked.

"No," he answered, then looked up at her with dark troubled eyes. "Will she be okay?"

"We're going to take good care of her," Lana said, then rose to her feet and headed for the door. "I'll let you know any news as soon as I can."

"And the baby? Will the baby be okay?" she heard him ask as she was leaving the room.

She wanted to ignore the question, knowing that her answer wouldn't bring the relief that this father wanted, but that was the cowardly way out and what he needed was honesty. He needed to be prepared in case the worst happened.

"I don't know," she answered quietly, then turned and headed for the scrub sink.

The operating room would have appeared to be in chaos to anyone who didn't know that every one of the staff members there was competently doing their job. As she dried her hands on the sterile towel one of the techs handed her, Lana turned in a circle so that one of the nurses could tie her up in a sterile gown.

Checking the fetal monitors, she saw that the fetal heart tones, which had been dipping down with the contractions earlier, were remaining low. They needed to hurry and get the baby out—but they had no choice but to wait for the surgeon.

She looked over as the swinging doors opened and Trent walked in with the neonatal team. They went straight over to the warmer unit and began setting up the resuscitation equipment. They had already opened the crash cart so that they would be ready as soon as the baby was handed to them. This was a situation where a few wasted seconds could be a matter of life or death.

"What do we have?" Trent asked as he moved over to her.

She had thought she would be uncomfortable the next time she saw Trent after their afternoon together, but right now all she felt was relief at the sight of him. If there was anything that could be done for this baby when they delivered it she knew Trent would do it.

"Patient's name is Joy. Past C-section times three... placenta abruption on arrival. She doesn't speak much English," she said.

She watched as he moved over to the neonatal team

and started giving orders. And the whole time, as people turned the woman from side to side, stuck monitor pads on her arms and chest and applied all the necessary monitors, she kept pleading with that sad voice for her child's life.

"Is everyone ready?" asked Dr. Bradley as he entered the OR and reached for a sterile towel to dry his hands.

Lana's breath came a little easier at the sight of the OB doctor entering the room. As the circulating nurse reviewed the patient's history and her presentation at the hospital he gowned and gloved. He called for the patient's name and then did a time-out, to assure everyone was aware of the procedure and the patient.

While everyone in the room listened to Laurie's report the staff positioned the instruments where they could easily be handed to the doctor. Debra from Anesthesia was injected some medicine into Joy's IV and then inserted the endotracheal tube, so that she would be able to control her breathing while she was under anesthesia.

Seconds after the team was in position Dr. Bradley made an incision into the abdomen. Lana operated the suction, trying to clear all the blood and fluid so that the doctor could see as he made his way through to the uterus. He cut into the uterus and removed a pale, still baby girl.

Lana remembered that Joy's husband had said they had three boys at home. This mother must be so excited about having a little girl. Lana felt the mask that covered her nose and mouth become damp as she watched Trent and the neonatal team begin to work on the quiet baby.

"We're not finished here, people," Dr. Bradley said, getting back the attention of his team. "Let them work on the baby. Our job is to fix this momma."

Lana quickly returned her attention to assisting while the doctor delivered the placenta and then repaired the uterus and closed the incision. Meanwhile Trent had quickly intubated the small baby and was working on getting intravenous access.

Finally the doctor closed the last layer of the earlier incision and the staff could relax.

"I have to go check on the staff," Laurie said as she pulled off her mask. "Melody, you take over here."

"I've got her," the nurse responded.

Lana moved over next to Trent as he finished putting a line through the umbilical cord. One of the respiratory team continued to bag the baby, but her color was still a dusky blue.

"Will she make it?" she asked him.

"I don't know," he answered. "Her heartbeat is still a little slow, but we've ordered blood to transfuse. The sooner we can get that in her the better."

A shrill alarm sounded and Trent quickly turned back as the monitor showed the baby's oxygen saturation falling rapidly.

"Rate?" he asked the nurse who was listening to the baby's heart with a stethoscope.

"Fifty-six," she answered.

"Start compressions," he ordered. "Where's that blood?"

"It's on its way up from the lab," another nurse said. "I'm drawing up the epinephrine now."

"Go ahead and give it," he said.

Lana watched as yet another nurse walked in with a small packet of blood and began setting up the tubing. She waited as all the nurses coordinated their compressions and ventilations, feeling helpless but knowing there was nothing she could do but pray for a miracle.

"Pulse-check," Trent ordered.

"One hundred and twenty," said the nurse checking the pulse.

"Let's go," he said to the team, and they rushed out with the new baby.

Lana looked down at the blood on her scrubs. Unless she wanted to give her staff and her patients a scare, she would need a new pair before she went back to her office.

She pulled out her beeper and was surprised to find that it had only been thirty minutes since she had walked onto the unit. It always felt so much longer when you knew there was a life depending on your speedy response.

Lana was just stepping out of the locker room when Trent walked in. He couldn't get his thoughts off the woman who had been on the operating table. He knew that she would be physically okay once she got into Recovery. It was the woman's emotional reaction to hearing that her baby was in critical condition that would affect the young mother the most.

Would she be able to cope if her baby didn't make it? What about Lana? Would *she* be able to cope if she lost Maggie?

It was thoughts of Lana that had sent him here, looking for her.

"The baby?" she asked when she saw him.

"Now that we've got a transfusion going her color is better, but it's too soon to know how she'll do. I just wanted to grab some new scrubs," he said.

"'Save my baby. Don't let me lose my baby,'" Lana quoted as she leaned against the locker room wall. "She kept telling us that. And I can't lose *my* baby, Trent. I can't lose Maggie."

He felt his heart break when Lana looked up at him, her eyes brimming with tears.

"Don't, Lana…" he said as he came over and put his arms around her. Pulling her down to the closest bench, he rubbed his hands up and down her arms, where goose-bumps peppered her skin.

"I don't know if I'm crying for her or for me," Lana said as she wiped away her tears with the back of her hands. "Selfish, huh? To be thinking about myself when that poor woman doesn't know if her baby is going to live or die?"

Trent moved her hands out of the way, then used the pads of his own thumbs to wipe at her tears. How could she ask that? She was the most unselfish person he had ever met.

He had watched her with her patients. She could be falling-down tired, but she remained at their side no matter how long they needed her. She thought of everybody's needs—even his—before herself. She only asked for one thing for herself. To be able to raise the little girl she had taken into her heart.

"No, I don't think you're selfish. I'm surprised you haven't broken down before now," Trent said as he held her face between his hands. "Look at me," he said when she tried to look away. "I came here without any thought of how it would affect anyone except me. But I think I have a way to make things right—to fix this. But I need a few more days to work things out."

"I stopped by to see her husband. He says the baby's name is Hope."

Trent looked down into those pure green eyes that swam with tears. There was hope there now. He couldn't let her down. A hint of doubt sparked through him. He had let Michael down, hadn't he? How could he know that he wouldn't fail Lana too?

"I've got to get back," Trent said, then pulled away from her.

As he opened the door he looked to where she sat on the old wooden bench. She was bent over, with her elbows resting on her knees and her beautiful blond hair falling around her face, staring down at the dull gray carpet on the floor. He was doing the right thing—the only thing he *could* do right now. But that didn't mean it was over. He would find a way to work this out. He just had to.

He had no doubt that she would agree to anything to keep his niece, but his plan would come at a cost for both of them. He felt the weight of guilt hit him at his thoughts of sacrifice. He should tell her about the stipulations of the will. But would she understand how important it was for him to be able to protect Maggie from his father's influence? Or would he lose the trust he'd just seen in her eyes?

He walked back into the nursery with new determination as he remembered Lana's face as she had looked up at him, with all her faith in him in her eyes. She trusted him, and the weight of that trust lay heavy on him.

He wouldn't let her down. This time he would protect those who were depending on him. He couldn't fail Lana and Maggie.

"Of course I understand that you want to know your granddaughter, Father."

Trent tried to relax his grip on the phone. He was getting nowhere fast in this conversation. But he had enough experience in dealing with his father that he knew not to push at this point. He'd let the man try to convince him that this was all about family. As if Calvin Montgomery knew *anything* about family…

Trent had been thinking a lot about his childhood since his talk with Lana. There had been times when he was young when his father had spent time with him and his brother. It had been his father who had taught him to ride his first horse. And there had been a few fishing and camping trips with the whole family together. He would have sworn that his parents had been happy then—would have sworn that his father had truly cared about his sons.

But things had changed when his mom had passed away. It had been as if his father had just given up on his family after that. They'd all been damaged, with his father devoting more and more of his time to the business and Michael getting into more and more trouble. And Trent had found himself hiding behind his school work and spending as much time at his uncle's house as possible.

Hitting the "end call" button on his phone as soon as his father had ended their conversation, he gave himself some credit for not throwing it against the wall. His father reaching out to him like this was just a sign of things to come. He could expect more pressure now that the lawyers would be getting involved. There were too many people fighting over one little innocent girl.

He'd realized the night before, while he was lying in bed, looking at his picture of little Maggie and Lana, that really none of them had taken into account the fact that not only did Lana love Maggie as if she was her own, but Maggie loved Lana too.

That was what Lana had been trying to tell him in the social worker's office, but he hadn't listened. He hadn't wanted to hear what she was saying. But it was there in the picture, where Maggie was smiling up at Lana with all the love in her little heart. What would Maggie think if they took her away from Lana? That her mother had just gone off and left her?

He'd remembered the feeling he'd had when he had realized his mother wasn't coming back. He had been so scared. The thought of Maggie being scared like that had tied his stomach into knots, and he had known he couldn't let anything happen that would leave the child feeling like that.

So he'd woken up this morning and decided to take action to protect both woman and child.

Now, after glancing at his watch, he poured the coffee he'd let get cold while he was talking with his father into the sink. He had half an hour to get to Lana's for his visitation with Maggie and he didn't want to be late. There were plans to be made and action to be taken.

Lana stopped and looked outside her window for the second time in as many minutes. At this rate she would never get anything done. She was in a bad mood today, and it was the irritating man who was supposed to be here at any minute who had her that way. One minute he was all over her—the next he was walking away. A woman could get permanent whiplash, trying to keep up with his coming and going. And what had he meant when he had said he could fix things?

"Maggie, I found your purple puppy!" she called out as she bent down to pick it up off the floor. The toddler was busy pulling out all of her toys, looking for the prized stuffed animal.

She remembered when she had bought the silly-colored toy dog. Maggie had just started to crawl then. She'd been so cute, trying to hold onto her puppy and crawl at the same time. The poor puppy was missing an eye now, and it needed one of its ears to be sewn back on.

She heard a car door slam and felt her body relax. He was here. She hadn't been sure if he would show or not after his cryptic vow to make things right yesterday. She had been afraid that he intended to walk out of her and Maggie's life, and the thought of something that a couple of weeks ago would have thrilled her now left her feeling empty and alone.

She tried to tell herself that the only reason she didn't

want Trent to leave was because of Maggie. Her daughter had become very attached to her uncle, and now that she had gotten to know him Lana knew she'd never keep him from seeing his niece.

Taking the stuffed animal into Maggie's room, she glanced at the mirror in the hall. It was a good thing that Amanda had decided to go out shopping with some of her friends today. Her babysitter would have seen right through her if she had seen her primping in front of the mirror.

So maybe she *had* spent a little more time on her make-up than necessary this morning? It certainly wasn't a crime to want to look good when you were doing housework and laundry, was it?

Who was she fooling? It had been years since she had been this concerned about how she looked. Trent had brought out the woman in her—the one that had been dead for the last couple of years. All those feelings of insecurity were almost gone now, and the excitement that filled her at the anticipation of seeing him was new.

She couldn't remember feeling like this even when she had been dating in college. It had to be the absence of a man in her life that was doing this to her. She had been wrong in thinking that since she had given up on marriage she didn't need a man at all. When Trent left she would have to find someone to take his place. She could do that. Couldn't she…?

"Who are you trying to fool? You've got it bad, girl." she said to her reflection, then looked down to see her daughter looking up at her. "Your momma's got to get herself together, Maggie-girl."

She picked the little girl up and gave her a big hug as the doorbell went.

"Now, let's go answer that door and see if we can talk some sense into your Uncle Trent."

She let Maggie greet him first. She couldn't help but smile when he picked her up and she gave him hugs and kisses. Maggie had always been a happy baby, but she had never been so comfortable around a man before. Lana had always blamed it on the fact that she had never been around a man except for Lana's dad, whom Maggie had loved immediately.

"Daddy!" the little girl said as she patted Trent's face with her small hands.

Lana felt the blood leave her face. Maggie had seen other children at daycare being picked up by their dads, so she must have decided that was what all men were called.

Lana reached out and took Maggie from Trent's arms. "I'm so sorry," she said. "I guess she thinks that's what men are called."

"It's no big deal," Trent said as he followed Lana into the house and shut the door behind him. "I've been called a lot of things, but I have to admit that is a first."

Lana looked up at Trent and noticed a tinge of color under his golden tan. Had he been embarrassed by Maggie calling him Daddy? But why? As he'd said, it wasn't a big deal.

"This is your Uncle Trent, Maggie," she told the little girl as she squirmed her way out of her arms.

Maggie immediately went back to Trent and pulled on his jeans leg, asking to be picked up. "Daddy?" she said in her sweet little voice.

"I'm sorry. She must be going through a phase," Lana said.

"It's not a problem, Lana," Trent said as he leaned down to pick the little girl up.

"So, what's the plan for today?" she asked. "Do you just want to hang out here with her or is there something you want to do?"

"I saw a park down the road," he said. "I thought we could go there. The weather is beautiful today, and we can talk while Maggie is playing."

"Let me grab a bag for her," Lana said, and headed down the hall.

So they were back to talking again. She didn't know why they bothered. She wasn't going to change her stand on Maggie's adoption. And he was too tied up with his feelings of being responsible for his brother's actions. They'd just end up chasing the same rabbit down a hole and they'd never come out in the same place together.

Trent watched the two little girls as they played in the sandbox. Even with a fairly small vocabulary the toddlers managed to communicate and play together. Kids were amazing. It was too bad that people seemed to lose that ability when they got older...

He and Lana had been sitting there watching the toddlers for several minutes and he still didn't know how to approach this. Would she go along with his unorthodox plan?

"I thought you wanted to talk?" Lana asked, then turned toward him.

He noticed the way she had pulled back her shoulders, as if she was getting ready for a fight. Well, either that or she was trying to show off the cleavage that was peeking out of the fitted pink tee shirt she was wearing today. He knew if he had to choose between a fight and looking at her breasts, the breasts would win every time.

He tried to smother the laugh he felt coming, but then decided he could use a good chuckle after the week he'd had, so he let go of all the happiness he felt in just this moment and enjoyed it.

"What's so funny?" Lana asked, then looked down to

where his eyes were still trained. "Trent Montgomery, are you staring at my breasts? This is not the time!"

Lana had leaned in to whisper, which just gave him a better view.

When she saw his eyes, still peeking down her shirt she laughed herself. "Behave! There are little kids all around us."

He watched Lana tug at the top of her shirt as she pretended to be scandalized by his behavior, but he wasn't fooled. Memories of her in his bed had his body responding in ways that definitely weren't appropriate, considering their location.

He shifted in his seat and crossed his legs so that he wouldn't embarrass her any further.

She peeked over at him from under her thick lashes while she pretended to take in all the people walking and playing in the tree-lined park—though he noticed she didn't let her eyes stray from Maggie for more than a few seconds.

She was such fun to tease, and it was such a beautiful day. He was a lucky man, to be sitting out in the sun with two of the prettiest girls around. Too bad he was going to have to ruin it.

"I talked to my father today," he said.

"Did he mention Maggie?"

"Yes, he did." He stretched out his legs as he turned toward her. "He fed me some bull about always wanting grandchildren. He even had the nerve to give me a hard time about not having any kids."

"Why haven't you?" she asked.

"What?"

"Why haven't you gotten married? Had children?" she asked. "You know—all the things people normally do by our age?"

Because the thought of living like his father and mother scared the life out of him. He would never be able to live like that. It was better to live alone than to spend his life on a rollercoaster of ups and downs such as his parents had called a marriage.

But maybe, for a little while, he wouldn't have to be alone. Surely if anyone could manage to make a temporary arrangement work for the security of little Maggie, he and Lana could.

"Why haven't *you*?" he asked.

"You know why," she said. "I can't have children."

Trent looked over to where Maggie played. "Would it make any difference to how you feel about Maggie if you had given birth to her?" he asked.

He watched her lips curve up in a smile as she watched Maggie playing.

"No, of course not. But it's not that simple," she said, then changed the subject. "What did you mean when you said you could 'fix things,' Trent?"

CHAPTER NINE

LANA WATCHED AS he cleared his throat. She sensed in him the same nervousness that she had felt while discussing her infertility. Was it something so bad that he was scared to tell her?

"I think Ms. Nelson is right. Maggie does need both of us. We need to get married."

The shock of his statement hit her instantly. For a second she thought she would pass out, and then she remembered to breathe. She tried to open her mouth and ask one of the hundreds of questions spinning in her mind, but her voice wouldn't come.

He couldn't be serious. Could he?

"Trent..."

She let him take her hands in his and waited. She had to have misunderstood him.

"Just hear me out, Lana," he said. "Right now we're fighting against each other, when we should be fighting together for what's best for Maggie."

"You know I only want the best for her," she said.

"And with both of us working together we can make sure of that," he said.

"But that doesn't mean we have to get *married*," she said. "This has something to do with your father, doesn't it?"

She couldn't understand what his father could want with

her little girl when from what Trent had said he hadn't cared for his own children, but it was plain to see that Trent thought his father was a real threat. Why else would he come up with such a hair-brained idea?

Marriage? To *Trent*?

She fought down a flutter of excitement that wanted to float to the surface. She couldn't let herself get pulled into that happily-ever-after dream again. Marriage was not meant for her. She had gotten her hopes up once, and when Joe had rejected her after he'd learned about her infertility it had nearly destroyed her.

She wouldn't go through that again. Better to accept that her future didn't hold any hope of the traditional family she had always planned on.

"What could be better than the two of us together?" he asked. "We've shown that we can work together and we get along well."

Yes, they did work well together—both in and out of bed—but that wasn't enough to build a marriage on. Was it...?

"And, yes, this has a lot to do with my father," he said. "There's something I should have told you—something you need to know that concerns my brother's will and is the reason I'm so worried about my father. I should have told you sooner—when we first met—but I didn't know you then. And later it always seemed the wrong time... No, that's not right. The truth is I was afraid you'd think I was just here trying to take advantage of you and Maggie and I didn't want that."

He pulled himself away from her, stretching his legs out in front of him as he looked out over the park.

"I'd never think that. I know you care about Maggie. Just *tell* me. What is it that I need to know?" she asked, knowing that whatever it was it had something to do with his desire for them to marry.

"When Michael died he didn't have much. He'd gone through most of the money we had inherited from our grandparents. But he still had the shares in the family business he inherited when our mother died. When he learned about Maggie he had his will updated, leaving everything to her. Those shares are worth a lot of money, Lana, but more importantly having control of them is worth a lot to my father."

"I don't care about any shares in your father's company, Trent. As far as I'm concerned he can have them. I just want to protect my daughter."

"The will specifies that Maggie is to keep them until she turns twenty-one. Then she can do whatever she wants with them. For now Michael's lawyers are in charge of them—till custody is decided by the courts. And that's where we are right now. The court can decide on only one of us. When my father decides to get involved in the custody battle—and he will, I promise you—we could both lose. This way we can both be there to protect Maggie."

"Of course after the case is settled we can both go back to our old lives, but until then we'd have to play the part of a loving couple for the court's sake."

Of course he would go back to his life in Houston. Had she really thought a man like Trent would be interested in actually setting up a home with her? It was only his sense of responsibility that had him willing to do something as drastic as marrying her.

She knew she shouldn't be hurt that he had come up with what might be the solution to all their problems. She should be happy that he was willing to go this far for his niece. But playing a part for the court? Living together day in and day out? How could she do that without falling for the man completely?

"I need to think about it," she said. "You should have told me everything before, Trent. For me to even consider this we need to be honest with each other."

"I'll do anything I can for you and Maggie," he said. "You know that."

Anything, but love us. How could she go into an agreement like this without her feelings for him getting stronger? But how could she not when this might ensure that Maggie would always be hers?

"I need some time," she said.

As she stood to leave she watched Trent as he walked over to the sandbox to get Maggie. He would be such a good father—a great father—but would that be enough?

She had so much to consider before she could make a decision of this magnitude. She would have to talk to Nathan so that she would know the legal requirements, and she would have to come up with some guidelines for their relationship. She knew she needed to protect her daughter, but if she was to survive this fake marriage she would have to find a way to protect herself too.

She had already let herself get too close to Trent. If she took this step it would just make her more vulnerable. Could she take that chance? Could she survive another heartbreak? She wasn't sure she would.

A scream cut through her thoughts and she turned to see Trent, still holding Maggie, running toward a young woman holding a limp child.

Lana caught up with him and reached for Maggie, freeing his arms to take the child. As he knelt beside him Lana looked up at the woman whose face was filled with horror. She knew her. Sally—or was it Sandy?—and her little boy came to the park often when she was there with Maggie.

They'd talked a few times, sharing something cute or horrible that their kids had recently done.

Shoving Maggie into the mom's arms, she leaned down to see if she could help.

"What happened?" Trent asked the mother.

Lana watched him check the child's breathing, then his pulse.

"Call 911," he said.

"He was playing, just running around like normal. Then he coughed…he kind of coughed… I don't know… he sounded funny… And then he fell… I thought he was playing…just playing." The woman sobbed as she clutched Maggie to her.

Lana watched as Trent assessed the child even as she gave their address to the operator on the line. "Pulse?" she asked.

"Too slow," Trent said.

"An ambulance is on its way," she told him, and she continued to hold the phone, giving the operator a play-by-play on the situation.

"Any history of asthma?" he asked the mother.

"No. He just fell down…" the mother said.

Trent was about to give the child a breath, then he paused. Lana watched as he glanced around the sidewalk. Following his gaze, she saw the apple core at the same time he did.

"Was he eating an apple?" she asked the mom.

"An apple?" the mom said.

Lana could tell the mother was going into shock, panic overwhelming her.

"Could he have choked on an apple?" Trent asked as he opened the child's mouth and looked inside. "Nothing," he said to Lana.

"Yes!" the mother said. "I gave him an apple for a snack. Oh, God, is that it?" The mother was now sobbing.

Maggie whimpered in the woman's arms and the woman held her tighter, unconsciously soothing her with her hands.

Trent positioned his hands on the child's body, then thrust up several times before returning to the child's mouth.

"I've got it," he said as he pulled out a piece of apple and threw it on the ground. Then he gave the child a couple of breaths and they both watched as the small chest rose with each one.

The child suddenly started to cough—a sound as sweet as the most beautiful music Lana had ever heard.

Trent checked the little boy's pulse then looked up to Lana and smiled. "His pulse is stronger," he said.

The child opened his eyes and then took in all the people surrounding him and started crying for his mother.

Lana took Maggie from the woman so that she could hold her son, then reached over and hugged Trent to her.

"I'm so glad you were here," she said, and reached over and gave him what had to be the biggest kiss she'd ever given him, ending it with an audible smack.

"Me too," Maggie said, and she planted soft baby kisses on Lana's laughing face and then Trent's, before he moved away to talk to the ambulance team who had arrived.

Lana held Maggie close as other people in the park approached her, asking what had happened, and watched Trent help the crew load the little boy on a stretcher. The mother gave Trent a hug and thanked him.

Trent was a good man. He had saved this woman's child. He was prepared to marry her so they could protect her little girl. The truth was that a fake marriage was more than she had ever expected. Yet the thought of faking something as important as marriage didn't sit right with her.

If she couldn't have the real thing, could she settle for an imitation?

Trent walked out of the nursery and felt like a jerk even before the door had closed behind him. He had been short with the nurses for days now. Baby Hope had not made the progress he would have liked to see, and that along with the pressure of waiting for his father to make his next move was getting to him.

Of course his bad mood didn't have *anything* to do with the fact that Lana hadn't jumped at the chance to be Mrs. Montgomery. Sure it didn't.

He decided that he would walk up to Labor and Delivery and check on the laboring patients there. And if he just happened to run into Lana up on the unit that would be okay. It was time for her to make a decision…time for both of them to move on to the next step that would secure the future for her and for Maggie.

"Kat told me you were on the unit," Lana said as she walked into the break room.

"How does that woman always know where I am?" Trent asked as he poured himself a cup of coffee. He started to offer Lana a cup, then remembered she preferred tea.

"I wouldn't be surprised if she knew where every good-looking warm male body in this hospital is right now. It's just a talent she has," Lana said.

"You doing okay?" he asked her as she moved from the table to open the fridge and then shut it. She was as nervous as the mares at the ranch when they were about to be mounted by one of the studs.

Suddenly memories of their lovemaking flooded his

mind. Okay, he really *didn't* need that in his thoughts right now.

"Lana, come here," he ordered her.

She was a nervous wreck, and he needed to find out what he could do to settle her down. Was this what the thought of marrying him did to her? So much for all his charm and good looks.

Pulling her close to him, he moved his hand down her soft cheek, then tilted her chin up till her troubled green eyes were forced to meet his. The feel of her body against him had his body responding instantly, while at the same time the emotional strain that had plagued him for the past few days eased away.

"Someone could come in," Lana said, and pulled away. "I got a call from Ms. Nelson," she told him.

"And…?" Trent asked as he moved closer.

"He's done it," Lana said.

She looked at him with eyes shadowed with the dark circles that told him he wasn't the only one not sleeping these days.

"Your father's lawyers contacted her today to see where the custody process stood," she said.

"She hasn't contacted me yet," he said as he pulled his phone out of the back pocket of his scrubs and checked to see if he had any missed calls. "Or she called my lawyer and he hasn't had time to pass on the information yet. I don't want to pressure you," he went on, "but if we're going to have any chance of pulling off this marriage for the benefit of the court you're going to have to make a decision soon."

Marriage to Trent. It was the only thing she had thought of since that day at the park. It wasn't a terrible idea. And she did see the advantages it would give them. With her history with Maggie, and Trent's biological relationship, together and presenting a happy home for her daughter, they would have a good chance against anything his father might throw against them.

But would she be able to pull it off? She wasn't a good actor. Her drama grades in high school would attest to that. But surely they should be able to play the role without much effort? She would have to be comfortable with Trent touching her in public, and with showing the normal affection a couple in love would share, playing the happy newlyweds. It would hurt, but she could do it.

Yet still she couldn't bring herself to say yes.

There would be real problems after the marriage was over and Trent went back to his old life, but that wasn't what was stopping her. The problem was that even after all the warnings she had given herself she was falling in love with Trent a little bit more every time she saw him. How was she going to be able to hide the way she felt from him if they were living together?

Part of her wanted to believe that he cared for her too. She had to believe that he cared for her in some way, or he wouldn't be willing to go to such extreme measures. And there was no doubt that they got along well together in bed. He had never mentioned that it would be a marriage in name only, and just the thought of being back in his bed made her want to agree, but she knew that the intimacy between them would just make it harder to walk away later, when the need for their marriage was over.

She was willing to sacrifice everything for Maggie, but surely there had to be another way.

"I know," she said as she pulled away from him. "I just need a little longer."

Trent threw his jacket across the back of the first chair he came to when he got home. An emergency Caesarean section had come in right when he had been about to get off, and he had volunteered to stay and help out.

He saw the blinking light flashing on his answering machine, but decided to get himself a cold bottle of water from the fridge before he checked to see who had left a message. He had given the number here to only a few people since he was only in town temporarily.

He took a refreshingly clean swallow of water, then picked up the phone to check the message. His stomach twisted itself into tight knots as he listened.

He ran his hands through his hair, then began to undress. His father was coming to town and there was nothing he could do about it. Lana would have to give him an answer—and soon. There was no telling what his father was planning and he would have to be prepared for anything—including telling Lana about what he intended for Maggie's inheritance.

But how did he bring that up with her? *Oh, by the way, I forgot to tell you that I plan to use Maggie's share of my family's oil company to get revenge on her grandfather for ruining her father's life.*

Would Lana really believe that a man she had known only for a few weeks was more concerned about his niece's welfare than an inheritance worth millions? Would *he* if he was in her shoes? Had he really come with Maggie's welfare as his priority he could have returned to Houston as soon as he had gotten to know Lana and seen how much she loved the little girl, but instead he'd let his own personal experiences with his parents cloud his judgment.

One look at Michael's little girl and he had been reminded of how his brother had been treated by their father, so he had continued with his plan to grab custody of Maggie before his father could get involved.

What had he been thinking?

* * *

Lana caught sight of Trent as he entered the cafeteria. He smiled at her as he headed over to her table, but she noticed his high-voltage smile had been turned down to just a low-wattage gleam today, and his eyes had the same look she was becoming accustomed to seeing in her own mirror.

Stress was beginning to take its toll on both of them.

"May I sit down?" he asked as he approached.

She wasn't sure what had him doubting his welcome. She was thinking about *marrying* the man, for heaven's sake, and yet now he was back to acting as if they were strangers?

"Sure. Is everything all right?" she asked as she watched him lay his tray on the plastic table and then arrange his food.

"Yeah—why?" he asked as he looked up at her.

"You just don't seem like yourself today," Lana said, and she reached out and covered one of his hands with her own. "What is it, Trent?"

Trent looked around at the other staff and visitors sitting at the tables and then back at her. Whatever was bothering him clearly wasn't something he wanted to discuss in public. Was it the fake marriage? Or was it something his father had done?

She placed her fork back down on the table, the thought of having to deal with more complications in her fight to keep Maggie dulling her appetite.

She started to remove her hand from where it lay over his, then stopped when he turned his hand over and gave hers a slight squeeze. She'd have to wait till they were alone to find out what had caused this change in him.

"Eat your lunch," Lana said as she removed her hand from his. "Though I'm warning you: the tuna surprise is a step down from the fried potato casserole."

"So I've been told," Trent said as he picked up his own fork and stared down into the pale-looking noodles and sauce.

They ate in silence, with Lana just moving her food around on her plate while she watched him somehow manage to finish the cafeteria's special of the day. As they went to drop off their dirty trays she tried to think of somewhere they could go and not be interrupted.

She needed to know what had happened to cause this change in him. And there was one place where no one in the hospital would see or hear them and they could have the privacy they needed.

It was risky, going down there, but it would be worth it if she could find out what was bothering him. They would talk, she promised herself as the idea formed. *Just talk.*

"You got a few minutes?" Lana asked as they walked side by side down the hall that led to the bank of elevators that went up to the patient care floors.

"I'm checked out on the roster for the rest of this hour," Trent said as he studied his watch. "Why?"

She could tell that he was shocked when she grabbed his hand and pulled him away from the main elevators and down the hall to where one old, dented metal elevator door stood.

Okay, maybe they'd do a little more than talk. Maybe she would kiss his sad mood away…just a few kisses to bring the warmth back into that spectacular smile of his… and then they'd talk.

They'd had such little time alone together lately, and she couldn't help but feel that he was pulling away from her. And if she decided that she couldn't go through with a fake marriage, where would that leave them? She'd had a taste of Trent and she wanted more. Whether or not she agreed to marry him everything between them would soon change. She needed just one more time alone with him before that happened.

"You want to show me the freight elevator?" Trent asked.

The doors opened and Lana pulled on his hand until he reluctantly got into the elevator. She pushed the button that took the elevator to the basement, and then froze when the reality of what she was doing hit her.

What she was doing was crazy and dangerous, but she wouldn't let that stop her. She'd have to give him an answer soon and then everything between them would change. She needed to be held in his arms one more time. Because she knew in her heart that it would have to be the last time, no matter what she decided about marrying him.

When the doors opened Lana poked her head outside to make sure there wasn't anyone around to see where they were headed. Looking both ways, she was relieved to see that they were alone. She pulled Trent out of the elevator with her.

"Okay, now I'm getting a little freaked out," Trent said as he pointed to the arrow indicating the hospital morgue.

"It's not that way," Lana said, and began walking down the opposite hall.

It had to be close to here. She had heard one of the nurses talking about it not long after she had come to work there, and then one of the labor and delivery nurses had dragged her along on a dare —to see if the room really existed or if it was just an urban legend.

"If you tell me what you're looking for maybe I can help you."

"It's right here," Lana said as she made one more turn and then saw the door she was looking for.

"What *is* this?" he asked.

Lana tried the doorknob and was relieved when it turned

easily. She had gotten her nerve up and she didn't want to lose it now. She pulled Trent in by the hand she was still holding, then shut the door quickly before she flipped the light switch and locked the door behind them.

"It's the hospital make-out room," she said, and smiled when she saw the shock hit his face.

Trent glanced around at the mix of broken furniture filling the room. Looking back at sweet, honest-to-the-core little Lana, he watched as she seemed to turn into a siren right before his eyes.

"We need to *talk*, Lana," Trent said as he pulled away.

"You see this door?" she said as she leaned back against it.

Surely she couldn't mean what she was about to say? With everything that was going on with them right now?

Guilt slammed through him as warning bells began to toll inside his overstimulated body. This wasn't right. He had planned to tell her everything—come clean about his plan to use Michael's will against his father, and tell her everything that he should have told her long before they had gotten to this point. He wanted everything out in the open so that there was nothing hidden between the two of them and the decision she had to make.

"We leave everything and everybody on the other side of this door," she continued. "Can you do that?"

"Lana, we need to talk." Trent said again.

He was going to tell her all the reasons this wasn't a good idea. He would swear in a court of law that he was. But then she walked over to him and laid one small finger against his lips.

"We'll talk later," Lana said. "I promise."

Trent tried once more to stop things from going any

farther, and then she stood on her tiptoes and whispered in his ear.

"I *need* you, Trent. Do you need me?"

Urgent desire struck him as her warm, sweet breath blew into his ear. If he'd been a better man then maybe, just maybe, he could have withstood the want that flashed through him as her lips worked their way down the side of his neck.

But he had a weakness where Lana was concerned. One moment alone with that sweet body of hers and he was done for. Somehow he had let his desire for her seep deep down inside him—until he could no longer control the need that flared up and consumed him.

"Yes," he answered as he lifted her up so that he could meet her lips.

The taste of her filled him as his tongue circled with hers. He had missed this—her—so much. He tilted his head to let his tongue delve deeper into her mouth, then crushed her body to his and took the weight of it.

The feel of her returning his kisses with the same feverish need that he felt had him losing control too fast, so he pulled back. Her moan of protest was almost too much for him, and for a moment he thought of just taking her right there, against the wall.

Barely managing to clamp down on his body's demand that he take her *now*, he pulled away from her. Looking around the small room, he saw a dilapidated plastic chair within reach. He used one of his feet to hook one of the chair legs and pull it close.

As he sat down with Lana in his arms he arranged her body so that she faced him, with her legs straddling his body. When her hand reached down between them and pulled the cord that held his scrub pants closed he lifted her and hiked up her skirt. He let his hand run down the thin line of her thong then pushed it aside so that his fingers could slide deep inside her.

A hot bolt of desire ran the length of him as her hand circled him and his groan filled the room. He ran his hand once more between her legs, then pushed her hand aside as he lifted her until he could feel his tip at her entrance. Thrusting up, he brought her down on the full, hard length of him in one swift move.

He stopped and took a moment to look at the flushed face and bruised lips of this woman who had clearly caused him to lose his mind.

And then she started to move.

This was so much more then she had planned but, oh, it felt so good to be with him like this again.

Lana eased herself down around him as she stared into his eyes. Never had she felt such an intimate connection as she did at this moment. In this stark room, totally absent of any romance, it was as if they were the only two people in the world.

She let him increase speed as he tightened his hands against her hips, and her breath caught with each stroke as she fought to keep her suddenly heavy eyes open. She loved the feel of him sliding in and out of her, loved the sweet, almost painful stretch of her body deep down inside her.

She could feel her body tightening around him, but she fought against it. She forced her eyes to stay open, letting herself drown in his deep blue eyes as his body stroked her into unbearable pleasure. His hands came up and cupped her breasts, then he bent his head and took her lips with such hunger that it destroyed her.

It was too much for her to take—too much for her to withstand. Her hands gripped his hair and she tried to pull his mouth closer. The demand of his lips, the hard length of him as he drove deep inside her, filled her completely. Her breath caught, then held. This was too much. He was taking her too far.

She felt herself losing her hold as she soared higher and higher, her core tightening, her body reaching for its climax. She tightened her arms around him, holding on to him as if her life was dependent on that connection between them, the joining of their bodies anchoring her to him. He thrust into her once more and her body shattered into a million pieces.

CHAPTER TEN

LANA, WHO HAD NEVER had the privilege of experiencing the walk of shame before, snuck into the back entrance of her unit. Trent had reassured her that she looked great, but she knew there was no way she could look the same coming out as she had going into that storage room.

Had she lost her mind? Thank goodness none of the other midwives she worked with, were in the office. They would have seen right through her casual act. All she would have had to do was look one of them in the eye and she knew she'd spill everything.

It wasn't every day that she managed to have mind-blowing sex in the most scandalous of places. Was it just a few weeks ago that she had been calling her life boring?

She knew that making love with Trent again had added more complications, but she would never regret it. She didn't even want to *think* about what the consequences of their getting caught together would have been. But at the same time it seemed she had spent too much of her time worrying about what the staff were saying about her and Trent. Why not give them something to really talk about?

Not that she would actually *tell* anyone about what had happened between the two of them, but she might as well be guilty of some of the rumors going around about them.

But what had been wrong with him today before the

mind-blowing sex? He had become known around the hospital for having a big smile and a quick sense of humor. Even in the fight they'd had in the court he had still been friendly to her.

Not that she had always been the same with him. And she wouldn't apologize for that. She'd had every right to be angry with him when he had first come to town. But she hadn't been able to stay mad at him for long. Watching the gentle man he was while caring for the smallest of babies, and the way he eased the concern of anxious mothers, and then seeing him interact with Maggie, it had just become too hard for her to hold a grudge against him.

He had looked much more relaxed when they'd parted—or at least until he had stopped her before she got on the elevator and reminded her that she couldn't avoid making a decision about their marriage much longer.

She'd seen the stress return then. Had he sensed the conflict inside her?

The consequences of *not* going through with the marriage were so high that she knew she shouldn't even be considering turning him down. She should agree to Trent's plan and just hope she would be able to find the strength to survive when everything was over between them.

But how would that be possible when her heart already hurt at the thought of him leaving?

If she'd felt that Trent had even the slightest desire to marry her for any other reason than to protect his niece, she would jump at the chance. But that wasn't the case, and she needed to get over any daydreams she was having of them being together as a family and accept the inevitable.

Trent was only interested in marriage because of his need to protect his niece—which was as honorable a sacrifice as anyone could make. But she had vowed after her break-up with Joe that she would never let someone make her feel that marrying her would be a sacrifice. She had always wanted to have someone love her just the way she was, but maybe it was time to accept that wasn't ever going to happen.

She grabbed the lab coat she kept hanging on the back of her office door and put it on to help hide the wrinkles that she had in her skirt and then headed down to the reception area to call for her first afternoon appointment. Everything in her personal life was coming to a head, but life kept going. Women continued to get pregnant, and that meant there were still babies who needed her to be there to deliver them.

As Trent rounded the corner of the Labor and Delivery nurses' station he saw Lana as she was coming out of one of the labor rooms, and he watched her as she spoke with the family members who had been waiting outside the patient's door. She was wearing scrubs today, so he knew she was planning on spending most of her time on the unit.

"Hey, Trent," one of the nurses called as they walked up beside him. "We're almost ready to go back if you want to meet us in the operating room."

"I'll be right there," he said, and turned to walk toward Lana.

She gave him a little wave, then walked back into the labor room. He'd have to catch her after they'd finished the next delivery.

The surgery went off without any problems, and in less than an hour another mother was holding a perfect little baby in her arms as her husband took pictures to show the rest of the family in the waiting room. He checked at the nurses' station and found that Lana had just gone into another delivery.

"You have a great team here," Trent told Dr. Miller as he joined him at the nurses' station to finish his paperwork.

"They're a great group of nurses," Dr. Miller said as he looked up from the chart he was checking for his notes. "I've heard you're here just for one a short time," the doctor said as he stretched back in his chair. "You ought to consider staying."

"I'm here for an eight-week assignment right now," Trent said. "I have a permanent position in Houston."

He turned as Lana came into the nurses' station. She walked over to some of the nurses who were talking.

"We'd be happy to have you stay," Dr. Miller said. "Good pediatricians are hard to find."

The doctor rose out of his chair, then turned to see where Trent's attention had gone.

"Just think about it," he said. Smiling, the man gave Trent a hearty slap on the back and left the unit.

Trent was glad to see Lana heading over to where he stood leaning against the station's countertop. He nodded his head toward the exit door and then accompanied her out of the unit. He only had a few minutes before he needed to get back and take the next case in the operating room.

"Lana, I—"

"Look, I've got to get back to the office right now, but why don't you come over tonight? You can see Maggie and I'll fix dinner."

They came to the elevator doors just as one opened its doors with the button's light showing it was headed up. A group of visitors bearing flowers and pastel-pink-wrapped presents walked out, pushing the two of them together. Her body brushed against his, sending a quick burst of desire through him.

Desire he couldn't act on. Not here, not now.

He reached out to tuck a loose piece of hair behind her

ear and let his hand linger on the soft lobe, then slide down the side of her neck.

"Trent...?"

The hoarse whisper of his name was too much. Before he could do something that would surely shock the staff he pulled away from her.

"Tonight," he said.

Turning away, he headed for the stairs. Maybe a little physical activity would get him cooled down before he made it to the OR.

Lana was in a better mood when she got home. She'd made peace with her decision concerning Trent's marriage proposal and, while she was nervous, she knew she was doing the right thing.

She'd taken Maggie with her to the grocery store, where she'd bought all the ingredients for one of her daughter's favorite pasta dishes.

"Hey, you're home!" Lana said as Amanda walked out of the house.

"Class was canceled tonight," Amanda said as she reached over and took the toddler out of Lana's arms.

"Thanks. I bought a few more groceries then I had planned." Lana juggled the bags in her arms, then reached back into the car for the last two.

"Yeah, it looks like you're going to feed an army," Amanda said. "Did Momma invite a football team over for supper?"

Maggie laughed up at her babysitter, then struggled to get down as soon as they made it inside the house. The toddler ran down the hall to her room as soon as she was let down, then was back in seconds, pushing her plastic play shopping cart around the kitchen, where the bags of food had been taken.

"No, but I did invite Trent," Lana said.

"Are you sure that's a good idea?" Amanda asked.

"Have you gotten a *look* at the man?" she teased her friend, and then stopped as she saw the look of confusion on her face.

"Okay, I know this is hard to understand," Lana said as she walked around the room, putting everything in its proper place.

"It just seems like you're getting more and more involved with him," said Amanda.

"Does it?" Lana asked.

She began sorting through the vegetables she would need to get ready for the evening's meal.

"Lana, are you okay?" Amanda had walked over to the sink and was staring at her as if she had grown a second head. "Oh, my God—you're in love with the guy."

"I didn't say that," Lana insisted.

She began slicing a tomato on the wooden butcher block, making sure that she had a good excuse not to look up at her friend.

"You didn't have to. I can see it," Amanda said.

Lana felt the heat of the blush that she knew stained her cheeks.

"Have you had sex with him?"

Looking up, she watched Amanda's eyes go wide before a big grin spread across her face.

"I can't *believe* it. You've had sex with the hunky Dr. Montgomery!"

"Hey, no S-word in front of Maggie," Lana said, hoping to change the subject—as if that was going to happen now.

"So the rumors about you two hooking up were true?" Amanda asked as she went over to the table to sit down. "I want details."

"I'm not telling you about—" Lana stopped as Amanda

doubled over with laughter. Crap—the brat had tricked her. She knew there was no way she would share what was going on between her and Trent.

She didn't even know for sure herself what it was that was happening between them. It was as if they had two separate relationships. In one they were talking about marriage as if it were a business arrangement between the two of them. In the other they weren't only friendly...they couldn't keep their hands off each other.

No—they both had to leave their personal issues out this. Maggie had to be their priority.

Lana ignored her friend's teasing for the rest of the day. Amanda was just having a good time, picking on her, but deep down Lana knew her friend was right. Even after all the warnings she had given herself, she had fallen head over heels in love with a cowboy doctor who had come to town to break her heart.

CHAPTER ELEVEN

LANA WAS SURPRISED at how smoothly the meal had gone. If only their next conversation would go as smoothly.

Dinnertime with a tired toddler could quickly turn into a messy, crying affair, but instead of running from the house screaming Trent had pitched in and helped.

Deciding to give him a realistic view of parenting, she had assigned him the task of bathing Maggie while she cleaned up the kitchen. He'd survived his one day alone with the toddler, but that was different from the day-in and day-out demands of parenting. The sight of him drenched to the waist and grinning madly as he held a sparkling clean Maggie had sent her into uncontrollable fits of laughter.

"She's really asleep this time," he said now, as he joined her back in the kitchen.

"You sure she's not playing possum again?" she asked.

"Hey, I happen to be an expert on child behavior," he said.

She looked up from the sink and raised an eyebrow.

"Okay, she fooled me once," he said, "but I'm on to her tricks now. She's definitely destined for the big screen when she grows up."

"I'm thinking more of her as a teenage drama queen," she said.

One look at his horrified face had her laughing again. "You do realize she's going to grow up some day?" she said.

"I don't want to even *think* about it," he said.

She didn't either. It seemed like only days ago that Maggie had learned to crawl. Now she was walking everywhere, and learning a new word daily. Next there would be school, then boys... *Boys?* She definitely wasn't ready to think about *that*.

"You were great with her tonight—well, except for the half-hour it took you to actually get her into her crib," she said, "But that's not really your fault. She knew you'd be an easy mark so she played you."

"But those were *real* tears," he protested.

"That she quickly turned off as soon as I walked into the room. Like I said—she played you."

Trent took the glass of tea Lana offered and sat at the small table, waiting for Lana to sit down too. Finally they would have a chance to discuss their plans to keep his father out of Maggie's life.

He knew Lana had reservations about the idea of marrying him, but he knew they would be able to make things work out together. They were both level-headed adults. There would be none of the dysfunction of his parents' marriage.

Still, it would be for the best if they ironed out some of the details. If they set up the terms of their marriage now it would be easier for both of them, but for some reason the more they tried to make this feel like a business deal the more uncomfortable he felt.

He put his hands in his pocket and felt for the ring he meant to surprise her with. He tightened his hand around it, then let go and pulled his hand out.

This was what he wanted. No drama, no chaos, no fights

that ended with one of them crying or, worse, one of them dead. They needed to keep this separate from any feelings they might have for each other. They were putting a good plan in motion and sticking to it so there would be no misunderstandings.

"So, have you come to a decision?" he asked. He felt his pulse quicken as he waited for her to answer.

From the hesitancy before Lana's response he knew she was uncertain, but that was to be expected. Most people didn't go into marriage like the two of them were doing. Of course most people weren't in the situation maggie were in either.

Trent watched her as she seemed to gather herself together. This wasn't going to be easy for either of them, but it would be harder if they didn't start off on the right foot.

"Trent," she said, "I want you to know how much I appreciate your offer. I know you'd do anything for Maggie."

Trent watched her as she took a sip of tea, a sinking feeling invading his chest.

"That's why I think we can work things out between us so that we don't have to do anything as drastic as getting married," she went on.

"I don't understand. If we married everything would be taken care of," he said.

"Stop and think about it, Trent. What about after the adoption? After you go back to Houston? We'd be right back at the same place we are now, trying to work out custody of Maggie. We can't do that again. It's not fair to either of us and it certainly isn't fair to Maggie."

"I promise this is not some type of trick. I'm not trying to take Maggie away from you, Lana. You're her mother. The only one she will ever know. I lived most of my childhood without a mother—I don't want that for Maggie. But I still want to be part of her life. This way I can be."

"And what are we going to tell Maggie when suddenly you're not there every day? How will that make her feel, Trent? She'll just be more confused. It's not right to do that to her. But if we work together and show the court that you support my adopting her we can both do what's right for her. Maggie can live with me and still have an awesome uncle who she goes to visit and who spoils her as any uncle would. Instead of being confused about your part in her life, she'll have the security of being loved by the two of us. And with you handling her inheritance I know she'll be taken care of just as your brother wanted."

He got up from the table, unable to sit still any longer. He didn't want to confuse Maggie—he just wanted to protect her. And Lana. Why couldn't she see that this was the answer to keeping Maggie safe from his father?

"We wouldn't have to end the marriage immediately," he said as he began to pace.

"Listen to yourself," Lana said as she stood up and joined him. "You're already changing things. Can't you see how complicated marriage would make things between us?"

"It wouldn't have to be that way. We can set out the terms of the marriage. Have a lawyer draw it up, if you like, to make it all legal if you don't trust me."

He heard the bitterness in his voice, but couldn't control it.

"It's not that I don't trust you—it's that I don't trust myself," she said as she shook her head.

"What does *that* mean?" he asked, even more confused now. If she truly trusted him why wouldn't she marry him?

Lana had expected Trent to try and get her to change her mind, to see the reasons he thought this was the best thing to do for Maggie, but she had never thought he would be this upset.

The man standing in front of her was not the Trent she knew, who always remained calm and controlled no matter what was going on around him. This man was anything but calm, with his body coiled tight, his face a beautiful mix of confusion and frustration, his hands running through his thick dark hair.

Hair she'd once run her hands through. Hair she'd never have the right to touch again after tonight.

Her body heated with memories of tangling her hands in Trent's hair as she pulled him closer, as she anchored her lips to his, felt his tongue deep inside her mouth, his hands roaming her body. Those were the other times she'd glimpsed this man in front of her now.

She watched as he took a deep breath, then walked over to her and took her hands in his. How could she continue this relationship without him utterly destroying her heart? How could she make him see that faking a marriage with him was impossible for her without telling him what she felt for him?

"What *is* it? What do you mean you don't trust yourself?" he asked, his voice now calm and caring. "I would trust you with anything."

"Anything?" she asked, her heart stuttering as she took the biggest risk she'd ever taken. "Would you trust me with your heart?"

"What?" he asked as he pulled his hands from hers.

"I don't want to settle for a fake marriage, Trent. I want a real marriage. A marriage like my parents', where you plan to grow old together, a marriage filled with love and respect."

"And what would *I* know about those types of marriages, Lana?"

She could hear the bitterness in his voice. She couldn't blame him for being bitter. He'd been given a raw deal as a child. But he wasn't a child any longer. He needed to see that things could be different for him.

"I know your parents' marriage wasn't perfect…"

"That's an understatement. It was a war zone, with me and my brother as prisoners. I'll never live like that again."

"But that's not what marriage has to be. When two people love each other they can make it work. Yeah, they might argue and disagree sometimes, but they also learn how to compromise and support each other. That's what I want, Trent. Not a marriage filled with lies. I want someone to be there when things are good, but also to be by my side when things go wrong. I want someone to love me no matter what. In sickness and in health."

"Till death do us part?" Trent asked, and the sarcasm in his voice was almost palpable.

"Yes, that," she said.

"And you think you could have that with *me*?" Trent asked, his eyes wide as he backed further away from her. "This was supposed to be about Maggie—not about us."

"And it was—until I fell in love with you," she said, her hands covering her heart, as if to protect it from the pain she knew would come.

It hurt to see the panic in his eyes, but she'd known before she'd admitted her feelings for him that he wasn't ready for this—not for any type of real commitment, let alone one that included messy emotions such as love.

How long had it been since someone had told him that they loved him? Months? Years? Had anyone really, truly, *ever* loved this man the way he deserved? She knew he could love—she'd seen it in his eyes every time he looked at Maggie—but did he know how to *accept* love?

"I love you, Trent," she said, and her voice was stronger

as she poured everything she felt for him into it. "I love the way you comfort your patients' parents when they're scared and worried, the way your eyes light up with laughter when you're playing with Maggie, and the way you want to protect her so much that you're willing to marry me—even if it is for all the wrong reasons. I love the way you make me laugh, the way you have of calming my worries, the way you make me feel like a whole woman when I'm in your arms."

"It's not you…" he said.

"I know it's not. It's about you being afraid to take a chance on us. Life's all about chances, Trent. Do you know how hard it is for me to stand here and wait for you to reject me like Joe did?"

"Joe was stupid," he mumbled.

"Yes, he was—but I didn't see that until I met you. You made me see that I could have it all if I was willing to take a chance. I just need to know if you can take that same chance with me."

She waited as Trent looked at her, sadness in his eyes.

"I don't think I can give you what you need," he said.

She watched him reached his hand into his pocket, then slide it back out again, empty.

"I don't know how to be what you want…what you deserve."

"Yes, you do," she whispered as he walked away from her. "You just don't know it."

Lana tried to keep her mind on the patient's chart that she was updating. She'd been having a hard time concentrating since the night Trent had walked out of her house. It had been two days now and she hadn't heard from him.

She'd spent hours second-guessing her decision to refuse Trent. Would it have been so bad to take what he had offered? To have what time with him she could have, even though she knew it would have ended with a broken heart?

A knock at her office door sent her thoughts back to the present, where they needed to be.

"Come in," she called as a second knock sounded.

"Hey, Lana, there's a Mr. Montgomery is here to see you," the young receptionist said as she stepped into the room.

"Send him in, Lily." Lana stood and removed her lab coat, then straightened her skirt, her hands unsteady. Trent had never been to her office before and she couldn't imagine why he was there now. Could he have realized that she was right?

The man who walked into her office wasn't Trent, but she had no doubt that he was a Montgomery. His face was so like his son's, in all its lines and angles, but it was aged and hardened. His brown eyes were cold, so unlike the warm blue of Trent's, and the straight line of his lips showed no hint of humor.

He wore an expensive suit that screamed power, and his large six-foot frame overwhelmed her small office. Now she understood why Trent had been so worried about his father's interest in Maggie. If this man wanted something, he'd take it. But he wouldn't be taking her daughter anywhere.

"Mr. Montgomery—come in." Surprised when her voice came out with no trace of a tremor, she indicated the chair in front of her desk with a wave of her shaky hand.

"Please have a seat," she said, then waited till he sat before sitting down in her own chair.

"Thank you," he said as he folded his body into the small chair.

She watched as he looked around the room, taking in the setting as if preparing for battle. His eyes stopped on the bulletin board behind her, where she displayed pictures of the babies that she had delivered. She knew the second his eyes found the picture she had added just that morning.

It had been taken on one of their trips to the park and it showed Maggie giggling with joy on one of the toddler swings. But it had been the look on Trent's face that had caused her to pull her phone out of her purse and snap the picture. He looked so relaxed and free. And *happy*—as if spending the day pushing a swing in the park was just what he wanted to be doing.

"What can I do for you, Mr. Montgomery?" she asked.

"I'm sure you know I'm here about my granddaughter," he said.

"Maggie's fine. She's a beautiful, healthy little girl," she said. "If you'd like to meet her I'm sure me and Trent can arrange it."

"I was under the impression that you had sole custody of the child at this time."

"I do, but Trent has become a very important part of our lives," she said. "We discuss everything concerning Maggie together."

His cold eyes melted with the heat of the temper that flared there now. *Why?* Why couldn't the man just be happy that his granddaughter was going to be taken care of?

Being studied like a bug under a microscope was uncomfortable and she was tired of it. "Mr. Montgomery, if you didn't come here to arrange to see Maggie then why *did* you come?"

The smile on his lips didn't touch his eyes. How could a man so cold and calculating have raised a son like Trent? Of course the obvious answer to that was that he hadn't raise him.

"I came to make you an offer."

An offer?" she said. What was he going to do? Offer to *buy* her daughter?

"My youngest son…"

"Michael… Maggie's father," she said, with a hint of annoyance evident in her voice.

"I do know my son's name, Ms. Sanders. No matter what *Trent* has told you…" he emphasized the name "…I do care for my sons. Both of them."

"I'm sorry," she said. "And I'm sorry for your loss."

He accepted her apology with a nod of his head.

"As I was saying, Michael made certain stipulations in his will concerning his daughter—Maggie."

His lips parted in a small smile at this acknowledgement of the little girl's name.

"My son apparently wanted to make sure his child was taken care of financially on a long-term basis. Simply put, he left her all his shares in my oil business—shares that could be used to gain control of the company. I'm willing to make an arrangement that would allow you to keep Maggie and still have the financial stability her father wanted for her. I just want the *control* of the shares—not the ownership."

Disbelief filled her. No, this man didn't want to *buy* his granddaughter—instead he was willing to sell her for the right to control some of the shares in his company. No wonder Trent was scared to trust anyone with a father like this man.

"I'm sorry." She stood up abruptly, surprising both of them. She grabbed the top of the, desk using it to steady her. "I'm going to have to ask you to leave. If you want to discuss Maggie's inheritance you'll need to talk to Trent."

He stood and reached into his pocket, then pulled a card from a case and laid it on her desk.

"Here's my contact information. Hopefully we will be able to come to an agreement. I'm sure neither one of us would like to have to take this to court."

CHAPTER TWELVE

TRENT PULLED THROUGH the gated entrance. He was tired and he needed to grab a shower. He'd barely slept since he'd left Lana's house two days ago, and his mind was swirling with thoughts of life without her and Maggie. The only thing that had gone right that day had been with baby Hope's progress. The baby girl was showing herself to be a fighter and if she kept up the progress she had shown in the last couple of days he had no doubt he'd be able to take her off the ventilator by the end of the week. He couldn't help but be inspired by the fight in one so small. He laughed to himself. Baby Hope gave him hope.

The long black car sitting in his driveway had him taking his foot off the gas pedal. There was only one person who would be waiting for him in that limo. His father was in town. That was *just* what he needed to have to deal with today.

He left the front door open for his father to follow him. It was rude, but it was the mood he was in. Why couldn't his father have called and at least informed him of his visit? Instead now he'd have to deal with everything between the two of them when he was already as tightly wound as a rattlesnake about to strike.

"And hello to you too," his father said as he followed him into the living room.

Trent turned around to face him. He tried to corral the anger that sprang up within him, but it was too strong. He'd held it under such tight control for so long that he was afraid of its power. But he couldn't afford to let his anger at his father take him back to that black hole he had been in when he'd left Texas—before he had met Lana.

Lana and Maggie. They were what was important now.

"Father, I wasn't expecting you." With his thoughts on Lana and little Maggie he felt the anger subside to a manageable irritation.

"Weren't you?" his father asked.

His father took a seat on the sole chair in the room, leaving him to the couch. It was a move he had seen him carry out before. His father was holding court and he was just another one of his subjects, expected to bow down to him.

Trent remained standing.

"I knew you'd be coming eventually, but I expected to hear from your team of lawyers first."

"I find out I have a granddaughter and you expect me to send my *lawyers*? This is something of a personal nature, wouldn't you say?"

Things of a personal nature? Was that what his father was calling family matters now?

"If you'd like to meet Maggie I can see that it is arranged," Trent said.

"The child's foster mother has offered to let me see her and, yes, I would like to meet her. But first I'd like to know what your intentions are concerning the girl and the shares she is to inherit."

"So you've met Lana?"

"Yes, she seems a lovely young woman who has no idea of the worth of my grandchild's inheritance."

"Lana doesn't care about Maggie's portfolio. She loves Maggie for herself."

Just like she loved *him* for himself, he thought.

He bit down on his anger as it returned. "She's one of the most caring women I've ever met and we both owe her our thanks for the way she has taken care of Maggie. She's a genuinely good person. And, unlike most of the people you're used to dealing with, she's honest and sincere."

He could go on and on about what a good person Lana was, but his father would never understand. In his father's world Lana would be considered weak and easy prey. But in the new life Trent had found Lana was all the good things he'd never had in his life. She and Maggie had shown him a whole new world that he could have if he was willing to take a chance.

"And what are your feelings for this woman?" his father asked. "Apart from gratitude."

"I..." He stopped with the word *love* sitting on his tongue. *Love*... Not a word he was comfortable with, or one that he really understood, but it had come to him so easily, so naturally. Was it possible that these crazy feelings he had for Lana were more than just friendship? More than just desire? *Could* it be love? *Was* he in love with her? How would he even know?

But he did. Somehow he knew—had known for a while, if he was honest with himself, that what he felt for her was more than he had felt for anyone else in his life.

"No, Father, it's not gratitude, and it has nothing to do with Maggie or with Michael's will."

He heard his voice rise as he felt joy such as he had never known fill him. *Hell, yeah, it was love.* How had he not known it? If just thinking about her made him feel this good, how could it *not* be? He *loved* Lana Sanders. Not only did he love her, but he was going to marry her if she'd have him. They were going to be a family—him and Lana and Maggie. *His* family.

He looked at the man sitting in the chair inn front of him. He had never understood his father—probably never would—but he couldn't help but feel sorry for him. With all his wealth and power, he was living his life all alone.

They'd both isolated themselves emotionally from others, never letting anyone get close. But then Lana had come into his life and now he was a different man. His life was nothing like his father's and it never would be again.

He needed to tell her. Let her know what she meant to him, how she'd saved him. That he was willing to take a chance on marriage even though it still scared him.

"Look, I don't have time to explain it right now. If the only thing you came for was to see what my intentions are as far as Maggie's shares in the company are concerned, you can relax. I no longer have any plan to use her shares to make a move against you. As long as you agree to let me and Lana adopt her, Maggie's shares will be under the control of the lawyers I'll be setting up for her trust fund. Neither one of us will be able to use them. I won't use your granddaughter against you unless you decide to fight us for custody."

He watched his father's shoulders relax and for the first time noticed how tired his father looked. The man was working himself into an early grave. And for what? More money? More power? Would this have been him thirty years down the road if he hadn't found Lana?

"And now that's settled, I really need to get a shower," said Trent.

He headed off down the hall, then turned around and caught up with his father, who was heading out the door. As his father turned toward him he felt a surge of guilt. He'd dug up a lot of memories lately, and he had to admit that not all of them had been bad. There had been a time before their family had been torn apart when his father had been close to both him and Michael. There was no going back to those times, but he owed it to his brother to give Maggie a chance at a relationship with her grandfather.

"Let me know when you want to meet Maggie. She's a special little girl. I think you'll like her."

"I'm sure I will," his father responded, then started back out the door.

"She has Momma's eyes," Trent said.

His father stopped, then turned back. The glimmer of dampness that filled his father's eyes told him what he needed to know. His father had loved his mother.

He watched his father get into the car, its door being held open by a uniformed driver. No, there was no going back. But maybe with the help of a little girl they could go forward on a different path than the one they had been following all these years.

Lana had folded the same washcloth three times, but she just hadn't got the energy to stop her toddler from playing in the clean laundry. The visit from Calvin Montgomery had sent her into autopilot. She couldn't even remember the trip home. And, while she'd tried to act normal while she fed and bathed Maggie, she just couldn't keep up the act.

She finally put the child to bed after a quick game of peekaboo with one of the clean towels.

Her whole conversation with the senior Montgomery had been surreal, the man's attention blinded by his greed. How could anyone be so calculating as to offer their grand-daughter to a stranger for strictly financial reasons? And how dared he threaten to cause trouble for her with the courts?

She had no intention of letting him intimidate her. She just hoped that she could still depend on Trent to back her up after she'd scared him with her confession of love for him.

A knock on the door startled her out of her dark thoughts.

Opening it, she found a different Trent from the one who had left her house two nights ago. His eyes were bright, his body full of nervous energy, and his smile was dangerous and sexy.

"Can I come in?" he asked as he stood there, one hand in his pocket.

"Of course," she said, and she stepped back from the door, turning her back toward him, unable to meet his eyes.

Having a man run from your house after a declaration of love had a tendency to make things a little awkward.

"Lana, I heard that my father came to see you. I'm sorry if he upset you."

"Upset me?" she said as she walked over to the couch and sat down. "The man was ready to bulldoze me, and when he couldn't do that he threatened to make trouble with my adoption case. I take it he came to see you?"

Trent took a seat on the other end of the couch. She noticed he didn't try to move closer. She'd known there would be no going back after she bared her heart to him. Their relationship was bound to change.

"You won't have to worry about my father anymore. We discussed his concerns and I settled things in a way that he understood. He won't get involved with our adoption of Maggie."

"*Our* adoption?" she asked. Did he still think she was going to go through with his fake marriage plan? "I thought you understood that I can't marry you, Trent?"

If she sent him away now he'd be lost forever.

"Lana, I will do whatever it takes to protect you and Maggie—that will always be a priority in my life. But I know I messed up, asking you to fake a marriage to me. You were right. A marriage built on lies wouldn't have been fair to either of us. I know that now. And that's not what I want."

Trent rose from the couch and looked down at Lana. What a lucky man he was to have a woman like her love him. He didn't know how to talk about his feelings. It was something they'd have to work on together. But for now hopefully the three little words that had scared him into running away from her just two days ago would be enough.

He knelt down in front of her and pulled the ring he'd been carrying with him for days from his pocket. "Lana, I love you. I want to marry you. And it has nothing to do with my father, the will, or even the adoption. I want to marry you simply because I'm in love you."

"Will you marry me, Lana? Marry me for real?"

Trent had reached out and taken her hand. He *loved* her? He was the prince she had always dreamed of and he *loved* her. The life she had always wanted was just within her reach. But she had to know for sure that he understood what he would be getting.

"We'll never be able to have biological children of our own," she said, feeling her wounded heart stutter as he raised her hand to his lips, then placed it over his heart.

"I'm sorry you had to go through so much when you were young, but I'm thankful that the treatments saved you," he said. "You and Maggie are more family than I ever thought I would have. More than I deserve. The two of you are all I need."

"Are you sure? What if you decide you want to have more children later?"

"We can always adopt—just like we're doing with Maggie," he said. "Lana, we can't build our family on a past that neither of us can change, but we can build it on our future together...on our love for each other."

Could life really be that simple?

"I love you, Trent," she said as she wiped tears from her eyes. "And there's nothing more I want than to marry you."

She watched as he took her hand in his and slid a sparkling ring on her finger. Standing up, he reached down and scooped her up in his arms, silencing her surprised scream with his mouth as he carried her down the hall.

She'd gotten her fairy tale prince and her cowboy all roped together in this man she would soon call her husband. And whether they rode off into the sunset or she was carried away in her prince's arms, she knew they would find their happily-ever-after together.

EPILOGUE

LANA RUSHED UP the courthouse steps. She was going to be late again.

"Don't even say it," she said to Amanda, who was standing at the front door waiting for her.

"Say what? That I told you running off to a delivery wasn't a good idea?" Amanda said.

"You know I had no choice. I've been there for every one of Lacey's deliveries. The fact that this one was going to be a Caesarean section was freaking her out," Lana said as she rushed down the hall toward the courtroom.

Stopping outside the door, she straightened the hemline of the tea dress, then checked her hair in the mirror that Amanda had pulled out of her pocket. The nurses on the unit had all helped her get dressed. Even Kat had helped with her hair and make-up.

"You look beautiful," Amanda said.

Lana smiled at the woman looking back at her from the mirror. It wasn't the perfectly applied make-up, or the hair combed into a flawless knot. No, what she saw was the beauty that only real happiness could bring.

"Ready?" Amanda asked.

"Definitely," Lana said as she opened the heavy wooden door—and stopped.

He wore the same dark suit he'd worn that first day

they'd met, with a thin string of a tie he called a *bolo*, and she knew that if she looked down at his feet she'd see a pair of black pointed cowboy boots. In his arms he held a beautiful little girl, dressed in soft pink ruffles.

The sight of the two of them together filled her heart with love. He turned as she entered and the force of his smile almost knocked her over. It was more than she could take. This was her life. How had she got so lucky?

As she walked toward the front of the room she saw her parents, and Trent's great-aunt and uncle, along with Ms. Nelson sitting to one side. They'd decided to make it a quiet ceremony, with a larger reception at the beach to follow.

"Well, here she is," said Judge Hamilton as she approached the bench.

"I'm sorry I'm late, Your Honor," she said.

"Well, I could hold you in contempt of court, I guess, but I think that would make this young man of yours very unhappy."

"Your Honor," Trent said as he shifted Maggie in his arms and took her hand. "I'd be beholden to you if you could show some leniency in this case."

"I promise it won't happen again," said Lana.

"In that case, let's get started," said the stately judge.

"Yes," Lana said as she looked up at Trent and her daughter, "let's get started."

They repeated their vows with hands joined and Maggie at their side, and her sweet giggles filled the courtroom as they shared their first kiss as husband and wife.

Then the judge called the court to order again.

"There's one more piece of business we need to handle," the judge said, "and that's the finalization of this little girl's adoption. Miss Maggie," he said, as Trent lifted her up in his arms so that she could see the judge up close, "do you take your mommy, Lana Montgomery, to be your forever mommy?"

Lana thought her heart would burst from her chest as she watched her little girl's curls bounce around her head as she nodded yes to the judge.

"And, Miss Maggie, do you take your uncle, Trent Montgomery, to be your forever daddy?"

Astonishment filled the little girl's face, then her mouth lit with a smile and she grabbed Trent's face between her hands. "Daddy!" she squealed, patting his face, and the whole courtroom broke out in laughter.

"You have to answer the judge," her new daddy reminded her.

Turning her head back to the judge, she nodded while Trent reached over and wrapped Lana in his other arm.

"Well, then, by the power invested in me by the State of Florida, I now pronounce you husband and wife, father and mother and daughter, and the cutest darn family I've ever had the privilege to unite."

Trent smiled down at Lana, his arms full of their daughter, his eyes full of love.

"Thank you, Mrs. Montgomery," he said.

"For what?" she asked.

"For loving me," he said, "for teaching me how to love."

"Oh, cowboy," she said as she grabbed his tie and pulled his lips down to hers, "you haven't seen anything yet."

* * * * *

THE BABY THAT
CHANGED HER LIFE

LOUISA HEATON

For Nicholas, James, Rebecca, Jared and Jack
xxx

PROLOGUE

CALLIE TAYLOR STARED at the pregnancy test kit. She felt the weight of it in her hands. There was no point in reading the instructions—she already knew what they said. Knew the simplicity of its words: *'One line indicates a negative result. Two pink lines indicate a positive result'*.

Simple words but such a momentous implication. Life-changing. Well, just for nine months, maybe—because, as a surrogate, she'd be giving the baby away after it was born. But even then…being best friends with the father of the baby meant the baby would *always* be in her life…

Callie opened the box, pulling out the thick wad of paper wrapped around the end of the two kits, and threw the instructions in the bin. She knew how these things worked. As a midwife, she conducted many a test—especially when she worked in the fertility clinic. She placed the second kit back on the shelf and tore through the wrapping around the first.

She had never considered for even one moment that she would be doing this test on herself, and yet here she stood.

What was she doing? Had she made the right decision to do this? To be a surrogate? What if things didn't work out? What if she fell in love with the baby?

No, course not…I'd never do that.

She splashed her face with cold water and dried her hands.

Pee on the stick. That was all she had to do and she would *know*.

Could there be any doubt? It had to be positive, didn't it? She already felt sick and tired all the time. And she kept eating biscuits.

Not much of a sacrifice, though, was it? A big waistline and labour. That was all she had to get through to give Lucas and Maggie their much wanted baby. Callie could do that. And she didn't have to worry about wanting to keep the baby because she'd never wanted kids anyway.

No biggie.

So why aren't I peeing on this stick?

She held the slim white plastic tube in her fingers, staring at it. Her bladder felt full. There was only one thing to do...

She did what she had to and put the cap on the stick, sliding it between the taps on her sink.

I'll look at it in a moment.

Just as she was finishing washing her hands her doorbell rang. They were insistent, whoever they were. Ringing constantly, a finger held on the button, determined not to stop until she answered the door.

'Oh, God... Who is it?' she called out. If it was someone she didn't know, then she wasn't going to bother answering it at all! Did they not know that she had a life-changing moment going on here?

Leaving the bathroom, she glanced around at the state of her flat. It wasn't too bad. There were cups here and there and on the coffee table, papers, magazines and an open packet of gingernuts. Clothes were draped over the back of the sofa, the radiator, and the whole place had a bit of an uncared-for air about it. It looked a mess.

Like me. Besides I'm in my pyjamas.

'Callie, it's me...Lucas!'

Lucas. The father. Maybe...

Okay, I have to answer the door for you, at least.

'Hang on.' Callie moved quickly down her hallway, grabbing stray items of clothes and tossing them all in her bedroom. She ran her fingers through her hair, hoping she didn't look too much like death warmed up, and pulled open the door, trying to seem casual.

'Hi,' Lucas said. He looked awful.

She frowned. Lucas looked pale, distracted. Not his usual self.

Callie followed him into her lounge. 'You okay?'

It wasn't like Lucas just to turn up like this. Normally he'd ring to let her know he was coming round, just to make sure it was all right and she wasn't going out.

Lucas stood in the centre of Callie's lounge, hands in his jacket pockets, looking very uncomfortable. 'No, not really—no.' He fidgeted in his pockets, bit his lip. Then, with nothing better to do, he sat down on the couch in a sudden movement, waiting for Callie to join him.

'What's up?' She hoped this was going to be a quick conversation, considering the state her stomach was in.

Lucas shrugged, unable to meet her gaze. 'Everything. Everything's up.'

Callie felt awkward. Normally in this situation a friend would reach out, lay a reassuring hand on a knee and say, *Hey, what's up? You can tell me.* But Callie didn't feel comfortable doing that. It wasn't who she was. She didn't do reassuring physical contact.

Except with her patients. Somehow it seemed okay to do it with them. It was her professional persona. It wasn't *her.* That was *Midwife* Callie, not *Real* Callie.

Lucas smiled at her, but it was strained—one of those brave smiles that people tried to put on their faces when in reality the last thing they wanted to do was smile.

Callie was even more at a loss.

'Hey…what's wrong?' She edged closer. She could manage that and resist the urge to put her arm around him.

'It's Maggie…'

'What's wrong?' she asked quickly. 'Is she sick?' Callie really couldn't imagine anything worse than that.

'No, not sick. That would be easy to deal with… No, she's worse than sick.' His voice had a tinge of anger to it now, and Callie found herself frowning.

'Then what is it?' She dreaded asking. What would he say? Had she been in an accident? Was she at death's door? In a coma? If it were any of these things, then how would the baby situation work? She'd only agreed to be a surrogate because there was no chance she'd be expected to take care of the baby…

Oh, God, I'm going to be expected to take care of the baby…

Horror and fear grabbed her in their vice and she began to feel icy-cold, almost to the point of shivering. She closed her eyes at the onslaught, hoping that when she opened them again everything would be good and Lucas would tell her something nice.

Lucas took in a deep breath. 'She left. Walked out.'

He looked at her in disbelief and waited for her reaction. His eyes were strangely empty of tears, despite the news.

'*Left*? But—'

'She's been having an affair, apparently. Some doctor in A&E. I don't know—I think that's what she said. She said I didn't love her enough, she wasn't happy, and she's gone.' He stood up then, unable to sit still a second longer, sighing heavily now that he'd told her the important news. He turned to her and did that brave smile thing again. 'Good thing you're not pregnant yet.'

His words echoed around her skull like a bully taunting her in the playground.

Of course. She'd told neither Lucas nor Maggie about feeling a bit dodgy these last few days. She'd kept it to herself so that if it *were* true that she was having a baby it would be the best surprise to give them…

Only now it was backfiring as a great idea. There was a test in the bathroom, currently marinating, about to tell them both their future. She *could* be pregnant. With Lucas's child and no Maggie to play the part of mother!

So who would be mum, then?

Callie recoiled at the thought, looking away from Lucas and shifting back in her chair. She nibbled on her nail, worrying about all the implications.

She'd never wanted to be a mother—that was the whole point! It was her gift to Lucas and Maggie: the most perfect gift you could ever give to your best friend. A baby. Ten tiny fingers and ten tiny toes…all for them to look after, allowing her to swoop in occasionally on visits and bestow a few 'oohs' and 'aahs' before sweeping out again. The perfect—and distant—godparent.

And that was all. Callie wasn't meant to have a bigger role than that!

Sitting there, she felt numb. She knew she needed to go to the bathroom. To check that result. All she had to do was excuse herself…

Callie leapt to her feet and turned to Lucas to say something, but he'd gone. Her eyes tracked a movement to her left and she saw him disappearing into her bathroom…

'No!'

The bathroom door closed and she heard him lock the door.

Oh, God…

She waited.

And waited.

She heard the flush of her cistern, then the running of her sink taps. Closing her eyes in disbelief, she could see in her mind's eye him picking up the test on the sink and finding out that…

That what? It could still be negative, couldn't it? There was every possibility that the egg salad she'd eaten last night had been off. And the day before that? Maybe that jacket potato had been past its sell-by date…

Lucas emerged from the bathroom. He held the test in his hand and came back into her lounge, looking perplexed. His every step was heavy. Then his gaze met hers. 'You're pregnant?'

She stared at him, hearing the words but needing confirmation still. 'It's positive? Two lines?'

He turned it round so she could see and, yes, there were two solid pink lines.

Callie's mouth went dry. Sinking back down onto the couch, she felt her head sink into her hands. Tears burned her eyes with a fire she'd never felt before.

'You're pregnant.'

This time it wasn't a question.

Callie sat numb, aware only of Lucas sinking onto the couch next to her, just an inch or so away.

She hoped he wouldn't put his arm around her, or tell her everything was going to be okay, because how could he? How could he know?

Neither of them had any idea.

So they sat in silence, staring only at the carpet.

CHAPTER ONE

Dr Lucas Gold sat next to Callie in the ultrasound waiting room, wishing he had something he could do with his hands. Nerves were running him through with adrenaline, and he had to fight the strong urge to get out of his seat and pace the floor.

He wasn't used to feeling out of his depth in the hospital. It was his home turf—the place he felt most secure. He knew what he was doing with work and he was looked up to and respected for it. But this situation was brand-new. Something he'd never experienced before. It was completely terrifying and he had no idea how to handle it. His insides were a mish-mash of conflicting thoughts and emotions, all jarring with each other and fighting for superiority, whilst on the outside he hoped he was maintaining an air of calm authority. As everyone was used to.

His best friend, Callie, was drinking water from a white plastic cup, an oasis of calm, whilst he sat there, rigid, a million thoughts running through his head.

'Callie Taylor?' A nurse in blue scrubs stood in a doorway.

He glanced at Callie, meeting her gaze and offering a supporting smile, although he knew he was probably just as nervous as she was. This situation was all just so... complicated! Not the way he'd imagined this time in his life being at all. But he tried not to show it. He didn't want Callie worrying. He didn't want her to think that he had any doubts at all.

Not that I do. *Have doubts, that is. Not about the baby anyway.*

And he knew that *she* just had to be as frightened of this as he was. The situation wasn't perfect, was it? For either of them. People didn't normally plan to have babies like this. But it was the situation they were in and he was going to make it work—no matter what. The important thing here was the baby, and he was determined to do right by his child as well as his best friend. After all, he was the one who'd got her into this mess. There were so many men who got a woman pregnant and then, when the circumstances changed, left them holding the baby.

Well, not me. I could never be that man.

They both stood and he reached out to touch her upper arm, just to offer her some reassurance. But something held him back and he stopped, letting his hand drop away, pretending not to have done it and hoping she hadn't noticed. She wasn't his to touch, after all.

'After you.'

He followed her into the darkened room and stood by her side. He held his hands out as she got onto the bed, to make sure she wasn't about to fall whilst she carried his precious cargo, before sitting down in the chair beside it.

The sonographer smiled at them both. 'Oh, Callie, I didn't realise it was you!' It was one of her colleagues: Sophie. 'Are you happy for me to perform your scan today?'

Callie nodded. ''Course!'

Sophie beamed. 'So exciting! Okay, can you confirm your name and date of birth for me?'

Callie gave the details.

'And it says here that this is your first pregnancy?'

'That's right.'

Callie's voice held a tremor and Lucas glanced at her, wondering what she was thinking.

'And when was the date of your last period?'

'February seventh.'

Sophie fiddled with the plastic wheel that Lucas knew was a predictor of delivery dates. 'So that makes you twelve weeks and two days today—is that right?'

'Yes.'

'Okay, so what I'm going to do is ask you to lower the waistband on your trousers. I'll put some gel on you, which might feel cold but will help the transducer move around easier and also helps with a better image. Now, do you have a full bladder?'

'Fit to burst.'

Sophie laughed. 'I'll try not to press on it too hard. So, do you want to just undo your trousers for me and lower the waist?'

Lucas glanced away, looking elsewhere to give Callie some privacy. He waited for Sophie to tuck some blue paper towel into the top of Callie's underwear before turning back. He watched the sonographer squirt on the gel, mentally hurrying her in his mind, but smiling when Callie gasped at the feel of it on her warm skin. Then he waited.

Sophie had the screen turned away from them both as she made her initial sweeps with the scanner, and Lucas had to fight every instinct in his body not to get up and go round the bed to have a look at the screen himself!

It was difficult to be the patient. To be the person on the other side. He was used to being the one who knew what was going on first. But he knew he had to wait. Sophie would be checking for an actual embryo first, then a heartbeat, before she turned the screen for them to see.

He'd have to learn how to be patient if he was going to be a good parent.

He glanced at Callie and noticed the frown on her face

in the half-light. He wanted to tell her it would be all right, to hold her hand tight in his and tell her that there was nothing for her to worry about, but he knew he couldn't. Not yet. What was the right etiquette in this situation? No one told you *that* at the clinic.

She's pregnant with my child and I daren't even touch her.

Besides, how could he tell her there was nothing to worry about? It wasn't true, was it? There was plenty to worry about. Like how this was going to work in the first place. Maggie was supposed to be by his side at this moment, both of them watching the screen with Callie, but Maggie was gone. That was still a shock. They were on their own now and he had no idea what Callie was thinking.

Then Sophie was smiling and turning the screen. 'There you are…your baby.'

'Oh, my God!'

Lucas couldn't quite believe it! After all the uncertainty—all the testing, the waiting, the drugs, the injections, the tests. After all this time… There it was. A tiny grey bean shape, nestling in Callie's womb, its tiny heart busily beating away. It was amazing. Surreal.

My child…

His eyes burned into the screen, imprinting the shape of his child, the beat of its strong heart, into his memory for ever. This was something that could never be forgotten. Pride filled his soul and he felt an instant connection and a surge of protectiveness for his little bean—and for Callie.

He'd waited so long for this moment…

To be a father…it's real…it's happening…

A laugh of relief escaped him and he reached out without thinking and grabbed Callie's hands in his, not noticing her flinch, forgetting that she wasn't good with physical contact. His prior fears were forgotten in the moment of joy.

'Can you believe it, Callie?'

She shook her head, not speaking, and he saw the welling of tears in her own eyes and was glad. He wouldn't normally be glad to see *anyone* well up with tears or cry, but this was different. They were in a difficult situation, the pair of them, thrown together into having a baby when they weren't even a couple. Now Maggie had gone they had to find a way through this situation themselves...

After Maggie had left them both in the lurch they'd initially struggled even to be in the same room as each other. It had been so hard to know what to do or say in their situation. And so wrong that they had to feel that way! They were best friends and always had been.

Maggie had been quick to see a solicitor and apply for a divorce. She'd said it was best for both of them. She'd been quick to sever all ties.

As the days had passed the atmosphere between him and Callie had got a little less awkward—though it still wasn't what it once had been. He knew Callie had as much adjustment to make to this situation as he had—if not more. It was a tough test of their friendship...one that neither of them could ever have imagined they would have to face. They were both testing the water like anxious ducklings, not knowing if they were going to sink or swim.

Each day that they worked together brought new challenges for both of them. He could sense her awkwardness each time she worked with him. Often he found himself craving the relaxed atmosphere they'd used to have with each other. The ability to laugh at the same things, to predict what the other was thinking.

Only last week he'd helped her out on a particularly difficult shoulder dystocia and, though they'd worked together efficiently for their patient, the old rapport had not been the same and he'd felt the tension between them return the second the baby had been delivered safely. When he'd left the patient's room he'd banged his fist against the wall with frustration at the whole situation.

But he was thrilled that seeing the baby meant something to Callie too. After all, he knew she'd never wanted to have a baby of her own. Not after the way she'd been treated by her own mother. Callie's childhood had been bloody awful compared to his. To see that she was just as affected as he was at seeing the baby onscreen was priceless.

'It's a baby,' she said.

Sophie laughed at them both. 'Of course it is!' She began to take measurements. She measured the head-to-rump length and then zoomed in on the nuchal fold, which was one of the measurements they took at the three-month scan to check the risk factors for Down syndrome. 'This all looks fine. Well within parameters.'

'That's good,' Lucas said, relieved.

'I had no idea you two were together. You kept that quiet,' Sophie said.

Callie glanced at him, a question in her eyes. Should they correct her?

'Actually…er…we're not…' He stumbled over the explanation, his words fading away as he recalled Maggie's impression of their relationship. '*You love Callie, Lucas! Always have! I could never live up to her, so now I'm giving you the chance to be together!*'

'We're not together,' Callie said. 'Just having a baby.'

Lucas gave a polite smile.

Sophie raised her eyebrows. 'There's no "just" about it—you two should know that. Having a baby is hard work.'

'You give all your patients this pep talk?' Lucas didn't want her attacking their decision, and he *certainly* didn't want Callie getting upset. She'd been through enough already, what with all the morning sickness and everything.

'I'm sorry. I didn't mean—'

Lucas shook his head, appalled that he'd been snappy

with her. 'I'm sorry. I didn't mean to be sharp with you/
It's just been a tough few months already.' What was he
doing? He wasn't normally this prickly.

But Sophie was obviously used to the up-down moods
of her patients and she smiled. 'That's all right. Here—
take these.' She passed over a long strip of black-and-white
scan photos.

Callie took the opportunity to pull free of his cradling
hand and took the pictures first. She held them out before
her, admiring each one, and then turned them so that Lucas
could see. 'Look, Lucas.'

His heart expanded as he looked at each one. He could
physically feel his love growing for this little bean-shaped
creature he didn't yet know, but had helped create. All right,
maybe not in the most ideal of circumstances, but they'd
find a way to make it work. They had to. Even though he
knew he and Callie would never be together *like that.*

'You okay?' He looked into her eyes and saw the tears
had run down her cheeks now. He hoped they were happy
tears. She *seemed* happy, considering...

'I'm good,' she said, nodding. 'You'd better take these.'
She offered the pictures to him, but he sat back, shaking
his head.

'Not all of them. I'll take half. You'll need some too.'

She looked puzzled, and he didn't like the look on her
face. It made him feel uncomfortable to think that maybe
she still didn't feel that the baby was part hers.

'It's your baby, too,' he insisted.

The smile left her face and Callie avoided his gaze, looking down and then wiping the gel from her belly using the
paper towel.

He helped her sit up and turned away so she could stand
and fasten her trousers. Then, when he judged enough time
had passed, he turned back and smiled at her. 'Ready for
work?'

'As I'll ever be.'

He thanked Sophie for her time and followed Callie, blinking in the brightness of the waiting room. He tried to avoid looking at all the couples holding hands. Couples in love, having a baby. The way *he* ought to be having a child with a partner.

Yet look at how I'm doing it.

He didn't want to think about how appalled his parents must be. He'd avoided talking to them about it, knowing they'd be sad that his marriage had failed. He was upset to have let them down, having wanted his marriage to succeed for a long time—like theirs had.

'Youngsters these days just give up on a relationship at the first sign of trouble!' his mother was fond of saying.

But I'd not given up. I thought everything was fine... We were going ahead with the surrogacy. It all looked good as far as I was concerned. And then...Maggie said it was over. That she'd found true love elsewhere because she'd had to!

Now he and Callie, his best friend in the whole wide world, were in this awkward situation.

We have to make this work.

I have to.

Callie had not expected to have such a strong emotional reaction to seeing the baby on screen. Why *would* she have suspected it? Having a baby had never been one of her dreams, had it? Not really. She'd always been happy to let other people have the babies. She just helped them along in their journey from being a woman to a mother. Others could have the babies—others could make the mistakes. Others could be utter let-downs to their children and be hated by them in the long run. Because that was what happened. In real life.

What did people say about not being able to choose your family?

So even though she'd *known* she was pregnant, logically, had *known* she was carrying a child, she'd still somehow been knocked sideways by seeing it on screen. Her hypothetical surrogate pregnancy had turned into a real-life, bona fide baby that she might have to look after! And seeing it on screen had made her feel so guilty and so upset, because she already felt inadequate. She feared that this baby would be born into a world where its mother was useless and wouldn't have a clue. Callie could already imagine its pain and upset.

Because she knew what it was like to have a mother like that.

Callie waited until the sonographer had led someone else into the scanning room and then she stopped Lucas abruptly. 'Hold this,' she said, passing him her handbag. 'I need to use the loo.' Her bladder was *killing* her! Sophie had pressed down hard, no matter what she'd said about being gentle.

In the bathroom, she washed her hands and then realised how thirsty she was and that she wanted a coffee. Her watch said that they had twenty minutes before they were due to start their shift, so when she went back outside she tried to ignore the anxious look on Lucas's face and suggested they head to the café.

'You okay with coffee?' Lucas asked with concern.

'I think so.' She'd been off coffee for weeks. But now she could feel an intense craving for one and ordered a latte from the assistant. 'This is so strange,' she said as she gathered little sachets of sugar and a wooden stirrer.

Lucas looked about them, glancing at the café interior. 'What is?'

'This.'

'Having coffee?' He smiled.

She gave him a look. 'You know what I mean! This. The *situation*. Me and you—having a baby. I mean…' She swallowed hard, then asked him the question that had been on her mind ever since Maggie had walked away. The question that had been keeping her awake at night. The question that she wasn't even sure she wanted answered. If he said he wanted her to be the mother... 'How's it going to work?'

She could tell her question had him stumped.

He was trying to decide how to answer her. After all, it wasn't an easy situation. After Maggie's big revelation they'd both been knocked for six—especially when Maggie had kept her word and disappeared out of their lives altogether. No one had heard a peep from her—not even the hospital where she'd worked. She'd really dropped them in it as they'd lost a midwife without notice!

For a while Callie had believed that at some point Maggie would call and it would all sort itself out again. That she and Lucas had simply had one giant misunderstanding and it would all be sorted easily. Because then it would be easier for *her. Callie.* And wasn't that how Lucas operated? Before Maggie there'd been other girlfriends. There'd certainly been no shortage of them during the time she'd known him. Which seemed like forever. He'd always been splitting up with them and then getting back together again.

But Maggie hadn't called. The situation hadn't changed.

Callie was pregnant with Lucas's child. But they hadn't slept together and they weren't a couple.

Lucas wanted a baby and Callie never had.

Yet here she was. Pregnant. And though she'd thought she'd be safe getting pregnant, because she wouldn't be in any danger of having to keep the baby, she was now in the predicament that she might have to. Or at least have more to do with it than she'd hoped.

It.

'Honestly, Callie...? I don't know how it's going to work. But I know that it *will*. In time. We'll sort something out.'

He stood opposite her and shook some sugar into his own drink, replaced the lid.

'But *how* do you know that?' She pressed him for more information. He was her best friend in the whole wide world and always had been—for as long as she could remember. There'd once been a moment—a brief, ever so tempting moment—when she'd considered what it would be like to go out with him, but she'd not allowed herself to do it. His friendship with her had been much too valuable and the one stable element in her wretched childhood.

Callie didn't do relationships. Not long-term ones anyway. She'd had dates, and gone out with someone for a couple of months, but once he'd started making mutterings about commitment she'd backed off.

Then one day Lucas had asked her out. On a date. In a boyfriend/girlfriend kind of way. He'd looked so nervous when he'd asked her. And though they'd been great friends, and she'd known she loved him a lot, she just hadn't been about to ruin their friendship by going out on a date with him.

Lucas had been her one stable choice through her childhood and she couldn't risk losing him if things went wrong between them. Besides, they'd both been about to go off to university—it would never have worked, would it? It had been a sensible decision to make.

She could still recall the absolute shock on his face when she'd turned him down. But then he'd left her that night and gone out and met Maggie and the whole thing had been moot, after all.

'I don't know it. But you're sensible—so am I. We're good friends. *Best* friends. I don't see why we won't be able to come to some arrangement.'

She watched him sip and then wince at his coffee. 'I wish I could be as sure as you,' she said. Because Callie wasn't used to certainties. All her life she'd felt as if she lived in limbo—nothing stable, nothing rooted, her mother going through bottles of alcohol as fast as she went through various men, all of them the latest, greatest love of Maria's life.

He put his coffee down and reached out to take her hand, knowing she didn't feel comfortable with personal touch but doing it anyway to make his point. His thumb stroked the back of her knuckles, gently caressing the skin. 'We'll be fine.'

Then he let go and went back to his coffee.

She was relieved he'd let go—relieved to get back control of her hand. Relieved the sizzling reaction to his touch—where had *that* come from?—had gone. Her hand had lit up with excited nerves as his fingers had wrapped around hers and her stomach had tumbled all over like an acrobat when he'd squeezed them tight before letting go.

She gave a little laugh to break the tension. 'Too big a subject when we're due to start work in ten minutes!' She grinned, but inside her mind was racing. She'd never reacted like that to Lucas before. Why? What was happening? Hormones? Possibly...

No, it *had* to be. No 'possibly' about it.

He smiled back, laughing too. 'Way too big.'

Callie laughed nervously. There'd been something reassuring and caring about his touch, and though she disliked physical contact something had changed since she'd got pregnant. It was as if she needed it now but didn't know how to ask for it, having gone for so long without it.

And how threatening was Lucas's touch anyhow? He was her best friend. It didn't mean anything. Not like *that*. And he knew it.

But I'd like you to protect me, Lucas. Promise me I'll be safe.

Lucas sat in his office, twiddling with a pen without really seeing it. There was plenty of work he knew he ought to be getting on with, but his mind was caught up in a whirl of thoughts and emotions. As it had been for many weeks now.

Maggie was gone. But if he was honest with himself that wasn't what was bothering him. Not at all. What bothered him was what Maggie had said on that final night before she'd walked out.

'I tried with you, Lucas, I really tried! But it was all pointless, wasn't it? You've never truly loved me. Not the way you should have.'

'Of course I love you—'

She'd half laughed, half cried.

'But it wasn't real, Lucas! You thought it was, and that was the problem. You lost your heart to Callie long ago and you can't see it!'

'Callie? No, you're wrong. She's my friend...that's all—'

'She's more than your friend and I can't be second best in your life. I need someone to love me for me. I don't want to be your substitute.'

'You're not! Maggie, you're being ridiculous. Callie and I are just friends and that's all we'll ever be!'

'But you still want more. Haven't you noticed how uncomfortable it is for me every time she comes round? How you are with her?'

He'd looked at her then, confused and still reeling from her announcement that she was leaving him.

'Well, yes, but—'

'I know you care for me, Lucas. Maybe you do love me—just not enough. And not in the way that you should.'

'But we're going to have a baby together, Maggie. Hopefully. One day soon!'

She'd looked at him then, her eyes filled with sadness.

'And look who you picked to carry your child.'

Why had he allowed Callie to get into his mess? His beautiful Callie. His best friend. That was all she was. He knew her situation, knew her background—with her awful childhood and her ridiculous drunk of a mother—and he'd stupidly let her get into this situation.

Why?

Was it because Callie always seemed to set things right? Was it because he only had happy memories with her, so he'd let her suggest the surrogacy in the hope that her involvement would somehow set his marriage right?

Maybe. He couldn't be sure.

But now his mess had got real. There was a *baby*. He'd just seen it. And though he was happy, and thrilled to be having a child—there was no disappointment in *that*— he wasn't sure how all of this was going to sort itself out.

He didn't want to pretend. As he had with Maggie. The fact that he'd hurt Maggie hurt him. Pretend to Callie that everything would be fine…? He couldn't be sure. Not really. Callie didn't think she could be a mother so it looked as if he was going to have to raise this baby by himself.

I could do that. Plenty of men are single dads.

But the realisation was there that he *did* want Callie involved. More than she had ever volunteered for.

Was that fair of him? To push her down a road she wasn't ready for? Did he want to parent a baby with someone who wasn't committed—like his father?

The pen dropped to the table with a clatter and he glanced at the clock. He needed to be with his patients.

I'll have to think about this later.

He and Callie could do this. He was sure of it.

Callie was running the booking clinic that afternoon, and there were twelve women booked in to be seen over the next four hours. Due to Maggie's unexpected absence they were still down a staff member and had had to rely on an agency midwife to step into the breach and help out.

Callie took a few minutes to show the new member of staff where everything was, and how to log into the computer system, and then pulled out the first file: *Rhea Cartwright. Sixteen years old.*

Callie checked to make sure she had all the equipment she'd need and then went to the waiting room and called out the girl's name. A young girl, who was there alone and looked far less than sixteen, stood up. Clasping a large bag in front of her stomach, she followed Callie into the clinic room.

'Hi, there. My name's Callie Taylor. I'm a midwife here at St Anne's and I'll be following your case throughout your pregnancy—hopefully right up to the birth. How are you feeling today?'

The girl was about eleven weeks pregnant, according to the notes from her GP, so Callie hoped she was no longer suffering the effects of morning sickness as she herself had done. Those few weeks when it had been at its worst had been just horrible!

'I'm all right.'

The girl answered tersely, without smiling, and didn't meet Callie's eye as she gazed about the room, taking in the breastfeeding poster, the framed black-and-white picture of a baby fast asleep surrounded by sunflowers in full colour.

Callie beckoned her to sit down and settled into a chair next to her. 'No one with you today?'

'My mum couldn't make it. She was busy.'

She nodded. Perhaps Rhea's mum *was* busy. Or perhaps Rhea's mum had no idea of the pregnancy—or, worse still, couldn't be bothered. Callie didn't *want* to jump to that conclusion, but she had personal experience of having an uninterested mother. It wasn't nice. But she couldn't judge someone she'd never met, and nor did she want to jump to conclusions.

'What about your partner? The baby's father?'

Rhea shook her head and looked at anything but Callie. 'I don't want to talk about him.'

She was going to be a closed book. Callie knew she would have to tread softly with Rhea and gain the girl's confidence if she was to learn anything. It was like this sometimes with teenage mothers. They suddenly found themselves in an adult world, living by adult rules, when all they wanted was to live by their own and be left to get on with it.

And in Callie's experience pregnant teenage mothers were often reluctant to show their trust until you'd earned it.

'Okay…well, take a seat.' Rhea still hadn't sat down. 'I'll need to run through some questions with you.'

She tried to keep her voice gentle and neutral. Nothing forceful. Nothing that would suggest Rhea was being ordered or expected to answer questions, as if she was taking some sort of test.

'Just some basic things about you and your last period… that sort of thing. Is that okay?'

Rhea sank into the chair with her bag clasped in front of her, still looking at anything but Callie. She shrugged, as if unwilling to commit either way.

'Well, we'll just start with some basics and see how we go on. Can you confirm your date of birth for me?'

Callie sensed it was going to be a long afternoon. Rhea was not going to give up any information easily. Small red flags were waving madly in her mind. Her midwife's sixth sense, developed over time, was telling her that there was something going on here that she didn't know about. She had learned that it was best to listen to it. It would be so straightforward if every couple or single mother she saw had a happy home life for a baby to be born into, but quite often that wasn't the case. There was a lot of poverty in London. There were a lot of drugs problems, lots of drink problems. Hadn't that been her own experience?

'April the first.'

April Fools' Day. Not a joke. It was confirmed in her

notes. Callie knew she didn't have the type of relationship with Rhea yet to make a joke about the date, so she kept a neutral face and voice and continued with her questions.

'And when was the first day of your last menstrual period?'

There was a moment of silence, as if Rhea was weighing up whether to give her the information or not, then she said, 'February the seventh.'

The same as me.

Callie smiled, about to say so, but decided to hold back. This young girl was so different from her in so many ways.

'Do you mind telling me whether this is a planned pregnancy, or were you using contraception?' she asked without thinking.

She'd not asked just because Rhea was a teenager. It was one of the questions that she always asked. It was important to know whether someone had planned their pregnancy. Whether they'd been actively trying for a baby, or whether the pregnancy was a complete accident and a surprise. It had a bearing on the mother's attitude to it all. Just because a mother was at her booking visit it didn't automatically mean that she wanted to keep the baby. Plus, she needed to know if Rhea had taken any prenatal vitamins.

'I don't see why that's important.'

Callie put down her pen. 'I'm sorry. I just wanted to know whether you'd planned the pregnancy or not.'

'Because I'm sixteen? Because I'm young it must have been a mistake? Is that what you're saying?'

Rhea met Callie's gaze for the first time, and now Callie could see how frightened and unsure this young girl was.

Where was her support? She was so *young*! It had to be scary for her. Callie herself was twenty-eight—a whole twelve years older than Rhea—and *she* was terrified of being pregnant. How could she even begin to imagine how this girl felt?

'No, not at all. I didn't mean that. It's a standard question—'

'Well, I don't want to talk about it. Next?'

Rhea folded her arms and closed up and didn't meet Callie's eyes again for the rest of the meeting.

It was obvious she was a troubled young woman, and if Callie was going to be there for her then she needed to get the young girl on side.

'Let's start again… Let's look at your family health. Any medical problems on your side of the family I should know about? Diabetes? Asthma?'

Rhea shook her head reluctantly. 'We're fine.'

'Again this is a standard question: any history of depression? Anything like that?'

'My mum has that.'

Right, okay—that's something.

'Do you know if your mum suffered with postnatal depression?'

'No.'

'That's okay.' Voice still neutral. Unthreatening. Soft. Rhea was answering the questions.

'What about the father of the baby?'

Rhea stiffened, still not meeting her gaze, shuffling her feet, twiddling with her bag strap with nervous fingers. 'What about him?'

'Any health issues on his side we should be concerned about?'

'I don't know.'

What is it about the father of this baby that she doesn't want me to know?

'How tall is he?'

'What?' Rhea frowned.

'His height? It can have a bearing on the size of your baby.'

Surely she can tell me his height?

'I don't know.'

Callie paused. What was going on here? How did she not know the boy's height? Or perhaps she did know but didn't want to give Callie any clues that might identify him? Perhaps he was an older man? Married? Or was he younger than Rhea? Which would be a whole different kettle of fish. Not that she wanted to think that way, but it was a possibility she had to consider.

'How did you two meet?' That *wasn't* a standard question, but Callie felt she needed to do some extra detective work on this case if she were to get any helpful answers.

'What's that got to do with anything?'

Callie shrugged. 'I'm just interested.'

'Nosy, more like. How I got pregnant has got nothing to do with you. You're a midwife. You should know how people get pregnant, yeah? So just tell me what I need to do next so I can get out of here.'

Callie shrank back from the anger, but she was getting really concerned for Rhea. The girl was so angry and scared. There had to be a way to help her. To get the young girl to trust her.

'Okay, okay… I guess what I really need to know is your intention. You're very young and I have no idea of your support system. I'm making no judgements, but I need to know what your intentions are regarding this pregnancy.'

'My intentions?'

'Yes. Are you keeping it? Are you here to ask about other options?' She didn't want to use the word abortion unless Rhea used it first.

She was quiet for a while, and Callie could see that Rhea's eyes were filling with tears. Her nose was going red and she was really fighting the urge to cry. All Callie's instincts told her to reach out and comfort her, to put an arm around her, to show her that someone genuinely cared. But it wouldn't have been professional to break that boundary—

and, besides, she wasn't comfortable being that person just yet with Rhea. Any show of affection might have the opposite effect and send Rhea running for the hills.

So she sat quietly and waited, her gaze on Rhea's face.

'I don't want it.' Her voice was quiet and empty of emotion.

'You don't?' This was what she'd suspected.

'No.'

'Then there are two options open to you, Rhea.'

Tears rolled down Rhea's cheeks. 'I can't have an abortion. I don't believe in it.'

'Right…okay.'

'I want to give it away. Get rid of it that way.'

It.

So impersonal. So unattached.

I called my baby 'it'.

There had to be personal reasons for Rhea's decision, but Callie truly felt that now was not the time to push for them. If Rhea wanted to give her baby away after it was born, that gave Callie six more months of learning about Rhea and working with her to find out what was going on and how best she could help her.

It was a big decision to give away your baby.

It was what I was going to do. Give the baby to Lucas and Maggie. Only it's not 'the' baby now. It's 'my' baby, isn't it?

Isn't it?

Callie wasn't sure. She and Lucas still hadn't discussed properly what they were going to do to sort this. But they needed to. They were on the clock now and time was ticking. Should she still give the baby to Lucas? Was it even her decision to make?

Callie decided that once the booking clinic was over she was going to call the fertility clinic and ask to speak to one of the counsellors there. She, Lucas and Maggie had each undertaken individual counselling before agreeing to the surrogacy, but the situation had changed now. Everything was different.

I was going to give my baby away. Happily. I was going to do it for Lucas and Maggie.

Who was Rhea doing it for? *What* was Rhea doing it for?

'Okay. We can talk about that. It's a big decision.'

'I know what I'm doing.'

'Have you talked to your family about it?'

'It's not their decision. It's mine. My body—my choice.'

'Of course it is. I'm not denying that.'

'Just put it in my notes that I'm giving it away. The Social can have it. I don't want to see it, or hold it. Just get them to take it away and give it to someone who doesn't know where it's come from.'

'Doesn't know where it's come from'? Why would she say that? Did Maria think that way about me? She never wanted me. Never wanted anything to do with me. Was my own mother like this young girl once?

'I'll put it in your notes. You do know that I'll be here for you throughout this, Rhea? Any time. You'll be able to call me, night or day. I'll give you my contact details.' She passed over a small card that had the hospital numbers and Callie's own personal mobile number on it too.

Rhea stuffed it into her bag. 'I don't want anyone judging me.'

'No one will do that.'

'You don't know what I've been through.'

'No. But I'm hoping that at some point you'll trust me enough to tell me.'

She meant it. Sincerely she meant it. And she hoped Rhea could sense that. It was at times like these that Callie's job meant the world to her. It was at times like these when she felt she could really help someone—and this young girl clearly needed help for something.

If only she'd let me in. If only she'd let me help her so that another baby doesn't grow up feeling like I did as a child. Unwanted and unloved.

'Don't you need to take my blood pressure or something?'

Rhea broke the silence and Callie nodded, glad that Rhea was offering her something.

'Of course. I need to take blood, too.'

'I brought this.' Rhea reached into her bag and took out a small jar with a urine sample in it. 'I washed it out before I used it.'

'That's great—thanks.' She would need another sample if this one was more than two hours old. It was hospital policy. However, she wasn't going to say that. Rhea had offered her a little something. That would have to do for now.

Rhea's blood pressure was fine, as was her urine sample. Nothing out of the ordinary and all well within parameters. Physically, she seemed fine. It was just emotionally that something was off.

'You know, I'm really looking forward to getting to know you better throughout this, Rhea.'

'Yeah, well, don't go thinking you'll get me to change my mind.'

'That's not my place.'

'No, it isn't. No one has the right to judge me for giving this thing away.'

'No, they haven't.' *I was going to give a baby away myself.* 'But please don't call the baby a "thing". Call it what it is.'

Rhea stood up to go and slung her bag over her shoulder. 'It's a *thing*. It will always be a *thing*. It'll never be anything else.' And she stormed from the clinic.

Callie watched her go, bewildered and amazed. In some ways Rhea seemed so strong, but in others she was just a tiny young girl, terrified and afraid.

And what am I afraid of?

Callie's hand went to her own stomach, as yet still un-changed in size. She didn't even know she was doing it until her phone beeped a text message alert and she was brought back into the present. As she rummaged in her bag for her phone thoughts echoed through her mind.

Don't go getting attached.

You have no idea if you're keeping it either.

CHAPTER TWO

THE NEXT DAY Callie was scheduled to work on a twin delivery. She could see that Lucas was on duty that day too, along with the senior consultant Dev Patel, though she hadn't seen him yet. They had four women in labour, most in early stages, and Callie had been assigned to a woman in her late forties, having her first babies. Callie hadn't been expecting to work with Lucas, but he was already in the room.

'There's been some decelerations,' he said, after saying hello and seeing her look of surprise.

Olivia Hogarth was on her knees, leaning over the back of the bed, panicking and almost out of control, showing real signs of not dealing with her labour at all. Every time a contraction came along a terrified look came into Olivia's eyes and she began to huff and puff on the Entonox as if for dear life. Her husband, James, stood helpless beside her. He was at a complete loss as to what to do, but kept rubbing her back for dear life as she held on to the support of the bed.

'Hi, Olivia, I'm Callie, and I'm going to be your midwife today.' Callie leant round the back of the bed so Olivia could see her face and not just hear a random voice.

'Hurgh!' Olivia's teeth gripped the mouthpiece and her frightened gaze practically begged Callie to do something. 'Help me!'

'Okay…slow, deep breaths…that's it. Slow your breathing.' Callie showed Olivia how to breathe in slowly through her nose for five seconds and then out through her mouth for five more seconds.

'I'm all tingly!' Olivia protested when the contraction was over. 'Pins and needles.'

'It's because you're not exhaling properly. Come on—practise with me whilst there's no contraction.'

As Olivia practised Callie took a moment to glance at Olivia's trace. There were some decelerations in the babies' heartbeats. Not by much, but they were definitely there. Each time Olivia's babies got squeezed by a contraction the heart-rate dipped, which meant they weren't liking labour very much.

Callie wasn't happy with the trace and glanced up at Lucas as he came to stand by her and judge it for himself.

Sometimes decelerations could be caused by there being a short cord, or a knot in the cord, or by the cord being tightly wrapped around the baby's body. It didn't mean that there was something wrong with the baby physically. But Callie knew it was never worth taking any chances. It was always best to call for help if you were working alone. If you weren't sure you got someone else. Fortunately she already had Lucas there.

He stood beside her, dressed all in black, in tailored shirt and trousers, and she could smell his aftershave. Since she'd got pregnant smells and aromas had seemed particularly pronounced, and his was delicious today.

Callie glanced at him sideways as he concentrated on the trace. Her heart skipped a beat—*palpitations?* She'd never had those before—it had to be the pregnancy. She supposed she couldn't help it, she thought wryly. He was a very attractive man after all. Hadn't she watched a multitude of women fawn over him?

He was tall, broad and handsome. It was hard to think

that the little boy she'd once known—the one with the spindly legs and constantly scuffed knees—had turned into this strong, mature, devastatingly handsome man. It never mattered what was going on in her own life—her mother letting her down yet again, her mother lying to her, someone treating her badly—she always brightened when she saw Lucas. He was her pillar. Her rock. Her safe place in stormy seas. He'd always been there for her and she hoped he always would be. Especially now. Now they were having a baby together—even if it wasn't in the traditional way.

He looked really good today. Fresher and brighter-looking than she'd seen him look these last few weeks. Maggie leaving the way she had, and admitting to an affair, had shaken them both. But even though Lucas had been shocked by the end of his marriage, he'd thankfully not been devastated. He'd coped with the change in his life amazingly well, and she couldn't help but admire him for his courage and resilience—as everyone did.

She could only assume that seeing the scan yesterday had perked him up. Either that or he'd managed a great night's sleep! His eyes were bright and blue, like cornflowers in a summer meadow, and there was colour to his cheeks. He'd even shaved! These last few weeks he'd been beginning to look like a mountain man.

She liked the fact that he looked bigger and stronger. It made her feel safe and protected, and she knew he'd move heaven and earth to do anything to help her at the moment.

Callie couldn't help but wonder what this pregnancy was *doing* to her? Her emotions and responses seemed hyper-aware, with all these hormones floating about, and she knew she needed to be careful that she didn't let them carry her away. He cared for her because they were good friends. Nothing more.

He's just my friend. Yes, he's the baby's father, but it's not like we slept together, is it? It was all done in a petri dish in a clinic—nothing romantic.

But just thinking about sleeping with Lucas made her cheeks flush with heat.

She knew she needed to focus on her patient and deliberately stepped away from him. Thoughts about sleeping with Lucas were dangerous and she'd never allow them to surface.

Olivia finished puffing on her gas and air and looked panicked, her eyes open wide. 'What's wrong? Is it the babies?'

Lucas pulled out the long white roll of paper and checked through the tracing with Callie. He gave a tiny nod. 'Olivia, Baby A seems to be a bit upset after each contraction and Baby B doesn't look too happy either. It may just be because of the reduced room in your uterus and the contractions, but I'd like to be on the safe side.' He turned to Callie. 'When was her last examination?'

She checked the notes. 'Four and a half hours ago. Would you like me to do another?' They tried to examine women vaginally every four hours during labour. This usually gave the cervix plenty of time to show the changes every midwife and mother wanted to feel.

Lucas turned the full beam of his attention on the mother. 'Sure. Olivia, we'd like to examine you, if possible, see how you're getting along. Is that all right?'

'Of course.'

Lucas looked at Callie and nodded.

'I'll be as gentle as I can…'

Callie washed her hands and then put on gloves, settling herself on the side of Olivia's bed as she did so. She felt as much as she could, her fingers sweeping the edge of the cervix, her eyes on Lucas.

He kept checking with Olivia to make sure she was all right and apologising for any discomfort she might be feeling, but Olivia was quite stoical. The most calm she'd been since Callie had met her. Perhaps she could cope better with men around, supporting her, rather than another woman?

As Callie removed her gloves she smiled. 'You're making good progress. Eight centimetres.'

'Eight!' Olivia began to suck in gas and air again as another contraction hit, so she didn't notice Callie take Lucas to one side of the room.

'I'm concerned there's some extra blood in the birth canal,' she whispered. 'I don't want to panic her, but I think we need to put a continuous CTG on her and the babies and keep it monitored.' CTG was cardiotocography—a technical way of recording the foetal heartbeats as well as any uterine contractions.

'Yes, we need to be alert for any signs of possible placental abruption.' He kept his voice low.

Placental abruption was a life-threatening condition in which the placenta detached itself from the uterine wall before birth, causing heavy bleeding and potentially fatal consequences for both mother and baby if not caught in time.

'Possibly.'

'Okay. I want to move her to Theatre, just in case.'

'I'll ring Theatre to let them know we're coming.'

And just as Callie said this blood soaked into the sheets around Olivia's legs.

Her husband, James, leapt to his feet. 'My God! What's going on?'

Callie and Lucas leapt into action. There wasn't much time. They had to act fast. They quickly unplugged Olivia from the monitors, grabbed the ends of the bed and began to wheel her from the room.

Lucas kept his voice calm, yet firm, as he gave an explanation to James and Olivia. 'Your wife's bleed may mean the placenta has detached early from the wall of her womb. We need to do an emergency Caesarean to get the babies out safely.' Lucas's controlled, assertive voice was an oasis of calm in a situation that could so easily be filled with panic or fear.

'Is she going to be okay?' The colour had gone from James's face.

Olivia looked pale and clammy and her head was beginning to loll back against the pillows.

'Just follow us. It's going to be a general anaesthetic, so you won't be allowed into Theatre, I'm afraid.'

They began to push the bed from the room and head up the corridors towards the operating rooms. Lucas called out to passing staff to help and they responded to his firm authority and helped them get Olivia to Theatre.

'And the babies?'

As they reached the theatre doors there was a large sign stating 'Staff Only Beyond This Point' and James slowed to a stop, looking lost and hopeless.

Lucas turned back briefly and laid a reassuring hand on James's arm. 'We'll do our best for all of them.' And then he and Callie pushed Olivia into Theatre, leaving James behind, bewildered and in shock.

They didn't like to do it, but James was not their first priority at this point. Time was critical now, and they couldn't waste it by stopping to talk it through with Olivia's husband. They could debrief him afterwards.

It was a mad rush of preparation. They'd not had time to call Theatre, so the first the theatre staff knew of an emergency coming was when they wheeled Olivia in. But they were such a well-oiled machine that they all knew what to do.

Within minutes, they had Olivia under general anaesthetic, drapes up, and Lucas was scrubbed and ready to go. The theatre staff were used to emergency sections, and they all liked working with Lucas, who was calm and fair and friendly—unlike some of the other doctors who operated.

Lucas could just give a look and everyone would know what he needed. His authority was not questioned, and everyone in his team looked to him for guidance.

'I'm going to perform a lower segment section.' He pointed the scalpel to Olivia's skin and in one quick yet sure movement began the emergency operation.

Callie stood by the side of the bed, her heart pounding, her legs like jelly. She really disliked occasions such as this. *Emergencies*. If she could have her way then all babies would be born normally, without danger, without the need for Theatre. Babies were meant to arrive in calm environments, with music softly playing in the background, and then to be placed in their mother's arms afterwards for that all-important cuddle and skin-to-skin contact.

General anaesthetics and emergencies took away all of that. Babies were separate from their mothers until the mother was awake enough to hold the baby without dropping it, and sometimes that initial important breastfeed was missed because the mother was unable to do it, or the baby itself was too drowsy from the cross-over of the drugs the mother had had.

Her lips felt dry beneath the paper mask. She glanced at Lucas, admiring the concentration in his gaze, his composure. Despite the emergency, he knew exactly what needed to be done and how. But as she stood there Callie realised she was beginning to feel a little bit woozy and hot.

The rush from Olivia's room and pushing the bed through the corridors wouldn't normally have taken its toll, but now that she was pregnant she felt a little more fragile than normal. She still felt out of breath from the sprint and her brow was becoming sweaty, as was her top lip. Her stomach began to churn like a washing machine, as if she was about to be sick.

It wasn't the sight of the blood. That sort of thing never bothered her. Nor was it the controlled tension in the room.

No. This was something else. She didn't feel right at all. She looked at Lucas over her mask in a panic, hoping he'd look up. See her. Notice that something was wrong.

She could feel something…a weird sensation beginning to overcome her. If she could try to focus on his calm, reassuring face she felt it might help, but her vision was going a bit blurry and the noises in the room—the beeping of machines—began to sound distant and echoing.

As she felt herself sway slightly she put one hand on the bed to steady herself. Lucas looked up from his work and frowned.

'Callie? You okay?'

But his words sounded as if they were coming from far away. She blinked to clear her eyesight, felt her heart pound like a hammer and then heard a weird whooshing noise in her ears. A black curtain descended and she went crashing to the floor, taking a tray of instruments down with her.

'Callie!'

Lucas was unable to catch her. She'd been standing on the other side of the operating table and there was a patient between them. Instead he had to stand there, horrified, his scalpel poised, as she collapsed onto the floor and lay there, despite the best efforts of the scrub nurse to try and catch her.

Her arms were outspread, her eyes closed.

I need to concentrate on my patient first. Her life is in my hands. I'll have to let the others take care of Callie.

The situation killed him, but what could he do? Just focus on delivering Olivia safely and *then* he could check on Callie.

How did I not see she looked pale? he berated himself inwardly.

The anaesthetist couldn't move either, but two other theatre assistants got Callie up onto a trolley and wheeled her from the theatre. He watched her go, his heart in his mouth, his mind whooshing with a million thoughts. But he pulled it back.

I need to be professional. Callie's in good hands. I know that. I can't do anything here but look after my patient.

The staff were great. They knew the situation—knew Callie was Lucas's surrogate, and knew how much it must be hurting him not to be with her—so they all did their best to help him work quickly, so he could be with her.

Lucas had to think fast and concentrate. All he wanted to do was leave Theatre and go and check on Callie, but he *knew* he couldn't! His professional integrity told him to stay with his patient. Her life and that of her babies were on the line.

Once into the uterus, he was able to deliver both babies quickly. They came out crying, which was great. A glance at the monitors assured him that Olivia was doing fine, despite the emergency.

A few moments later the theatre assistants returned.

'How's Callie?' he asked, busy removing the placentas.

'Coming round. We left her in the staffroom with one of the midwives looking after her,' the assistant called, her back to him as she assessed the babies at the Resuscitaires.

'How are the babies?'

'Pinking up—we'll get there,' confirmed the paediatrician, and then there was a lusty cry and Lucas was able to let out a breath he hadn't realised he'd been holding. He glanced at the anaesthetist at the head of his patient.

'Sats ninety-seven per cent, BP dropped. But she's stable…she's good.'

That was good to know. He'd expected Olivia's blood pressure to drop with the bleed, but if she was stable then it looked as if both mother and twins were going to get through this.

Once both the placentas were out Lucas began to stitch,

sewing together all the layers of muscle and fascia that made up the abdomen, finally closing Olivia's lower belly about forty-five minutes after he'd first had to open her.

It had been nearly thirty minutes since Callie's collapse and he was desperate to see her. His stomach was in knots, but he sewed quickly and efficiently. He kept clenching and unclenching his jaw as he thought of all the things that were worrying him.

Why did she faint? *Was* it a faint? Or something else? Perhaps she'd not eaten properly that morning? There had to be a reason, and he intended to do a full medical check-up on her when he got out of Theatre.

Why was everything going wrong? Having a child was meant to be one of the happiest times of his life! Yet it was all such a mess. He still didn't know what was going to happen after the birth, and now Callie had collapsed. He hated not being able to be there for her and he wanted to be. Every step of the way.

Finally Olivia was ready to go through to Recovery. The assistant and porters wheeled her away and he thanked the staff, seeing their appreciative smiles and nods, then scrubbed clean, quickly changed his scrubs and hurried off to find Callie.

He found her looking pale and ashen in the staffroom, feet up on the chairs and her hands shaking as she nursed a hot sweet tea.

He rushed straight over to her, kneeling by her side and feeling her forehead. 'Are you all right?'

She looked sheepish and slightly disturbed by his hand on her head, so he removed it.

'I'm fine.' Her voice sounded weak and shaky.

'You passed out.' He knew he sounded angry and was stating the obvious, but...

'I'm fine.'

'How do I know that?' Next he reached for her wrist and

felt her pulse as he glanced up at the clock in the room. Her skin was cool and soft, but her pulse was going quite fast. She pulled her hand free.

'Honestly, Lucas. I'm fine.' She sounded angry.

He knelt next to her, filled with concern, wanting to ask her a million questions, wanting to know if she'd hurt herself when she fell. He checked her over—skin pallor, pupil dilation, carotid pulse, respirations.

'You've no pain?'

'No. How's Olivia and the twins?'

'All doing well. Which is the least that can be said for you.'

'I missed breakfast, that's all.'

'That's *all*? You know how important breakfast is in your condition.'

'I know!'

'And yet you missed it? Why? What were you doing?' He tried his best not to sound angry, but knew she could hear it in his voice.

She shrugged, looking guilty. 'I slept in.'

'You *slept in*?'

'I was late getting up. I hit the snooze button a few times and then it was too late to eat breakfast, so I came straight to work. I was going to grab a banana or something.'

'So all you've had is that tea?'

'Yes.' She at least managed to look shamefaced.

He frowned, thinking of how he could immediately put this right. 'Wait there. Don't move.'

Lucas disappeared from the staffroom, headed for the stairs and ran down two stairwells, jumping the last couple of steps and skidding out onto the ground floor of the hospital. Women looked at him as he passed, but he didn't notice.

There was a store selling most things—mainly for visitors—and he grabbed lemon and raisin pancakes, a banana, chocolate and a snack pack of fresh strawberries, and headed back upstairs with his carrier bag full of goodies.

In the staffroom, Callie watched him thoughtfully as he arranged everything on a plate—slicing the banana and strawberries, pouring her a glass of milk and laying out the food as if it had been served at a hotel.

Then he turned to her with a smile, a towel folded over his arm as if he was a waiter. *'Voilà!'* he said with a flourish.

She laughed as she took it from him, and he grinned at her delight. Her laughter and pleasure made him feel good in a way he hadn't felt for some time. But Callie had always been able to cheer him up. She'd always been there for him. And there was something about her smile and childish delight that touched his heart.

'Now, you're not allowed to complain—in this situation I get to look after you,' he said.

Callie stabbed a strawberry with her fork and popped it into her mouth. 'I could get used to it.'

He nodded, his eyes shining with pleasure, and then a serious thought shot to the front of his head. It was a huge decision—a huge idea—but it felt so right and he just let it out.

'Then let me do it.'

'Do what?' she asked quizzically, another strawberry piece halfway to her mouth, suspended on the end of her fork.

'Move in with me. To the spare room,' he added, feeling his cheeks colour as he realised just what a huge thing he was asking.

Where had *that* idea come from? Okay, he hadn't liked the idea of not being there for every moment of her pregnancy, but he'd resigned himself to it. Hadn't he? It was what he would have had to do if Maggie had still been around. Or would it have come to this anyway? Her moving in to his spare room?

'No strings—nothing like that. Just a friend sleeping over. Just…let me look after you.' Suddenly he needed her to agree to this. And why not? They were best friends—how hard could it be? They'd spent years together, they knew each other inside out, and it wasn't romantic or anything. He knew that would never happen—she'd always been clear on that.

She slowly chewed the strawberry before swallowing. 'But why?'

'Because I shouldn't have to be worrying about you all the time!' His exasperation burst from him unexpectedly. 'I think about you constantly, Callie!' It was true. His mind was always on her just lately. Since the pregnancy, anyway. 'Whether you're okay, whether you're sick, if you're having pains, if you're bleeding and not saying anything. I worry, okay? It *is* natural—you *are* carrying my child.'

Callie stared at him, saying nothing. She wasn't used to people caring about her.

'I never wanted it to be this way.' He brought his voice down an octave or two, even though they were alone in the room. 'I thought I'd have a child the normal way, you know? Married…living with the woman who was carrying the baby…being there for everything. Missing nothing. The first kick. The first movement. The Braxton Hicks. The real contractions. The rush to hospital for the birth.' He let out a big sigh. 'I don't want to do this from a distance.'

'Do what?'

'*Fatherhood.* I can't do it from a distance, Callie. I'm not my father. At least consider it. Please?'

She stared long and hard at him and he wasn't sure whether to say any more. He decided to remain silent. He'd not meant to say *anything*! But it was tough, being a dad-to-be and not being allowed to hold the woman carrying your child. Not to be involved. He'd thought he'd be able to handle it, but what if he couldn't?

How had his own father done it? Eight kids in total, eight pregnancies, and he'd been away on duty in other countries for most of them. How had he got on with life? By not being there for it all? Easily. That was how. Because his father was a totally different creature. A man who liked to have the knowledge that his wife was forever pregnant, so other men knew she was taken, was unavailable, but without the day-to-day drudgery of being at home himself. He thought it was boring.

Callie was his best friend but the lines between them were blurring now, because of the baby she was carrying. She had always meant so much to him, but now she meant *everything*. She was precious and fragile and carrying his child—and he wanted to be there. Was that so wrong?

He couldn't think about what Maggie might have said if they'd still been together. How would she have reacted to him asking Callie to move in with them?

Not very well.

'I'll think about it,' she said, eating a slice of banana.

He nodded, satisfied with that answer for now. 'No strings. Strictly spare room stuff. Just…in the same home. That's all. Think of it as a long-term sleepover at a mate's house.'

Callie put down her fork as he reached out for her and wrapped his arms around her shoulders, holding her close, squeezing her gently, enjoying the feel of her next to him, knowing that this was as close as he would ever get.

'You worried me. I don't ever want to have to see you that vulnerable again,' he whispered into her hair. He felt her hot breath against the side of his head and realised he had to fight to not turn his face to her.

'I'm sorry.'

'Let me look after you. It'll be fun.'

She pulled back and looked at him, laughing. *'Fun?'*

It was good to laugh with her, to see the happiness in her eyes. 'Why not?'

Callie tilted her head to one side and looked at him strangely. 'I'd need to pay rent.'

He nodded. 'Fine.'

'And I'll do my own laundry.'

'Double fine.'

'And I get to cook sometimes.'

'Hmm…'

'Oy!' She gave him a prod. 'I'm not that bad!'

'Okay. Deal.' He held out his hand and she took it.

It had been a difficult time—a difficult event, seeing her collapse like that. But in these last few minutes he had his best friend back. And it felt good. Being close to her once again.

The only problem, Lucas began to realise as he sat facing her, was that he wasn't sure if he wanted to let go of her at all.

What mess had he got them both into?

CHAPTER THREE

CALLIE HAD MANAGED to get hold of Rhea on her mobile phone and persuaded her to come in. After Rhea had stormed off the other day there were still lots of things that Callie needed to do to make sure she was looking after Rhea in the best possible way. That meant doing blood tests and asking some of the questions that she hadn't got to ask in the first place.

As an incentive, she'd arranged for Rhea's first scan, hoping that the sight of her baby might make Rhea open up a bit more.

When she arrived, Callie noted that Rhea was wearing the same dowdy pink top and jeans as before, and was looking a little bedraggled. She invited her into the clinic room and offered her a cup of tea.

'I can't drink tea at the moment, thanks.'

'Me neither. Would you like coffee?'

Rhea looked at her, head tilted to one side. 'You're pregnant, too?'

'I am.' She smiled, hoping that this sharing of a confidence might provoke the same in her patient. 'Just out of that horrible first trimester. The sickness was awful—I tell you, it certainly made me think twice. How about you?'

Rhea nodded. 'I never wanted to be pregnant in the first place. The sickness was like extra punishment.'

Callie could empathise about the sickness. She smiled reassuringly. 'So the pregnancy is unplanned?'

'I didn't ask for it.' Rhea was instantly abrupt.

It was an odd response, and Callie wasn't sure what to make of it. 'What *did* you ask for?'

Again Rhea couldn't meet her eyes, but there were tears threatening again and Rhea was struggling to hold them back. Callie knew she had to offer Rhea something, in the hope that the girl would open up to her.

'Last time we met you mentioned you wanted to give the baby away. Have it adopted.'

'So?' The response was almost a challenge and Rhea glared at her, as if daring her to criticise.

'So...' Callie took a deep breath and plunged in. 'I want you to understand that adoption is a huge thing. It's difficult for the birth mother. You know...having carried the baby for nine months. Felt it kick, felt it move, gone through labour for it. I want to know that you've thought it all through.'

Callie didn't feel there was any need to mention that she was in a similar situation. For now, she needed Rhea to think hard about her choice, to look at her decision carefully. Without rushing.

Rhea looked at her with barely disguised curiosity. 'Yeah? I thought the Social would just take it away if I didn't want it.'

'Yes, they would. But they'd *also* give you the time to say goodbye. See the baby. Hold him or her. Some mothers who choose to have their babies adopted keep the baby for a few weeks, just to be sure of their decision.'

'I don't want to look after it! I don't want to see it!'

Callie frowned at such a strong, determined response. She wasn't judging Rhea's decision. She was free to make the choice to have her baby adopted. But Rhea was so young—only sixteen—and Callie knew she had to be sure that Rhea had thought this through properly and not just rushed into a decision because the pregnancy was still a shock.

'Okay, and that's fine—you don't have to if you don't want to. But, Rhea, you have to understand that, as a midwife, I know many women feel emotional after giving birth. It's such an arduous thing. It hurts, you're exhausted, but at the end of it—for most women—there's the prize, if you like, of a baby. They *need* to hold it. Need to see it. Smell it, touch it. See that after all those months of watching a bump grow their baby is real and that they're different people now. Mothers.'

'There's nothing you can say that will make me change my mind.'

Callie held up her hands. 'I'm not trying to. It's not my place and it would be totally unprofessional for anyone to do that. This is your choice, and whatever you choose will be fine by me.'

Rhea nodded firmly.

'As long as I know that you've thought through the consequences of your choice properly. It's not something you'll be able to just forget. It will always be with you.'

Rhea pulled her mobile phone from her pocket, checked the display and then put it away again. 'You're trying to make me feel guilty.'

'No. Absolutely not. But I *will* be devil's advocate and make sure you've thought through your choice—because, Rhea, you don't want to get a couple of years down the line and suddenly be filled with regret, with no way of reversing your decision.'

'You think I'll want it later on?' she scoffed. 'You've *got* to be kidding me.'

'I don't know how you'll feel later on. But I want you to think about it. I want you to imagine you give up this baby and a few years pass by, life carries on, and then you find yourself wondering about your daughter or your son.'

Rhea shook her head. 'I won't.'

'Okay, but I want you to think about it. You've got time, after all, if you're going to go through with the pregnancy.'

Rhea shrugged. 'I appreciate what you're doing, okay? You're a midwife. You must love babies to do this job. But I'm not you. I don't live in la-la land, where everything is right and beautiful. Where I come from it's tough and hard and life is cruel. I don't need to be saddled with the burden of a baby in a fourteenth-floor flat reached with a broken lift that stinks of old pee.'

'I know what it's like to have a tough life, Rhea. My childhood was no bed of roses, believe me.'

Callie bit her lip. This wasn't the time to be sharing personal information with Rhea. It wasn't professional. But she needed to get through to her somehow.

'Let me guess…your parents got you the wrong type of doll?'

'Actually, my alcoholic mother dragged me through childhood. Reluctantly.'

She regretted her words as soon as she'd said them. Callie knew better than to share that much personal information with a patient. But there was something about this young girl that called out to her.

Rhea stared hard at Callie, assessing her words, judging if she thought they were real. But she must have seen the truth in Callie's eyes, because she looked away and then apologised.

'It's okay. I'm sorry. I should never have said that.' Callie told her.

'I'm glad you did. Made you seem a bit more real.'

'Worldly-wise?' Callie smiled.

Rhea managed a small smile, the corners of her mouth turning up. 'Yeah.'

'It's easy to assume that everyone else's life is better than ours, but sometimes it just isn't.'

'No.'

Callie gathered the notes on her desk, taking a deep breath, and changed the subject slightly. 'Do you have support, Rhea? Family?'

'My mum—though she's as much use as a chocolate chisel.'

Callie smiled. Snap. Her own mother was now supposedly a *recovered* alcoholic, rather than an 'active' one, but Callie wasn't sure whether she was or not. Maria *said* she was off the sauce, but Maria was a born liar and Callie had heard enough lies to last a lifetime.

It was the one thing she couldn't stand more than anything. Liars. There was just something so horrible about them. Being untruthful. Taking you for a fool. Not respecting you enough to give you the truth. Assuming you were stupid enough to fall for the fallacy. Everything Callie's mother now said she took with a pinch of salt.

It was why she tried her hardest to have as little to do with her as she could, despite Maria's constant efforts to get in touch. The times Callie *had* bothered, the times she had made the effort, had always been in vain and dealing with the constant let-downs was just getting too much. It was easier not to try.

'Your dad? Brothers? Sisters?'

'Just mum.'

Like me. And Rhea is pregnant—like me. And both our mothers are useless and both of us are pregnant in difficult circumstances.

Tears began to prick and burn her eyes and she quickly turned away, pretending to look for something in a drawer. She felt a tap on her arm and turned back to see that Rhea was holding a box of tissues out to her. The box of tissues that Callie usually offered her patients, only now the situation was reversed.

'It's okay,' Rhea said softly. 'These hormones make you crazy, don't they?'

Callie half laughed, half cried and, nodding, she took a tissue.

What is the matter with me?

'Sorry, Rhea. This is very unprofessional.'

'Don't be. I should be the one saying sorry. I was being harsh.'

'But if you have reason to be—'

'There was no need for me to be rude. You were trying to help.'

Callie nodded, sniffing, and dabbed at her nose with the tissue. Letting out a breath, she relaxed her shoulders, sat forward and laid a hand on Rhea's knee. 'How are you coping?'

'I'm okay.'

'Are you doing this alone? Is the father in the picture?'

She couldn't help but think of Lucas, the father of her own baby. She'd agreed to move in with him! Would she regret that? Had *she* made a decision without thinking it through? What would it be like, living with Lucas for all those months, only to move out when the baby was born? Would he even want her there?

Of course not. It's the baby he's after. I'm his friend, but that's all. This was always about giving Lucas the baby—nothing's changed.

The thoughts made her feel sad again, but she bit the inside of her lip and tried to concentrate on that rather than allow herself to cry again. She'd already embarrassed herself once today…

'I need a biscuit. Something with chocolate. You?'

'Yes, please. I'm ravenous.'

'Are you eating properly?' Callie got a packet of chocolate chip cookies from her drawer and opened them, offering them to Rhea, who took three.

'I haven't got much money.'

'But you live with your mother?'

Rhea nodded.

'Does she cook for you?'

'She isn't in often.'

No. Callie knew what *that* was like. She'd lost count of the amount of times she'd come home from school to find nothing in the house but empty beer cans or discarded bottles. Plenty of empties, but not much else. She recalled one dinner time when the only thing she'd been able to find in the cupboards was an old tin of custard powder. She'd made herself custard for lunch, just to have something hot before she went back to school for the afternoon.

Callie shook her head. 'My mother was never the best.'

Rhea shrugged. 'But I bet *you'll* be.'

'Rhea! Are you trying to tell me I'd make a good mother?'

'Sure. You're a midwife. You're caring. How much better could you be?'

How about how wrong could I be? What about being in a committed relationship? Raising a child together?

But it was the first time Callie had seen Rhea smile. Properly, anyway. Perhaps they'd made a connection after all?

She laughed, thinking of Lucas. His blue eyes and the way he looked at her. The way his dark hair always looked tousled, no matter how much he combed it. The way he made her *feel*. Before all of this Lucas had been her best friend and, yes, she loved him. *As a friend.* But her pregnancy was changing things. Her hormones were changing things. Maggie leaving had changed everything and it was all up in the air now.

Callie didn't know what to think. What to feel. Before Maggie had left it had all been straightforward. Get pregnant, have the baby, give it to Maggie and Lucas and then play doting godparent or something. But now…?

'I shouldn't have told you any of that, you know. Not very professional.' She wiped her eyes dry and smiled.

Rhea nodded, seeming to be thinking deeply. Then she took a deep breath and said, 'My mum's thrown me out.'

Callie was shocked. She'd not been expecting that. 'Oh, Rhea…'

'I'm sleeping on a friend's couch. Have been for a week or two.'

'She knows about the pregnancy? That's why she threw you out?'

Rhea nodded and grabbed a tissue from the box for herself. 'She thinks I'm a tart. That I got pregnant deliberately, that it's all my fault. And it wasn't! It *wasn't*…'

Callie offered fresh tissues. 'What happened? Will you tell me?'

Rhea met her gaze and eventually nodded. 'I was at a party. At a friend's house. There was alcohol and I'd never really tried it before, so I think it went to my head quite quickly. I went to lay down in her room—try and sleep it off because I felt awful. I woke up in the dark and there was someone on top of me. I tried to stop him. I really tried. But he was stronger than me…' She sounded so matter-of-fact.

Callie stared on in horror. 'You were *raped*?'

'Mum reckons I asked for it. She's disgusted with me.'

'Did you go to the police?'

'Yes. But I'd already had a shower and they reckoned I'd washed away a lot of the evidence.'

'Oh, Rhea, I'm so sorry! Did they test you for STIs?'

'They came back negative.'

'But you were pregnant?'

'Yes. That's why I want to get rid of it.'

Callie could now understand why Rhea had been so uptight, so resistant to her prying questions. She felt glad now that she'd confided in Rhea herself, because it had shown Rhea that Callie could be trusted.

'That's why you don't want to keep it?'

Rhea shook her head. 'How could I? Every time I looked at it I'd be reminded. I'd see its eyes looking at me and—'

'And it would love you. The child. The baby would have no idea about its conception. It would just see you as its mother. It would *love* you.'

Rhea shook her head, violently disagreeing. 'No.'

Callie sat silently for a moment. They'd both shared an awful lot. She'd said something herself that she'd not meant to say. Certainly not to a patient. Even if it *had* been to get Rhea to open up and trust her.

'Let me arrange some counselling for you.'

'I don't need it.'

'It can help to have someone to talk to.'

'I've got you.'

Callie nodded. 'Okay. But I'll need to take some blood from you today. I should have done it last time.'

'What for?'

'To check your blood group. Check your rhesus status—that sort of thing.'

People could be either rhesus positive or rhesus negative, depending on their blood type.

'Right. I see.'

'I've booked you in for a scan as well. We need to do certain checks on the baby—check its growth and health. It's an ultrasound. Will you do it?'

'Do I have to look at it?'

'Not if you don't want to. But aren't you curious to see it?'

'No. I don't want to get attached to it.'

The walls had gone up again.

'In case it makes it harder to give away?'

Rhea met her gaze, nodded, and quickly looked away.

Callie could understand her reasons.

Rhea lay down on the same couch that Callie had just a few days ago and had gel smeared onto her abdomen. The sonographer spent a few moments getting her bearings and then turned to look at Callie, who was sitting in. 'Well, everything looks just fine.'

Callie reached for Rhea's hand and squeezed it. 'Do you want to see?'

'But if I see it—'

'Rhea...please...let me turn the screen. You need to see this.'

The teenager gave in and nodded, the expression on her face turning from a mix of apprehension and fear to one of confusion and wonder. 'What is that?'

Callie wasn't sure whether to smile or not. 'That's your baby.'

How would Rhea react? What would she feel?

At her own scan Callie had felt awe and a little afraid, if she were honest with herself. The pregnancy was *real*. No longer a hypothetical situation.

Rhea would have no choice now but to face facts.

Lucas sucked in a breath, then sighed heavily down the phone. 'I've asked Callie to move in with me.' He waited for the reaction from his mother, not knowing how she'd be.

'Right. Well, that makes sense.'

She still didn't sound too pleased, but then again she hadn't been happy with him ever since he'd mentioned the divorce and the surrogacy.

'And how's she doing?'

'Callie's doing well. She was a little faint at work the other day, so I suggested she move in so that I can look after her.'

'And that's all this is?'

He rubbed his forehead roughly. What *was* it with everyone suggesting there was more to their relationship?

'Yes! She's just my friend. There's nothing untoward about this.'

'Moving in together is a big deal, Lucas. You two have known each other for years and I know how you felt about her once and what it did to you when she turned you down. Are you sure there's nothing else going on?'

'Mum—'

'Maggie never liked her, did she? Always suspected your friendship was more than that?'

His mother was right. Maggie had never liked Callie very much. Or his friendship with her. It had been a difficult line he'd had to walk when he'd still been married to Maggie. Every phone call or conversation with Callie had had to be explained in minute detail, as if she'd suspected him of wanting to jump into bed with Callie at any moment.

Maybe once he'd wanted that, but they'd both been very young then. He'd adored Callie. Had been able to picture them both together as a couple and been excited to think that she'd say yes.

When he'd asked her and she'd got all upset before telling him no, they could never be together that way…*ever*…his heart had been broken. Never had he imagined that she'd turn him down. So he'd gone straight out and at the first club he'd gone into he'd met Maggie and bought her a drink.

Maggie—whom he'd treated appallingly by trying too hard to love her. Forcing feelings that had never been true…

Callie wouldn't risk their friendship back then and she sure as hell wouldn't now! So his mother had nothing to worry about. He knew where he stood with Callie. It had been clear then and it was clear now.

'Well, Maggie's not here anymore, is she? It doesn't matter. Callie and I are friends. I just thought I'd let you know what was happening.'

There was a pause. 'I see. And have you decided what's going to happen when the baby's born? Does she move out then?'

Lucas refused even to think that far. He certainly didn't like the idea of thinking of her moving out before he'd even got her moved in! 'I don't know.' He knew he didn't like the idea of her leaving.

'Well, you need to decide. Before that poor baby is born.'

'My child is not a "poor baby". It will be cherished and adored. You've no need to feel sorry for it.'

'Of *course* I feel sorry for it. It might never have a mother.' She sighed. 'Why didn't you marry Callie in the first place? You know that's what your father and I wanted for you.'

Lucas gritted his teeth. Of course he knew. Because he and Callie had been friends for so long they'd always hinted at it, or joked about it, but he'd seen the look on Callie's face every time they did. Shock…fear. Didn't they know that it had killed him to see her look that way? Didn't they know that it had destroyed him to know he couldn't have her? That she'd never contemplate it?

He refused to lose his temper. There was no point in going over old ground. Callie would never look at him in that way.

Ever.

Callie opened up the suitcase on her bed and stared at her clothes hanging in the wardrobe. She was meant to be packing. Getting ready for moving in with Lucas—just whilst she was pregnant—so that he could be there for her and the baby.

There's nothing romantic about this, so why do I feel so strange? So nervous?

She didn't want to call her mother—Maria was usually the last person she turned to—but she needed to talk to someone and it couldn't be Lucas. After her time spent discussing what had happened with Rhea, she felt as if she needed the connection that family gave. Even if Maria *was* useless, she could still be a sounding board—so she picked up the phone and dialled.

It rang for a long time, and just when she thought her mother must be out or in a drunken stupor somewhere it was answered.

'Yes?'

'Mum? It's me—Callie.'

'Oh, hi. I thought you might be someone else.' As always, her mother's regret at being connected to Callie shone through.

'Sorry. I can go if you're waiting for another call.'

'No, it's fine. I'm glad you rang. I've been wanting to speak to you.'

Well, then, you could have called me, couldn't you? Busy getting to the bottom of a bottle?

'I just wanted to talk…speak to you…let you know that…um…I'm having a baby. I'm pregnant.'

There was silence at the other end of the phone for a moment, though Callie felt sure she heard the slosh of a bottle being upended.

'A baby? Congratulations.'

Maria didn't sound thrilled. But what had Callie expected?

'I didn't even know you were in a relationship.'

You never called to find out.

She closed her eyes with dismay and hurt. What had she really expected from her? Support? Happiness? Joy at becoming a grandmother?

Who was I kidding?

'No, no, I'm not. I…er…just thought I'd tell you that you won't be able to get hold of me at this number for a while.'

'Oh?'

'I'm going to be moving in with the father… It's Lucas, by the way. This is his number, if you want to contact me there.' She read off the number, knowing in her heart that her mother would not be writing it down.

'You and Lucas? That's great. I always thought you two would end up together.'

It was too complicated to explain. 'Okay. I guess that's it. Take care.'

'Callie, wait!'

'Yes?' *What now?*

'He's been your best friend, hasn't he, all these years? I guess it was to be expected you'd have a baby with him.'

'Well, it's not straightforward.'

'What is in this life? Well, I'm happy for you both. I have some news too.'

'Yes?'

'I've met someone. Someone special to me. His name's Gareth and I'd like you to meet him.'

Callie had lost count of the number of 'someone specials' she'd had to meet over the years. This Gareth would surely be just another man in the long list of men that her mother hung around with—hangers-on, fellow drunks. She wasn't desperate to meet him at all.

'Well, I'm very busy at work.'

'Oh, I see.' Her mother sounded disappointed.

'I'll try to come over soon, I'm just not sure when.'

'Things are different now, Callie. I've changed. Gareth's helped me change. I haven't had a drink for six months.'

Lies. All lies!

Callie had heard all this before! She almost couldn't bear it—the way her mother handed out the same old patter all the time! Expecting her to believe it!

What sort of a fool does she take me for?

'Really? Well…keep it up.'

'I will. I *am*. I mean it this time, Callie. I really do.'

'I hope so. But you've said all this before, Mum.'

'I know I have, and I know it's difficult for you to believe me, but this time I'll prove it. In actions *and* words.'

Callie couldn't speak. There was too much emotion flowing through her at that moment. If she did speak, she'd cry.

'So I'll look forward to seeing you soon?'

She sucked in a deep breath and gathered herself. 'Sure. Bye.'

Callie put the phone down and shook her head at her own stupidity.

What was I thinking? She isn't going to care about a grandchild! She could barely care about her own child! She hardly said anything when I said I was pregnant. She cares more about this Gareth person!

'She's still drinking,' she announced to the empty room, to her empty suitcase, and she began to well up, then cry, as she pulled her clothes from the wardrobe and shoved them haphazardly into her suitcase.

Lucas would be round soon. He'd said he would be there about five to pick her up and take her to his.

It had been a long time since she'd last been at his place. She'd liked it there. It was safe. Homely. Not like her own. It would be nice to come home from work and not find an empty flat. There'd be someone to talk to. Someone to share her day with. They could each get exasperated about work and know where the other one was coming from.

Like a couple.

Now where had *that* thought come from?

Wiping her eyes, she sat down on the bed and thought about him. Did she like Lucas? In *that* way?

He is gorgeous. Kind and funny and caring and...yes, okay, he's hot.

But he was a friend. A friend she was now having a baby

with. Moving in with until it was born. She couldn't risk losing his friendship by having romantic feelings for him!

I'm not feeling that way. I'm not! It's just hormones, that's all.

Will I have to move out when the baby's born?

They hadn't spoken about it. She hadn't asked. But now she needed to know. What *did* Lucas expect of her after the birth? Anything? The original plan had been that she would be like an aunt, or a godmother or something. She'd be in the baby's life but on the edges, the fringe. *Maggie* was meant to have been the mother, but she'd gone now.

Does Lucas want me to be the baby's mother?

She knew she'd have to ask him. This was too big a deal not to get cleared up, too big a question not to ask. She couldn't assume. She'd have to ask him.

But what do I want to hear? I've never wanted to be a mother. But I know I want the best for this child.

She folded her jeans and placed them into her suitcase, absentmindedly laying a couple of reading books in the suitcase, a small toiletries case, a camera.

The clock said five past five when the doorbell rang.

It's him.

She got up and checked her reflection in the mirror. 'Bad hair, red eyes, chafed cheeks. I look great,' she muttered, and headed for the front door.

When she opened it she saw him take one look at her and read her face, but instead of the joke that she was expecting about how awful she looked he simply dropped the bouquet of flowers he was holding and pulled her into his arms, crushing her against his broad chest. He squeezed her tight and she could feel his lips in her hair, kissing the top of her head, whilst she inhaled his heavenly scent as if he was oozing pure amber nectar.

'What's wrong? Has someone upset you?'

She could hear his heart pounding through his strong

chest and it felt good to stand there, wrapped in his embrace, protected and warm and safe. He smelt amazing, and it would have been so easy just to stand there and let him hold her and never let go. So easy just to melt into him and stay there. Never moving, never letting go.

'I spoke to my mum…' she mumbled into his shirt. 'You know what she's like.' She pulled away, smiling sheepishly, and tucked a stray strand of hair behind her ear.

He walked with her into the flat, closing the door behind them. 'You told her?'

With reluctance, she nodded and sat down on the couch opposite. 'Yep. She reacted pretty much how I expected. You'll probably be pleased to know there'll be no pushy grandma from *my* side of the family.' She smiled, but the smile didn't reach her eyes. Then, as an afterthought, she asked, 'Were those flowers for me?'

'Dammit!' He leapt over the couch in one fluid movement and went back outside, picking up the flowers he'd dropped. Brushing off imaginary fluff, he presented them to her. They were beautiful! Lots of tiny pink roses, mostly still in bud. 'Flat-warming. I thought you could put them in your new bedroom.'

She lifted them to her nose and inhaled their delicate scent. 'They're lovely—thank you. You always know how to make me feel better.'

Lucas smiled. 'I try. So what did Maria say, exactly?'

'Well, I got a "congratulations" but she was too busy telling me about her new man to offer anything else.' Callie fiddled with the pink roses. 'She wants me to meet him.'

'But you don't want to?'

'I've met too many of her men. Oh, and she saw fit to inform me she's been off the booze for six months.'

'That's good, isn't it?'

'It'll be a lie.'

Lucas looked grim. 'Maybe, but what if she is telling the truth?'

Callie looked at him in disbelief and laughed. 'Hardly!'

Lucas persisted. 'But if she *is*...don't you think you should give her that chance? She's your mother. That's not a relationship you can just ignore.'

'Why not? She's done a good job of it for all these years. Why do I have to be the responsible one?'

He shrugged. 'Because you're about to be a mother yourself?'

There. He'd said it. But Callie still didn't know if she *was* going to be a mother, did she? Lucas and she hadn't discussed, yet, just exactly what her role was going to be now.

We need to clear this up soon.

'I think you ought to go and visit her. See for yourself.'

'I don't see the point, Lucas.'

'She's your *mum*.'

'Yes. She is. But only in title. I've always had to look after myself.' Her answer was final, suggesting the conversation was over where Maria was concerned.

Lucas let out a big sigh and looked around. 'Is there anything you need help with? Or are you already packed?' He was eyeing her flat, and she had to admit it didn't look as if she'd packed much.

'It's pretty much done. I was just finishing my suitcase when you rang.'

'So you're still happy to move in?'

She nodded. 'If you're happy—though I think there are a few things we still need to talk about.'

'I agree. But we've plenty of time to iron out the wrinkles in this situation. Let's not rush into making life-changing decisions straight away.'

She was glad to hear that he must have been thinking things through, too. 'Okay, so let's start with an easy one. Who's cooking tonight?'

He laughed and she smiled at the sound, enjoying the way his eyes twinkled with merriment. Glad that they were back on easier territory. Lucas had always tried to get her to be closer to her mother. Probably because he had a close relationship with his own mother. Well, he was lucky. Not everyone had that.

'Someone else will... I thought we could make it special. Our first meal together. At a nice restaurant... Because I'm damned sure I'm not going to have a baby with someone who I haven't taken out to dinner.'

It had been ages since she'd last been there, but his flat was exactly as she remembered. There'd once been a time when she'd felt she could pop round whenever she needed to, but when Lucas had got together with Maggie that freedom to visit had ended. She and Maggie had got on okay, but there had been a sense of 'stay away' that she'd got from Maggie when it came to visiting. Almost as if Maggie was laying claim to Lucas—especially after she'd married him.

Lucas had always told Callie to come round, but she hadn't called in as often as she'd used to, and she'd always made up some excuse. There was no way she would have caused problems in his marriage with Maggie.

But now she was looking forward to reclaiming her friendship with him. Regaining the closeness they'd once had.

All the photos that had once been there of him and Maggie were gone. Thankfully. It would have been disturbing if they'd still been there. At least it showed that he didn't still need her picture about, reminding him of their shared past.

Lucas gave her a quick tour, though she pretty much already knew where most things were. But she hadn't seen the spare room before. It was bigger than she'd realised, and decorated in a beautiful pale blue. A large double bed dominated the centre of the room, covered in a gorgeous crocheted creamy-white throw.

Callie raised an eyebrow at this, looking for Lucas to explain. It seemed a very girly decoration.

'Before you say anything, I bought that for you. Maggie took all the pretty covers we'd bought and left me with my old black and grey ones, and my inner interior designer made me go out and get something a little more feminine.' He grinned and heaved her suitcase into the room before depositing it on the bed. 'Want a hand to unpack?'

'I'm all right, thanks.'

'Okay. Dinner reservations are for seven-thirty.'

'Where are we going?'

'Gianni's. It's Italian—I'm sure you said you liked that once.'

She smiled. He'd remembered. 'I love Italian.'

'Great. I'll leave you to it, then.'

'Are we getting dressed up?'

He hovered in the doorway, his hands casually in his pockets. 'We can do. Might be nice. We *are* celebrating.'

'Okay.'

It would be nice to get dressed up, and she hadn't been out to eat for ages! Two months' worth of morning sickness had put paid to any appetite she'd had, but that was gone now. Callie was feeling much better, and she finally understood why some of her women were so glad to get that first trimester out of the way!

'Wow...you look...*amazing.*'

Lucas couldn't believe his eyes. Callie was wearing a gorgeous figure-hugging dress, all red and flowing, close-fitting at the hips and loose around her legs.

And what a pair of legs! Her calves were shapely and toned—and he wasn't sure why he was so surprised.

I guess I'm so used to seeing her in scrubs.

She'd obviously been keeping her figure a secret beneath the shapeless hospital garb. But there was a lovely gentle rounding around her abdomen, and he knew it was caused by the fundus of her womb spilling over the pelvic cavity and rising up as it swelled in size.

My baby.

She looked great. Blooming and healthy and…

Gorgeous!

There was no other word for it. She'd done her hair and put on make-up and he couldn't recall ever seeing her looking like this! She was glowing! As she smiled shyly at his response, her cheeks flushing, he had to fight the desire to reach out and stroke her cheek.

What's that all about?

He cleared his throat, trying to tamp down the physical response his body was having to her sensual curves.

She'd done something to her hair, too, curling it, sweeping it up, but letting small pieces hang down here and there. She looked tousled—as if she'd just had a good session in bed!

Calm yourself, Lucas, this is Callie…

Yes. It most certainly was Callie. She'd always been pretty, though she'd never played up to it as far as he could recall. But for some reason looking at her tonight, right now, she was more than just a pretty friend…she was beautiful and alluring…

'Wow…' he repeated.

'Thanks. You don't scrub up too badly yourself.'

He'd put on a dinner jacket and white shirt, though he hadn't bothered with a tie. His suit was tailored and well-fitting, and he was glad he'd put it on after seeing the effort she'd gone to.

Escorting her down to his car, he held the door open for her and waited for her to get in. He tried not to take advantage of his position, but he couldn't help getting a good view of her legs again and inhaling the scent of her perfume. He took a deep breath to try and regain control of his raging senses as he walked to his side of the car and then drove to Gianni's. He felt as if he was on a proper date.

Gianni's was a small Italian restaurant on the edge of London. It had had some excellent reviews by restaurant critics and he'd been there once before with some friends. Inside, it was dimly lit by wall sconces and individual candles on each of the tables, and a guy at a real piano played soft background music. No schmaltzy taped music here!

'Wow, this place is gorgeous,' Callie said.

'I'm glad you like it.' They went up to the maître d', who was waiting by a desk. 'Table for two under the name Gold.'

'Certainly, sir. This way, please.'

The maître d' led them to a small table for two, situated at the back of the restaurant. French doors near their table opened out onto a balcony, covered with bougainvillaea and filled with pots of flowers and a small water fountain. The view looked out over the lights of London.

'This place is amazing, Lucas,' Callie said in awe, draping her wrap over the back of her chair as he held it out for her.

He tried not to smell her hair as she stood before him, and he really struggled to keep his hands off her. He felt guilty. Maggie's words were haunting him.

When she was seated he quickly settled himself into his own chair opposite, glad to put some physical distance between them. Seeing her all done up like this was great and all, but…it was making him think crazy things! This was *Callie*! Not a date. Nothing romantic. But, by God, she was doing something crazy to his insides…

'I'm glad you like it.'

Callie wouldn't drink any wine, so they ordered soft drinks whilst they perused the menu. Lucas couldn't help but sneak peeks at her over his own menu whilst he pretended to read, and his stomach was in knots with nerves. He had to break the tension he felt inside, so he laid his menu down to reach across the table and take her hand.

He stared at her fingers within his own and played with one of her rings, pondering his question for a moment. Then he looked up at her and said, 'I've always meant to ask you something.'

She looked slightly afraid, worried about what he'd ask. 'Oh...?'

'Yes...it's something I've been meaning to ask you for a long time.'

'Yes?' Her breath sounded as if it was caught in her throat. What did she think he was going to ask?

He paused for a moment, dragging the tension out. 'What's Callie short for? Is it Calista? Something like that? In all these years we've known each other you've never said.'

She laughed with visible relief, squeezing his fingers and shaking her head as if in disbelief. '*That* was your big question?'

'That was my big question. For now.' He grinned.

'It's not Calista.'

'No?'

'No. And you don't really want to know what it's short for. There's a reason I've never told you, you know.'

'Is it something weird? Like Caligula? Be honest with me—are you named after a Roman emperor?'

They both laughed, and she took a sip of fruit juice before answering. 'I don't know why I've never told you. Actually, I *do* know—it's because I'd be embarrassed.' She took a deep breath. 'Promise me you won't laugh if I do.'

'I promise.' He mimed crossing his heart across his chest and smiled at her, loving the way she looked, so soft and gentle in the candlelight.

She looked at him carefully, weighing up his promise. 'You know what my mother was like, right?'

'Yes.'

'A drunk…an alcoholic. She never wanted me. Hardly bothered to acknowledge me sometimes. So she didn't even bother thinking of a name for me when I was born. *But…* she had to register me. Obviously she needed the child benefit money for drinking. So she went to the register office and when they asked her for my name…'

He was listening intently, wondering about the possible outcome.

'She looked about the room for the first thing she saw. There was a calendar on the wall and so she called me… Calendar. Calendar Taylor.'

Lucas didn't laugh. He'd promised. And there was something so inherently sad about the story that it didn't seem the slightest bit amusing now. He'd hoped it would be something exotic—Calliope, or something like that—something interesting. But instead it was simply a very sad story about a mother who seemed to care nothing for her child.

'I'm so sorry.' He reached out and tightened his grip around her fingers once again. He realised that he suddenly wanted to kiss her. Kiss her madly to take away the sadness and the pain that she'd experienced over the years at the hands of her mother. Crush her against his body, his lips to hers, with so much passion that neither of them would be able to breathe until it was all over and they had to break apart for air. Kiss her the way a lover might…

A lover?

The realisation startled him, so instead of holding her tightly he let her hand go. He took a sip from his drink, feeling the condensation on the glass, the drops of water, giving himself a chance to cool down. There was no way *that* was going to happen. Not with Callie. He knew that.

When he felt he might have control over his voice box he called the waiter over so they could order.

Callie had told him what she'd like and he ordered for them both: pan-fried tiger prawns in butter and chilli for a starter, *agnello* for main—which was a braised lamb shank in tomatoes and a red berry jus. When the first course arrived he heard her apologise. 'Sorry if I've ruined the evening. Mentioning my mother does that a lot.'

'I always knew you and your mother didn't get along. That she was an alcoholic. But I guess if you never have high expectations of her she can't let you down.'

'I suppose.'

'But, you know, even normal families have their issues.'

'Really? Are you trying to cheer me up?'

He smiled at her over the candlelight. 'I am. Both my parents were sober, but I had six sisters! Being the seventh child and the long-awaited son, in a family whose father was always absent for one reason or another, didn't always make for a great time either.'

'But you were the only boy. They'd wanted a son all that time. You *have* to admit you were a little spoilt!' She smiled to show she was joking.

'Are you kidding me? I had to fight for any attention that came my way. Positive attention was rare and negative was in great supply. My father, when he was there, was always quite happy to use his belt and make me into a man. My parents had all these dreams for me and they pushed me hard. *Very* hard. Sometimes nothing I did was right. All my life they'd wanted me to be a doctor and so that's what I became—just so they would be proud of me. I sometimes wonder what I might have been if they hadn't steered me in that direction.'

Callie frowned. 'But you love being a doctor, don't you?'

He nodded. 'Absolutely. I *do* love it. But that's just luck, isn't it? My parents wanted the best for me—a career, mar-

riage with children—but only when the time was right…
when my career had taken off. They didn't like Maggie,
they didn't like me choosing to marry her, and they let me
know about it.'

'How?'

'They initially told me they wouldn't come to the wedding. That I was making a mistake.' He chose not to explain
that his parents had actually told him he was marrying the
wrong woman and that *Callie* should have been the one in
a veil. 'And look at how *that* turned out. They were right.'

He sipped at his drink.

'You rushed into the marriage?'

'Maybe. You turned me down!' He laughed to lighten
the atmosphere, not referencing the great pain in his heart
at the memory. 'So I had to look elsewhere. I met Maggie
and down the aisle we went, without thinking about what
we were doing until it was too late. I should have waited,
maybe, but I thought I knew what I was doing. I was never
in love with Maggie. Not the way I should have been. I see
that now.'

Callie was listening intently, her heart saddened by these
revelations. She should have known about this, but hadn't
because she'd been so wrapped up in her own problems.
'I never realised.'

'Why would you?'

'Well, I'm your best friend. Perhaps I should have known
instinctively? Perhaps you should have felt able to tell me?'

'Neither of us are psychic, Callie. You had too much
going on in your own life to be worrying about mine. I
didn't want to burden you. At the time all this was happening your mum was in hospital with that liver complaint.'

'I do feel like maybe I let you down, though. You should
have been able to talk to me about it.'

But he knew that he wouldn't have. Why would he?
He'd had those intense feelings for Callie, which had slowly

developed over time, without him realising, and when he'd finally discovered the nerve to ask her out she'd turned him down! He'd been heartbroken. In all his imaginings he'd never expected her to say no. The let-down had been devastating and he'd reacted by going out to a club. That was when he had run into Maggie.

'People make you hurt,' she said with understanding.

Once again, she'd hit the nail on the head. She'd always understood him so well. 'I guess both of us would have changed things if we could.'

'Oh, I don't know. If my mother hadn't been the way she was then I might never have become a midwife.' She looked up and smiled. 'And we get to work together.'

'I love that we're still together. After all this time. So many people lose their childhood friends when they become adults. Move apart.'

'I'm glad too.' She looked into his eyes. 'I would like to discuss our situation, though, Lucas. We've got a lot to sort out, you and me.'

'I know.'

But he was afraid of letting her down. He'd let Maggie down by treating her badly, by not loving her the way he should have and driving her into the arms of another man. No wonder she'd gone looking for love elsewhere if she'd thought that he loved Callie. What woman would stand for that?

He'd tried so hard to make his marriage work, to make Maggie happy, to give her the child she wanted so badly—but he'd been doing it all for the wrong reasons. His heart had always been with Callie, even though he knew nothing could come of it.

Maggie had been right to leave him.

For a while they ate in companionable silence. The food was delicious—not too rich, yet full of flavour, with explosions of taste on their tongues.

'What we're doing…it's a big thing,' she said.

Lucas put down his knife and fork and dabbed at his mouth with his napkin. 'Moving in together?'

'The baby. It seemed a simple thing for me when Maggie was still going to be the mother, but she's gone now and I can't help but wonder…' She looked down at her lap, almost afraid to say her next words.

He waited for her to finish, but it seemed she couldn't say what she wanted to say. He leaned forward, looking past the candles, past the small posy of flowers on the table and deep into her eyes.

'I'd like you to be involved,' he said softly. 'As much as you'd like.' He paused for a moment before continuing. 'Actually, that's not true. I want you to be involved a hundred per cent. I know you've always said that you've never wanted to be a mother, but…'

'I never felt I could be what a child would need me to be.'

'But why not?'

He could see her eyes filling up. She was trying her hardest to blink away the tears, but couldn't stop a solitary tear from rolling down her cheeks.

He hated that she was upset. That she was hurting.

'I just…I wouldn't know *how* to be a mother.'

'Does anyone?'

'It should be instinctive. I never had that instinct. Never felt it. Never experienced it.' The tears trickled freely down her cheeks now 'Damn…I'm always crying just lately.'

He reached out with his napkin and dabbed at her cheek. There was so much he should be saying to her. That she still looked beautiful even if she was crying. But instead he went with, 'It's hormones. You can't help it.'

She hiccupped a laugh.

The waiter came and took away their starter plates and they sat quietly at the table. Lucas held her hand. How could he not? He didn't want to see her upset or crying, but he knew she must be scared because he was too. Every time he touched her now it was getting harder and harder to let her go. They'd always been close, but now that she was carrying his baby...

Moving in together, although it was just as room-mates, *was* a big deal. He was welcoming Callie into his life so that he could be there for them both, and he hoped that by doing so she would become happy and feel safe.

He knew she didn't want to be a mother. Was scared about being a mother. It was why she'd sworn off children. But she'd become a midwife—a profession where caring for others was tantamount. Could she not see that? She was one of the most caring people he knew and he felt instinctively, even if she didn't, that she would be a great mother. He knew she could be if she gave herself that chance.

He wanted his child to have a mother like Callie. For Callie to consider herself to be its mother. All his life he'd insisted that whenever he had a child it would be in a stable relationship, hopefully he'd be married, but whatever the situation it had to be stable and strong and definitely with a mother as well as a father. Parents who were around for their kids every day.

It was something he hadn't had with his own father. And when his father *had* been around he'd been angry and had had little patience with a young boy who'd craved his approval... There'd be no getting out the belt for *his* child. His and Callie's baby.

Would Callie agree to be that parent?

He wouldn't ask anything of her apart from that. There'd be no demands on them to become an actual couple. They didn't have to start 'going out'. She'd already turned him down once before and he knew she wouldn't let that happen anyway. It was totally out of the question for her. Wasn't it? And he could keep his feelings separate. Somehow. Callie could be a mother without being his partner. Although...

I wouldn't stop it. I think Callie and me would be good together. I always have.

But he knew he couldn't press her that way. She'd turn tail and run for it—as she had before when he'd tried to ask her out. That had been years ago now, and she hadn't wanted to risk their friendship. But things were different now, weren't they? They were both adults, for a start, and they knew what they were doing. Supposedly.

Their lamb shanks arrived and they tucked in with gusto. The meat was tender and just melted in the mouth. The green beans were perfectly *al dente* and the potatoes soft and full of flavour, with butter and mint melting over them.

They kept the conversation neutral for the rest of the evening. One set of tears had been enough for them both and Lucas didn't want to upset Callie any more about anything. They talked about films they'd both seen, which led to Callie announcing that a new documentary about midwifery was going to start on television and she wanted to see it.

'Should be interesting. It's meant to be real-life fly-on-the-wall stuff.'

'Could you imagine if they filmed in *our* hospital?'

She laughed. 'Oh, my God! That would be priceless!'

Their puddings came and went, the evening rolled on pleasantly, and much too soon it was time for home.

When they got back to the flat Callie kicked off her heels and stumbled onto the couch. 'I'm beat.'

'What shift are you on tomorrow?' Lucas asked.

'I've got three night shifts in a row. You?'

'A late shift tomorrow, then two nights.'

'I guess we'll run into each other, then.'

'Guess so.'

They were staring at each other. Uncomfortably so. As if each of them was expecting the other to say something or do something definitive.

But when Lucas didn't make a move Callie stood up

with a sigh and went to pick up her heels, then she turned to walk to her room. 'I'm going to bed. Thanks for tonight. It was lovely.'

Lucas stood up and nodded. 'It was my pleasure.'

She looked at him from across the room. Was there tension between them? Sexual tension?

She walked over to give him a friendly peck on the cheek, her lips caressing rough stubble. 'Good night.' She paused again, as if she was thinking of something, but then smiled and turned away before he could process it too much.

'Goodnight, Callie.'

He watched her go and he could feel the burn on his cheek where her lips had touched him. He ached with longing for more. He switched off all the lights, grabbed a drink from the kitchen and headed for bed himself. After hanging up his suit, he pulled back the duvet and slumped into bed, one hand behind his head as he stared up at the ceiling.

It had been an interesting night with his Calendar Girl.

I wanted to kiss her.

But she's my friend.

I can't lose her as a friend.

I wouldn't be able to bear it.

But what if they gained so much more?

Sleep was a long time coming, and by the time he finally drifted off into the land of nod he'd pretty much memorised exactly how his bedroom ceiling looked in the dark.

In the next room, Callie also lay staring at the ceiling. Her stomach was comfortably full with rich food and she felt a nice warm buzz from the evening. It had been good to spend some time with Lucas away from work, away from the hospital, out on a social basis. They hadn't done that for...

God...years!

They'd had a nice night. He'd looked totally amazing too! When she'd come out of her room and seen him standing there in the middle of his flat in his dinner jacket she'd practically melted with desire. Where had this *sexy* Lucas emerged from? He could have been James Bond, he'd looked so yummy!

It's just hormones. You know it is. You tell women that every day.

Didn't make it easy, though. He'd kept taking her hand at dinner and it had been *so difficult* to remember that they were just friends and nothing else.

Her hand went beneath the covers and rested on her barely-there bump. She spoke to it, whispering soft words that meant so very much.

'I'll not hurt your daddy. I'll make sure I do right by him. Even if that means I have to walk away.'

For Callie, sleep didn't come easily either.

CHAPTER FOUR

THE NEXT FEW weeks were strange as they got used to living with each other. Waking up in the morning and finding Lucas in the next room, ready to have breakfast with her, seemed odd, but enjoyable.

She liked the way he was always there when she needed someone to talk to. She didn't have to phone him and make a time to come round, she didn't have to seek permission to be with him, and she didn't have to make an appointment—like she had to if she wanted to see her mother.

He cooked her some delicious meals, and once he even rubbed her feet after she'd had a particularly exhausting day. That had been surprising. Not the foot-rub, but the thoughts that had gone through her head as he'd done it! He had a wonderful way with his fingers. His large hands had enveloped her feet individually, their warmth caressing her tired muscles as his fingertips pressed and glided and worked out the knots. Firm where they needed to be, gentle and delicate in other places.

Her thoughts had run to how Lucas might be as a lover, though it had felt strange to allow herself even to think of him that way when he'd always been her friend. He'd had a masterful way with her feet, anyway, and she could only imagine the wonderful sensations he'd produce if his hands were let loose on the rest of her body!

And every night she'd chastely wish him good-night and go to her room feeling alone.

Odd how I feel alone even though I'm living with someone.

Callie had just turned eighteen weeks in her pregnancy, and was beginning to show much more. She went into work most days feeling tired and sleepy. Sleep had evaded her for many of her nights, and she didn't think it was because she was sleeping somewhere different. The bed in her room was comfortable, the mattress firm. She was warm enough. It was just that her head was brimming with too many thoughts…

Would she be a mother?

Wouldn't she?

Where were things heading with Lucas?

What would this do to their friendship?

She hoped it would strengthen it. After all, they'd been best friends for years and now a baby was involved…half her, half Lucas.

If I had ever changed my mind about wanting a child I'd have wanted it to be with Lucas.

That was the main thought that kept spinning round her head, rattling its way into all the corners like a whirling dervish. Not that she'd admitted to that at the fertility clinic when they'd all had to go through counselling. She knew she could never admit that.

Her thoughts were spilling over into her consciousness and making her fret and worry over lots of little things. Neither of them had come up with many answers, though she now knew that Lucas would like her to be involved as much as possible.

And that's the big question for me.

Can I be involved? And by how much?

What form would that involvement take? Neither of them

had been specific, and the idea of being a full-time mother scared her still.

I don't know if I have it in me to do that. What if I get things wrong?

Originally she'd have been on the sidelines. The baby would have been Lucas and Maggie's child and Callie would only have been involved whenever she'd visited them, or if—as Lucas had once suggested very early on—she'd became a godparent to the child.

She'd agreed to that. After all, how many godparents actually ended up having to look after a child because something tragic had happened to both its parents?

Hardly ever. In fact she knew of no circumstances in which that had happened to *anyone*. So for her it had been an easy thing to agree to. A godparent could be as close as he or she wanted.

But an actual *mother*?

I wouldn't know what to do. If I get things wrong... I have no frame of reference for what a good mother is...

And now Maggie was gone. Lucas would happily raise the child on his own. She knew in her heart that he would be more than capable of doing so. She still didn't have to be involved. She could still be a godparent.

But it's different now. If I'm to be its mother, then I want it to have the best childhood. Nothing like mine. And how could I explain to that child why I walked away?

What would Lucas think of her if she *did* walk away?

Maggie was gone and Lucas wanted Callie to be involved and, damn it, her hormones were affecting her more than she'd ever thought that they would! On the scan day she'd been so determined not to get attached, not to get excited at what she might see. To keep her distance just as Rhea had wanted to.

After all, hadn't she been taught how to do that by a master? It should have been easy...

But then the baby had been there, right before her eyes, on the screen. Curled up, rounded like a bean, softly nestled safe in her womb, its heart beating away, unaware of the situation its parents faced.

Totally innocent. It had no preconceptions. It was simply a baby. A baby that would be born into the world not knowing whether it would have one, two or any parents to care for it.

Callie changed from her day clothes into scrubs, attached her name tag and filled her pockets with all the paraphernalia she carried with her at work—scissors, pens, a small notepad, tape measure... She pinned her pink fob watch to her top and clipped her hand scrub to the bottom, where it was easily accessible. Then she pulled her hair up to keep it out of her face and headed to the reception area of Antenatal, where the staff hand-over at shift-change took place.

The supervisor of midwives, Sarah, was leading the hand-over and she stood in front of a busy board. All the rooms were filled with labouring mothers and Callie sensed a hectic shift.

Sarah turned to Callie. 'Callie, I'd like you in Room Six. Dr Gold will be assisting. In fact he may already be in there. Jenny Cole—she's thirty-six and a first time mother. She's diabetic and we think it's a very large baby. She's got no birth partner. There doesn't seem to be any close family.'

'Okay.'

Callie loved working with Lucas. He was just so good and efficient. Yes, all registrars were probably the same, but she *knew* Lucas and that made it different. Though she was a very capable midwife on her own, she felt safer knowing that he was in the room, backing her up. There had been so many times when he'd been there for her. And not just for her but the whole team. Calm in a crisis, efficient, direct when he needed to be, and an absolute rock in an emergency situation. Everyone knew they could rely on him and Callie had never heard anyone say a bad word about Lucas Gold.

In Room Six, Callie nodded to Lucas as she entered and then introduced herself to Jenny. Her patient appeared to be coping with her contractions well and was simply breathing her way through them.

'I'm just going to have a quick read-through of your notes.'

Callie stood at the end of the bed as Lucas checked the trace. It all seemed to be going well. According to Jenny's notes, at her last scan just two weeks ago her baby had already been estimated to be at ten pounds. Callie had a quick feel of Jenny's abdomen. Baby was head down, engaged almost four-fifths, and definitely felt extremely large.

As Jenny put in earphones to listen to soothing music Callie stepped over to Lucas. 'What's your idea for delivery?'

'I think when the time comes we'll have everyone on standby. If this baby is as big as we think it is I want to know people will be available if it becomes an emergency.'

Callie nodded. 'How come she's not having a C-section?'

'She was offered one in clinic, but she insisted on trying for a natural birth. She was adamant.'

Fair enough. Callie felt that a mother *should* try for a natural birth if that was what she wished. Though she had reservations about that if there was a risk to either mother or baby. Still, it was not her place to make a judgement. She was there to support Jenny in her wishes.

Jenny removed one of her earbuds. 'Is that a little bump I see?' She nodded at Callie's stomach.

Blushing, Callie nodded. 'Still a long way to go yet.'

'It's exciting, isn't it?'

Exciting wasn't the word... It had been a real roller-coaster since Maggie had left. Callie made a non-committal noise. It was difficult to answer with Lucas in the room. If she said it *was* exciting would he think she was thinking of being there for the baby? If she said it wasn't, then what would Jenny think?

'I've waited an age to have a baby…' Jenny breathed out happily.

'I saw in your notes you used a sperm donor?'

'Best decision I ever made. No health problems. An academic. Similar physical attributes to me. And no worries about anyone making demands to be involved. Perfect.'

'What does everyone else think of your choice?' Callie was curious.

'Mum and Dad were very supportive once they got over the shock. They wanted me to be in a relationship, you know?'

Callie nodded. Wasn't that how everyone expected it would go?

'Lots of good friends?'

'Loads. All dying to be aunts and uncles.'

Lucas came to stand by the bed. 'It's good to have a large support network. I grew up in a big family, so I can't possibly imagine what it might be like to not have anyone.'

Jenny looked at him, blushing slightly. 'Are you married, Dr Gold?'

Since becoming pregnant with his child Callie was beginning to notice the effect Lucas had on other women. It was something she'd always been aware of but hadn't really paid attention to. But now it was different. She could see them looking at him. Sizing him up. Noting the absence of a ring on his finger. And she wasn't sure if she liked it.

He glanced at Callie. 'I'm not, no.'

'But you have a big family? That's good.'

Callie wondered what it might be like to have a supportive parent? How did that feel? To have a parent on the other end of the phone you could just talk with or pour your heart out to? What would it feel like to know you could just call round to your parents' house and *know* that you'd be welcome? That they'd make you tea, serve you biscuits, tell you the latest about so-and-so down the street?

It was so different for Callie. She couldn't imagine having that kind of relationship with her mum at all. Maria had never, *ever* been there for her on the end of a phone.

'What about you, Callie?' Jenny asked.

Callie glanced at Lucas and saw that he was staring at her with an intense look in his face. She could see he was intrigued to hear her answer, but she felt like a rabbit caught in the headlights.

What could she say? That she had an alcoholic mother, no siblings, and no idea if she was keeping the baby she was carrying? That she was considering giving away her own child? That she might have to?

How easy it had seemed months ago to agree to that. Whilst she wasn't pregnant. Whilst Maggie and Lucas were still together and married. It had been a future event—one that hadn't actually seemed real. And what maternal instincts had Callie had? None. Zero. And she'd been happy for it to be that way. Which was what she'd told everyone.

She could still enjoy babies. Other people's babies. Which was why she'd become a midwife. Callie was fascinated by pregnancy—how a woman's body nurtured and grew a baby in order to birth it and create brand-new life. A pure life, unburdened by worry, regret, selfishness or ego.

And each baby would go home with its mother and she would help another woman. And another.

Each case was different, but mostly she got to share in the joy of creating a child. Bringing a brand-new person into the world, their pages unwritten.

It was the hope she loved. That each new baby she saw would go home with its parents and have a fabulous life. The kind of life she'd never had herself.

Callie's cheeks flushed under the intensity of Lucas's gaze, the heat searing her skin as if she was being roasted on a spit over a flaming hot barbecue.

'I...there's just me, really.' She smiled and fiddled with Jenny's bed sheet, making it lie flat on the bed.

Lucas raised an eyebrow at her and she felt her heart skip a beat. She was having palpitations over Lucas as she stood at a patient's bedside!

What was happening here with Lucas? How had he gone from just being her friend to being this *man*, this *sexy, alluring guy*, since she'd conceived his child? She'd understand it if they'd slept together, or something, but they hadn't. Their baby had been conceived in a laboratory—the most unsexy, least alluring conception you could ever imagine. The most he'd done was hold her hand as the fertility specialist had positioned the fertilised egg in her womb.

Hand-holding! That was all! But now the morning sickness had passed, coupled with the fact that he was now a single man and she was carrying his baby—which was also hers as she'd used her own eggs—it was as if her body *knew* that this was the man she should have. The man she caught looking at her oddly at times...the man whose sofa she shared, whose genes she carried. Technically she should let him take her to bed and have him make her tremble and quiver with delight...

How had that happened? One minute Lucas was her best friend, a good laugh, a dependable guy—yes, he was good-looking, but she'd always believed herself immune to those good looks of his—and then the next minute, when she was knocked up with his baby, Lucas became this scintillating, sexy, so-hot-he-looked-airbrushed kind of guy, whom she lived with, slept in the next room to...a please-can-I-get-into-your-bed kind of guy.

It was madness. Madness!

Dragging her eyes away from Lucas's steely blues, she blushed once again and smiled at Jenny.

'I'm going to be the best mum this little girl could ever have,' Jenny said.

'I'm sure of it,' Callie said. Though part of her wondered how she could be so sure for someone else but couldn't apply that certainty to herself.

Jenny delivered her baby girl some hours later. Ten pounds exactly. She gave birth beautifully and it was a very smooth delivery, even though there'd been a fear that there might be a shoulder dystocia when the baby's shoulders had got stuck in the birth canal. But everything had gone well.

Only when Jenny and her daughter, Camille, were settled on a postnatal ward, with the baby feeding well, did Callie go for a sit-down in the staffroom.

She was tired…exhausted. It would be so easy to close her eyes. But as she sat there with her feet up she felt a little something swirling around in her stomach. She laid a hand on her round abdomen.

Was the baby kicking?

She must have had the strangest look on her face, for when Lucas came into the staffroom to grab a coffee and saw her frozen, waiting for something to happen again, he asked, 'You okay?'

'I felt something.'

'Pain?' Fear was etched into his features.

'No, not pain…'

'Is the baby moving?' A beam of a smile broke out across his face and he shot across the room to join her.

'I don't know…' She moved her hand to feel again.

'Is it doing it now?'

He reached out and laid a hand on her stomach—the first time he'd done so. She could feel the heat of his hand through her scrubs and found herself hoping the baby would make one of its swishing movements.

It did.

'Oh, my God!' He pulled his hand away, his face lit up with delight. 'I felt that!'

So had she. And though she was delighted the baby had moved for him she found herself wishing he'd lay his hands on her again.

Oh, my goodness, these pregnancy hormones!

She flushed and had to use a piece of card to wave at her face and cool herself down.

'Are you all right?'

'Absolutely. Just a little hot flush.'

Putting her feet up, she lay back on the chair and ran her hands over her growing baby bump. She was quite happy with her bump. Pleased that as yet she had no stretch marks.

Inside, her baby gave her another little swirl and she gasped out loud as she felt it through her skin. She wanted to see if she could *see* the baby move, and raised her scrubs over the bump to reveal her bare belly.

This time there were no scrubs between them. This time Lucas had his hands on her bare abdomen, cupping the small mound of her growing uterus as the baby flipped and swished and generally swam about inside.

'That's amazing!'

'It knows you're its daddy.'

'Maybe.' He nestled closer to her and laid his head against her stomach. She could feel the bristles from his jaw prickling her skin. 'I can't hear it.'

'Give it a few months.'

He looked up at her, one hand still on her abdomen. 'I'm glad I'm having the baby with you.'

Callie looked back at him, shocked at his words. For weeks they'd danced around the subject, since that night at Gianni's, but now he was getting all serious again. 'Are you?'

'Yes. I couldn't have wished for it to be with anyone else.'

She gulped, her face flushing with heat and tension. 'Really?'

'You're my best friend.'

'I'm not very maternal.'

He looked deep into her eyes. 'You are. Or you wouldn't worry so much about doing the right thing.'

'You know I worry?'

'Of course. I worry too. We didn't get ourselves into this situation in the conventional way, did we?'

'I guess not.'

'I don't want that to matter anymore.'

She sat there, tummy exposed, his hand still resting on it just above the belly button, aware of his touch, aware of his nearness, and aware that his lips looked ever so kissable!

He got up off the floor and sat on the sofa next to her. He was close. Unbearably so.

Her heart began to pound as her breath caught in her throat. Her skin had come alive at his touch, tingling and yearning for more.

He's going to kiss me!

And she realised she wanted him to. Wanted it more than anything else in the whole wide world!

She sat up slightly and met him halfway, wrapping her hand behind his neck, embedding her fingers in his tousled hair and pulling his face towards hers, meeting his lips with hers, indulging in a wonderful, tentative, exploring first kiss.

Fireworks were going off throughout her body. She felt tense and relaxed and excited all at once. Her hands itched for his touch, to be holding him. Their mouths opened as the kiss deepened and his tongue took hers, and then she was breathing him, kissing him, holding him, in a way she'd never felt with a man before. His bristles scorched her face and it was a sweet agony as passion took them both by surprise and hunger for each other burned them to their very core.

This is Lucas!

Of course it was! He'd been there in front of her all this time, the man for her, and she'd let him be just a friend for all that time—not knowing, never allowing herself to think about it. *Why* hadn't she thought about it?

Perhaps I did. In fact, I know I did!

She'd once let the thought of what it would be like to sleep with Lucas occupy her mind for many a night.

But she'd not wanted to risk their friendship. She'd not allowed herself to linger on the prospect. She'd always dismissed it. It had been wrong before—he'd been with someone else, and she'd been his friend.

I need to breathe.

She couldn't remember how. Instead she continued to kiss him, to feel his soft hair in her fingers, his chest against hers, the yearning for more… She moaned softly and it seemed to increase his ardour. He mumbled her name.

For so long she'd wondered what it would be like. This moment. This kiss. Yet never in her wildest dreams had she thought she'd be thinking about ending it.

She knew she had to stop it. Knew she had to let him go. Because this wasn't meant to happen! If she lost him as a friend they would endanger everything they'd held dear about their friendship. And if she let things continue in this vein and it didn't work out… Well, where would they be then? Parents living in separate houses, meeting in rooms where the tension would be so thick it would need to be chopped with an axe, not sliced with a knife.

She knew that was what happened. She'd experienced that when her mother had broken up with her many boyfriends. When Lucas had broken up with girls in school and he'd confided in her about how awkward a particular class had been.

It never went well. People would *say* they'd remain friends, but that never happened in her experience. They separated. Pretended for a while and then drifted apart. Far apart.

She could never allow that to happen with Lucas.

Callie pulled back and stared into his eyes. Absently, she touched her swollen lips with her fingertips and then she stood up quickly, putting physical distance between them as she pulled her scrubs back over her stomach and put her hands solidly into her pockets.

'We shouldn't do that.' She sounded breathless. 'We can't risk it… There's a baby now—we have to think about that.'

Lucas looked hurt, but then the shutters came down. 'Sure.' He licked his lips. 'Not a problem. I'd better get back to work.'

She watched him go, her heart breaking, wishing she could take back her words but knowing that she couldn't. But he must have thought the same thing as her. Why else would he have backed off so easily?

We have to be sensible about this. We can't risk what we have…

The baby began to swish again with all the excitement. Callie laid her hand on her stomach. 'I can do this,' she said.

Callie wished she could be sure of that. She was certain Lucas would make a good dad—she believed in him. Knew he would be.

It was her own maternal instincts she doubted.

Lucas stood in Theatre, suturing a wound, his face a mask of concentration. Anyone on the outside looking in would think that he was simply concentrating on the task at hand—and he was. It was just that he was also thinking about what had happened with Callie.

She let me kiss her!

She'd more than *let* him. She'd *welcomed* it! Hadn't she? At first? Just after the baby had started kicking and he'd been touching her belly?

His hands had felt alive at the softness of her skin and the roundness of her belly, each nerve-ending dancing with excitement. Not just from feeling the baby move, but from touching *her*.

When had he ever touched her so intimately?

Never.

Callie didn't invite touching. Never had. He'd always known to keep his distance in that way. But with the baby moving…

They'd been able to share a wonderful, cherished, delightful moment—each of them feeling the child they had created together. But it had also been the first time he'd ever properly laid his hands on her.

The way she'd looked at him! He would swear blind she'd had something akin to desire in her eyes! Her pupils had widened, her breath had hitched in her throat and he'd sensed her pulse beating rapidly… It had been too magical a moment *not* to kiss her.

And what a kiss!

He'd never felt that way from just a kiss before. It had been like waking up from a deep sleep and realising that after all this time, all the years with Maggie, the kisses meant nothing compared to this one. With Callie it had been so special, so tender—as if his lips had discovered what they were truly meant to do. They were meant to be connected to Callie. They were for her and her alone.

His whole body had come alive. Each nerve-ending tingling, every synapse in his brain firing away like a space rocket. His heart had pounded and adrenaline had rushed through him, awakening every muscle, every intention, daring him to touch her more, to wrap his arms around her and pull her close, to envelop her as much as he could.

Fighting that had been difficult. Because there'd been fear there, too. Fear that she would stop him. Fear that she would break away. And if she did what would she say? What would she do? She was so afraid of losing their friendship and he…he was afraid she'd push him away. She'd already done it once, broken his heart once, why wouldn't she do it again?

And she had.

She'd stopped the kiss, shut them both down, before he could get carried away.

Perhaps that had been wise? Perhaps it was good that she'd put the brakes on? After all, he had no real idea of what she actually *felt*. Hadn't he already rushed into one relationship? Look how that had turned out! Wouldn't he be foolish to do the same thing with Callie? The one person who mattered the most to him.

The suturing done, he snipped the stitch and pulled down his mask. 'I'm done.'

The theatre assistants nodded and watched him walk away.

But as he stood at the sink, firmly scrubbing his arms with iodine soap, he knew—just knew in his heart—that this time, no matter what, he would treat Callie better than he had his wife.

The kiss—though heart-poundingly amazing—had been wrong. Callie had been right to stop it. They could never be together in that way and no matter what he felt for her he had to get over it—or he knew he'd get hurt again.

CHAPTER FIVE

OVER THE NEXT couple of weeks Callie realised that the baby's movements were going from being 'swishy' to definite kicks. Their baby liked moving. *A lot.* She knew she had to keep track of the movements and make sure she felt ten or more each day—and as the days passed she had no problem surpassing that total.

She had a very active baby, and she enjoyed nothing more than lying in the bath and watching the somersaults going on inside, as her belly wobbled from one side to the other, or was poked up in one area as the baby stretched its legs. There were times when a foot would press up against her belly and she could push it back down with her finger. Other times the foot would keep pressing out, as if the baby were playing with her.

Every evening they were at home together Lucas would sit with her, his hand on her belly, and talk to the baby. They were moments that she treasured, not knowing for how much longer this closeness might last, so she eked out every last second of the time.

They jokingly referred to the baby as 'Bean', and there was nothing she enjoyed more than to have Lucas tell the baby a story. He'd once read *Jack and the Beanstalk* to it, and every time he'd got to the *fee-fie-fo-fum* the baby had kicked madly and wriggled, making them laugh with delight and joy.

They both thought they were having a boy, but the discussion came up as to whether they ought to find out at the next day's twenty-week scan.

'It might be nice to know for sure,' Callie said. Then she'd know what she'd be giving away. A son? A daughter?

'I don't know. I kind of like the surprise.'

'Well, it's going to be one or the other, isn't it? If you find out what sex it is then you can start thinking about names and how you might want to decorate the nursery.'

The nursery was going to be the room that Callie was currently staying in. It was currently a pale blue, but they both knew that babies preferred strong colours to pale ones, so it would need redecorating.

'Don't you want to know if you're having a son or a daughter?'

'I'll be overjoyed either way.' He shrugged. It was a simple matter for him, it seemed. 'And *we* will pick names and *we* will think about how *we* want to decorate the nursery. I don't want to hear any more of this "you" stuff.'

'But it's *your* baby, Lucas. I was never meant to be involved.'

He shook his head defiantly. 'But you *are*. Things are different now and I want your input.'

How could she explain? If she got involved—if she started making choices—then she might get too attached. What would happen then if it all went pear-shaped? If it all went wrong? She couldn't bear to lose him.

'I'm not sure that I should give it.'

He looked at her sideways. 'Why are you afraid, Callie?'

'I don't know! Because I'm not sure how good I'm going to be for the baby. What role model did I have? A lying drunk who couldn't even be bothered to think of a proper name for me. A sly, selfish monster who loved alcohol more than she did finding food for our table. I don't know how to connect with a child—'

'Ridiculous! So Maria was an awful mother? You think that will make *you* a bad one too? You see women at work every day from all social backgrounds, having been through neglect and abuse and poverty, and they prove that they can be the best mothers *because* they had such an awful time themselves. Look at how Jenny was. She didn't even have parents, and yet she knew she was going to be the best parent she could for her little girl. You can do that too.'

'I know. I know you're right. But I still worry. I never thought that I'd have a child, and now that I am I need to know that I'm doing the right thing for it.'

'If you really were such a cold fish—if I thought in any way, shape or form that you were a cold-hearted, selfish monster—do you think we would have stayed friends as long as we have? You're *lovely*, Callie. You're kind, and you have the biggest heart of anyone I know.'

He was looking into her eyes so intently it was difficult to stop the somersaults in her tummy. Ever since they'd kissed that time his close proximity, his intensity when he looked at her, sparked her awareness of him. The way he moved, his scent, the way he gazed at her when he thought she wasn't looking… She knew there was the possibility of something else developing between them. And that scared her too.

'Really?'

'Do selfish people offer to have babies for someone else?'

She could see his point. But she'd never told him that she'd once entertained the idea that they *could* get together. That she'd thought if she was ever going to have a baby with anyone she would have chosen him. She'd not told the clinic. Had deliberately lied to them all. Because when he'd asked her out it had been the toughest thing for her to turn him down. Because she'd known she had to do something she didn't want to do. To the one man she'd wanted to say yes to!

But she'd not wanted to lose him as a friend if anything had gone wrong. All his relationships with women up until that point had been short ones. They'd all started with passion and *'Isn't she amazing?'* and then they'd all ended.

Callie couldn't have borne to be one of those girls.

Couldn't have borne to lose the one rock who had always been there for her through her childhood. Her one shoulder to cry on. The one person who would actually listen to her. Comfort her. Hold her.

Did he know that he was the only person who had ever held her? Properly? Just to enjoy holding her and not want something else?

It had been a big thing for her to offer to be his surrogate—especially when she'd known she'd be using her own eggs…that the baby she'd be giving away would be biologically half hers.

'Talking of Maria—she rang this morning and left a message. I think you ought to go and see her. She clearly wants to make amends.'

Callie visibly sagged. 'I can't bear to be let down again, Lucas.'

He touched her hand and she squeezed his fingers in response. 'But if she really has turned a corner—if she really has been off the booze for six months—you could have that relationship with her you've always wanted.'

He was looking at her strangely again. Was he thinking about *them*? About the relationship that he'd once wanted?

But he was right. Her craving for a relationship with her mother had been long buried, but it was still there. If there was any chance at all that Maria had turned a corner…

'Would you come with me?'

'Of course I will.'

There was an intensity in their stares as their gazes locked, and suddenly Callie was aware of how close Lucas was. It would be so easy to lean forward and kiss him again, to allow themselves to lose each other in the moment again, but she knew she couldn't let that happen.

She pulled her hand free and stood up. 'Cup of tea?'

He looked disappointed at her putting distance between them, but then his face went serious, and she hoped he realised she was doing a good thing by keeping her distance.

We can't be together like that, no matter how much we want it. But, damn, it's so hard to get to sleep at night, knowing he's just next door...

By the next morning, the day of the scan—a day off for both of them—they still hadn't reached a decision. They sat in the same chairs they'd sat in at the first scan, waiting nervously.

'Can you remember the last time we sat here?' Lucas asked.

She nodded, watching a mother opposite them try to play with her toddler, who'd found a set of bricks and was stacking them rather unsuccessfully. 'Seems such a long time ago. So much has changed since then.'

He reached over to grab her hand. 'Good changes?'

She smiled back and squeezed his fingers. 'Definitely. But if you'd told me weeks ago that it would end up like this...I would never have believed you.'

He smiled. 'But I'm happy it has. Aren't you?'

Callie shrugged, noncommittal. 'Just...you know...at the beginning the set-up was different, wasn't it? I went into this pregnancy knowing I was going to give away the baby, and then everything got thrown up into the air. That was what I meant.'

'So *are* we finding out? The sex?' he asked. 'I'll let you choose.'

It was a nice gesture. But she knew he didn't want to

know and so decided to side with him. 'We'll leave it as a surprise.'

'Okay.'

They waited another ten minutes or so before they got called through, during which time the toddler tottered over, grinning and dribbling, grabbing on to Lucas's legs for stability.

'Hey, hello there.' He smiled at the little boy and Callie loved watching them interact.

He's so good with him! Lucas is going to be a great dad! But how does he make it look so easy?

She was glad the toddler hadn't come to *her*. She'd have felt awkward and the toddler probably would have cried—she knew it. She still wasn't sure what type of mother she'd make as she had no frame of reference as to what a good mother was.

Lucas had told her once that she didn't need a frame of reference. That she could learn as she went and that, seeing as Callie wasn't an alcoholic or anything like her own mother, the likelihood of her being a good mother was strong.

'Being a parent doesn't come with an instruction guide, Callie. People learn as they go. You think no one else is afraid?' he'd asked her once. He'd really got angry. Frustrated that she just wouldn't agree to the possibility that she might be a good mother.

She hoped beyond hope that he was right.

Eventually, her name was called and they went in. It was Sophie again.

'Hi, guys, nice to see you again. You're looking well, Callie. Blooming.'

Callie smiled and heaved herself onto the bed. 'Bigger this time.'

'Definitely. You've been okay? Everything normal?'

'Oh, yes.'

'Baby moving lots?'

'Like a trapeze artist.'

Sophie grinned. 'That's what we like to hear. Okay, same procedure as before. Lie back, I'll put the gel on and then we'll have a look around. It'll be a longer scan this time, because we use this one to check for any anomalies or soft markers that might indicate a problem.'

'Sure—I know.'

'Of course. I'm so used to explaining everything I forget this is probably old hat to you.'

'Not really. It's all quite scary when it's your own.' She reached out for Lucas's reassuring hand, surprising herself. Where had 'hands-off' Callie gone?

Sophie nodded and tucked paper towel into the top of Callie's underwear.

'Right…we'll have a general look round first, then I'll take four measurements today. The biparietal diameter to measure the baby's head, the abdominal circumference, head circumference and femur length. We'll check that against gestation and decide which percentile your baby is in. Do you want to know the sex today?' They looked at each other to confirm what they'd decided earlier. Lucas gave her a nod. Callie turned back to Sophie. 'No, we don't. We want a surprise.'

'Excellent. Okay. And so we begin…'

As before, Sophie kept the screen to herself until she'd found the heartbeat and could see the baby moving, and then she turned the screen so that both of them could see.

Callie gasped aloud. 'Wow! It's so big this time!'

'Baby's grown beautifully,' Sophie agreed.

Lucas squeezed her hand. But Callie couldn't take her eyes off the screen. There was their baby! Their beautiful baby! Moving and tumbling and sucking its thumb. It was all so clear! A real person. A new human being. *Theirs*.

Sophie was clicking and moving the mouse around, looking at the head, the brain.

'Beautiful butterfly patterning—just what we'd expect to see.'

Then she went down through the baby's body, checking various organs and pointing them out: the kidneys, the heart. Even their baby's bladder, which had some urine in it, was sweet to see! She checked legs and feet, then arms and hands, and then she turned to the blacker parts of the scan.

'I'm just going to measure the amniotic fluid around baby first.' She moved a small white cross from one side of the expanse of black across to the other and clicked again. Then she moved the transducer and took another measurement. 'Fluid's good.' As she worked she kept clicking to print the pictures. 'No soft markers that I can see. I'll do the measurements now.'

Callie gazed on in awe.

You're my baby. Our baby. The last time I saw you I had no idea if you'd be mine. Now... Well, now I'm allowing myself to think that you might be.

The thought didn't surprise her. Which *did* surprise her. It seemed natural to want this baby.

'So, how far along are you now, Callie?'

'Twenty weeks and six days.'

'Okay. That's good. I can use that against the measurements in a minute. I just need to check where the placenta is lying.'

Callie knew this was very important. Not that the other measurements weren't important too, but if there was a problem with the position of the placenta it might jeopardise her chances of a normal delivery. If, for example, the placenta was low down and covering the cervix, the baby would not be able to come out of the birth canal. What they needed to hear now was that the placenta was posterior, or placed high.

'It's just slightly covering the cervix, but you've got time for it to move up, out of the way. We'll keep an eye on it. Arrange for another scan.'

Callie let out a breath she hadn't known she'd been holding. 'Right.'

They both watched intently as Sophie carefully skirted around the pelvic area of the baby—without giving the game away—and took abdominal and femur measurements. Then she did the head, taking the two measurements she needed to check for proper growth.

Sophie wrote everything down in Callie's notes and then plotted the measurements onto a graph. She showed the results to them. 'Everything's perfect. Baby's on the seventy-fifth percentile for all of these, so he or she is growing properly in all the right places, and for the right gestation.'

'Good.' Callie took the long stream of photos that Sophie had printed off for them. 'Thanks.'

'Do you want a 3D picture of baby's face?'

They looked at each other. Then Callie turned back to Sophie. 'Yes, please.'

Sophie pressed a button to change the scan picture from two-dimensional to three. The grainy black and white disappeared and was replaced by a sepia-type colour as Sophie brought the transducer up to their baby's face. Part of it was obscured by a hand and the umbilical cord, but most of it could be seen.

'Oh, my God!'

Sophie clicked and a picture slid out of the machine.

Callie held it so Lucas could also see. He couldn't stop grinning.

He leaned down and kissed Callie on the cheek. 'Beautiful—like you.'

She flushed at the compliment—and at the burn of his lips on her skin.

Sophie smiled. 'Everything's normal. Progressing as it should be. Now, do you have any questions?'

They didn't.

'Can't think of any.'

'Okay. So we'll arrange for another scan in a few weeks—just to check the placenta has moved off the cervix. But if you have a bleed you must come straight in. Although at the moment I couldn't see any reason why that might happen.'

'You have to warn us just in case. Don't worry—we understand.'

Sophie nodded. 'Okay. Have a nice day, you two.' She stood and opened the door once Callie was cleaned of gel and covered up again.

They walked out into the light of the waiting area and hugged each other. The moment had been perfect.

'Do you think *she* knows?' Lucas asked.

'Knows what?'

'The sex of the baby.'

'Probably.'

'Hmm, I thought so too. Seems kind of odd that she knows and we don't.'

Callie looked at him thoughtfully. 'Do you want to go back and ask? I won't mind.'

Briefly it tempted him, but then he shook his head. 'No. We agreed on a surprise and a surprise we'll get. Let's get home and have something to eat. I'm starving.'

'I thought we could go over to Laurie Park. The weather's nice—we could go out on the boating lake.'

'Sounds good.'

Lucas drove them home and they packed a picnic for Laurie Park. It was a beautiful place, filled with fruit trees and harvest bushes. It was a 'free food forest'—following an idea that had started in Seattle, America, and travelled across the pond. It had been specifically created and designed to be filled with fruit-providing trees and shrubs and plants, so that people could pick and harvest for free. Callie thought it was an ingenious idea, but hadn't been there yet.

In the centre of the park there was a boating lake, with an island at its centre established as a nature reserve, where you had to keep to certain paths and picnic areas. This was where they headed.

The weather was beautiful and sunny, and Callie couldn't help but admire Lucas's muscles as he rowed the boat. His short-sleeved shirt showed off his tanned skin and muscular arms to perfection and it was nice to see him relaxed—not the intense Lucas she usually saw at work, with a stethoscope draped around his neck.

They moored the small rowing boat at one of the wooden jetties and Lucas got off first, then reached down to help her out so she didn't slip or fall. She tried not to pay too much attention to how she felt whilst he held her hand, deliberately ignoring the wish that he would continue to hold it.

The boat wobbled as she stood, scaring her for a moment, but Lucas kept hold of her firmly until she was off. He took the picnic basket in one hand and walked beside her as she delighted in the different berries and fruits she saw, picking some for their meal.

The sun was hot and it was the type of weather in which you might easily burn. She was glad she'd chosen her summer dress. The dress was the first bit of maternity clothing she'd ever bought, knowing she would be carrying her baby through the long, hot summer months.

There weren't many people about on the small island, and no one else in the picnic area they chose. They spread a tartan blanket on the ground and began to lay out their food.

'It's beautiful here.' Callie remarked, looking out over the fresh green grass and through the woodland glade to the calm water of the lake. There were swans gliding smoothly over the surface, two grey cygnets behind them.

'It certainly is. You'd never imagine we were in London.'

'No.'

He reached out to smooth a tendril of hair away from her face and she awkwardly tucked it behind her ear, flushing slightly at the intimate touch. What was he doing? Didn't he know he shouldn't touch her like that? They'd kissed once, but that had been a mistake. It couldn't happen again. They were just friends.

Callie finished laying out the picnic: baguettes, cheese, fruit, fruit juices, deli meats and strawberry jelly—her current craving. Lucas laughed when he saw she'd brought it.

'I couldn't come out without it.'

'Our baby is going to have a sweet tooth.'

'Oh, I don't know…my mum drank all that alcohol and I'm not an alcoholic.'

She knew she shouldn't have said it. It had put a dampener on things as soon as it was out of her mouth.

'Sorry. Forget what I said.'

'We can talk about it if you want?'

She shrugged. 'I was being flippant.'

'But it's important to you. It's part of your history.'

She poured out some fruit juice. 'Okay…where do I start?' She shielded her eyes from the sun, wishing she'd brought sunglasses. 'Well, I guess I was lucky I didn't have foetal alcohol syndrome when I was born. I was small—only about four pounds, though I was full term—and they reckoned I had a small heart murmur, but that was it. The murmur's gone now, thankfully, but I was so worried about today's scan.'

'Even though you don't drink?'

'Even though I don't drink. I was worried that because I got away with it as a child there might be a problem with *your* baby instead. Jump a generation—that sort of thing.'

He smiled. '*Our* baby.'

'Yes.' She nodded quickly, feeling awkward.

'But you know that's unfounded?'

'I know, but I can't help myself worrying.'

Lucas wafted a fly from his leg. 'You never raised this at the clinic.'

'I did. I told my counsellor when we had one-to-one sessions.'

'And what did she say?'

'Same as you. That it doesn't work that way, and that, besides, when they choose the egg and the sperm in the dish they pick the healthiest, best-developed ones. The chances of us having a problem was going to be minimal. And they'd done the genetic testing, too. I'm just an old worrywart.'

He leaned forward. 'It's because you care. You're going to be a great mum, Callie, because *you* have that quality. Your mum didn't for a reason. Her alcoholism is a disease which you don't have. Please don't worry about what sort of mum *you'll* make. I *know* you'll be fine.'

It was sweet of him to say it, but he was her friend—of course he'd say that. There was still that deep-down worry that she would be an awful mother. Like Maria had been. It didn't matter that she wanted to make amends. She'd still got it badly wrong to start with.

'We'd better eat before the wasps beat us to it.' She laughed, but the laughter tailed away when she saw the stern look on his face.

'Why do you always change the subject, Callie?'

'I'm not sure I know what you mean.'

'Your being a mother. I give you a compliment, tell you you'll be fine, and you change the subject. Or you argue with me. Tell me I'm wrong.'

She shrugged. 'I was taught avoidance by a master at the craft.'

'For someone who's so afraid to be like her mother, you frequently admit her influence on you, happily accepting it.' He sounded annoyed.

'I'm not happy to accept it, Lucas. It's just the way my life was. You wouldn't understand.'

'Wouldn't I? You weren't the only one with a difficult childhood.'

She looked at him askance. 'I don't remember *you* having an alcoholic mother.'

'Don't be pedantic, Callie. I meant my father. I hardly ever saw him, and as a boy I craved that connection. When he did come home he would be angry and resentful, and smack me more times than I could count just to "make me into a man". He hated the fact that I was surrounded by nothing but women, and knew how to sew and cook rather than fish or hunt. Even my best friend was a girl, and my father hated that too. He couldn't understand why I wasn't this football and rugby-playing army cadet, ready to follow in his footsteps. Instead he'd come home from Malaysia or Singapore and find me cooped up in the kitchen with my mother and sisters, covered in flour and other baking ingredients.'

Callie looked upset. 'I'm sorry. I didn't mean to be flippant.'

'I'm just saying you weren't the only one with a bad childhood.' He sighed. 'I craved my father's approval and attention just as much as you craved your mother's. Neither of us got what we wanted.' He looked at her as the wind billowed her hair around her face. 'Or *who* we wanted.'

There was an awkward silence filled only by birdsong and the gentle humming of nearby bees.

Lucas got up and walked to the water's edge, his hands in his pockets.

Callie looked at his back as he stood by the water. So alone and remote. She felt bad, and knew she ought to go to him and apologise. This was supposed to be a nice day out for both of them. A day off from work. A day off from pressure. Time to give them both the opportunity to talk about what would soon happen.

And I've messed it up.

Callie got up from the blanket and went over to where he stood. There were some ducks happily paddling, and further along a moorhen. She reached out to touch his arm and slid her hand into his.

'I'm sorry.'

When he turned she could see the anguish on his face.

'I am too. I didn't think anything could spoil today.'

She was going to make a comment about being taught how to do that, too, then realised that it was just the sort of thing Lucas had been referring to.

'We need to talk, Lucas. Properly. About everything. The baby, the surrogacy… Everything.'

'The future?'

She nodded, blinking in the bright sun. 'Yes.'

He looked her straight in the eye. 'I want you involved, Callie. I want you to be there for our baby. I know you can be. I know you're capable. I just want you to persuade *your-self* that you can do it just as much as I know that you can.'

She wanted to believe him. She really did. But years of doubt and second-guessing everything she'd ever known was a hard habit to break. 'When you say "involved", what does that mean? Occasional visits? Being a godparent?'

'Being a *mother*.'

There. He'd said it. Out loud. Asked for a huge commitment from her. A commitment she'd not expected when she'd first gone into this surrogacy.

'But what if—?'

He grabbed her arms. 'No "what ifs", Callie! Okay, you were only going to be the surrogate to start with, but that's all changed now. We're in this together and we're best friends. I don't see why we can't do this!'

She looked deep into his eyes, aware of how firmly he was holding her, aware of the proximity of his broad chest, those strong arms that had rowed them across the lake, the healthy brown glow of his sun-drenched skin. How could she tell him she was so afraid? Afraid that she'd lose him as her friend if they took their friendship to the next level and it didn't work out.

She knew she'd just die if she didn't have him in her life, and if he stayed just a friend then she could keep him there. Anything more than that would put them at risk.

She shifted her gaze and focused on his lips. His beautiful mouth, his strong jaw. He was gazing hungrily at her, like a man who couldn't bear not to touch, and before she knew what was happening he'd pulled her against his chest and pressed his lips to hers.

She sank into his embrace, tasting him, submitting to him, sinking against his body and feeling his arousal as they kissed.

Why have we been fighting this?

It felt so natural. It felt so *good!*

Kissing Lucas felt so damn *right*, and her hands went into his hair, clutching him to her as their mouths opened, deepening the kiss, their tongues entwining. A fiery heat spread up her body, electrifying her skin with his every tender touch.

The sun beat down upon them as their own fires burned within them.

She could barely breathe. She didn't want to stop kissing him just to breathe but she had to, and as she pulled away she saw the dazed look in his eyes and knew he'd been just as physically affected by the kiss as she had.

'Lucas, we—'

He shook his head and kissed her again. More tenderly

this time, cupping her face, sliding his hands down her neck, over her shoulders, down her arms, until he pulled her firmly against his arousal once more.

Callie groaned his name as his tongue wrapped around hers searing his touch into her memory banks for evermore.

Oh, God, why can't I have him like this?

She felt dizzy. Hot. Swept away on a tide of passion that she'd never felt before. The heat deep within her began to burn, awakening after many years of being kept hidden, trapped inside, bursting forth to scream its very nature to the world.

Everything around them was forgotten. The lovely island, the beautiful warm sunshine, the romanticism of the lake. All there was—was his kiss.

Her need for Lucas was frightening, overwhelming, and suddenly she felt scared by what they were doing. She pulled free and stepped back, breaking their contact.

'Callie—'

'We should stop.' Her hands hung limply at her sides, her hair was ruffled by his hands, and the memory of his touch was burning a trace across her heart.

He looked at her, hungry for more. 'Why?'

She couldn't answer him. Why *was* she stopping them?

Because you're my friend, Lucas, and I dare not lose you if this goes wrong! I couldn't bear to be without you.

'I need time to think.' She saw the disappointment in his face, so she reached out for his hand and took it in hers. 'I'm not running away. I just…need time to absorb this.'

He nodded, reluctantly, and they went back to the blanket together. They sat and nibbled at their lunch, no longer hungry for food, looking over the water, talking about nothing. But the atmosphere was strained by what was not being said.

A mallard glided by followed by six young ducklings, all brown and yellow and chirping. Squirrels jumped from tree to tree above them, and all around was birdsong and sunshine and warmth and bees flitting from flower to flower.

It should have been perfect. It should have been easy.

She'd ruined it and hurt him again.

Eventually Lucas broke the silence. His face was grim. 'If your heart isn't in this, Callie, then I'd rather you stepped back.'

'What?' She wasn't sure she'd heard him correctly. What did he mean, 'step back'?

'If you can't commit to this one hundred per cent, then I'd rather you didn't commit at all.'

'Lucas—'

'I mean it.'

He stared at her. His eyes were telling her he would not budge on this. He would not make allowances for her. She had to decide. She had to let him know what her plans were.

A cooler breeze came along and Callie felt cold. She'd not brought a jacket or cardigan and neither had Lucas.

'We ought to head back,' he said.

'I'll gather together the picnic things,' she mumbled, but he blocked her with his arm and said he would do it.

She watched him tidy away. He was so good. He'd been so patient with her. She knew he wanted more for them and that she was unable to give it. Or too scared to give it. But she hoped that in time he would understand. Surely he valued their friendship as much as she did?

'I'm glad we came here today,' she said, trying to brighten the mood.

He nodded. 'Me too.'

'Perhaps another day we could go to Windsor Castle? I always wanted to go there, but my mother never took me.'

He sat back on his haunches, blinking in the sunlight. 'I remember. She always let you down, didn't she?'

He wasn't just talking about the castle, though, was he?

He was letting her know that he understood. About how hard it was for her.

'I'll definitely take you.'

Their eyes met and she wondered if he was still talking about taking her to the castle or *something else*? Feeling all hot and bothered suddenly, she smiled and helped him pack away the last of the things.

It would be nice to go to Windsor Castle one day.

Perhaps they'd make it?

As friends, if nothing else.

Back at the flat, Callie unpacked the picnic, put the things they hadn't used into the fridge, then headed into her room for a cardigan. As she stood by her wardrobe, deciding which one to choose, she became aware of Lucas filling the doorway.

'You okay?'

He was looking at her strangely. His beautiful blue eyes all intense and serious and dark.

'I need to tell you something, Callie. Something I wanted to say at the park, but...'

Callie closed her wardrobe and threw on the cardigan, then sat down on her bed, rubbing her abdomen as the baby kicked. 'What is it?'

He came in and knelt down in front of her, looking up into her face. 'I'm getting strong feelings for you, Callie. Feelings I never thought I'd feel again. And I want us to be honest with each other at all times.'

She nodded slowly, afraid of what he might say. He'd said 'again', reminding her of the first time he'd asked her out and she'd turned him down. But she'd been so young! As had he. It had been too scary to take that step with him then and it was even more so now! So much was at stake— not just their friendship, but the baby. Their innocent baby.

'You can be honest with me.'

'I think you ought to go and see your mother. Get some closure. See if she really has turned a corner.'

She sighed. 'I'm not sure I can cope with any more of her lies, Lucas.'

'I know. But if she's *not* lying, Callie...if she really has been on the wagon for six months and this new man has made a difference in her life...you'd be a fool to let that relationship go.' His voice softened. 'She's your *mother*. And that's a bond that can never be broken. Besides...people can change.'

He let her go and went back into the lounge, leaving her thinking over his words.

He might be right. If Maria *had* been dry for months, then didn't she owe it to her to give her another chance? Even after all her lies? After all the let-downs? If she turned away now, when there was the chance of reconciliation...

But what if Lucas was wrong? If she was still lying...?

Then I won't have lost anything. It'll just be the same as before, won't it?

But she knew he'd also been referring to her. Saying that *she* could change. That she could be the mother he believed she could be.

CHAPTER SIX

THE BANANA TASTED odd in her mouth, and after a brave attempt to finish it she pushed it away, half eaten. Life was beginning to bother her. Thoughts were keeping her awake. Feelings and physical pangs kept her hungry in more ways than one.

Lucas had said she needed closure with regard to her mother. Well, maybe she needed closure in other ways too.

When Lucas came in from work he was exhausted and needed a shower. She found herself twiddling her thumbs, then cleaning out a cupboard and reorganising a bookshelf before he emerged, hair wet, a towel around his neck and another at his waist, his bare chest and legs pebbled with moisture.

What are you doing to me?

He looked delicious. Delectable.

Edible, even.

Licking her lips, she tried to calm her twitchy fingers and the pang in her stomach that cried out for some physical contact from him. Perhaps another kiss like that one at the park, by the lake?

That had been a toe-curler in all the right places!

He had a nice flat stomach—nothing too ripped, but not flabby either. And from his belly button there was a smattering of dark hair leading down to…

To distract herself, she tried to think of Maria. Memories of her were usually perfect for dampening her mood. She spotted her favourite teddy bear, lying at an awkward angle on the table, and she reached for it to straighten it, remembering another teddy bear she'd once made.

As a child, when she'd outgrown a nightdress, rather than throw it out she'd cut it up into squares and circles and hand-sewn it into a teddy-type thing. It hadn't been pretty, or neat, but it had been girly and pink and she'd stuffed it with filling from her pillow, hoping her mum wouldn't notice the crudely cut hole in the pillow covering.

Of course her mum hadn't noticed.

Callie hadn't named it, but she had cuddled it. And for a long time she'd thought she'd known what it was to cuddle.

Until Lucas had held her.

Stop it, Callie!

Then the importance of being held by someone who loved you had suddenly became important, and she'd realised just how much she'd missed as a child.

'I'm glad you're home.'

He looked at her face and frowned. 'Sorry. I got called away. You got my note?'

'Yes. Thank you.'

She stared at him, wondering how to start, but with him dressed like that he was too much of a temptation and she took a step back.

He raised his eyebrow, then grabbed the towel around his neck and began to ruffle his dark hair.

'We've never really discussed Maggie properly, have we? When she left, I mean?'

That was it. Best to come straight out with it. Not beat around the bush.

'I didn't want to burden you with my issues about Maggie.'

'I'd like to talk about her now, if that's alright?'

He nodded. 'Okay. I'll make us some tea and bring it through. You go and sit down—put your feet up.'

'Will you…erm…' she licked her lips and eyed that smattering of hair on his abdomen '…get dressed?'

He looked down at himself and then back at her, raising a sardonic eyebrow. Then he smiled and nodded. ''Course.'

Callie waited for him in the lounge while he disappeared off to his room. Soon enough he came back through—dressed, thankfully, in jeans and a white tee. He moved into the kitchen and came back with a tray of tea and a small plate of biscuits.

'Hungry?'

Definitely. But not for food…

'I couldn't eat.'

'I could make you an omelette?'

She shook her head. 'This is fine. I'll eat properly later.'

Callie inhaled a deep breath. She wasn't sure she wanted to hear some of the answers, but there were questions and she had to ask them.

'So tell me about you and Maggie.'

'What do you need to know?'

'What went wrong?'

He shook his head as if he didn't know himself. 'We should never have married. Plain and simple.' He shook his head, disgusted with himself. 'I was stupid. On the rebound. When we first got together, everything seemed fine. Or I pretended it was, I guess. I was so determined to make it work with her, and love her, and give her anything she wanted to make her happy.'

On the rebound? 'So what went wrong?'

He shrugged. 'I really thought I loved her. I thought I was proving it to her every day. She seemed happy, for a few years, at least, but then she started looking at me strangely and asking me weird questions.'

'Like what?'

'Questions about you. Us. Our friendship. There was a distance coming between us and I panicked. I didn't know what to do. I knew she felt that there was something missing, and when she mentioned children I was determined to give her the child that she wanted.'

'But that didn't happen.'

'She learnt she couldn't have children. When we couldn't conceive the distance between us became greater. Because of her infertility, I believed. She was so sad, and I so wanted to make her happy. When you suggested the surrogacy I leapt at the idea.'

'*You?* Not both of you?'

He shook his head. 'Not at first. But I persuaded her it was a good idea. She had doubts, but she agreed to let us look into it. When she started to have counselling at the infertility centre…that was when it all started to go wrong.' He took a sip of his tea. 'There were issues in our relationship from the start. I truly believed I loved her, and she insisted that I didn't. But that wasn't true. I *did* love her…in a way…just not in the way I should have.'

Callie nodded in understanding, sad that he'd never confided in her about this before. 'When I worked with Maggie on the ward she kept questioning me about the surrogacy. About my feelings about it. My feelings for you.'

Lucas looked at her. 'Did she? What did you say?'

'That of course I was happy to do it. That I loved you. That I couldn't imagine not giving you the greatest gift a friend could give. She looked so sad.'

'It's hard to work in Maternity and then discover you can't have what's in front of you all day long…' He shook his head. 'I felt so sorry for her.'

'Perhaps you shouldn't have?'

Lucas nodded. 'I know. She told me the night she left that my pity was so obviously just for *her*, not for us as a

couple. That I was truly showing her I wasn't connected
to her in the way I should have been.'

Callie felt sick. Why hadn't he confided in her about
all of this? She could have helped them both! Given them
space, distance, time. Whatever it was they'd needed.

'And then she had her affair?'

'Yes. She told me she'd found love in the arms of someone who put her first for once. That she'd found someone
who was willing to treat her right.'

'But you *did* treat her right.'

'No. I didn't.' He looked at her and smiled sadly. 'I
thought I had. I truly did. But she was right about me, and
I feel terrible for treating her in such a way. I know now
that I'll never do that again. It's all my fault.'

He slid over to the couch she was sitting on and put his
arm around her shoulders.

Callie sank into him. 'But it *wasn't* your fault! She
should have said something! She had a voice. You were
trying to make the best of what you had. You acted with
good intentions—'

'I so wanted to put it right. In all of this I was trying to
prove something. To myself, to my parents, to Maggie. I
should have been thinking of you, and I want to put that
right too.'

'You haven't hurt me, Lucas,' she said gently.

'I never want to—'

Callie heard the crack in his voice. Her heart swelled
with concern and she hated the fact that he was hurting
over what he might have done to her. She turned to hold
him, comforting him, hoping her arms around him would
convince him of her forgiveness. She kissed the side of his
face, his cheek, his jaw.

Her lips were moving ever closer to his mouth and he
pulled back, looking at her, searching her face with his eyes.
'Callie, don't do this if you're going to stop me again—'

But she leaned in and closed her eyes as his lips brushed hers. A fire ignited within her and she didn't fight it this time. This time she welcomed it, falling into his arms, falling into his strong embrace.

He kissed her as if the world was going to end, and when he stopped she was gasping for breath.

'I should have been stronger. I shouldn't have allowed you to be dragged into my mess.'

'But we're working it out, aren't we?'

He stroked her hair back from her face. 'Yes. But I need you to know, Callie.' He held her hands in his. 'I will never hurt you. I will never lie to you. I will be here for you, always.'

She had to blink back tears at his words. 'I still have doubts.'

'Why?'

'Because…because you've never had a relationship work out! At school, at college. Plenty of girls, plenty of dates, but never a commitment. And then with Maggie…even that was wrong…even that failed.'

'But I was so young then! You can't hold relationships I had at sixteen against me? They were all wrong for me. And I've just *told* you about Maggie…'

'And the others?'

He looked at her, his face a mask. 'I was a teenager. A young teenager. Hardly anyone has successful relationships at that age. Besides…the one woman I truly wanted turned me down.'

Callie stared, his words echoing in her skull, accusing her, blaming her. Asking why she had turned him down? She'd told him why! Did he not realise? Understand? Did he truly not appreciate just how much he meant to her?

He leant back against the chair and sighed. 'You should hate me,' he said quietly.

'But I don't. You can't take all the responsibility here,

Lucas. We went into this process with our eyes open. So you knew things weren't great between you and Maggie and you didn't say? Well, what about what *I* knew? What *Maggie* knew?'

'What do you mean?'

'You weren't the only one in that relationship—she knew how bad it was, too. She was even sleeping with someone else, for goodness' sake! And I was her husband's best friend and she still allowed me to get pregnant with a baby when she was messing around with someone else! You didn't do that.'

Lucas lifted her hands in his and kissed them, his lips caressing the backs of her fingers with a tenderness that broke her heart. 'We were all in the wrong. I'm sorry. With all my heart, I'm so sorry.'

'Don't be. Because you're *you*. Because you're truthful. Without this situation I would never have had a baby. I would never have been able to consider the possibility that I'm able to be a mum. I would never have tried to be. And I can only contemplate it because you'll be at my side. There are no doubts in my mind about what a committed father *you'll* be.' She stroked his jaw. 'You're nothing like your own father.'

'You'll be here with us?'

His eyes lit up with hope, and the realisation that he wanted her to be there so much almost broke her heart.

It was terrifying to say it, but she knew in her heart that she could. 'I'll try. If you want me to be.'

'I want nothing more than for you to try. Because I'm living my life for *me* now. Not for Maggie. No one else. Me. And this baby.'

As they sat next to each other Callie circled the few hairs in the middle of his forearms. 'I love it that we can be honest with each other.'

'Me too.'

'I don't regret the surrogacy, Lucas. I knew then and I know now that you're going to be the best dad in the world to this baby.'

She looked deep into his heart and saw that her words meant the world to him.

They decided to paint over the pale blue with a pale green, so that they could paint a jungle mural on the upper parts of the wall: tree foliage, brown monkeys hanging down from the branches holding bright yellow bananas, snakes with red and blue stripes wrapped around tree trunks, a bright yellow sunshine in one corner and some red macaw parrots flying from one side of the room to the other.

It was an ambitious project, but Callie had agreed to it after seeing Lucas's draft drawings. He was a pretty good artist and could sketch what he wanted to perfection.

'You weren't kidding about having an inner interior designer, were you?' Callie laughed. 'I don't suppose you've got an inner chef, too?' She was starving.

She was wearing an old shirt of Lucas's, tied in a knot below her bump, with some old jeans. He wore an old tee shirt with jeans and both of them were pretty much covered in paint. They'd been working hard on the room for hours.

The nursery was really beginning to take shape and Callie could picture herself there, holding the baby. She could imagine looking down and feeling something. Love, devotion... That bond that had always been missing from her daydreams before.

Everything seemed to be coming together. It was all starting to look rosy.

Lucas flicked some paint on her. 'Hey—planet Earth to Callie?'

She looked at him and smiled. Could a man look more delicious, wearing scummy old painting clothes with a smear of green paint across his forehead? 'What?'

'I said I've made arrangements for us to visit the castle. Didn't you say you wanted to go?'

Windsor Castle was one of the oldest castles in Britain, and it still stood in its entirety in the centre of London. Queen Victoria had gone there on her honeymoon with Prince Albert. The pictures she'd seen of the inside on the internet made the place look so romantic—like a real life fairytale castle, right in the heart of the capital. People could hire it out for celebrations, and last year couples had started getting married there.

'That's great! When?'

'After the next scan. I thought we could go as a treat—before the baby's born. I'm not sure we want to negotiate turrets with a baby buggy in tow.'

No. Those turrets looked narrow.

'That's great! Oh, I can't wait! I was always asking my mum to take me and she never did, and then one day at school we were all given a letter to take home about a school trip they were organising to go there.'

He listened intently. 'I think I know what's coming.'

She nodded. 'You're right. She gave me two pounds for the deposit, which I paid, finally thinking I'd get to go on a school trip, but then she never paid the rest. I stayed at school, doing algebra and factoring equations, whilst everyone else had a lovely time.'

'Oh, Callie…'

'My classmates came back full of it. Since then I've always meant to go, but when you live in the heart of somewhere you tend not to go to the touristy places.'

He put down his paint and held both her arms, looking her straight in the eyes. 'Well, we're going. After the scan to check the placenta we are most definitely going to the castle.'

She smiled at him, and this time she hoped he would kiss her. She wanted it to happen. If he did she wouldn't fight him or step away. Not today. Today she deserved to be kissed.

Lucas didn't disappoint her. He pulled her closer and dipped his head to hers.

Callie closed her eyes in expectation. This felt so natural to her now, and she wanted him so much! She'd denied herself years ago and kept Lucas stored in a box marked 'friend' for too long. She wanted his lips on her, his hands touching her, caressing her. She wanted to feel the love that he could give. To have that release. Just once.

As their lips met sparks flew. A barrage of sensations ripped through her body. It was like waking up after centuries of being asleep—every nerve-ending was alive and just waiting for him to caress it.

His hands cupped her face as their lips made sweet music and she inhaled him as if he were her only life's breath. Tenderly and slowly he removed her clothes, as if he expected her to stop him at any moment. He didn't rush her, but moved at her pace.

Callie helped him pull off his tee shirt to reveal his broad, muscular chest and she ran her hands over parts of him she had never seen, as if privileged now to do so. He was so perfect—so right. A delight to look at and to touch.

Briefly she wondered why she had denied herself this for so long. She wasn't thinking about what she was risking any more. Somehow she'd pushed those worries to one side, as if she was allowing herself this one night. Those thoughts were too burdensome, too disappointing, to let them rule her head now.

Her heart was in charge and she wanted Lucas. Hadn't they both wanted each other for too long? Well, dammit, this time it was going to happen!

Callie's fingers undid his jeans and they dropped to the floor. Lucas scooped her up to take her to his bed. This room smelt of fresh paint and they didn't want any distractions.

She laid her head against his chest as he cradled her to him before gently lying her down on the bed, lowering himself onto her, holding his weight off her round belly.

'You're so beautiful, Callie,' he murmured, kissing her skin in feather-light touches, trailing his lips down her body to envelop her peaked nipples. 'If you're going to stop me, then do it now.'

She gasped at the sensation, gripping his back, hungry for more. More than anything she wanted him inside her… To feel him filling her, to enjoy that ultimate surrender…

She wasn't going to stop him. Not today. Not any more.

He took her gently, but still she cried out his name. He stopped briefly to check she was okay and then he was moving. Rhythmically. His mouth claiming hers. Her body was his to control and she cried out in ecstasy as he brought her to her peak.

Her hands gripping his back, pulling him tighter against her, she went with him on his own journey to climax. When he finally collapsed above her, spent and sweating slightly, he kissed her once again and then just held her, as if she was the most precious thing he'd ever owned.

Callie kissed him back and he fell asleep in her arms.

CHAPTER SEVEN

It took Callie a while to fall asleep, and when she did she dreamt in fits and starts. Dramatic, terrible dreams in which she was on a small boat out at sea in rough weather. High waves kept crashing down into the boat and all she had was a small delicate china teacup to bail out the water. Just when she thought the boat was safe from sinking another wave would crash down, or she'd notice shark fins in the water and the music from *Jaws* would inexplicably be heard.

In the dream, her panic was rising and rising, and then in the distance, beyond the high waves, she spotted another boat—a larger, stronger boat. Lucas was aboard, with all his sisters, and they were waving and calling at her to come to them. But no matter how hard she rowed her stomach would start to hurt and she would have to stop.

When the biggest wave of all came crashing down upon her head Callie woke with a start and sat up, gasping, her eyes taking in the familiar room. She was safe and on dry ground. Beside her, Lucas slept peacefully, his face relaxed, his hair tousled and gorgeous.

Thank God for that. Just a dream...

She ached in places she'd never ached before, and she remembered last night and how Lucas had touched her... Why had she made them both wait for so long?

She wiped the sleep from her eyes and ran her fingers through her hair. Glancing at the clock, she saw it said six-thirty a.m. She had to be at work for eight a.m. Throwing back the covers, she went to swing her legs out of bed—but stopped when she saw all the blood.

'Oh, my God! *Lucas!*'

Lucas leapt up beside her. 'What is it?'

'You need to call an ambulance.'

'What?' Then he noticed the large pool of blood beneath her. 'Are you okay? Are you in pain?'

She hadn't thought so, but now that he asked she was aware of some cramping. 'A bit…'

Lucas leapt from the bed, pulling on his jeans and throwing his old painting tee shirt over his head. He grabbed his mobile from his jacket pocket and dialled 999. 'Ambulance, please.'

'What is the nature of your emergency?'

'My partner's bled overnight. She's twenty weeks pregnant.'

In both their minds they knew that twenty weeks was much too early for their baby to survive if he or she arrived now. They needed to remain calm, but it was hard.

'I need to put on some clothes.' Callie said, about to get up.

'No! I want you to lie still. I'll give you one of my tee shirts. Do nothing until the paramedics get here.'

'Am I losing it, Lucas? Am I going to lose the baby?' she asked in a timid voice. This was the most frightened she'd ever been in her life.

He came to sit beside her on the bed and laid his hand on her belly. 'We can't know. But you do know as well as I do that this can mean nothing. Just a breakthrough bleed.'

'But there's so much…'

Callie began to cry. What had they done? She knew they should never have done what they had—knew they should never have overstepped that mark. Look what had happened!

'Hey… Shh… Come on.' He leaned into her and put his arm around her. 'Have you felt the baby move?'

She thought for a moment. Had she felt anything since being awake? 'No—nothing.'

'That still doesn't mean anything.' But his face hardened, his mouth a bitter line.

It was the worst seven minutes of their lives, awaiting the ambulance. When the two guys in green made their way into the flat, carrying their big packs and smiling reassuringly at her, Callie couldn't help but burst into tears again. It was all so scary. She had no idea what was happening to her baby and wouldn't know until she got to hospital and got them to do a scan.

The paramedics were very kind, and they tried to keep her spirits up as they wrapped her in a cream blanket, strapped her into a portable chair and wheeled her down to their vehicle. In the ambulance they attached monitors and checked her blood pressure. It was a little low, but nothing significant that would indicate a major blood loss, which gave them a little hope.

Callie lay on the trolley after they'd transferred her over, concentrating like mad on her insides, hoping and waiting for baby to kick, to give her a sign that it was all right. That it was still there…that its heart was still beating.

Why won't you kick? You're always kicking me…

But she felt nothing, and by the time they wheeled her into the St Anne's Hospital, she was despondent and very upset. Convinced that because she'd slept with Lucas she had somehow killed her baby.

'This is my fault.'

'It's not.'

'I'm being punished, Lucas. It's because I never wanted to be a mother. It's life's cruel trick.'

'No, Callie, it's not. It's nothing to do with that.'

'How can you know? I never wanted to be a mum, and just when I manage to persuade myself I could be one life strikes a blow and takes the baby away anyway!'

'You don't know that.'

'The baby hasn't moved! And it's always kicking me. *Always.*'

Lucas felt helpless. And angry… Angry at the world. He knew what she'd be thinking. How she'd be blaming herself.

All he could do was hold her hand, when what he wanted to do, as a doctor himself, was take over and order a fast scan so that they could get the status of the baby. She hadn't continued to bleed, which was a good sign. The bleeding had happened overnight and then stopped for some reason.

But inside his rage was building. Rage at life playing cruel tricks. Finally he'd been allowed to have Callie and now they were being punished for it. He knew what she'd start to think. Start to believe. That their lovemaking was somehow to blame. That it had been wrong. He cursed the world for doing this to him. Letting him have a taste of her. A taste of what it could be like for them together. And then swiping it away before he could hold on.

The doctors took her blood pressure again and it had stabilised. They also brought a portable ultrasound machine to Callie's bedside.

Lucas took hold of Callie's hand and gripped it hard. He was trying to tell her through touch that he would protect her, that no matter what the result he was there for her and they would get through it.

The doctor added some gel to the transducer and slowly drew it over Callie's abdomen. It seemed to take an age, and then the doctor turned the screen for them to see.

There was a heartbeat.

'Oh, thank God!' Callie began to cry again, with relief,

and Lucas reached to embrace her and kiss away her tears 'So it's all right?'

'Baby's fine. Heart-rate is good—about one hundred and forty a minute, which is average.' He swirled the transducer around some more. 'Placenta is still in position—no sign of early abruption.'

Abruption would mean that the placenta was coming away from the uterine wall early.

'It's possible you had a breakthrough bleed—dramatic as it was. If it's okay with you I'd like to do an internal and just make sure the cervix isn't opening.'

Callie nodded. 'Check everything. I don't mind.'

She was happier now that she knew her baby was safe, and as if in response to her strong emotions the baby kicked.

She laughed. 'Ha! So *now* you start! You couldn't do that earlier?'

Lucas had felt the kick too and audibly exhaled, his own heart reassured that he wasn't about to lose the two most important people in his life.

'I'll call everyone—let them know it's okay.' By 'everyone' he meant his sisters and his mother, as he'd called them earlier from the ambulance, to notify them that they were on their way to hospital.

He left the cubicle, so Callie could have privacy for the examination, and used his phone.

Callie meanwhile was reassured to hear that her cervix was tightly closed, was not effaced or thinning out in any way, and that she was showing no signs of labour.

'There is a small spot of cervical erosion. That could have been the cause of the bleed.'

'Erosion? Right…' Lucas had been so gentle, though, and careful. Had she bled because she'd slept with him? Was this her punishment?

But of course it could just be 'one of those things'. Unfortunately for her, and everyone else who experienced it, 'one of those things' could be quite dramatic.

'Is it because the placenta was covering the cervix?'

The doctor seemed undecided. 'It hasn't yet moved up off the cervical opening, so it's a possibility, but with erosion we can't know for sure. It does look like it's recent.'

The doctor suggested that she stay on the maternity assessment ward for the day, just to make sure she had no further bleeds. It would also allow her to rest.

'You have a stressful job, Miss Taylor, and you said you were decorating the nursery. Perhaps you just overdid it a bit?'

She accepted the admonishment. She *had* been up and down the stepladder a lot. And she *had* made love with Lucas. What had she been thinking? A day of rest was probably a good idea. Though she felt a little embarrassed that her colleagues would have to look after *her* when they were overworked already.

They soon dismissed that silly idea. They were overjoyed to be looking after one of their own.

'It's so special!' one of them said.

Callie wanted Lucas to get some rest too, so she asked him to go home.

'No, I'll stay with you,' he insisted.

'No, Lucas. Go and get some rest. I mean it. I'm fine now, and everyone else will look after me. Please.'

She didn't tell him it was because she wanted him to go. She felt so guilty about having sex with him. As if they'd been punished for something they should never have done.

Would she have felt different today if there'd been no bleed? Possibly. But she *had* bled, and they *had* slept together, and it was clearly a sign that what had happened was wrong. It could never happen again.

Lucas did feel tired. So he agreed and kissed her goodbye. Their lips lingered as they kissed each other, not wanting to part. But part they had to, and he stroked her face, deep in thought, his fingertips tracing the soft curves of her skin as if memorising the contours of her face.

She watched him go and closed her heart once again.

By the time he got back to his flat Lucas was exhausted. He changed the sheets and then lay on his bed for ages, hoping to sleep, but the last few hours kept running through his mind. Hearing Callie's scream, the fear in her voice when she'd called his name. Maybe on the outside he'd looked calm, but inside he'd been a mess.

The fear of losing either of them had almost killed him and the knowledge of that had made him realise something.

He loved Callie. Not just because she was carrying his baby. Of course he cared for her because of that, but this felt deeper. Something that had been awakened after a long time. Something that had always been hidden there inside him, but had masqueraded as his friendship with her.

Lucas loved being her friend—yes, he did—but...he wanted more than friendship with her. He wanted to love her properly, in the open, not just as friends but as lovers, as a couple, as a committed partnership.

He'd seen her darkest days. He'd seen her go through so much. And each time it had hurt him and he'd been there for her—if only to hold her hand or to listen as she'd cried, wept with despair or anger. They'd shared good times too. Her getting into university, then qualifying as a midwife; himself qualifying as a doctor.

They had a shared history. Had shared so much together.

Now they were having a baby.

Surely two people could not be connected more than to have created a life together?

He got up and began to pace. Wanting Callie home.

Home.

They lived together. They were best friends. Were having a baby.

And he loved her.

But he knew she was afraid. Afraid of jeopardising their friendship. How could he make her see that she meant the world to him?

There had to be a way.

There had to.

Just thinking about her and the baby made him feel good, and his heart soared so high it might have been up in the stratosphere.

The baby meant so much to him. He loved it—he knew he did—that was without question.

I love Callie too. I do.

But could he have her in the way he wanted?

He needed to know that she would give him the commitment he needed. Not just to him but to the baby too. He'd lived his entire life wishing his own father would be more committed to him, rather than just being a disciplinarian and an occasional parent who swooped in from overseas for a week or two at a time…

Lucas needed to know that Callie would be there one hundred per cent. Not a weekend mother, not a godparent, not an 'aunt'.

A mother. A wife.

My first marriage might have been a dreadful mistake, but I could damn well be sure my second won't be.

He picked up his phone and dialled a number. A number he'd put into his phone just a few days ago. As it rang he hesitated, just for a moment, and wondered if he were doing the right thing. But then he thought of Callie and he just *knew.*

This was the right thing to do. But he'd keep it a secret for now. Surprise her.

As the phone was answered at the other end he grabbed his car keys and walked down to his car, making arrangements as he went.

He'd had a very productive evening with Sienna from the castle. Walking through the doors of the hospital the following afternoon, he felt less anxious. Hospital could be a frightening place for most, but for him, it almost felt like home. He liked working there—liked the people, the place. His work. He knew the team and he knew that Callie would be looked after well.

Upstairs in the maternity assessment suite Callie was sitting upright in bed and looking much better. There was colour to her cheeks and her face lit up when she saw him.

His relief at seeing her was overwhelming. 'Callie...' He kissed her and sat down in the chair beside her bed. 'How are you doing?'

'All right. I've had lunch, and the doctors say if I don't have any more bleeding in the next few hours I can come home.'

'That's fantastic.'

But he was looking about the ward, not looking at her. Distracted. Something had changed with him. What was it?

She looked at him, concerned at the odd tone in his voice. He didn't seem his normal self.

Something was wrong. Lucas was hiding something—she knew it. She could always spot someone lying to her or hiding something from her. She could smell a woman's perfume. She could also smell alcohol. On *Lucas*? What did that mean? Had he been drinking?

For some reason Callie chose not to say anything, but inside she hurt. Had Lucas been drowning his sorrows? Self-medicating with alcohol? Why would he turn to booze? She'd never known him to drink before.

She'd confront him later. Not here. Not in the hospital where they both worked.

'Did you get some sleep?'

'A bit.' He changed the subject. 'Have you spoken to your mum?'

Callie looked at him with a raised eyebrow. 'No. I figured because we're going to see her in a few days I could tell her then. If she's interested.'

'I'm sure she will be.' He squeezed her hand. 'Can I get you anything?'

The truth… 'You can get me out of here.'

He laughed. 'Soon. I *have* missed you, you know.'

Have you? 'I've only been gone a night.'

Lucas nodded. He knew that. They'd been the most unbearable few hours he'd ever spent.

Although Callie had her suspicions, she had to let them go for now—even if they *were* eating her alive. She would remain friendly until she had proof. She couldn't believe he was making her think like this! Making her suspicious. How *could* he? After all this time, after all her worrying about losing him as a friend, now he'd slept with her he'd gone out and celebrated, or something, and probably hadn't done so alone! That had to explain the perfume smell. The aroma of alcohol on him.

Why wouldn't he? He was a good-looking man. Charming. Women gravitated to him, didn't they?

She hoped her suspicions were wrong. Because if they were right then that meant Lucas was keeping things from her. *Lying to her.* She'd been lied to her whole life by the one person who shouldn't have. She couldn't do that again.

Not with him.

Not ever.

Lying was the worst kind of betrayal she could imagine.

* * *

They were just about to leave the hospital to go home, and were standing by the midwives' desk saying their good-byes, when the telephone rang. One of the midwives answered it, listened and then put her hand over the speaking part of the phone.

'Callie? I know you're not actually on duty, and you're going home, but it's someone called Rhea on the phone and she says it's urgent. She's been trying to call you on your mobile.'

Callie's mobile had been left at the flat. She reached over the counter for the phone while Lucas rolled his eyes in dismay. She shouldn't be working.

'Rhea, it's Callie. What's up?'

'You said I could call you any time, but I couldn't get hold of you on your mobile.'

'I left it at home. Is something wrong?'

'I've been having some pains. Tightenings, really. I don't know what to do.'

'Have you had a show or anything?'

A 'show' was part of the mucous plug that sealed the cervix, and it could sometimes be seen before labour started to show that the cervix was beginning to soften and dilate.

'No. I had a bath, though. It didn't help.'

'Well, are these tightenings strong? Are they painful?'

'More achey. A couple of them have taken my breath away.'

Callie thought for a moment. 'It could be Braxton Hicks, but you're very early on for them. Is the baby moving?'

'Like a trooper.'

'Well, that's good. It's up to you, Rhea. You can come in and let us monitor you for a bit—maybe run a trace to be safe—or you can stay at home and see what happens.'

'I think I want to come in.'

'Okay, you can do that.'

'Will you be there when I get there?'

Her heart sank. 'I'm sorry, Rhea, I'm on my way home now—you've just caught me. But the other midwives here will look after you just as well as I would.'

'But you *know* me. Know my situation.'

'I'll tell them.'

She got off the phone and explained the situation, and then she and Lucas headed home.

He was happy in the car, whistling or singing along to the radio. She couldn't be sure of what was going on, and she needed evidence before she confronted him. Besides, she felt so tired from the last twenty-four hours that she didn't want to ask.

When they got home she went straight to bed, on Lucas's orders, and fell fast asleep.

Lucas watched her sleep. He was glad he'd stripped the bed earlier and replaced the sheets with fresh ones. Callie looked as snug as a bug in a rug, her face relaxed and free of the worry lines she'd had over the last few days.

She'd seemed a bit odd in the car, and he'd thought about asking her if everything was all right, but he'd decided not to push her. He didn't want to hear that maybe she was having second thoughts about their having slept together.

That night had meant so much to him, and he loved her even more if that was possible. It had been a real fright to think that they might lose the baby, but everything had turned out fine in the end. Besides, if he started asking questions she might tell him what he didn't want to hear. Not now. He'd be giving her ample opportunity soon to declare her intentions. Fully. For the whole world to know.

Just thinking about that churned his stomach. Everything would change on that day. Either his world would fall apart or he would get everything he had ever wished for. And by arranging a surprise proposal at Windsor Castle he would know for sure whether Callie's commitment to them both was a hundred per cent. He didn't want a part-time parent for his child. He wanted a mother.

But he also wanted Callie for himself. As his wife. As he'd wanted her years ago. If she turned him down...? Well, he'd be devastated, but he'd survive. He'd done it once before and he supposed he could do it again. Though it would be harder this time.

But he couldn't see how she *could* turn him down. Weren't they perfect together? Hadn't they always been great together? And some of the best relationships came from being friends first... By being committed to each other they could know that they would always be together. As Callie wanted. She'd never lose him.

Unless she got cold feet.

What if she panicked? What if she backed off? What if the proposal scared her?

He was trying to arrange the perfect conditions, so that there wouldn't be a crowd to pressure her into saying yes. He wanted her honest answer. If she said yes it would be because she truly wanted to be with him—great—but if she said no...

Lucas tried to imagine hardening his heart. Being stoic at the disappointment. But he couldn't. It would just seem so devastating.

Was he ready to endanger himself like that? Was it worth the risk? What if she *did* say no?

It was like being on swings and roundabouts. One moment his heart was all for it, the next his need to protect himself swung into play.

But it's not just about me any more. This is about our child too!

He *had* to do right by his child.

His secret plans were starting to come together and he

could only hope she didn't suspect what he was doing—because he wanted it to be the biggest surprise of her life.

The stress that the bleed had caused both of them had been awful, and he knew she'd not been sleeping well lately. But as he sat looking at her now, the woman who was carrying his beloved child, he vowed not to lose her. To prove to her that they had a future together.

Lucas switched off the small bedside lamp and curled on to the side of the bed next to Callie. The last forty-eight hours had been awful. Terrifying. But they'd got through it—and they'd got through it stronger than they'd been before because they'd pulled together. It was what people did. People who loved each other.

A few days had passed since the bleed, and Callie and Lucas were sitting in Maria's lounge. Callie felt awkward. The strained atmosphere between her and Lucas had developed more and more, and once when he'd been in the shower his mobile had rung and she'd seen the name 'Sienna' when she'd looked to see who was calling.

Who was Sienna? Callie didn't know of anyone at the hospital with such a name, and she'd not heard him mention a patient called Sienna. None of his sisters or family was called Sienna, and it was hardly an *old* woman's name, was it? Sienna was a young woman's name. A *pretty* young woman's name. How did he know her? How involved were they?

She'd been tempted to look at the contacts list in his phone but had quickly put it down, not wanting to be that kind of woman who checked her partner's phone.

But then a text from the lovely Sienna had popped up. It had read: Fabulous! You're brilliant! Can't wait to meet again. Sienna xx

Her heart had been ripped in two. Had he cheated on her? The night she'd been in hospital?

Although grief-stricken at the thought of having lost him already, she'd pulled herself together, determined to get through the rest of her pregnancy with dignity. She would have this baby and give it to Lucas and then she'd walk away.

It was what she'd been going to do in the first place, wasn't it? Lucas and this Sienna woman could play happy families. It was nothing to do with *her*.

She must have been in a weird mood since, because Lucas had kept asking her if she was all right. She'd kept answering that she was 'fine', and now she had to get through this visit to her mother.

As Callie was having difficulty driving, and not feeling comfortable behind the wheel, she'd had to let Lucas bring her.

She hadn't been to her mother's home for years and, truth be told, the last time she'd seen it, it had been a bit of a dive. Clutter and rubbish had been piled up everywhere, as if she was a hoarder, with surfaces overflowing with empty cans and bottles. The odd plate of food mouldering. They'd had a massive row the last time Callie had been here.

The last time I was here I stormed out.

But now the flat looked totally different. It was clean...it was neat and tidy. The walls had been given a lick of paint— 'Gareth did them...'—and the hallway had been freshly wallpapered. There were pictures of Maria and Gareth up in frames, and one of Callie as a baby in her cot had been given pride of place in the centre of the mantelpiece.

'The place looks great.'

Maria smiled, inordinately pleased that her daughter approved. 'We've worked hard to change it around. Money's tight, but it's amazing what a bit of spit and polish and a dozen or so bin-liners can do.'

Maria placed a tea tray on the low coffee table and poured them all drinks, offered round a plate of biscuits.

'I'm just sorry Gareth couldn't be here, but he got called to work on an emergency.'

'What does he do?' Lucas asked, thinking someone ought to show an interest, and Callie was oddly quiet. She'd been strange for days now, and he wondered if she suspected what he was up to. He hoped it *was* that. Because she was starting to pull away from him. The way Maggie had in the last few days of their marriage.

'He works for a counselling line. For ex-alcoholics. Because of his background he's got a lot of experience with helping people, and sometimes when they get a crisis call he goes in and helps out.'

'A counsellor? Wow...' So Gareth was used to helping out people in crisis? What had made him fall for Maria?

'Gareth is an alcoholic too,' Maria explained, seeing the question in Callie's eyes. 'But he's been on the wagon for twenty years. He still goes to AA meetings and that's where we met.'

'Two alcoholics together? Is that a good idea?' Callie asked.

'A lot of people may say two dependents living together is a recipe for disaster, but we don't think so. It's down to the individuals at the end of the day, and Gareth was determined to help me kick the sauce. And he did. Over six months now, Callie.'

She nodded. 'That's good, Mum. Long may it continue.'

Maria smiled, looking at both of them. 'It's a new start for me. Like this baby is for the pair of *you*. I'm so glad you two got it together in the end. I don't know why it didn't happen earlier.'

Callie and Lucas looked at each other. But it was awkward. Uncomfortable, somehow.

Lucas spoke. 'Things are complicated. We're taking it slow—not rushing into anything. We don't want to get it wrong.'

Callie rolled her eyes. It was twice now that Lucas had told people he and Callie were together, and each time she heard it she still felt scared by it. Did he still think everything was okay? There was a baby involved here—they couldn't afford to screw this up!

'How are you anyway, Callie?'

It was the first time Maria had shown concern for her and something inside Callie softened. She had to fight tears for a moment as the one thing she'd craved from her mother—attention and concern—was finally given.

'I'm all right. We had a little scare and I was in hospital for a few days, but I just needed to rest.'

'Oh...I do hope you're okay? Having a baby is a truly life-changing event—one that I got badly wrong. But I'm sure that you two will love this baby in a way I never could.' She turned to her daughter. 'I need to apologise to you, Callie. For everything. For the way I mistreated you. The way I put alcohol first. The way I neglected you. But it was a disease I couldn't fight at the time. Thank God for Lucas, here, because without him around as your friend I don't know how you might have turned out.'

'Wow...' She'd never expected an apology. She'd never expected this. 'Thanks... I guess I turned out all right...'

'All right? You're an amazing person, Callie, and I can't say enough how proud I am of you, and how sorry I am that alcohol took me away from you and stole the mother you deserved.'

Callie swallowed back tears. 'Well, thank you for the apology. It means a lot.'

The rest of the visit was spent with Maria showing Callie a scrapbook she'd managed to put together with scant pictures of Callie through her childhood and some of Maria and Gareth together. They spoke of the years of Callie's childhood, telling stories, sharing snippets of what they remembered.

There were lots of tears.

But there was lots of forgiveness and love too.

Callie got into Lucas's car for the drive home, feeling that bridges were now being forged that would hopefully never break. There was some hope for the future with her mother at last, but even though she'd made a good start today there were still many more days when it could all still go wrong.

Past experience had taught her that.

And present experience.

But she was hopeful.

And yet cautious.

I may be losing Lucas, but I'm getting my mother at last.

More weeks passed and Callie didn't have any more bleeding. But she made it quite clear that they would not be sleeping together again. She kept Lucas at arm's length.

Lucas understood her reticence and accepted it, though it was killing him not being able to touch her. He had even accepted her explanation of why, but he'd seen that she was being quite clipped with him, and sharp. He was beginning to fear that she was putting distance between them in time for the big day, so that she could still disappear and leave him holding the baby.

She was at thirty-four weeks' gestation and that day was getting closer. She had two more weeks left at work before she went on maternity leave. The nursery was all done and painted, a pram had been bought, and lots of tiny baby clothes in neutral colours. Lucas had bought some cuddly toys to go inside the cot which he'd spent the previous night building—with much swearing and cursing and dropping the Allen key constantly, or catching his knuckles on the wood.

The future was looking good for baby Gold, even though

he wasn't sure if Callie would be a part of it—and that broke his heart.

He knew he ought to be resigning himself to her leaving. All the signs pointed to it. His dad had been the same when he'd been at home and was about to leave again for foreign climes. He'd get sharp with everyone, snappy, find reasons for arguments. Callie was behaving the same way. Maggie had done it—why wouldn't Callie?

Everything was going really well pregnancy-wise. She'd even been receiving calls from her mother every week! Asking how she was and everything! Maria was certainly making an effort and trying to prove what she'd said to Callie.

'I'm going to be dry now, Callie. For ever. You can depend on me.'

'Wow. That's great, Mum. That would be amazing, in fact. But you've got to do it for yourself—not for anyone else.'

'I *will* do it for me. And for you. I know I wasn't the best mum in the world to you. I was no mum at all.'

Callie's eyes had welled up at that point and she'd found it difficult to speak.

Lucas had wanted to lay his hand on hers, to offer support, but that was difficult now. He knew Callie wouldn't appreciate it.

'Well, I'm behind you. You have my support. And I think I'd like to meet this Gareth who's made you like this.'

Maria let out a breath. 'I'd like to come and see you. When the baby's born. Perhaps I could bring him then?'

Callie had agreed. 'That'll be nice. I'd love that.'

When she'd told Lucas of the call he'd been just as shocked as she'd been, at first, but then he'd been so pleased! Especially when she'd mentioned that she'd invited Maria and Gareth to come after the baby was born. He'd picked her up and whirled her around the room, with her shrieking and squealing at him to put her down. How could he not know that it hurt for him to touch her and try and kiss her?

'Is everything okay?' he kept asking.

'It's fine. I'm just hormonal,' she'd reply.

When he wasn't looking she'd glance at him and feel sad. He'd let her down so badly. She'd not got an opportunity to look at his phone again for more messages from this Sienna person, but occasionally a text message would pop through and he'd look at it and smile before texting back.

Each time her heart would break a little more, and she'd dread when the time would come for them to part.

CHAPTER EIGHT

WHEN CALLIE GOT into work the next day she was informed that her teenage patient, Rhea, had been admitted in early labour.

'She had a show last night, and then her waters broke this morning. She's in Room Two and she's waiting for you,' said Sarah, Callie's supervisor.

Callie was surprised. Rhea was at the same gestation as she was—thirty-four weeks. That was six weeks earlier than expected. Not drastic—the baby would more than likely be fine, although depending on its condition when it was born they would decide whether it needed to go to the Special Care Baby Unit or not.

Premature labour in teenagers was common. More common than most people knew. Lots of people assumed that teenage mums were healthy because they were so young, and would easily be able to carry a pregnancy to term, but unfortunately statistics and evidence didn't bear that out.

Callie grabbed Rhea's notes, quickly skimmed through them and saw that she'd been four centimetres dilated at her last check, which her colleague Donna had done only twenty minutes ago. Rhea had had a good night, had managed to get some sleep and was not using any medication—not even gas and air just yet.

She headed on down the corridor and got to the door of

Room Two. She tapped on the door gently and then popped her head in. 'Hiya—it's me. Can I come in?'

She was shocked to see a woman seated in the corner of the room, writing in a file. Who was *she*?

But Rhea was sitting on the bed in a beautiful red nightshirt and pink bed socks, one ear plugged into an iPod. She pulled the earphone out and smiled when she saw Callie.

'Thank God you're here! I was beginning to wonder if you'd ever make it.'

'I had no idea you'd come in.'

'I came in first thing.'

'Well, I only discovered that about twenty minutes ago. How are you doing?'

'All right. They don't hurt too bad at the moment.'

Callie nodded, then turned to the woman who was now smiling at her. 'Hi. I'm Callie, and I've been looking after Rhea throughout her pregnancy.'

The woman smiled politely. 'I'm Jessica. I'm the social worker assigned to Rhea's case.' She indicated Callie's bump. 'You look ready to have one yourself.'

Callie ran a hand over her burgeoning bump. 'Six weeks left. Looks like Rhea's going to beat me to it.'

'You can't stop babies when they decide to come, can you?'

Callie smiled. 'You certainly can't.'

Callie went over to Rhea and began to prepare the CTG machine. 'We need to run a trace for a little while. About thirty minutes. Is that okay? It's just with you having gone into labour early we need to make sure baby's okay.'

Rhea nodded and lifted herself so that Callie could get the straps behind her before applying the sensors to her abdomen and strapping them tightly. The baby's heartbeat was registering in the one hundred and thirties and the lower sensor measured the contractions.

She gave Rhea a push-button device. 'Record any movements you feel, okay?'

Rhea nodded, looking nervous.

'Don't be scared. This is all normal.'

'I bet *you'll* be scared when it's your turn.'

She laughed and smiled in sympathy. 'I probably will. And they always say medical personnel make the worst patients. I'll probably be a nightmare for whichever poor soul has to look after me.'

Rhea smiled nervously. 'What if I can't do this?' she asked in a small, terrified voice.

Callie sat herself down on the side of Rhea's bed. 'You? Not do this? Rhea? The brave girl who faced me off in her booking visit? What you've been through makes you the strongest girl in the world. You're here, you're a survivor, and you can and will do this.' She patted Rhea's hand, but Rhea grasped it, and Callie could feel her nerves. 'It's okay.'

Rhea met her gaze and nodded. But there were tears in Rhea's eyes.

'Look, I have to go and fill in your notes and then get Lucas. So I'm going to leave you for a bit whilst we get the trace. Try to use the time to relax. You'll need all your strength later. Can you do that for me?'

Her patient nodded.

'Put your head back, listen to some music, close your eyes. We'll be back in a jiffy.'

She quietly left the room, sighing deeply. Her own stress was building on Rhea's behalf. The time for her delivery was getting closer. Time for her to make a choice about her baby. They should have had more time. Another six weeks to get her to see that there were other options open to her. But time had been taken from them all. Was Rhea going to give her baby over to Social Services?

Sitting at the midwives' desk, she was writing up the notes when she felt Lucas's hand come over her shoulder.

She froze. Lucas had continued to try and touch her these last few weeks. It was baffling. Their relationship was seemingly just the same to him. Had he not noticed that she was trying to break away? So that when they did part her heart would remain in one piece?

She shrugged off his hand. 'Rhea Cartwright is here. Remember her? She's gone into early labour. Waters have broken, she's four centimetres, and she's in Room Two as scared as anything.'

'Don't you want to be with her?'

She nodded. 'She's got a social worker in there. I think she's going to take the baby if Rhea sticks with her decision. But whilst she's on the trace I thought I'd give her a break, you know?'

He looked at her, curiously. 'Give *her* a break or *yourself* a break?'

'How do you mean?'

'Well, I know how you feel about her case. Her giving the baby away. It has to resonate with you—it was what I was asking you to do.'

'But for completely different reasons. I hadn't been through what she'd been through.'

'So it would have been less traumatic for you to give away a baby because you hadn't been raped? Come on— you know that's not true. It would have been hard and diffi- cult and heart-breaking, no matter what the circumstances.'

Callie rubbed her belly, feeling their child move and tumble around. There was less room inside now, so she felt every little stretch, every little movement, every little hic- cup. It still could be heart-breaking. She had no idea if she would try to keep the baby herself now or give it to Lucas. She would most probably be giving it away. Unable to keep it or even be in its life.

Best not to think about that right now.

Was Rhea still okay about giving her baby away? Or was

she getting attached? Having doubts? Did she feel pressured to give up her baby because Jessica was in the room with her?

'I need to get her out.'

'Who?'

'The social worker. I need time to talk to Rhea.'

I may not be able to keep my baby, but Rhea could still keep hers.

'You can't persuade her to keep it, you know. That's not your decision.'

'I know, but I at least need to know that she's looked at all her options.'

'So what do you want to do?'

She looked at him for back-up. 'Come with me. Into her room. We'll say we're about to do an internal, or something, send her for coffee—anything to get her out of the room. I need to know that Rhea has thought through *everything* before she gives that baby away.'

Lucas breathed in deeply through his nose, thinking hard. 'Okay.'

They headed into Rhea's room and managed to persuade Jessica to go for a coffee whilst they ran some tests and examinations. Callie sat once more on Rhea's bed whilst Lucas stood by the CTG, looking at the trace.

'Hello, Dr Gold.'

Lucas smiled back at her. 'Hi.'

'Rhea, I'd like to talk to you,' said Callie.

'What about?'

'Your decision. About what happens after the baby has been born.'

'Oh.' Rhea looked down at her lap, fiddling with her earphones.

'Have you had any more thoughts about what you want to do?'

Rhea shrugged. 'I don't know.'

Callie didn't understand. 'You don't know? Whether to give it up?'

When Rhea looked up her eyes were full of tears. 'I don't know what to do! I was doing fine to start with. I was going to give it away—end of story. You know what I was like.'

Callie nodded.

'But then you bloody well made me see the scan! In 3D! I saw her *face*! Her sweet face… And you know what it made me think? That she *didn't* look evil. That she *didn't* look like a monster. It'd been so easy to think that she was.'

'Easier to separate yourself from it?'

Rhea nodded and sniffed. 'Yeah. But by then I'd got *them* involved, hadn't I? The Social.' Rhea wiped at her eyes with the back of her hand, then was gently handed a tissue from the box by Lucas. Rhea took it and blew her nose, wiping her face clean. 'I don't know what to do.'

She looked at Callie.

'How did *you* know you wanted to be a mother?'

Callie knew that was too long a story to go into. And if she was truthful about her own doubts that wouldn't help Rhea with hers.

She glanced at Lucas. 'I don't know… I guess it happened quite slowly. I had to get my head around the idea. It was frightening.'

'You were scared? But you're a midwife.'

'Worst patients, remember? I don't want to be flippant. It's an individual decision. But I think you know if you want to be a mother deep in your heart. Sometimes you think that you don't—that it'll be too hard, or it'll be too painful—but that's just a reflex reaction. It's not until you think about it…and I mean *really* think about it…that you know for sure. What's in your heart, Rhea?'

A contraction hit then.

They waited whilst Rhea breathed through it, and when she was done she let out a huge breath. 'Whoa! I think…I think I might like to try. When I imagine her life, lost in the system…'

Callie looked at Lucas hopefully. This was the sign she'd been after.

Rhea had another contraction then. A painful one.

Callie and Lucas looked at the CTG and saw that it was strong, lasting a lot longer than the others—nearly a full minute.

Callie got the Entonox ready and asked her if she wanted it for the next one?

'Are they all going to be like that?'

She smiled. 'They might get worse.'

'Then give it to me.'

Rhea took the tube and mouthpiece and waited, and another contraction came hurtling along, only thirty seconds since the last one.

Lucas looked at Callie. 'Things are moving on?'

She nodded. 'Definitely.' A glance at the clock told her that technically there were still two more hours to go before Rhea needed to be checked internally once again, but if she continued to have contractions that quickly, and for that length, they might not have them.

Rhea groaned. 'Here comes another one!'

She started breathing on the mouthpiece and Callie laid a hand on Rhea's stomach to feel the contraction. It was strong. *Very* strong. Rhea was gasping and panicking now, rolling around on the bed.

Lucas glanced at Callie, then whispered, 'What you said just now…about knowing in your heart whether you want to be a mother…'

She looked uncertainly at him. 'Yes?'

'Don't *you* know?'

Callie was saved by a knock at the door and Jessica was there, poking her head in. Callie asked her to wait outside for a moment. 'She's just about to have an examination…'

Jessica happily stepped back into the waiting room.

Callie asked Rhea if she could do an internal to check her progress.

Rhea nodded, and Callie began her examination to feel for the cervix.

But that wasn't what she reached first.

There was part of the umbilical cord visible.

'Prolapsed cord!' she stated.

Lucas quickly hit the emergency button. An alarm sounded and the bed was tilted backwards.

Callie warned Rhea that she was going to have to keep her hand inside her to keep the baby's head off the cervix.

'What?'

'You've got a prolapsed cord—we're going to have to take you to Theatre and do a Caesarean section.'

'Why?' Rhea began to cry.

'If the baby's head presses on the cord it'll cut off the blood supply and oxygen. I need to support the head and keep you tilted back so that gravity will help until we get you into the operating room!'

'But, Callie…'

There was no time for more conversation.

Other midwives came pouring into the room, along with maternity support workers and any paediatricians who'd happened to be present on the ward at the time. The general rule on Maternity was that if an alarm bell sounded you responded—no matter *who* you were!

They raced Rhea through the corridors, past a confused and shocked Jessica. Callie called out to her, to try and explain what was happening, but they were going past her so fast there wasn't time to check whether she understood what was happening.

Rhea was crying and gasping and trying to fight another contraction. 'Callie, what's going to happen?'

'We're going to give you a general anaesthetic.'

'Can't I stay awake?'

'I'm sorry, Rhea, it's an emergency.'

'But I want to *see* her! Don't let her take her away!'

She meant Jessica.

Callie nodded her understanding quickly and promised Rhea. 'No matter what, I won't let anyone take your daughter—not until you've seen her first.'

'And I hold her first. No one else gets to do that.'

Callie nodded. 'No one,' she agreed.

The anaesthetist quickly got a general anaesthetic into Rhea, and inserted an artificial airway to keep her breathing properly during the operation. Callie still knelt on the bed, holding the baby off the cord. She ached and hurt, and her belly was being kicked and punched from the inside by her own baby. All she wanted to do was sit back and relax and breathe a sigh of relief, but she knew she had to stay there until the baby was lifted out by C-section.

Lucas was scrubbing up, along with another consultant, and it wasn't long before he strode into the theatre. They made their incision, the seconds ticking away as they cut through the layers, burst her bag of water and lifted out the baby.

Rhea's daughter screamed her head off indignantly at being brought out into the very brightly lit room. She continued to cry until she'd been thoroughly wrapped in blankets and a towel and had her hair dried. Only then did she settle and go to sleep.

Callie climbed off the bed and went to the station where the paediatricians were working to see how the baby was getting on. Her knees hurt. Her lower abdomen ached from the position she'd had to be in. But none of that mattered. Rhea's baby was fine—only needing a little bit of oxygen to assist with her breathing. She looked a good size too: maybe even four or five pounds already. She didn't expect her to stay in SCBU for long. Not if she had the same determination and grit as her mother.

Lucas peered over at her. 'Is she okay?'

'Doing well.'

'And you?'

She turned and beamed a big smile at him. 'Fine.'

His eyes crinkled in the corners and she knew he was smiling back, even if she couldn't see it.

She informed the SCBU nurses that Rhea had insisted that Social Services were not allowed to see or touch the baby before Rhea had done so first.

'Social Services are around, and I don't know how pushy they'll be, but Mum gave strict instructions,' Lucas said, and Callie was glad and proud that he'd insisted on Rhea's wishes for her as well. He knew how important it was to Rhea.

'Don't worry—we'll look after her,' one of the nurses replied.

Callie discarded her gloves and washed her hands. Then she went to see Jessica.

'Everything's fine. Rhea's doing well—as is the baby.'

Jessica smiled and nodded. 'That's wonderful.'

'Rhea will be asleep for some time. She's insisted that she wants to see and hold her baby first. You won't be able to see her until she has.'

'I thought Rhea didn't want to see the baby?'

'It's Rhea's wish. She changed her mind and made it quite clear,' Lucas stepped in. 'We have to honour the wishes of the mother.' *As should you,* he wanted to add.

Callie went to get a drink, and had just made herself a cup of tea when Lucas joined her in the staffroom.

'Rhea's in Recovery. Doing well.'

'Excellent. I almost can't believe she's had her baby. We were going to be in it together until the end.'

She rubbed her stomach, aware that this was her last

few weeks of being pregnant. Would she ever experience being pregnant again? Was this going to be her only baby?

Crikey, I'm thinking too far ahead, here!

Lucas cocked his head. 'What's the joke?'

'Nothing. Just thinking about these last few weeks. Only six more weeks of being pregnant. It's scary.'

She chose not to mention all the other terrifying things. Losing him…

'Because you know all the things that can go wrong?'

'Because it's something I denied myself, not even considering it for so long. Now it's nearly at an end and I'm not sure how I feel about it. Whether I really *can* do it.'

He frowned. 'Be a mum? I thought you'd got your head round that?'

'What if I've been kidding myself? I'm good at doing that. What if this *doesn't* work out?'

'Why wouldn't it? So what if you get things wrong? Mothers do that all the time. So do fathers. But they carry on because they know that no one is a perfect parent, and that no one can do parenting without making mistakes.'

'Why are you so knowledgeable? You seem to know what you're talking about.'

'Because I believe in you. If you didn't care then you would have something to worry about—but you *do* care and so you don't. If that makes sense.'

She could see the pulse throbbing in his neck. He was clenching and unclenching his jaw. What she wouldn't give to touch him once more. Feel his lips on hers. The physical ache of longing for him almost knocked her off her feet.

'So, what are you going to do with your morning off tomorrow? Put your feet up? Knit bootees?'

She sighed. 'I thought I'd go into town. One last look around before I'm burdened with a buggy and have to hope people will hold doors open for me.'

He laughed and offered her a biscuit from the packet

on the table. 'Shall I meet you in town? I could be free around lunchtime? Maybe we could make it over to Windsor Castle?'

His face was flushed and she looked at him oddly. Why did he seem uncomfortable mentioning that place? Had he been there before? With this Sienna person? Maybe he'd met *her* there?

Maybe she *should* meet him tomorrow. There were a few things they needed to discuss. Time had not given her any answers. Any explanations. And it would be good to be on neutral ground.

'I'll meet you at the coffee shop opposite Laurie Park.'

She munched down four more of the biscuits before realising they weren't hers. They were *so* yummy.

'Oh, God,' she said, changing the subject. 'I'll buy some tomorrow. Replace the packet.'

'They're mine. Don't worry.'

But she *did* worry. She worried a lot.

Rhea was soon sufficiently awake and well enough to be wheeled down to SCBU. Lucas and Callie went with her.

They had to wait for someone to let them in, and then they manoeuvred Rhea round to the unit that contained her baby.

Baby Girl Cartwright.
Born: 2.37 p.m.
Weight: 4 pounds, 13 ounces.

'She's a good size,' Rhea said, peering through the plastic. 'Can I touch her?'

'How about holding her?'

The SCBU nurse got Rhea's daughter out of the unit and laid her in her mother's arms.

Rhea's face was a picture. It was a delightful mix of love and confusion and fear and excitement. And hope.

Rhea ducked her head to inhale her daughter's scent and examined her thin fingers and tiny nails. 'So little. So perfect.'

'And totally healthy for her gestation,' the SCBU nurse said. 'She's only here until we can be satisfied her oxygen levels are being maintained without assistance.'

'What is she on?' asked Callie, wanting to know the amount of oxygen assistance. The lower the number, the better.

'Only ten per cent.'

'That's good, Rhea. She won't be here long at all.'

Rhea smiled, but couldn't take her eyes off her daughter.

Callie reached out and touched the baby's cheek, wondering if *her* baby looked like this inside her. 'She looks like you.'

'She does. She's…beautiful. How could I ever have thought she was a monster?'

'You don't have to make any decisions you don't want to, Rhea. You can change your mind. You can ask for time. Social Services will hold off until you're ready to make a firm decision.'

Rhea's face darkened. 'I already told them, though. That I wanted to give her up.'

'But that was before. This is now.'

Rhea looked up from her daughter's face. 'But I'm on their radar now. Won't they think I'm a bad mother for wanting to give her up?'

'Of course not!'

Lucas knelt down in front of them. 'Have you thought about a name for her?'

Rhea looked shy. 'I thought of some. After the scan, when I knew she was a girl, I played around with a few names—you know, just in case.'

'No matter what path you choose for her, you can still name her,' Callie said.

Rhea smiled. 'Yeah? Okay. Then her name's Rosie. Rosie May Cartwright.'

Lucas smiled. 'That's beautiful. She's clearly a Rosie.'

'We'll leave you alone with her for a while. Let us know when you want to go back to the ward,' said Callie.

Rhea nodded.

Callie and Lucas walked away, standing at a distance in the corridor beyond the room where Rhea and Rosie were.

Looking through the window Callie saw all the other incubators, some covered with blankets to protect the babies' eyes from the overhead lights, and all the tiny babies—the ones fighting for life, the ones so small they were almost transparent. She saw the parents beside them, the fear on their faces, the grit and determination in the furrow of their brows that their babies *would* get better. She hoped that they'd all have positive outcomes for their stories. Unlike her.

'Look at them, Lucas. We're so lucky not to be in there. It must be horrible for some of them.'

He put a reassuring arm around her shoulders and she wanted to shrug him off. 'A lot of them will have been prepared for it. But you're right. And we shouldn't have to worry about coming here. Our baby is happy and well.' He reached over to rub her stomach and felt a reassuring kick in response. 'See?'

'Rhea's got a big decision to make. I hope she makes the right one. For her *and* for her daughter.'

'What do you think she'll do?'

'I honestly don't know. But I do know she's finally connected with her. It's what she needed to do. She needed to see that what she was giving away wasn't evil. I wish her well. I wish her happiness in whatever she decides, and I'll support her. She knows that.'

'And you know that I'm here for *you*, don't you?'

He turned Callie's face with his finger on her chin and made her face him. Looking into his blue eyes, she knew that she could never get tired of looking at them. They were a vibrant blue, like the down of a kingfisher as it sat above the water. The glint of sunshine was always reflected in them, no matter where he was.

'You've been odd with me ever since the bleed and I need to know, Callie, if you're here for the long haul or not? If you can't be—if you have any doubts—then tell me now, so I can be prepared. It's all of you or nothing. No half measures.'

She had to say something. Now was the time.

So she was blunt. 'I don't trust you,' she said, as simply as that.

Her doubts about him overwhelmed her. She couldn't stand it anymore! Keeping up this pretence, this façade that everything was okay and hunky-dory. She *had* to know if he'd lied to her! She needed to ask him. Because they couldn't move forward unless he told her the whole truth.

There could be no other way for them.

'Have you lied to me, Lucas?' She turned to face him, a whole yard of empty space between them. Her stomach was churning in anticipation of his answer. Would he try to lie even more to get himself off the hook?

'What?' Lucas looked shocked at her question.

'Did you *lie* to me?' Her voice rose slightly and she saw him glance around to see who might be listening.

'No!'

He sounded angry. With himself…?

But she could *see* the lie in his eyes, and the knowledge that he was keeping something from her broke her heart. She physically felt the pain in her chest.

'You have, haven't you?'

'No, Callie!'

'And now you're lying about lying! That's what happens when people tell untruths. They twist themselves into knots and show those around them that they have no respect for them!'

'I respect you more than anyone!'

'But not enough to tell me the truth? Why not, Lucas? Is it because you're afraid to tell me? You haven't been honest with me. I thought you cared for me…I thought…I began to believe I was good enough for you!'

'You are—'

'No! I'm *not* good enough for you because you've lied to me. Easily, it seems. My mother did that. I wasn't good enough for her to bother about and she lied to me. Every single day. Do you know how that feels? To be worthless?'

'I have *not* lied to you! And if we're going to play the blame game, what about you?'

'What *about* me?'

'You know I needed one hundred per cent commitment from you—but could you give it? Ever? You blow hot and cold, like a bloody kettle, and I never know where I stand from one moment to the next! One day you want to be a mother—another day you doubt it. You let me sleep with you one minute, then push me away the next.'

'You're blaming *me*?'

'Well, who else is there?'

She laughed harshly. '*You*! You and bloody Maggie, for getting me into this mess in the first place. If you hadn't been so keen to prove your marriage to yourself none of this would have happened!'

'None of this would have happened if you'd said yes to me in the first place!'

She stared at him. What he'd said… Was that true? Had him asking her out all those years ago truly meant something to him? She'd thought he'd asked because he'd been out with most of the girls he knew and she was the only one left!

He shook his head, upset, and then something came into his eyes. Knowledge. Knowledge of what she was talking about—about his keeping something from her. He tried to hide it.

'All these weeks you've been off with me...I thought it was because you've had second thoughts about us sleeping together...'

'Oh, I have. I regret it completely!'

'Callie—'

'I never thought that *you* would lie to me. *Ever*!'

'Callie, it's not what you think—'

'No? You came to the hospital stinking of booze and perfume! There were strange messages on your phone! Who's Sienna?'

His face blanched white. 'She—'

'No! I don't want to hear it! I can't bear to look at you right now...leave me alone!'

She turned from him and began to run away, back to SCBU. Lucas called her name, then ran down the corridor to grab her arm.

She shook him off. 'Leave me alone, Lucas!'

People were looking, watching them, so Lucas hung back, his jaw clenching, frustrated with himself for answering her with a knee-jerk reaction and saying he hadn't lied. He knew he should have told her the truth.

I will tell her the truth. I'll tell her the truth and make her listen to me.

Rhea waved at Callie through the glass to come in and she entered slowly, taking in the lovely sight of mother and daughter. 'Are you ready to go back?' she asked, and sniffed, determined not to show Rhea that she was upset.

'I've made a decision.'

'Yes?' Callie's heart was in her mouth. Whatever Rhea decided she would back her one hundred per cent, but there *was* one direction she was hoping Rhea would take more than any other.

'I'm keeping her. Even though I have nothing. No equipment. Nothing. I'm keeping her.'

Callie gasped with delighted surprise, letting out all the pent-up breath she'd not known she was holding. Then she was smiling and laying an arm around Rhea's shoulder, hugging her, trying her hardest not to cry even more.

'Well done. I'm so pleased for you! Do you want me to tell Social Services?'

'No, it's all right. I'll do it. They need to hear the truth from me.'

'I'm sure it'll be fine. They can still help you.'

'I hope so. My daughter is going to know her family. Be loved. That's what matters at the end of the day, isn't it?' Rhea looked up at Callie.

She nodded.

Yes it was.

More than anything.

Callie hadn't come home. He'd waited and waited, but there'd been no sign of her. He'd called her phone, but it either kept ringing or was switched off. He'd thought about going round to her mother's to see if she was there, but anger had stopped him.

Why was he so cross?

Okay, so he'd kept a secret—but it was a small secret, and it was one worth keeping for the surprise it would cause. It was a *good* omission of truth. He couldn't tell her he was going to propose!

And what had she done? Overreacted. That was what.

Instantly blamed him, not giving him a chance to explain himself, and then running off like…like someone in a dramatic movie.

Well, this wasn't a movie—this was real life. And he was mad at being tarred with the same brush as her mother.

One tiny mistake. Just one. That was all he'd made, and now Callie was using that to punish him for someone else's mistakes.

It was more proof to him that she couldn't commit the way he needed her to. Was she so frightened of commitment that when she actually had the chance of it she threw it away? Was she unable to recognise just what he'd been about to do for her?

There was no other way he could prove his commitment to her. Apart from being there every day. And he couldn't prove that ahead of time until he was actually doing it! But by proposing marriage, by showing her that he wanted that commitment from her…

He loved her! Plain and simple. That was how it had always been with him. But after that time she'd pushed him away he'd been cautious about showing it. Yes, there had been girlfriends at school. But he'd been so young! There had even been Maggie. But that had all been a façade to hide the fact that there was only one true love that he'd always wanted and craved.

Callie.

And she was unable to see it.

Why couldn't he make her see it?

Lucas lay in his bed and stared at the ceiling. Sleep wasn't coming easily.

By morning he was exhausted, and desperate to talk to her, but he had to go to work. He'd been paged with an emergency and had no time to try and find her. Hopefully she'd call later, because he *had* to get this sorted with her. He had to know whether she wanted to be with him or not.

Because he wouldn't lay his heart on the line a third time.

CHAPTER NINE

THERE WAS A book in her bag and Callie began to read as she waited, but she was so tense and nervous none of the words would go in. She kept reading and re-reading the same passage over and over again, until she gave the book up as a bad job and put it away again.

She was just closing the zip on her bag when the door-bell sounded as someone entered the café and she looked up, hoping to see Lucas, but it wasn't him.

She wondered if he'd remember that they were supposed to meet today in this little coffee shop opposite Laurie Park.

He probably wouldn't arrive. Not after their argument. She'd run out on him and not gone home, instead getting a taxi and going to her *mother's*, for crying out loud!

When had her mother ever been there to support her? Never. And yet…the world had gone topsy-turvy. Lucas had lied and let her down and the one person who'd never been there for her suddenly was. Life was screwed up and she couldn't possibly see how it would ever right itself.

She missed him like crazy. This was her most dreaded situation. To have lost Lucas. To have lost her best friend. Her pillar. Her rock. Her heart. She would give him his baby and then leave and go…where?

She wrapped her hand protectively around her baby, her feelings torn.

Where did you go when your heart was torn in two? Was there a place that could heal that? She didn't think so.

Her coffee sat untouched and cold on the table and she stared at her phone. Perhaps she could ring him? He was meant to be at home, unless he'd been called in to work, so he should answer. Perhaps she should hear his explanation? Though she couldn't imagine how he'd wriggle out of this one!

But she'd dialled his number without thinking.

He didn't answer for ages. She could imagine him standing in the hospital corridor, or at home, his hand rubbing at his eyes, pacing the floor, staring at nothing as he focused on the terrible question she'd posed.

Was he going to answer? It was taking him a long time...

'Callie?'

'Lucas.'

'Where are you? You didn't come home last night.'

'I stayed with my mum, but I'm at the coffee shop now.'

There was a pause. 'Of course. We were meant to meet there today. Before we went to Windsor Castle.'

She nodded, hearing the sadness in his voice.

'I don't know how this went so wrong. I want it all back to how it was before.'

'You mean before you lied to me, Lucas? You had an affair—'

'An *affair*? Hang on—what are you talking about?'

She closed her eyes in despair that he could still be trying to wriggle out of it. 'I know about Sienna.'

A shocked pause. His silence spoke volumes.

'You do?'

'I saw her message on your phone. The day after you came to me in the hospital, stinking of alcohol and her perfume.' Her voice broke and she hiccupped back a sob. She was *not* going to let him hear her cry.

'Oh, Callie, you've got it all so wrong!'

'I don't think so...'

'Callie, listen to me. I am not having an affair with Sienna! I was planning to propose to you! At Windsor Castle. She's the events manager there and she arranged for us to have a private part of the castle opened just for us so I could ask you to marry me! She served me champagne—that was why you could smell alcohol on me!'

What? A proposal? To *her*? To Callie?

'I was meant to be proposing to you today, Callie! At the castle! I was going to meet you at the coffee shop and then suggest we go for a walk around, only to surprise you!'

'But—'

'Everyone else knew about it! My family, your mother—they were all going to be there. But I had to cancel because I thought you'd fallen out with me.'

Oh, no!

Could it all be true? Her mother had kept trying to get her to call Lucas, but Callie had ignored her...

The baby gave Callie a hard kick to her bladder and she held her stomach, gasping... She felt sick. To her very core. She dropped her mobile. It began to ring again and she could see it was Lucas, but...

The whooshing noise in her ears was getting louder and she leant against the table as the world began to grow dark.

'I...'

She'd leapt to conclusions. Terrible conclusions. Because that was what she was used to! People letting her down. Lying to her. Treating her like a fool. And she'd accused him of having an affair...

She'd been so wrong. How could she have got it so wrong? She should have trusted him, given him the chance to explain... He'd promised he would always be truthful to her...

Her face grew hot and as she lifted up her hand to wipe at her forehead she stumbled forward, hoping to go outside to get some fresh air. But her legs were weak and jelly-like, and before she knew it she'd gone crashing down in the café, smacking her head violently on one of the tables.

Lucas was suturing in Theatre when the internal phone rang. A theatre assistant answered it, and Lucas expected it to be a quick reminder from his lead consultant about their meeting that afternoon. He really wasn't in the mood for it and he didn't want to go. All he could think about was that call from Callie.

Callie had rung off and then hadn't answered his calls. The urge to go and find her and right the wrong of having lied to her was strong, because he knew how she felt about liars. Her own mother had lied to her throughout her life and it was something she couldn't tolerate. He knew that.

I should have told her the truth from the beginning.

But he'd been trying to protect her and had thought a little white lie wouldn't hurt. How wrong he'd been! And now he hadn't been able to get away. There'd been emergency after emergency in Maternity that day. He was hoping for a break after he'd finished up here, so that he could grab a coffee and try and see if Callie would answer her phone yet.

When the assistant brought the handset of the phone over to him and held it to his ear he got a call he'd never expected.

'Dr Gold?'

'Yes? Who is this?'

'My name's Dr Alan Carter. I'm an emergency doctor down in A&E.'

'Yes?' Perhaps he had a maternity emergency down there and wanted some advice?

'We've had a patient brought in, thirty-four weeks, who's received a serious blow to the head and abdomen. There's internal bleeding and we need to deliver.'

'Right. I'm just finishing up in Theatre…'

'The ID in her bag states her as being Callie Taylor, and you're the ICE number on her phone.'

The ICE number was an 'In Case of Emergency' number that police officers liked everyone to have on their phones in the event of situations such as these.

'Oh, my God…how is she?'

'She's currently unconscious. We're having her rushed to Theatre Two now.'

'The baby?'

'We have to deliver the baby or she could bleed out. The trauma has caused a heavy bleed and we've had to rush her in for an emergency section.'

Lucas stared at the needle and suture in his hand. Two more stitches and he could be gone. But he didn't have time for two more stitches. He looked up at his foundation year one doctor and passed him the tools. 'Finish off.'

He ripped the mask and scrubs from himself, flinging on new ones and scrubbing his hands clean, then dashed from the department and hurtled down the stairs, not bothering with the lift. The doors banged as he slammed them open and raced down the long corridor. Staff and patients stared in wonder. It had been maybe five minutes since the call.

Lucas grabbed a nurse—any nurse who was walking by—and explained who he was. 'Callie Taylor. In surgery. Where?'

She seemed to look him up and down, saw his ID tag, noted he was an actual doctor and not just some weirdo off the street and pointed down towards where the emergency theatres were. 'But you can't go in!'

'Try and stop me.'

He pushed past her but was stopped at the security doors. There was a viewing window, and he planted both hands on the glass like a prisoner and stared through.

He could see Callie. Well, her head, anyway. One eye was swollen and starting to blacken and her other eye was taped over. She had a tube down her throat, helping her to breathe. An anaesthetist sat by her head, measuring all her responses and saturations, and by looking at the monitor Lucas could see she had very low blood pressure. Anything beyond that, he couldn't see.

The surgeons were beyond a green scrub screen, but he could see a baby monitor in the corner, manned by two women, and there was a flurry of theatre staff, all doing various things, concentrating hard on their patient.

There was a speaker button by the glass and he pressed it. 'I'm Dr Gold. The patient is my partner. How is she?'

The surgeon turned and peered at Lucas over his mask. 'She's in a bad shape, but we're doing our best.'

'How's the baby?'

'We're just about in. We'll let you know in a moment or two.'

It was an agony of waiting. They seemed to be moving so slowly at times. There didn't appear to be any urgency and it was all he could do to fight the urge to get scrubbed up and go in there himself! But he knew, sensibly, that he'd be no use. In fact he'd be a gibbering wreck!

I can't lose them. I love them.

I love her too much to lose her! And I never got the opportunity to show her!

What if she died? What if he lost her now and he never got the chance to prove to her that he'd been committed to them working out?

There was a weak cry and Lucas looked up, hope flooding him. The baby! The baby had been born!

It was handed over to a nurse, who took it away into the far-off corner. The staff stood over it whilst they worked. Lucas could see them using suction and oxygen and towels to rub some life into it. But the baby looked floppy. Unresponsive.

No! No, come on, baby! Cry again! Cry! He jabbed the communication button hard. 'What's going on?'

'She's weak, but we've got a heart-rate,' the nurse said.

She? I have a daughter?

'And Callie?'

The surgeon didn't look at him. 'We're still working on her. If the bleeding doesn't stop we may have to do an emergency hysterectomy.'

The baby let out a louder cry and Lucas exhaled heavily, slumping against the glass. He'd literally not been able to breathe and was winded now, as if he'd taken a sucker punch to the stomach. On shaky legs, he stood once again, just in time to see the baby wheeled out of Theatre.

He stopped them. 'Is she okay? I'm the father.'

She was a perfect pink bundle, wrapped up and swaddled in towels within a large incubator.

'She'll be okay. But she needs to be kept warm.'

'Where is she going? SCBU?'

They nodded and pushed past him. He let them go.

He was thrilled she was fine—thrilled to be a father finally, after all this time—but what mattered to him right now was Callie. He had to know she was all right. He had to be able to talk to her. To get a chance to put things right between them. He sensed they could have a great future together and he wanted to ask her something. To let her know that he would look after and love her always.

But it was awful to stand there and see her looking so lifeless and broken on the table.

But I will bear it. If she can, then so can I. Fight it, Callie. Fight it like mad.

He rested his forehead on the window and waited.

They fixed her skull and her womb before wheeling her through to recovery. He sat beside her bed, holding her hand and staring at her pale face, willing her to wake up.

Lucas kissed his beloved's fingers and reached over to kiss her face. 'Come back to me, Callie. Come back to me so I can tell you the truth. I love you. Do you hear me? I love you. We have a daughter who needs you. As do I.'

The machines continued to beep as Callie slept on. Her vital signs were good, he convinced himself of that, though he wondered how Callie might cope with a newborn *and* a bad head. It wouldn't be a problem the first two weeks, when he was at home, but he'd have to go back to work eventually... Perhaps he could get his sisters round to help? They loved babies. They'd fight each other for the opportunity.

He smiled and stroked Callie's hand. 'We're all waiting for you. And your daughter is waiting for you to hold her. She's waiting for her mum to name her, though if we could refrain from naming her after items in the room...' He laughed and felt tears as he recalled Callie's memory of how her mother had named her.

It would all be so different for their daughter. She was loved already. She was wanted. She would have a beautiful name and a beautiful mother.

And if Callie gave him the chance, then they could have a beautiful future together too.

After a few hours in Recovery, they decided to wheel Callie up to Maternity. The neurosurgeons had offered to visit her there, to monitor her, thinking she'd prefer to be by her daughter when she woke up.

Lucas had visited their baby briefly and put his hand through the little round window. His daughter had clutched his finger, breaking his heart and then swelling it to twice its size with love for her. She truly was a beautiful baby, and showed no signs of being harmed in the collapse—which was a miracle. She had dark hair that was quite thick, like Callie's, and when she'd briefly opened her eyes to squint at the world Lucas had seen they were a beautiful dark blue. Violet-blue, he thought to himself.

The staff had weighed her and discovered that she was six pounds four ounces—a good size for her gestation. The small birth-card read *'Baby Girl Taylor'*. He wanted to get that changed. He wanted to name her. Give her an identity. But he still *knew* her. Here was the little girl who had kicked him through Callie's abdomen, who had responded to his voice when he'd leant over Callie's belly and read her bedtime stories.

'I know you!' he'd whispered. 'Remember? *Fee-fie-fo-fum!'*

He'd not been there but a brief moment when he'd felt a gentle hand upon his shoulder. Expecting a nurse, he'd turned round, then smiled in surprise. 'Rhea! How are you? How's Rosie?'

'Doing well. They say she can go home soon. Is this yours? Is it Callie's?'

He'd looked back at their baby and nodded, unable to speak.

'She had a section, then?'

'Unexpectedly.' He couldn't say any more as his throat clogged with a lump.

'She'll make a great mum, Callie.'

'She will.'

'What are you calling her?'

He shrugged. 'We haven't decided. I said Callie could choose. To right a wrong from her past.'

Rhea frowned, not knowing what he meant, but she wasn't about to pry. 'Well, I'll probably be gone by the time she's come round. Will you thank her for me? Tell her how much I appreciate her? I got her this card.'

Rhea handed over a small pink envelope.

'Of course,' he said softly.

If she'll let me.

CHAPTER TEN

SLOWLY, SOUNDS AND sensations began to become clear. There was the beep of a heart-rate monitor and occasionally the cuff around her left arm would be inflated.

Measuring my blood pressure.

Hmm... Why's that?

And then, as she opened her one good eye and began to see the interior of a hospital room, she began to remember details.

She'd been at the coffee shop and then... Callie blinked and looked down. Her pregnancy bump was gone, though there was still some roundness, and by the side of her bed, fast asleep, sat Lucas, his hand still holding hers.

Where's the baby? Is it okay?

Her need to know about the baby made her speak.

'What's happened?'

Callie inhaled deeply through her nose. She could feel a small nasal cannula there that she hadn't noticed before. More and more sensation was coming through now. Looking at his sleeping face, so innocent, only made her feel like weeping. He'd lied to her, yes, but it hadn't been what she'd thought. Years of being messed about by her mother had made Callie instantly think the worst! But she'd been so wrong. So terribly wrong!

He mumbled slightly, then blinked slowly and looked up, his gorgeous blue eyes widening at the sight of her awake.

'Callie...'

'Where's the baby?'

He reached for her hand again and clasped it tightly, kissing her fingers. 'In SCBU. We have a daughter, Callie. A little girl. And she's beautiful, like you.'

Tears pricked at her eyes at the thought of a daughter. A baby girl! Oh, how differently she would do things! Her daughter would be loved and cherished and know deep in her soul that she was the most precious thing to her mummy.

I'm a mum...

'Callie, I'm so sorry I tried to keep the proposal a secret. I just wanted to show you how much I love you and want to be with you. For ever.' His eyes were dark and full of love. 'That you'll never lose me. That we'll always be together.'

He's never let me down in all the years I've known him.

'I do love you, Lucas...'

'And I love *you*—more than words can say. Can you trust me? Can you believe in me?'

She thought quickly, knowing in her heart what her answer was.

Yes... I can believe in you. I do believe in you.

'I'm so sorry!'

The pain lifted from her heart at her words. She reached out for him.

Lucas took her hands in his and leaned forward to kiss her.

She closed her eye, accepting the kiss. His lips touched hers so lightly it was as if he was afraid to kiss her harder in case she broke. She had to laugh, and then winced as a pain stretched across her stomach.

Of course. I must have had a Caesarean.

'Callie, I—'

'Shh. Don't talk. Let me speak. I'm sorry I got angry with you.'

'I'd never—'

'I know! I know. But back then… I should have trusted *myself* more. I'm so used to being lied to by people who are supposed to love me. When you told me about Sienna it was my fault I didn't give you chance to explain.' She sighed heavily. 'The fault was with me. I'm sorry. I should have trusted you more.'

'*I'm* sorry… We should never have secrets from each other. Planning the proposal the way I did, in secret, was a bad idea.'

Callie smoothed the hair on his head and cupped his face. 'It was a wonderful idea.' He was so gorgeous. So handsome. And he was all hers. Mind, body and soul. She knew that now. 'So…we have a daughter?'

He nodded, smiling, his eyes lighting up. 'She's gorgeous and she's absolutely fine. When you're stronger, we can go and see her.'

'I want to see her today. I need to hold her. Feel her in my arms.'

'I'll check with the nurses—see if we can arrange it.'

'I love you, Lucas Gold. But you're going to need to know that I may just love our daughter a bit more.'

He smiled. 'I can deal with that. But there's something *you* need to know too.'

'What?' she asked sleepily.

'I'll be damned if I'll have a baby with the woman I love and not marry her…spend the rest of my life with her.'

Callie smiled, her grin stretching her face. 'Are you asking me to marry you?'

He slipped from his chair and got onto one knee. 'I am. Calendar Taylor…I love you more than the world can ever know and I would be the proudest man alive if you would agree to be my wife.'

She nodded, smiling, her face aglow from happiness and the assurance of trust. 'I will.'

Lucas got up and kissed her again. Her mouth, her cheeks, her neck, her mouth again. 'You've made me so happy.'

'Me too.'

After that, she didn't remember much. The anaesthetic was still in her system and she must have fallen asleep again.

When she woke, some hours later, it was dark outside and Lucas still sat beside her bed. He reached into his pocket and pulled out a small box.

'I was going to give this to you when you went into labour, but seeing as you skipped that step...' He opened the small velvet-covered box to reveal a beautiful platinum ring, with sapphire stones set in an oval shape, surrounded by diamonds. Callie held up her left hand and let him slide the ring on. It was a bit small, so she had to put it on her little finger.

'Wait for the pregnancy fluid to disappear. It'll fit then,' she said.

'The nurses say if you give them the nod we can go and see Baby Girl Taylor.'

'Baby Girl Taylor-Gold,' she corrected.

'I like that.'

It was a bit of a squeeze, getting Callie's bed into SCBU, but they were used to adjusting the space for mothers in beds or wheelchairs who were eager to see their babies.

Lucas propped some pillows behind Callie's back so she could see into the incubator properly.

'Oh! She's amazing!'

Lucas looked through the little cot. 'Isn't she? Do you want to hold her?'

She looked at him. 'Have you?'

'No. I wanted her mother to be first.'

Callie smiled with happiness. 'What shall we call her?'

The SCBU nurses helped them open the incubator and they delicately laid their daughter in Callie's arms.

'You name her. I think it's only right.' Lucas held his daughter's foot, fingering her small toes as they peeked out of the blankets.

'She's so pretty.'

'I know. We make good-looking babies, me and you.'

Callie gazed at her daughter's face, seeing similarities with herself and Lucas. The eye-shape was all Callie, as was the nose, but she had her father's mouth and ears.

'So much hair, too... I'm so glad this worked out between us, Lucas, because I'm telling you now I don't think I'd ever have been able to give her away.'

He kissed Callie's cheek. 'You don't have to worry about that any more. You've given me a gift so wonderful I can never thank you enough.'

Face to face, they looked down at their daughter. Callie could feel the roughness of his stubble against her cheek and smell his familiar aroma, and she felt safe and secure, despite the fact that her head was throbbing and she had a wound across her stomach that would make bikini choices in years to come an interesting challenge.

'What do you think of Isabella?'

He nodded. He liked it. 'It's beautiful.'

'Isabella Marie.'

'After your mother?' He'd not expected that. But it was a measure of how much was changing now. Even Callie's mother had changed since meeting her new man.

'Isabella Marie Taylor-Gold. I love it. I love *you*.'

She smiled, and then bit her lip in surprise when Isabella opened her eyes and snuffled, her mouth opening as if searching for something. 'Do you think she wants a feed?'

He shrugged. 'You could try.'

'Her suck reflex might not be ready.'

'But the skin-to-skin will be good for her.'

Lucas helped Callie undo her hospital gown, so that she could lay Isabella inside her clothes, against her skin. Isabella seemed a lot happier and was soon rooting around, searching for the nipple.

'Amazing.'

Isabella managed a quick feed and then dropped off to sleep.

Callie just wanted to hold her for ever, and Lucas just *knew* he'd get to hold them both for ever. He would get to make Callie and his little girl the happiest people alive.

He'd prove it to them.

Every second of every day.

EPILOGUE

THEY PICKED A date in June for their wedding. They'd
planned to get married as soon as possible, but Callie
wanted the bruising gone from her face first. Then when
they did enquire at the castle about dates, they had to wait
another year to get the perfect summer wedding Callie
dreamed of. Mother Nature smiled down on them with
beautiful sunshine, warmth and birdsong. The little chapel in Windsor Castle was bedecked with white flowers,
and the place was filled to capacity with family, friends
and work colleagues.

Everyone was there to share in their happy day.

Callie walked down the aisle in a simple off-white dress,
strapless, with a tight bodice and flowing skirt, and behind her toddled their daughter, just short of two years of
age, assisted by Marie Taylor, her grandmother, who held
the basket of rose petals that Isabella was tossing all over
the chapel floor.

Lucas looked at them both as they entered through the
archway and knew that he could never be happier. Coming
towards him was the woman of his dreams, gliding along
the floor, her hands holding a delicate posy of pink roses.

She looked gorgeous, and when Callie stood by his side
he reached out to take her hand. He laughed with delight

as Isabella took her place next to Callie and peeked out at her father from beyond Callie's skirts.

'Boo!' she said, making everyone laugh.

The vicar intoned her solemn words as the sunshine shone brightly through the stained glass windows and filled the chapel with bright light and blessing.

They turned to each other and said their own vows, staring deeply into each other's eyes. Callie's voice broke at the beginning, but she ended strongly. Lucas was the other way round. His vows rang out loud and true and steady, and then, as his thoughts focused on how he'd nearly lost her and Isabella once, he faltered. He had to take a breath, take a moment to gather himself, before continuing on in a quieter, but deeply determined voice.

No one had any objections to their marriage.

No one burst through the church door at the last minute to protest.

No one laughed or gasped at Callie's actual name.

They exchanged rings, held hands and looked deeply into each other's eyes. Callie wondered how she could be so lucky. If someone had told her a few years ago that she would be marrying a man with whom she had a daughter she would have laughed in their faces.

What? Me? Married? A mother? Don't make me laugh.

Yet here she was, and she was happy beyond imagining.

Lucas looked so handsome in his wedding suit—a dark charcoal-grey. He had matched her pink posy with a pale pink tie and pink rose buttonhole. As he looked down at her she could read every emotion in his face. Happiness, love, joy, devotion.

It was how it was meant to be, but there was one more secret she had to tell.

The vicar pronounced them husband and wife. When Lucas leaned in to kiss her Callie closed her eyes and allowed herself to sink into the bliss of their connection as their lips touched.

The congregation cheered and clapped, and after they'd signed the register they walked down the aisle together, this time as man and wife. They stood outside as confetti rained down upon them.

Isabella ran around their feet in delight at the cascade of fluttering paper in pink and yellow and white, scooping it off the floor and throwing it back into the air. Lucas bent down to pick her up, not knowing she still had a handful, and when he had her in his arms she let the confetti go above his head.

What could he do but kiss his beloved daughter and then his wife?

As the photographer snapped pictures Callie leaned in to her husband and began to whisper something.

He didn't quite catch it and had to ask her to repeat herself.

'I said, I'll be damned if I'm going to be married to you and only have *one* child.'

He hefted Isabella into a more comfortable position and frowned, his brow furrowed in an amused question. 'You want us to have another?'

Callie leaned in close and whispered in his ear. 'We already are.'

Lucas stared at her as the realisation sank in. Overjoyed, he leaned in and kissed her, passionately this time, as if he could consume her. The crowd of onlookers cheered and whistled.

When they broke for air he looked into her pale blue eyes and told her he loved her. 'More than words or actions could ever prove.'

'And I love *you*—and Isabella—and whoever is yet to come.'

He grinned and nodded his head at the crowd. 'Should we tell them?'

Callie shook her head. They were already sharing this wonderful day with the people they loved. This new secret was one she wanted to treasure for themselves just a little while longer. 'Soon.'

'All right. At least you're not sick yet.'

She laughed. 'Oh, yes. I must admit I'm not looking forward to *that* part again.'

But she didn't have to worry. This time her pregnancy didn't make her regret her decision. There was only a little nausea—no clutching of toilet bowls for Callie Taylor-Gold.

And when their baby boy, Benjamin, was born, seven months later, they knew their family and their happiness were finally complete.

* * * * *

LET'S TALK
Romance

For exclusive extracts, competitions
and special offers, find us online:

MILLS & BOON

THE HEART OF ROMANCE

A ROMANCE FOR EVERY READER

MODERN

Prepare to be swept off your feet by sophisticated, sexy and seductive heroes, in some of the world's most glamourous and romantic locations, where power and passion collide.

HISTORICAL

Escape with historical heroes from time gone by. Whether your passion is for wicked Regency Rakes, muscled Vikings or rugged Highlanders, awake the romance of the past.

MEDICAL

Set your pulse racing with dedicated, delectable doctors in the high-pressure world of medicine, where emotions run high and passion, comfort and love are the best medicine.

True Love

Celebrate true love with tender stories of heartfelt romance, from the rush of falling in love to the joy a new baby can bring, and a focus on the emotional heart of a relationship.

Desire

Indulge in secrets and scandal, intense drama and plenty of sizzling hot action with powerful and passionate heroes who have it all: wealth, status, good looks…everything but the right woman.

HEROES

Experience all the excitement of a gripping thriller, with an intense romance at its heart. Resourceful, true-to-life women and strong, fearless men face danger and desire - a killer combination!

To see which titles are coming soon, please visit

millsandboon.co.uk/nextmonth

JOIN US ON SOCIAL MEDIA!

Stay up to date with our latest releases, author news and gossip, special offers and discounts, and all the behind-the-scenes action from Mills & Boon...

 millsandboon

 millsandboonuk

 millsandboon

It might just be true love...